LOVERS' ROCK

Ravi Bedi, ex-Air Force engineer, musician, painter, and now a prolific writer, lives with his wife of forty-nine years in Jodhpur.

LOVERS' ROCK

Ravi Bedi

RUPA

Published by
Rupa Publications India Pvt. Ltd 2014
7/16, Ansari Road, Daryaganj
New Delhi 110002

Sales centres:
Allahabad Bengaluru Chennai
Hyderabad Jaipur Kathmandu
Kolkata Mumbai

This is a work of fiction. Names, characters, places and incidents are either the product of the author's imagination or are used fictitiously, and any resemblance to any actual persons, living or dead, events or locales is entirely coincidental.

ISBN: 978-81-291-2479-1

First impression 2014

10 9 8 7 6 5 4 3 2 1

Printed at Parksons Graphics Pvt. Ltd, Mumbai

To Munu, Sheenoo and Lio
With Love

'Life is not measured by the number of breaths we take,
but by the moments that take our breath away.'
—Hilary Cooper

1

Had Flight Lieutenant Mani Shankar Varadharajan, a decorated fighter pilot, not visited the railway club that evening, nothing much would have changed in his life. He'd have won a few trophies, married a distant cousin chosen by his parents and lived on idli-vada-sambhar for the rest of his life.

But he did, and his life changed forever.

Life in the Air Force was one great party, especially at Kalaikunda airbase (Kkd for short) in the eastern part of India. There was never a dull moment. In the sixties, the railway officers' colony near the base still had a sizeable Anglo-Indian community boasting of long-legged beauties in miniskirts who loved to have fun. And the fun came mostly from the young, dashing fighter pilots, looking for some action.

Flight Lieutenant Mani Shankar, the only son of the headmaster of a municipal school down south in Poddukkottai, didn't quite fit into the scene. An accomplished fighter pilot, he was much admired and celebrated for his professional excellence. He had won the prestigious gunnery-meet trophies over two consecutive years, a rare feat. He knew more about his machine than the engineers on the ground did. But he was a loner. When others went to town to have their fun over the weekends, Mani got busy with his paints and canvas—his second love after flying. He rarely felt the need to leave the camp, and spent his free time painting or at the bar in the evenings—his third love.

Young pilots, having cleared their solos, never tired of bragging about their three-point landings, low pull-outs and close formation take-offs. They gesticulated with their hands, simulating vertical take-offs, dummy-dives and dogfights, reliving the thrill and pride of flying the Hunters, the front line fighter aircraft of the sixties, and logged more hours demonstrating their skills in the bar than they did in the air.

When tired of blabbering about their dual sorties in the air, the boys invariably switched over to the more enterprising ones they had on the ground—in the railway colony at Kharagpur. And the 'debriefing' usually took place in the bar.

'Hey, Pits, I heard you had a bad landing last Sunday?' Bozo yelled from a corner of the crowded bar.

'Yeah, the poor fellow overshot,' Dodi said blowing smoke rings into the air.

'And the crash barrier failed,' Bozo added with characteristic laughter that sounded more like the way his battered bike did while idling.

'Shut up, you buggers,' grunted Pits.

Dodi shouted from the back, 'I told you not to go solo, man.'

'Come on, Dodi, have a heart,' said Bozo. 'Remember the last time we went dual? Your engine packed up on the taxi track itself.'

The bar reverberated with a crescendo of laughter.

Dodi grit his teeth and threw his fist in the air. 'You bugger… you…'

Bozo ducked behind Pits in mock defense.

Mani listened to their banter, sipping his drink in a corner of the bar, without participating.

It was fashionable to give pet names to the freshmen soon

after they arrived in a squadron. Before he realised, Mani Shankar became 'Shanks', David became 'Dodi', Preetam Singh became 'Pits', and so on.

On weekends and holidays, the younger lot invariably headed to the railway colony. Saturday dance sessions in the club attracted hordes of young lads from the airbase. The club provided a fertile ground for the young pilots to chase pretty girls—they needed target practice anyway. Fighter pilots, with their glamour value, were the favoured lot. They maintained a generous supply of rum for the elders, which became a calling card of sorts, and they easily charmed their way into the hearts of the 'uncles' and 'aunties' in the colony.

The social interaction provided ample opportunities to harried parents looking for prospective matches for their daughters who were growing faster than the Frontier Mail. Sure enough, many of the hunters became the hunted, and eventually landed up in matrimony, for better or worse.

Mani had kept away from it all until one day, when the boys ganged up and pestered him to accompany them to a dance session. Growing up in a small town, Mani had hardly ever talked to a lady other than his mother, let alone danced with one.

'Come on, man, it'll be good fun,' Bozo cajoled him.

'No thanks.'

Dodi sneered, 'Be a sport, man. Grow up and have some fun for a change.'

'I don't know any bloody dancing,' Mani protested. 'What do you think I'll do there? Count pairs?'

Dodi patted Mani's shoulders, 'No sweat, you just have to hold the girl close to your heart and she'll do the rest.'

'You're pulling my leg, aren't you?'

'I'm not pulling your leg. It's time you came out of your shell and exposed yourself to the good things in life before it gets too late.'

Pits, the youngest and the most sober of the lot, came to Mani's rescue. 'Sir, I'll teach you a few basic steps. It's not difficult.'

'It's easier than handling the joystick in the cockpit.' Bozo grinned.

Mani shook his head. 'I don't want to make a fool of myself, thank you.'

'You won't,' said Pits. 'I promise.'

❧

Mani eventually relented and agreed to learn a few elementary steps in the privacy of Pits' room, before venturing out with the gang on the weekend. The railway colony had quaint barrack-type bungalows with picket fences in the front. Tall eucalyptus trees lined the avenue. Ladies in their colourful frocks, smelling of Evening-in-Paris, roamed the street. Nimble-footed girls, doused with talcum powder, chased their dogs. Mani hesitated, but there was no going back now.

Entering the dance hall, he drew in a long breath, and then let out another. He had never seen so many beautiful girls mingling freely with the boys, dancing to a gramophone record playing over the loudspeakers. After introducing Mani to their dates, Bozo and Dodi turned around and followed their dates to the dance floor, without looking back.

Abandoned so brazenly by his comrades, Mani was lost. Even Pits, the most trustworthy of the lot, merrily danced with a pretty young thing, without as much as a glance in Mani's direction. He would have removed himself from the scene at once, but for the sudden arrival of a long-legged beauty in a black leather miniskirt and tight-fitting blouse that left little to the imagination. His eyes opened wide and his breath caught in his throat.

Mani had never seen anything more beautiful in his life. Tall and slim, she had long, jet black tresses that reached straight down to her slender hips, blue eyes that sparkled like sunlight-kissed waves and a figure that a master craftsman would have loved to sculpt in solid gold. She could have charmed even the most pious of saints in the Himalayas. Decorum should have forbidden Mani from gawking at her so obviously, but Mani felt paralysed by this vision. Even when he forced himself to look away, her image danced in front of him.

Mani caught her eye and felt goose pimples break out all over his body. He turned away, but only for a second. When he looked back again, he found the angel dancing with a tall, handsome boy.

Swaying with his partner, Bozo paused near Mani. 'Don't just stand like a lamp-post, you dope,' he said, gyrating to the tune. 'Go and tap somebody for a dance.'

Familiar with only the tap in the bathroom, Mani cursed himself for falling into their trap. Feeling vulnerable, he withdrew into a corner and wondered if he should quietly slip away.

He was flabbergasted when the girl in the black leather skirt approached him and flashed a smile that sent his heart soaring.

'Hello.'

He stared. Had *she* really addressed *him*? He glanced over his shoulder and saw no one. He turned around and found her still smiling.

'I'm Grace, Grace Wilson, and you are?'

'F-f-light Lieutenant Shankar,' he stuttered, barely able to hear his own voice.

'Haven't seen you around, you must be new here.'

'This is my first visit to the club.'

She fluttered her eyelashes, 'Care for a dance?'

'Oh, well…I…' His voice cracked.

The gorgeous lass raised her eyebrows.

'Err...I would be delighted...but I don't know much about dancing.'

Sensing his dilemma, she came to his rescue. 'Oh, come on. It's no big deal.' She took his arm and guided him to the centre of the floor.

Her touch sent a thousand watt current flowing through his body and challenged his primal senses. He was as scared as when he first went solo on the Hunter aircraft. Was he dreaming? Was this really happening to him?

Miss Wilson placed Mani's right hand gently on the back of her slim waist and began to gyrate to a soft number playing on the gramophone. Mani felt stiff as a log. With the lessons he had learnt from Pits, he barely managed to sail through.

The proximity and the scent of her body intoxicated Mani. Such a phenomenal beauty was beyond his reach even in his wildest dreams. The little favour he received could at best qualify as common courtesy, or was perhaps meant to tease someone else in the crowd. He persuaded himself not to believe in the unthinkable, despite the tumult she unleashed in his heart.

When the song ended, Mani blushed as a child would on his first day at school. He thanked her and slipped into a dark corner outside the hall when someone tapped her shoulder. He took a quick swig of vodka from his hip flask to regain his senses and returned to watch the proceedings of the evening from a safe corner.

She approached him again. 'Come, let's have another dance,' she said, and took his hand in hers. A hand that felt as soft as the icing on a cake.

Mani followed her in a daze, like a puppy on a leash. Fortified with vodka, his legs moved a little more fluidly than before.

She gazed into his eyes. 'You're doing fine, Flight Lieutenant.'

Mani smiled, perhaps for the first time that evening. 'Thank you.'

Mani caught Bozo and Dodi staring at them from the other side of the hall, their faces flushed. He raised his chin and pulled her close.

'It was nice meeting you,' she said, when the session ended.

'Thank you for the lovely evening. It's wonderful to have met you.'

'I hope to see you again next week.'

Back in the officers' mess, the boys looked enviously across the dining hall and whispered to each other. They probably found it difficult to believe that he had won the favour of the best looking girl in town on his first outing.

❧

The next day, Bozo approached Mani at the bar. 'So, old chap, you seem to be on top of the world.'

Mani finished his drink and signalled the bartender for a refill.

'Better watch out, man, that girl is danger spelt with a capital *D*.'

Mani ignored him.

'It won't be long before we hear "mayday... mayday".'

Bozo chuckled.

'Get lost,' Mani said and toddled out of the bar, carrying his drink with him.

Mani lived every moment dreaming about Grace Wilson. He took dancing lessons from Pits more seriously and practiced his steps for hours in the privacy of his room, counting each day, impatient for the long week to end.

When they met at the club, Grace arrived in a beige skirt and a green blouse. A single yellow rose clipped to her hair enhanced her beauty.

Mani felt taller than his five-feet-seven-inch frame when she greeted him with a smile.

'Hello, Grace, you look absolutely stunning.'

She blushed. 'Thank you.'

Dressed in his bland regulation whites, Mani could hardly expect her to return the compliment. He felt awkward and resolved to replenish his wardrobe before the next weekend.

'Shall we dance?' She asked.

'Sure.'

They took to the floor and began dancing to a foxtrot number.

She arched an eyebrow. 'You're a fighter pilot, right?'

'Yes. I fly the Hunters.'

'It must be very exciting.'

'Of course, it is.'

'And dangerous?'

'Not really. If you know what you're doing.'

'Can't you take me for a ride in it?'

Mani chuckled. 'You must be joking.'

'No, I'm not.'

Mani wished he could smuggle her into a trainer aircraft and take her for a spin, but he couldn't risk a court-martial so early in his career. He shook his head. 'I'm afraid that's not possible.'

'How sad.'

'I can take you for a ride on my bike, though.'

Grace laughed, revealing her pearl-like teeth.

Mani ignored his buddies and enjoyed every moment with Grace Wilson, who stuck to him throughout the evening. At the end of the dance, Grace sprang a surprise. 'I would like you to have dinner at my place next Saturday.'

'Oh, I'd love to.' Mani was excited. 'What's the occasion? Are you having a party?'

Mani wondered if the invitation was meant to solicit a gift from him. He couldn't shake off his parsimony, even though he would have willingly sacrificed his left arm to win her heart. He had heard that the girls from the colony had taken many a Romeo for a ride, soliciting gifts on a regular basis. Birthdays, anniversaries and the like provided good excuses to expect gifts. He tried to rid his mind of such negative thoughts.

'No, no, nothing like that. I want you to meet my folks,' she said.

'I'd be delighted, but...'

'What?'

Mani hesitated. 'Err... I hate to bother you, but I'm vegetarian... eggetarian to be precise.' He sighed, as though being a vegetarian would have disqualified him for further invites. He had started eating the forbidden eggs only after joining the Air Force—a serious lapse according to his Dharma. He couldn't bear the mashed potatoes or the boiled vegetables served routinely in the mess in the garb of 'English food'.

She flashed a smile. 'No problem. My mother can do wonders with eggs.'

Mani started preparing for the day in earnest. One look at his wardrobe, however, left him despairing. He couldn't think of presenting himself at the Wilsons' door in those rags he had been wearing for several years. The regulation whites, the standard evening dress prescribed for the officers' mess, was out of the question. He wished he could share his predicament with his trusted friend, Pits, one of the best dressed among the gang who could surely suggest a thing or two. But he wanted to keep his visit a secret. So he decided to go to the market by himself.

When it came to civilian clothes, Mani had pedestrian tastes. He never looked beyond his uniform, his flying overalls or the whites. After browsing through many shops, he bought a pair of fawn-coloured trousers, a maroon shirt and a new pair of brown shoes. A yellow and green striped tie completed the picture. He felt uncomfortable while parting with a handsome amount on his indulgence. But when he put on the new clothes and looked into the mirror in his room, he forgot all about the hefty bill. For the first time in his life, he thought he looked presentable, if not handsome.

❧

On the appointed day, Mani sneaked out of his room and rode his bike straight to the railway colony to meet his dream girl. Dressed in a cream-coloured skirt and a black sleeveless blouse, Grace greeted him at the door. 'You're looking great today. Please come in.'

Grace introduced him to her parents, Mr Robert Wilson, the stationmaster, and Mrs Sandra Wilson, a tall, striking woman who looked a lot younger than her age.

Mani presented the gift-wrapped bottle of whiskey he had brought with him to Mrs Wilson. He had acquainted himself with the usual tactics employed by his enterprising mates in the squadron.

'Oh, that's very kind of you, Flight Lieutenant,' said the lady. 'But this wasn't necessary.'

Standing behind her mother, Grace pursed her lips—she obviously knew the standard operating procedures.

Sporting a French beard and thick moustache, Mr Wilson extended his hand.

Mani shook the stationmaster's hand, which felt a size too large compared to his own. 'Glad to meet you, sir.'

'Me too,' said the towering man squeezing Mani's hand.

Had the old man not joined the railways, he would have made an imposing character in a Hollywood movie.

Mrs Wilson welcomed Mani with heart-felt warmth. 'Please

make yourself comfortable.' She ushered him to a worn-out sofa.

Mr Wilson pulled out a bottle of rum from the cupboard, ostensibly received from a previous contender Mani couldn't help but wonder, as Grace set the glasses on the table. 'I hope you're comfortable with rum, Flight Lieutenant?'

'That's my usual, thank you.'

The old man poured the drinks. 'You fly the Hunters I believe.'

'Yes, sir.'

'Ah, how I wanted to be a fighter pilot,' he said, caressing his beard. 'But Sandra didn't quite like the idea. 'Too risky, she would say.' He threw a sideways glance at Mrs Wilson. 'I wouldn't have done anything without her express permission.'

Mrs Wilson shot him a look. 'Come on, Bob, I never objected. Why don't you say you never got a call?'

Mr Wilson cleared his throat. 'That's because I never applied.' He chuckled.

Mrs Wilson rolled her eyes. 'You wouldn't have fit into the cockpit anyway. Even if you did, the airplane couldn't have lifted off the ground with your bulk.'

Mani could barely suppress his laughter.

Sitting across from Mani, Grace said sharply, 'Mother, that's enough.'

The stationmaster said fondly, 'That's my girl.'

Mrs Wilson turned to Mani. 'Sorry, we keep pulling each other's leg all the time. The truth is, I wasn't comfortable when Bob wanted to join the Air Force.'

'Ma'am, Mr Wilson would have been an Air Marshall by now,' Mani said. 'And I would be shitting in my pants, sitting here with him.'

Everybody laughed, Mr Wilson the loudest.

Grace leant back in her chair and crossed her legs. Her skirt rose up to expose her supple thighs and a flash of black satin panties. Grace caught his eye and straightened. Feeling the rush of heat, Mani looked away and tried to join in the laughter.

The conversation drifted from the latest movies, Grace's college, to Mani's flying activities, and Mani and Grace stole a few glances. By the time Mrs Wilson laid out the dinner, the bottle of rum was more than half gone.

Mani found the food delicious and the company heartwarming. Compared to the environment back home, where a stern father ruled by the stick and a submissive mother didn't dare raise her voice, this was a different experience. The warmth with which the Wilsons treated him suggested that he had left a good impression.

Grace followed him to the gate when Mani took their leave. 'Care for a walk?'

'Sure.' Given a chance, Mani would have liked to walk the distance to the moon with her. The empty street, the trees swaying in the gentle breeze and her enticing scent intoxicated Mani. Walking alongside, he took a deep breath, and then another, as he stole furtive glances at Grace's slender behind. Her hips swayed majestically and challenged his senses. He wanted to pull her into his arms and kiss her, but he lacked the courage to do so.

'So when are you taking me for a ride on your motorbike?' Grace asked.

'How about tomorrow evening?'

'Suits me fine.'

'Seven o'clock, at the club.'

❧

Back in his room that night, Mani was ecstatic, as though he had conquered Helen of Troy. In the days that followed, he took her for long rides on his bike, and Grace gave him a few lessons in dancing. Clumsy in the beginning, Mani's proven skills with the controls in the cockpit of a Hunter aircraft helped him learn the basics rather quickly.

One day, Dodi cornered him in the bar. 'Shanks, don't get me wrong, but you better be careful with that female.'

That female. Mani clenched his jaw. First Bozo, and now Dodi. Mani didn't want to hear anything adverse about Grace from his jealous mates. 'What did you say?'

Dodi cleared his throat. 'The Wilson girl has quite a reputation, if you know what I mean.'

Mani glared, 'Excuse me?'

Dodi swallowed his drink and went on regardless. 'Grace Wilson is remarkably adept at falling in love when it suits her interests. She's an old hand at picking up unsuspecting dudes and then dumping them by the wayside. And now, it seems, she's found a new victim.'

Mani lit a cigarette and gave him a hard look.

Dodi went on. 'I mean, it's okay to have some fun, but you seem serious.'

'Why don't you mind your own business?' Mani said testily, blowing smoke into Dodi's face.

'Relax, man, no harm listening to some friendly advice. I'm sorry if I offended you, but I mean well.'

Mani signalled the barman for another drink and faced Dodi. 'Thank you very much, Mr Wise, I'll seek your advice if I need it.'

Dodi shrugged his shoulders and leant on the bar counter. 'Very well then, have your way. If you've decided to jump into the fire, I won't stop you, but don't say I didn't warn you.'

'Who the fuck do you think you are, my mother?' Mani snapped. 'You're all jealous, and I don't give a damn.'

Dodi picked up his glass and slipped out of the bar.

Left alone, Mani pondered for a moment. Indeed, Grace was a blazing fire, and he was ready to burn in it. Rumours going round the camp hinted that Grace was a known flirt and scandal suggested that she had dumped a few lovers in the past. But all of Mani's defensive armour failed against the onslaught of her potentially lethal, seductive charm. Her sexual appeal was the defining attribute of her personality. Fatally obsessed with Grace, Mani did not care what people said.

Grace and Mani met regularly, even on weekdays. Mrs Wilson went out of her way to pamper him with homemade cookies and cakes whenever he visited them. He forgot all about his Dharma and even succumbed to the taste of meat at the hands of Mrs Wilson. He particularly relished fried fish. The two went to movies, to dance sessions in the club and on long drives on the scenic highway out of town. The stationmaster never once raised the 'Red-flag'—it was 'Green' all the way.

Mani began to dream of grand entries at Air Force parties with Grace on his arm. He knew she would excel in social graces, which mattered a great deal in the Air Force. He shuddered at the thought of his distant cousin, Bhanumati, whom his father relentlessly championed as a prospective match for his son. Of all the cousins, distant or otherwise, he had seen but the least of Bhanumati. And the little he had seen of her presented a dismal picture. He could not imagine escorting her wrapped in a seven-yard Kanjeevaram sari to a social event, her long, greasy hair, smelling strongly of coconut oil and hugging her extra-large behind.

He made up his mind. He wanted none other than Miss Grace Wilson by his side, at any cost. To win the consent of his mother was easy, but to obtain it without the express permission of the headmaster would have been sacrilegious. After a great deal of thought, he gathered enough courage to write to his father about his desire to marry the Anglo-Indian girl. The reply came promptly in the form of a stern warning, threatening not to see his son's face again were he to think of marrying anyone other than Bhanumati.

❧

Breaking the news to Grace was not easy, but he did, on a rainy day when they took shelter under a tree during a long drive out of town.

'I'm not surprised,' she said, wiping her face with a handkerchief.

The clouds thundered ominously. Lightning struck at a distance, sounding like a warning. But Grace looked ever so charming.

She ran her hand through her hair. 'Why not seek your mother's intervention? She might be more understanding.'

Mani gazed at the dark clouds. 'My mother would never go against the wishes of my father.'

Grace knit her eyebrows. 'I don't understand why elders in your society are so domineering. Why can't they accept the choices you make in your life? You're not a baby.'

'I've made my choice and no power on earth can change it.'

Grace looked up.

Mani took her face in his hands. 'No one can separate us now.' He kissed her full on her mouth. She responded with equal hunger.

A week later, Mani proposed and the Wilsons approved. The news travelled fast and occasioned quite a few raised eyebrows in the officers' mess. When Pits announced their engagement during the weekly dance at the railway club, a hush fell over the hall. Girls whispered amongst themselves and boys looked dazed.

'I don't believe this,' someone whispered behind Mani's back. That the two of them had been going around together for some time was no secret, but the news of their engagement seemed to astound everybody. The immediate reaction of disbelief, and the uneasy silence that followed, tested the limits of decency and decorum. It took a while before a few half-hearted congratulations came their way.

Mani and Grace got married in the local church in a brief ceremony attended by a handful of the Wilsons' friends, with no representation from Mani's side of the family. For their honeymoon, they went to Digha, an isolated sea resort not far from the base and, from Mani's point of view, quite economical. His frugality nearly always got the better of him.

The glitz and glamour of the Air Force parties suited Grace perfectly. On special occasions, when senior commanders visited the station for inspections, gala parties were organised. Such events presented grand opportunities for the officers' wives to make fashion statements in their floral chiffons and colourful silks. Fancy lights illuminated the sprawling lawns and the finest service adorned the dinner tables . The VIPs, normally content with rum in the privacy of their homes, were pampered with the finest brands of scotch from the cellar.

The ladies strategised well in advance. Recognition in the right circles helped in the long run. Points scored on the dance floor added to one's overall grades. Grace bought an expensive evening gown from Calcutta on credit, prior to an important event. When she presented the bill, Mani knew it would take an entire month's salary to pay for the damn thing. 'Don't you think it's rather expensive?'

'I hardly have anything decent to wear for the occasion, darling,' she said. 'And I bought this at a sale at substantial discount.'

'How am I going to pay for this?' he muttered, thinking of other bills that had escaped her notice.

'All the girls are buying new dresses for the event.'

Mani sank into the nearest chair.

Grace put her hands on her hips. 'You wouldn't want me to

look like a maid, would you?'

Grace's tastes, Mani realised, were not cultivated with wisdom.

However, when he appeared at the venue with Grace on his arm in her glittering gown, all eyes turned in their direction. The conversation ceased. People thronged to greet her and the visiting dignitaries waited to gain her acquaintance. In those blissful moments, he forgot all about the bills. Grace became the centre of attention and glowed in the company of the big shots through most of the evening. She exuded such charm that even the VIPs did not leave her side. Mani could not but admire her from a distance as she danced by turns with honoured guests who waited on her throughout the evening.

❧

When sobriety returned in the morning, the pile of bills troubled Mani. A financial crisis seemed imminent. Mani had already given up his vodka and settled for rum to cut down on his bar bills. He carried on with the same drab lounge suit he had worn since his commissioning. Even the Kit-Maintenance-Allowance, which he claimed after completing seven years of service, went towards clearing some of the outstanding bills. The fading uniforms and the whites, he thought, were good enough for another seven years.

'Grace, do you mind having a look at our bills?' Mani asked one day as he brought the morning cup of tea for her highness, a routine that almost became a rule.

Grace didn't show any sign of having heard him.

'It's time to be serious,' he said.

Grace yawned and lazily reaching for her cup on the side table, asked, 'What time is it?'

Mani put his cup of tea on the table. 'I said it's time to be serious.'

She sipped her tea. 'I heard that.'

'So, what are we going to do about it?'

'Come on, Shanks, don't start the day with the bloody bills.'

Mani gaped at her in disbelief.

Grace picked up her cup and disappeared into the bathroom. He knew she wouldn't surface before he left for the squadron.

When it came to tactics, Grace was not found wanting.

2

Mani soon realised that Grace's slender legs had walked into his life with a whole lot of unpaid bills. He wondered how he had succumbed to the charms of a Marilyn Monroe conducting herself like the Princess Grace of Monaco despite hailing from the railway barracks of Kharagpur. The tenth of each month saw them practically broke. Thereafter, they lived on credit, or free invites, which were aplenty. Grace maintained a busy social calendar. Her presence at parties was in great demand, with or without Mani—preferably the latter.

And one day, while having dinner, she dropped a bombshell. 'Don't you think it's time we had a car, darling?'

The *darling* sounded like a 30 mm bullet into Mani's chest. Without four wheels, her majesty's comfort level was far too short of her aspirations.

Mani sensed immediate danger. 'Are you out of your mind?'

Grace passed a plate of salad to him. 'Why? All your friends have one, including some of your juniors.'

'So what?' he snapped. 'I wasn't born with a bank balance.'

Grace was not one to give up so easily. 'Why can't you raise some loans like others?'

'Fine, and who do you think will pay the instalments—Mr Wilson?'

Blood rushed to her face. She pushed her chair back and stomped out of the room.

For the next two days, Grace sulked with a face longer than a pregnant cow's and remained uncommunicative. Mani tried to reason with her, but patience was not one of her virtues. She knew what she wanted, and employed her charm to advantage.

Grace was difficult to handle and Mani stopped short of taking firm action for fear of losing her. He was holding a goldfish that could slip away any moment. After much dilly-dallying, Mani relented and applied for a car loan. Within a couple of months, he managed to get a second-hand Standard Herald car from Calcutta and drove it home with pride. Excitement gripped him when he turned into the driveway and honked.

Grace appeared at the door in a sexy mini skirt. Mani jumped out and leant against the bonnet, hoping to delight her.

He should have known better. Mani could hardly recall an occasion when Grace rewarded him with gratitude. That day too she lived up to her reputation.

'What the hell is this?' Grace recoiled.

Mani didn't expect such a hostile reception from the woman who had not used anything other than a battered bicycle in her father's home. He wanted to crash the damn car against the nearest pole. 'What did you expect, a Rolls-Royce?'

That should have silenced her, but Grace was made of different timber.

'No,' she shrieked, 'but certainly not this piece of shit from some junkyard.'

Her arrogance was appalling. For a moment, Mani considered driving the car back to where it came from. However, after seven hours of driving through rough terrain, he did not have the heart or the energy to do so.

Seeing some movement in the neighbouring house, Mani lowered his voice. 'It has four wheels, and it runs.'

'I hate to see this trash in my driveway. Take it away and dump it somewhere else.'

Mani's face grew hot and his shoulders tensed. 'Excuse me, you didn't marry an Arab Sheikh for God's sake,' he yelled, loud enough for the whole neighbourhood to hear.

Grace turned and stormed angrily into the house. Mrs Khan, their immediate neighbour, peeped over the fence, staring disapprovingly at the new contraption that stood in the driveway. Ignoring her, Mani got into the car, slammed the door hard and parked it in the garage.

It remained there for almost a week.

Grace hated the lacklustre grey of the car and the drab upholstery. Mani raised an additional loan from his provident fund for a fresh coat of paint—a blazing red—and new covers for the seats, before her majesty considered it fit to display it in her driveway or ride in it.

Grace took driving lessons from Mani and when his firm commands became unbearable, she switched over to the younger lot in the squadron, who willingly obliged. She picked up fast. While Mani continued using his old bike for his trips to the squadron, Grace drove around the camp, visiting friends and attending kitty parties wherein a select group of ladies assembled routinely to gossip about the latest scandals over tea. Grace constantly complained about Mandira, the Squadron Commander's wife, who commanded more authority outside of flying than her husband.

'I hate that snooty woman,' Grace said after returning from a party.

'Better start loving her,' Mani said, 'even if you don't like her mug-face.'

'I don't care if she's the boss's wife,' she snapped. 'You can lick her ass if you like.'

Mani's face knotted at the dreadful suggestion.

Grace scrunched up her nose. 'Once that woman gets going, there's no alternative but to listen to her babble without interruption.'

'Then why go to these parties?'

'She constantly bitches about everything and everyone,' Grace flapped her hands in the air. 'The bloody woman is loudest in self-praise.'

The haughty woman belonged to ordinary stock from Kapurthala in Punjab, but her long tenure in the service had taught Mandira enough to hold her court with authority. Grace threatened to put the annoying woman in her place, but Mani warned her to never do so if she wanted a peaceful existence at the station and avoid packing her bags in a hurry.

Mani drummed his fingers on the table. 'I'm sure we could save some money if you stop hosting kitty parties.'

Grace fumed. 'Money, money and money—that's all you can think of.' She threw her purse on the table and disappeared into their bedroom.

'Grace, for heaven's sake, look at our bills,' Mani pleaded. 'How are we going to pay for them?'

'What do you expect me to do? Wear payjamas to your parties?'

'Come on, Grace, let's be sensible. We have to cut down on our spending if you want us out of trouble.'

She cocked her head, 'Oh, so I'm responsible for all the trouble, am I?'

Mani's patience had long been tried. He threw the stack of bills on the table. 'See for yourself.'

Grace swiftly removed herself from the room, wiggling her

shapely behind as she did, without looking at the bills.

He knew he had married a live bomb, ready to explode at the slightest provocation. It wasn't easy to defuse her.

❧

Grace took up a teaching job at the camp school, not so much to contribute to the kitty but to kill the boredom at home. It provided Mani some relief, but only temporarily. She continued living beyond their combined means, which lead to acrimonious debates. When matters came to a head, Grace simply walked out and went to her parents in the railway colony—a clever diversion she often employed. Back in familiar territory, she visited the club regularly and danced with the fighter boys from the base until late into the night.

That horde also included Squadron Leader George—a known flirt. George had recently joined the squadron as the Flight Commander, Mani's immediate boss. His reputation as a ladies' man travelled faster than the Hunter aircraft with the afterburners on.

Mani's official duties often took him away from the base for short periods of time. Grace usually went to her parents in his absence, but stopped after George appeared on the scene. Mani discovered that Grace had been partying with George at their home in his absence.

Returning from one such trip, he confronted her as she was changing for the night. 'What's going on here?'

'Like what?' she asked.

'Between you and that bloody George.'

'What do you mean?' she retorted, sliding out of her dress in front of the full-length mirror. 'There's nothing going on.'

'Don't give me all that crap. You damn well know what I mean.'

She gazed into the mirror. 'No, I don't.'

'If that son-of-a-bitch walks into this house ever again,' he yelled, 'I'll break his legs and give you a permanent dent on your beautiful nose, you hear me?'

Grace frowned. 'You've gone nuts.'

Looking at the reflection of Grace's gorgeous figure in the mirror, he was tempted to pin her down on the floor and take her there and then. But his rage overtook his urge.

'People are talking, dammit.'

She reacted sharply. 'To hell with people, I don't give a damn. What can I do if people gossip about me?'

'I'm warning you, Grace, don't try to mess with me.'

'Oh come on, man,' she screamed back. 'If you're so damn hung up about it, why didn't you marry that Bhanumati? She would have suited you well.'

Mani didn't have an answer to that.

❧

A year after Mani and Grace's marriage, Mr Wilson retired from the railways and moved to Pimpri, near Poona, where his father had left him a small dwelling. Mani and Grace paid them a brief visit. While Mani kept himself busy with his painting, Grace didn't seem to enjoy her stay in that sleepy town.

'Don't you think we've had enough of this place?' she asked one day, looking out of the tiny window that opened out to a garbage dump. 'I would rather we go home.'

'But we still have another ten days to go before my leave expires,' Mani said, without lifting his head from his canvas.

'I've had enough of this place already.'

Mani missed his flying too, but he kept quiet and continued to paint.

Grace glowered. 'Are you listening?'

'Yes.'

'I said something about going home.'

'You're the boss, why ask me?'

'Then go and book the seats.'

'All right, if you wish,' Mani put down his brush and looked up. 'I was wondering if we could spend a day or two in Bombay to visit an old friend of mine, if that's okay with you?'

'Of course, that would be fine. Any place would be better than this hole.'

❧

They took leave of Grace's parents and left for Bombay. To economise, Mani decided to stay at the officers' mess at Cotton Green. He informed his old friend, Rusi Shenoy, that he was in town with his wife and keen to meet him.

Having flown the dilapidated Dakotas with the Air Force for a number of years, Rusi had resigned and joined the Indian Air Lines. He arrived at the officers' mess with his wife, an air hostess, in a gleaming, cream-coloured Jaguar to take them home for dinner. When introduced to Grace, Rusi couldn't take his eyes off her. Mani was all too familiar with the kind of impact Grace had on people. Rusi's wife, Monaz, clad in jeans and a loose shirt, surprised him. With her hair cut short and a lean face, she could easily be mistaken for a boy.

After exchanging preliminaries, Monaz turned to Grace. 'You should've come to our flat instead of staying in the mess,' she said, in a less than enthusiastic voice.

'Absolutely,' added Rusi.

Mani shrugged. 'It's only for two nights.'

'I'm not concerned about you, Shanks,' Rusi said, his eyes still riveted on Grace. 'You can sleep on the railway platform for all I care. But I dread to imagine how this young lady is going to stay in these barracks built to house troops during the Second World War.'

Grace tilted her head and smiled.

Mani ignored Rusi's impertinence and resisted the urge to remind him that they had spent months in worse conditions during their training days. 'Thanks, maybe next time.'

Monaz didn't press the matter further as Rusi opened the rear door of the Jaguar for Grace to get in.

A whiff of rich perfume filled Grace's nostrils as Monaz sat by her side. The car surged forward with a soft purr and rapidly gained speed. The richness of the leather upholstery and the plush interior made Grace feel out of place. Thinking of her jalopy back home that rattled even while idling, Grace felt small. This thing moved like a boat cruising through calm waters.

'Is this your first visit to Bombay?' Monaz asked.

'Yes.'

'Rusi told me about your visit only this morning when I flew in from Paris.'

Grace responded with a weak smile and turned to look out of the window, wondering how this matchstick-like lasso had hooked such a dashing chap. The Jaguar, and then Paris—it was enough to bring a lump to her throat. Coming from a backward place like Kkd, the glitter on the streets of Bombay overwhelmed her. She wondered if she would ever get a chance to live out of the woods where the Air Force built most of its bases.

Seated in the front, the old buddies exchanged news about the-good-old-days and common friends. Grace caught Rusi peering at her through the rear-view mirror. She turned away.

❧

Another shock awaited her when they arrived at the Shenoys' duplex flat at Worli. Thick rugs, plush furniture and heavy silk drapes presented a picture of affluence. Elegantly framed paintings adorned the walls. Souvenirs from across the world graced every nook and cranny of the spacious room. The magnificent view of the ocean through the large living room window and the elegant bar with its vast range of liquor astonished her. Back home, all she could display in her dining room cabinet was a bottle of rum and a half of whiskey.

Monaz led Grace towards the couch. 'Come, let's sit here. It has a better view of the ocean.'

Grace stole an envious glance at her hostess. The Plain-Jane made an odd pairing with the debonair pilot, but then her own pairing was no better.

'I wish I could have shown you around,' said Match Stick. 'Unfortunately, Rusi's flying to Delhi tomorrow, and I'm off to London the day after. Our schedules are so tight. Things are getting on my nerves.'

Given the choice, Grace would've willingly traded her own nerves with that of her hostess. She surveyed the well-decorated room again. The only decorative pieces in her drawing room were the Gunnery-Meet trophies Mani polished regularly as though they were family jewels, and a couple of unframed paintings Mani had done in his spare time. Her heart ached when she thought of the cheap five-by-eight rug and the drab curtains they had bought at a sale. Grace's stomach churned as wildly as the waves in the ocean. She remained withdrawn for most of the evening, wondering if she too should have joined an airline rather than settling into dreary matrimony.

'Would you like some wine?' Monaz asked.

Grace didn't register the offer at first. Her response came, but after a pause. 'I wouldn't mind.'

'What's your preference?'

Before Monaz could suggest any exotic names to mock her, Grace replied, 'Anything will do, as long as there's alcohol in it.'

Monaz chuckled and asked Rusi to pour wine into two glasses. She picked up an album from the coffee table to show their photographs taken in London, Paris and a whole lot of other places Grace had never heard of. Grace went through the motions of viewing the pictures with an occasional nod, allowing their hostess to do most of the talking.

As the evening wore on, a housemaid in spotless whites served food on the thick glass-top dining table. Despite the tantalising aroma, the elaborate spread left a bad taste in Grace's mouth. She could hardly relish the food because of sheer jealousy and didn't wish to stay longer than necessary. She swallowed her food silently, without taking part in the conversation she found utterly boring.

After exhausting the stories of their glorious days and the variety of food on the table, the old buddies poured another round of scotch for the road.

Grace couldn't bear it anymore. 'Let's make a move now.' She rose from her chair. 'It's getting late and I'm tired.'

Rusi glanced at his watch. 'It's only half past ten. How about some liqueur and cheese? We've saved some exotic stuff for special occasions.'

Special occasion be damned. 'No thanks, I'd rather leave now.'

Mani had to take leave of his friend rather unceremoniously. A driver drove them back to Cotton Green. Grace kept gazing out of the window nonchalantly, as brilliant neon lights of the streets faded into late-evening smog.

The uneasy silence on the drive back made Mani uncomfortable. It was not the best time to engage Grace in conversation, but he ventured, 'Are you okay?'

Grace dismissed the question with a wave of her hand without turning her head.

Mani considered it prudent not to ruffle her nerves further, especially in the presence of the driver. His thoughts wandered back to Rusi. How could this man, who had failed to make it to the fighter-stream of the Air Force, live in such splendour? Even with limited hours of flying in the comforts of the cockpit of an airliner, Rusi clearly earned much more than Mani did. He was anguished at the glaring disparity.

Back in the barracks, it was dark, hot and humid, with no electricity. Taking his own time to come out of his slumber, an orderly managed to produce a stub of candle.

'Good lord, what a contrast.' Grace's voice dripped disgust. 'It beats me why you didn't think of joining an airline like your friend, instead of sticking to the Hunters and bragging about your trophies.' She snatched the candle from Mani's hand and vanished into the bathroom.

Mani swallowed his pride with some difficulty, and decided not to create a scene at that late hour. He quietly slipped onto the lawn outside. Arguably, he wasn't doing all that bad. He'd come a long way from Poddukkottai, where most of his schoolmates had settled into insignificant jobs. And he had a full career ahead of him. From Grace's point of view, however, he was nobody, especially after the distressing visit to the Shenoys. He realised it had been a mistake to visit his friend with Grace.

Dressed in a white nightgown, her hair falling free, Grace emerged from the bathroom, holding the candle in her hand. Despite the frown on her face, she looked alluring. Mani's heart melted instantly. Perhaps she deserved better in life. Had she competed in a beauty pageant, she would've walked off with the crown and moved on to bigger things in life. Mani Shankar Varadharajan from Poddukkottai would've had no chance with her whatsoever.

'Sweetheart, there's something called destiny,' he said, trying to pacify her. 'I hope you understand that. We should be thankful to God for what we have, rather than brooding over what we do not.'

She flared. 'Yes, and what we have here is this shithouse which stinks, soiled linen, the sagging beds, mosquitoes for company, and no light—and you call yourself officers? What bloody officers?'

Mani couldn't take it anymore. 'That's enough. I didn't promise you the moon in the first place. You knew perfectly well what you were getting into.'

Grace shoved the candle into the ashtray. 'I wish I had known.'

'Stop cribbing for God's sake,' he yelled, flapping his hands in the air. 'At least I'm not carrying those red and green flags on the railway platforms like your father did all his life.'

Mani couldn't see her face in the dark, but it seemed to have silenced her.

3

Back in Kkd, the squadron was celebrating its anniversary at Digha, an isolated beach resort on the eastern coast, a three-hour drive from the base. Several rooms were booked in the only hotel in the sleepy town. Soon after arrival, the whole bunch went straight into the tempting waters of the sea, a welcome relief from the hot June evening.

For the next hour, people sang, danced and played games. Beer flowed freely. With George at his flirting best, Grace seemed to enjoy every moment. After a while, Mani saw Grace and George drifting away from the crowd, frolicking in the waters. Grace's wet blouse, with the top button undone, clung to her body, leaving nothing to the imagination. Mani felt awkward as people exchanged furtive glances.

Unable to bear it any longer, he confronted Grace. 'Aren't you ashamed of parading your body?'

George slipped away.

'What do you mean parading? Should I wear a breastplate?'

'No, you might as well remove your blouse for all I care.'

'I will, if I want to.'

'Shut up and behave, will you?'

Grace knit her eyebrows. 'Excuse me. We aren't in a church, for God's sake. Why don't you have some fun for a change?'

'I'm not going to tolerate this shameful act of yours.'

Grace looked him in the eye. 'What's your problem? I didn't come here to sit with a long face in a corner.'

'That's enough.'

Grace sauntered off with a hip-swaying stride.

'Hey, Shanks, where's your beer?' George yelled from a distance, with a condescending grin.

Mani ignored him and turned away.

'Come on, Bozo,' shouted the obnoxious fellow. 'Get him a bottle of beer, will you?'

Bozo pulled out a chilled bottle from the icebox and handed it to Mani.

Mani snatched it from him and moved away.

Seeing him alone, Mandira, the squadron commander's wife, came to his rescue–or so he thought.

'Hi Shanks, why aren't you joining in the fun?'

'Thank you, ma'am, I'm enjoying myself.'

'I can see that,' she said, pointedly looking at Grace who was jumping around with a bottle of beer in her hand. 'Grace's having a lot of fun…the life of the party as usual.'

Mani cringed.

She nudged him. 'Come on, join us.'

'I'd rather enjoy the show from here, if you don't mind.'

She rolled her eyes. 'Quite a show, I must say.'

It hurt. Before he could react, a few revellers pulled Mandira away, carrying her in their arms and dropping her with a splash in the water. The crowd clapped and cheered. They lifted all the other ladies by turns, Grace the highest.

The partying went on till the early hours of the morning. Mani sulked in his corner for most of the time, guzzling beers, hardly talking to anybody. He had already downed two bottles and asked for more.

'You've had one too many, Shanks,' Bozo said. 'You should have something to eat so you don't get sick.'

Mani staggered and glared at him. 'Don't you mother me, you fucker. Just get me the damn bottle, or else...'

'Or else what?'

'I'll knock your brains out, that's what.'

Bozo sniggered at him. 'You better take care of your wife before somebody knocks her.'

A surge of anger hit him hard. He raised his fist and charged at Bozo.

Dodi immediately restrained him to prevent a brawl. A few eyes turned their way. The boys dragged Mani to his room before things became worse. Grace followed them.

❧

'You're nothing but a slut,' Mani shouted at Grace, as soon she entered the room.

Pits and Dodi immediately withdrew from the scene. Grace shut the door behind her and faced Mani.

'A downright tramp, that's what you are.' Mani continued spitting fire.

'Hold your tongue,' she retorted.

'You don't give a damn how I feel,' he shrieked, staggering into the toilet to empty his bladder. 'A bloody whore,' he muttered from inside the toilet.

High on booze and low on self-control, he blasted her as he came back into the room, his fly open. 'I'm warning you. If you don't behave...I'll...I'll shoot you...I'll shoot both of us...yes, both of us.'

Grace put her hands on her hips. 'Stop it. I'm not about to take any bullshit from you.'

'Fuck you,' he mumbled and dropped down on the bed, face down and boots on.

❧

Grace ignored him, boots and all, and went to take a shower.

Unable to sleep, Grace tossed and turned on the bed, while Mani snored like an exhausted pig. Deep down, she knew that George had charmed her like no man had ever done before. She regretted having married Shanks in haste, bowing to the pressure from her parents.

She remembered her father's words in his characteristic railway jargon. 'My dear, you've missed out on the Mail, and if you miss the Express, you'll have no option but to settle for the Passenger, in which the journey of life can become cumbersome.' Her father's prophecy seemed to have come true. Her journey in life with Mani had started wobbling, like a passenger train rattling on metre gauge rails.

The morning after, Grace left the room before Mani woke up. She sat under the garden umbrella on the sands, with a cup of tea and a newspaper. She knew Mani was hurting, but she had never learnt to apologise for anything. The memory of Dave, her first boyfriend, flashed through her mind. Young and dashing, Flying Officer David had died in a motorcycle accident following a nasty quarrel with her. Then came Sexy, Flight Lieutenant Saxena, suave and mature beyond his years, ideal husband material. But she dumped him in favour of the more flamboyant, Garry. The affair didn't last long. When she learned about Garry's inclination towards the plump, overfed daughter of the base commander—for reasons other than love—she discarded him. The bloody man saw an obvious advantage in marrying the daughter of a rising star in the Air Force hierarchy.

'You are not getting any younger,' her father constantly warned her. Grace had to settle for someone fast, and in walked Mani, humble and sober, and different from the others who came with bottles of rum and false promises. Mani seemed more committed. Coaxed by her parents, she gave in. After all, a matrimonial alliance with an officer in uniform was no less an achievement. Besides, Mani was the only one who had proposed, unlike the others who came only for fun.

Mani approached, jolting her out of her thoughts. He pulled up a chair by her side and sat down. She hid her face behind the newspaper.

'Morning,' he said.

She turned the page, ignoring him.

After a long stretch of silence he muttered, 'I… I'm sorry, Grace.'

She instinctively knew she had won the first round by making him apologise first.

'Come on, angel, be a good girl,' he pleaded. 'I'll make up for it, I promise.'

Grace remained unmoved. Mani lowered his head to catch her eyes, but she didn't oblige.

Suddenly, she threw the paper on the table and looked him in the eye. 'Why the hell do you drink so much if you can't hold it?'

Mani locked his fingers and straightened up in his chair. 'These boys, you know… they forced it on me.'

'Like hell they did. Don't lie to me. I'm warning you once and for all that I will not tolerate such nonsense from you anymore.'

Mani lowered his voice. 'I'm sorry, I just lost my mind, but you crossed the limits.'

'What limits? We came here to enjoy ourselves, not to brood in a corner like you did the whole evening.'

He kept quiet.

Grace knew she had won the second round also. Despite a niggling guilt, she handled the situation quite deftly, transferring the blame onto Mani. She dug her lead further, 'I was ashamed of your conduct last night.'

'I wasn't too proud of yours either.'

'That's your problem, not mine.'

'Let's leave it at that, Grace, no point arguing.'

Grace thought likewise and looked the other way.

After a while Mani rose from his chair. 'Let's go for a drive and pack our breakfast for a private picnic away from the crowds.'

'First, you insult me in front of everybody, threaten to shoot me, and now you expect me to go for a picnic with you? What do you think I am? A dummy?' Grace fumed.

'Come on, sweetheart. Forget about what happened last night. It's a new day.'

'New day for you, but it's the same old story for me.'

Mani raised his hands. 'I said I'm sorry.'

She turned her face towards the sea.

'What shall we order for breakfast?'

'I don't care.'

Mani summoned the waiter and ordered him to pack Grace's favourites: stuffed paronthas, egg bhurji and assorted pickles. He borrowed Dodi's motorbike, and they set course on the smooth sands of the beach, carrying a couple of beers in a picnic basket.

They drove for a few miles on the shore without encountering a single soul. The sheer vastness of the horizon, sky simply merging with the sea, left Grace breathless. They sat on the rocks by the sea to enjoy their beers and the constant roar as waves crashed against the rocky shore. When the sun rose high, they moved under the shade of palm trees on the shore.

'Look at that,' said Mani, pointing to the twin rocks where they had sat a minute ago. 'Don't those looks like two lovers from this distance, sitting side by side, with the woman resting her head on her lover's shoulder?'

Grace, now mellow, gazed at the figures. 'Yes indeed.'

'I'd like us to be like that forever.'

'Not after what you said last night.'

'I swear I didn't mean what I said.'

She rolled her eyes. 'Like hell you didn't.'

Mani leant back on his side and faced Grace. 'Have a heart, Grace. I'm your husband. I hate to see anybody fooling around with you, especially that George. Don't you understand?'

'He wasn't fooling around with me. We were all having fun.'

'And people were making fun of me, because of the way you were jumping around.'

'Oh, come on. Let's not start all over again.'

Mani took a deep breath and lapsed into silence.

'Enjoy the scene,' Grace said, sipping her beer.

Mani sat up. 'Indeed, what a spectacle. Nature is the biggest sculptor of all. You see figures in the clouds, the mountains... like those twin rocks.'

'Let's give this place a name.' Grace suggested brightly.

'Like what?'

Grace gazed at the rocks. 'Mmm..."Lovers' Point"... maybe "Lovers' Peak".'

Mani thought for a few seconds. 'How about "Lovers' Rock"? I think it fits very well.'

'Cool. "Lovers' Rock" sounds nice.'

❧

In that vastness, Mani felt as if they were two tiny pieces of straw, about to be blown away any moment by strong winds. The insignificance of living beings, viewed in the context of the immense universe, had never been so glaring. But he refused to blow away just like that—he had much more to accomplish in life.

'Just imagine,' he said after a long stretch of silence, 'the gigantic sea out there can easily swallow a whole aircraft like a small toy, without anyone knowing about it.'

Grace turned around. 'Can't you think of anything better in the morning?'

Mani continued, 'The ocean has actually swallowed a whole lot of ships in the past. Most of them disappeared into its depths without a trace. People are still hunting for lost treasures in its belly. Maybe we too should give it a try.' He chuckled.

'How brilliant; go ahead, who's stopping you?'

'Maybe I should.' She missed the graveness of his tone.

'I hope you find something worthwhile.' She stood up and ambled towards the shimmering waves.

Mani allowed his thoughts to wander about the vast sea and the total isolation it provided. Gradually, an idea took shape in his mind. He mulled it over. An ideal setting... so vast and isolated... and not a soul in sight... just a toy disappearing into its belly!

The enormity of his thought sent goose pimples crawling up his arms. He lit a cigarette and took a long drag, gazing at Grace. The strong winds blew her skirt high, revealing her slender legs. He was noticing her legs without thinking about unpaid bills after a long time. He didn't want to lose her at any cost, and was prepared to do just about anything in the world to make her happy. Swiftly moving towards her, he pulled her back towards the shadows, and took her into his arms, kissing her passionately.

❧

A week later, Mani and Grace drove back to Digha, this time on his motorbike.

'A small airplane can easily take off or land on these smooth sands.' Mani accelerated on the isolated beach as though preparing to take off.

'Slow down, will you? I'm scared,' Grace screamed sitting pillion, her voice nearly lost in the roar of the bike and the constant thunder of the crashing waves. Mani continued speeding the bike at full throttle. Grace hid her face behind his back, clutching him tight, until they gradually came to a stop.

'Are you mad?' She trembled with rage. 'You don't care, do you? I'll never ride a bike with you again,' her eyes were blazing while dismounting from the rear seat.

'Oh come on, Grace, it's no big deal, I'm sure you enjoyed it.'

'Enjoyed my foot, dammit. I was scared to death.'

'Trust me, sweetheart, you're in safe hands. Let me show you how thrilling it is. Come and sit in the front.'

Grace's eyes turned wide. 'You must be joking!'

'No I'm not, just hop on. I'm sure you will love it.'

Despite her protests, he persuaded Grace into the driver's seat, while he took the controls of the bike from behind. It must've scared the hell out of her, but she took her position holding the handlebar firmly. When they gained considerable speed, Mani left the steering column in Grace's hands. Due to sheer momentum, the bike maintained a steady course.

'Oh no… I'm dead!' Grace cried out. Finally, Mani cut the engine and slowly glided the bike to a halt near his destination—the Lovers' Rock.

Grace dismounted unsteadily. 'You're mad.'

He smiled. 'Tell me honestly, didn't you enjoy the ride?'

'Never again. I don't wish to die in this wilderness to provide food for the vultures.'

'Don't be silly, I know you're thrilled.'

'Like hell I am.'

They walked over to the rocks and viewed the ocean.

'It's breathtaking,' said Grace. 'I wish I could live here in a cottage overlooking the sea ... and lots of creepers, climbing all over the slopping roofs ... with canopied windows jutting out.'

Mani peered at her. 'Dreams can come true, if you have the will and courage to achieve them.' He waited for a few seconds and then slowly unfolded the plan that had been brewing in his mind since their last visit.

Grace's jaw dropped, her face turned pale. 'How outrageous, man, have you gone nuts?' she blurted. 'Is this a bloody joke? How could you ever think of such a ridiculous thing?'

'I'd do anything in this world to make you happy.'

'This is bullshit. Don't give me all this crap.'

Mani often marvelled at how quickly the women in the squadron picked up the crew-room jargon and crude slang. 'Bloody', 'bullshit', 'crap', the 'F' words and the like never seemed to have existed in their vocabulary before their marriage. Grace too adopted them with remarkable flourish and never shied away from using them liberally—so much so that Mani was terrified of leaving her unsupervised.

'This crap has nearly two hundred thousand rupees waiting at the end, if you're willing to cooperate.'

Grace caught his eyes. 'What do you mean?'

'Two-hundred-bloody-thousand, nothing less,' he said. 'And total freedom to start a new life somewhere.'

Grace gasped, 'You don't say...'

'I see a nice big cottage on the shore covered with lush green creepers, a beautiful Ford Convertible with tail fins standing in the porch, and us playing with our kids in the front garden, or bathing in the sea.'

The corner of her eyes crinkled. 'This is crazy stuff, for God's sake.'

'Imagine what we can do with that kind of money…live like kings.'

'What if…'

'There're no ifs and buts,' he said. 'You've got to trust me. If you do as I say, we can pull it off.'

Lost in her own thoughts, Grace remained a mute listener for the rest of the evening as Mani narrated the finer points of his plan.

❧

During the next two months, Mani flew solo over Digha a couple of times on aerial reconnaissance. Later, on a full moon, he biked to Digha—alone, this time, carrying with him essential supplies. He drove straight to Lovers' Rock, fully prepared with his camping gear to spend the night on the beach.

Under the bright moon, he didn't need the bike's headlight to negotiate his way on the deserted stretch along the coast. Reaching his destination, he selected a slightly raised bit of ground under a cluster of trees, some hundred yards behind Lovers' Rock, to camp for the night. He fixed himself a stiff drink of rum and, glass in hand, strolled towards the whispering waves that glistened under the moonlight.

Once again, he marvelled at the magnificent landscape, far more enchanting than what he had seen in daylight. It was pure joy to watch the silvery moon and listen to the constant play of waves. He resolved to capture the beauty of Lovers' Rock on his canvas some day. After his second drink, he ate dinner and slipped into his sleeping bag.

He woke up at first light and surveyed the general area through his binoculars. Not a soul anywhere. Satisfied, he drove his bike in the southward direction to familiarise himself with the terrain. Six miles down the coast, the long stretch of sandy beach terminated in huge rocks at the foot of a hillock. He parked his bike and climbed the hill. He didn't see any sign of human habitation for miles.

Back at his camping site, he hid his equipment in a ditch, and covered it with foliage. Later, when he drove back to Digha, he stopped near the bus stand to buy cigarettes from a vendor.

Lighting up, he asked, 'By the way, what time does the morning bus leave for Nurpur?'

'Usually at seven,' the vendor answered, 'if the driver is not too drunk.'

'He couldn't be drunk that early in the day.'

'That bloke is perpetually drunk. I wouldn't step onto his bus if I were you.'

'Is there any choice?'

'Yes, you can swim,' the vendor laughed out loud.

Mani smiled. 'Thank you for the information.' He kick-started his bike and roared out of the sleepy town.

4

At long last, D-day arrived on a cold November night. The squadron was engaged in night flying exercises during the moon phase. Mani changed into his flying overalls, ready to leave for the flight, when a sudden apprehension gripped him. He looked at his reflection in the mirror, not quite believing that he was about to do what he had planned for months. It was one thing to plan—to execute, quite another. He shuddered to think of the 'what if...?' It was too late to worry about the consequences. He slipped a photograph of Grace into his pocket and came into the living room.

Grace stood with a glass of wine. 'I'm scared, Shanks... not sure if we should go through with this... it's too frightening.'

'Believe me, everything will turn out fine. Just follow each step carefully.'

Grace lit a cigarette and took a few quick drags, avoiding Mani's eyes.

'Relax, will you? There's no going back now.' He caressed her cheeks. 'Everything's been worked out well.' He looked at his watch, and then at Grace. 'It's time to go, sweetheart.'

She stood motionless, gazing at the door. Mani knew he would never walk through that door again. He pulled her closer. 'Remember, one wrong move, and we're done.'

She took a deep breath and nodded. 'Be careful out there.'

'I will, I promise.' He lifted her chin and kissed her. 'How am I going to survive three months without you?'

Grace buried her face in his chest.

Mani reached for his helmet and stopped at the door. 'Stick to the plan, no matter what.'

'I will,' she mumbled, with the hint of a smile at the corner of her mouth. 'No matter what.'

He rushed out of the door. Grace followed. Mani kick-started his bike and left with a thunderous roar, looking back for a fleeting moment at the bend, to wave at Grace. Standing near the gate, she waved back.

❧

Grace took a deep breath and gazed at the full moon, ever so bright and shining. She wondered if her life would be as bright and shining as the moon. She sat on the steps of her verandah and shuddered against the cool evening breeze—or was it the fear of uncertainty? After waiting for a few minutes she returned and refilled her glass.

A little later, the deafening sound of the after-burners jolted her. She dashed out into the open and gazed at the lone fighter aircraft zooming high into the sky, leaving a trail of fire in its wake. Her eyes remained glued to it until the aircraft became a dot, finally disappearing into the horizon.

Back in her room, she didn't believe it was really happening. A hundred thoughts raced through her mind. She felt restless and switched on the radio to distract herself. What she heard sent shivers down her spine. John F Kennedy had been shot dead in Dallas, and the whole world grieved. Her heart sank. For a few moments she forgot about Mani, and mourned like any other on earth. Shaking with anxiety, she slumped into a sofa and wondered at the strange coincidence—a catastrophic moment for the world, and a life-changing one for her.

Later, when she heard the haunting wail of sirens cutting through the quiet of the night, of vehicles moving about in the distance, a helicopter taking off, she knew it was time to brace herself for her act.

❧

She hurriedly ate her dinner and waited. Soon, an unusual calm descended on the base—like the ominous lull before a storm. She switched off the lights in her bedroom and lay on her bed, listening to the tick-tock of the wall clock. Minutes later, a staff car pulled up at her gate. Grace wasn't surprised, but her heart started pounding against her chest. The doorbell rang once, and then again. She rose, and took a deep breath. When she opened the door, Wing Commander Randhir Singh, the Squadron Commander, stood in semidarkness, his wife a step behind him.

Grace switched on the lights. 'Sorry, I had dozed off.'

The man in flying overalls removed his cap and cleared his throat. 'I'm sorry, Grace…there's been an accident.'

Grace stood still.

The officer hesitated. 'I'm afraid…it's Shanks…his aircraft is missing.'

'No!' she gasped, leaning against the door.

'Shanks reported control failure.'

'No…'

'I'm sure he ejected safe somewhere. We're taking every possible measure to trace him and are confident of getting some news by morning, if not during the night.'

Grace's knees buckled and she shook her head. 'I don't believe this…I…'

Mandira put her hand on Grace's shoulder. 'Please don't panic, Grace.'

'Shanks knows the emergency drills better than anybody else in the squadron,' the Wing Commander said. 'I'm sure he's ejected safe.'

Grace staggered into the living room and slumped into the sofa, burying her face in her hands. Mandira followed and sat next to her. 'Everything will be fine, Grace.'

Within minutes, ladies from the colony descended, whispering in hushed tones.

'It's going to be all right,' said the Wing Commander before departing.

Grace's closest friend, Sheila, escorted her into her bedroom.

The crowd dispersed as the evening wore on.

There was no news of Mani that night or the next day. Grace remained closeted in her bedroom, declining to meet visitors. Sheila stayed with her throughout and made sure nobody bothered her. Feeling drained, Grace poured herself a stiff drink of rum.

'Can I fix you a drink?' she asked.

'No, thanks.'

'I'd go mad if I didn't.'

'Go ahead. I'm sure it'll do you good.'

Grace walked to the window and gazed at the moon. She thought of Mani and wondered what fate awaited the poor fellow. She couldn't imagine anybody on earth doing something so horrific. But then, it was his idea, and she saw no point in stopping him.

'Did you hear about JFK?'

'Of course, I did.' Sheila shook her head. 'It's terrible.'

'Isn't it strange? I mean Shanks...and JFK, going down on the same day?'

'Shanks hasn't gone down, for God's sake.'

'I feel so sad for the president's wife and little children.' She turned to face her friend. 'What is the world coming to?'

'It is destiny, my dear, and nothing can change it.'

Destiny! Grace repeated the word in her mind and sat down on the sofa. What they were doing, or would do in the future, was not on account of destiny, but by choice. One makes choices in life, and the rest is determined by actions. And she had made her choice... ready to write her own destiny.

'Do you believe in God?' Sheila asked.

Grace thought for a moment. 'Not really. I think God is the biggest weakness man invented out of fear of the unknown.'

'I believe in God. And I strongly believe prayer does sooth a troubled mind.'

The only prayer Grace had recited was in her school, out of compulsion. 'Prayer provides a convenient diversion from the inevitable—an excuse to escape from reality.'

Sheila narrowed her eyes, 'Didn't you ever go to church?'

Grace shrugged. 'I did, but mainly as a social event.'

'I prayed for Shanks this morning.'

Grace swallowed her drink. 'He's not coming back.'

Sheila sat down beside her. 'Don't say that, Grace. There's always hope.'

Grace gazed at Mani's photograph on the sideboard. Standing next to his aircraft in a G-suit, helmet tucked under an arm, Mani smiled at her. 'He's gone, Sheila, I know it.'

'I've a gut feeling he will be back.'

Grace closed her eyes. 'Maybe he will, but in another life.'

Just then, the thunderous sounds of aircraft taking off sliced through the quiet of the night and shook the window panes in the room.

Grace rose from the sofa and paced around. 'They are at it

again ... waiting for the next.'

'Come on, Grace,' Sheila snapped. 'I know what you're going through, but think positive.'

'It's all over, and the earlier I accept it, the better.'

'Miracles do happen. You never know, he might just walk in through that door.'

Grace turned her back to Sheila and smiled to herself. Yes indeed. Miracles do happen ... and it would be the greatest of all if Mani Shankar walks through that door, ever. 'What happens tomorrow is not what destiny decides,' she said, turning back, 'but how I decide my destiny.'

'I admire your strength in coping with such a calamitous situation. I would've died of shock.'

'Don't speak like that, Sheila,' Grace said, downing her drink. 'It's not the end of life.' It may only be the beginning!

❧

After Sheila left, Grace took a long shower and changed into her night dress. She switched off all lights in the house and slipped into her bed. The intermittent sounds of aircraft taking off or landing haunted her as she considered the things she would have to do in the coming weeks.

A jeep stopped at her gate.

Damn, who could it be at this hour? Why can't they leave me alone ... or was there some news of Shanks? She tensed and held her breath. Heart thumping, she tiptoed into the study and peeped through the gap between the curtains. It was George. She withdrew and waited in the darkness. The bell rang once, twice, and then again, but Grace didn't budge. At another time, Grace would've been thrilled to invite him in, but not anymore. She heard the bell once more, but didn't open the door.

With no sign of Mani or the wreckage of his aircraft, even after four days, the officials declared the pilot 'Missing, presumed dead'. Grace went into her shell, refusing to meet anybody. The Wilsons arrived two days later. Grace's cousin, Ron, and his wife, Susan, came over from Calcutta. Mani's father, Mr Varadharajan, was airlifted from Madras, and arrived just in time for the ceremonial funeral. The stubborn man did not come anywhere near Grace, or the Wilsons, and stayed at the officers' mess. Grace didn't bother to meet him.

The funeral took place with full military honours. Mr Varadharajan stood like a rock throughout the ceremony. In less than an hour, everything was over. Flight Lieutenant Mani Shankar Varadharajan was officially dead and buried forever.

The Wilsons returned to their home, and Grace went to Calcutta to spend a few days with Ron and Susan. There, she visited the Insurance Company to file her claim. The amount involved was enough to keep her in good shape for the rest of her life. A sympathetic official, moved not so much by her plight as her cleavage, promised to speed up the process. After all, Grace knew how to allure men. A couple of weeks later, she returned to Kkd and passed the word around that she wouldn't be receiving any visitors. Her wish was honoured. A few days later, a note arrived in the morning.

I know this is not the best time to bother you. But
I'm dying to meet you…just once, if you don't mind.
George.

At first, she rejected the idea, but on second thought she saw no harm in meeting him, perhaps for one last time to clear the air. The man deserved a polite goodbye, if nothing else.

8.00 p.m. tomorrow, and make it short—She wrote back.

George arrived at the appointed time. It was a windy day. Grace left the door open for him to walk in, as she sat on her sofa. He entered silently and sat across from her.

Grace gazed at the floor. Minutes ticked by without any exchange.

'I feel sad for what happened, Grace.'

No response.

'This is the worst—'

'Cut the crap.'

He took a couple of minutes to get his voice back. 'What are your plans?'

Grace avoided his eyes. 'I don't know,' she said, a trifle uneasily. 'I just want to be left alone for a while, before thinking of the future.'

'Still, where do you plan to go from here?'

'I haven't decided.'

'Look, it's not the right time to bring this up, but sooner or later you have to settle down. It's tough being alone in this world, if you know what I mean.'

Grace knew exactly what he meant, but decided not to respond.

He hesitated and cleared his throat. 'I do not wish to upset you in any way, but should you ever consider, I'll be waiting for your hand, no matter how long it takes.'

It didn't surprise her. She remembered how he had once told her at a party that he was envious of Mani, and regretted having not met her earlier—and that he would have gone down on his knees to seek her hand in marriage had he known her before. At present, however, she had other things on her mind. No doubt, she was hugely infatuated with the man, and the offer was tempting, but now her destiny had changed drastically. She was no longer interested in counting change by the tenth of the month, or living a nomad's life, raising children and moving from place to place. Her dreams comprised Jaguars, plush apartments, full-time maids and other such luxuries that life had denied her so far. She could not abandon her dreams for the sake of her past inclination towards the fellow sitting opposite her, which she now considered as largely transient in nature.

George leant forward. 'Are you listening?'

Grace reached for her filters and lit one. 'It's too early to think on those lines,' she viewed George through the cloud of smoke that obscured his profile.

'Take your time; I'm willing to wait.'

Grace showed not the least bit of interest in his proposal, even though it was perhaps the best under the circumstances. She looked out of the window, eyes fixed on a distant picture, where the likes of George didn't exist.

'Please don't,' she said. 'I want to get away from the Air Force once and for all.'

The colour drained from George's face. His voice returned, but after an uneasy pause. 'I don't believe this.'

Grace had hoped that her denial might shorten his visit, but George didn't seem affected by her cold response. He continued to stare at her, which made her uncomfortable. She was herself surprised, for not too long ago such a gesture from him would have been most desirable. But things were different now and she didn't care about the past. She was looking at the future through a prism tinted with the colour of money, lots of it.

'Maybe you could think it over in your own time... in case you change your mind. I've very strong feelings for you and you cannot deny your own toward me.'

Grace took a long drag on her cigarette and then crushed it

in the ashtray, sending a strong message to George. 'I don't think I'll change my mind.'

❧

George had never been rebuffed so summarily in his entire life. And to receive it from Grace was a monumental shock he found difficult to digest. The stiffness of her manner and the silence that followed suggested that he should not linger there any longer. It was not in his nature to pursue someone beyond a certain point, no matter how tempting. He always believed in a 'take-it-or-leave-it' policy, but Grace was not one to let go of easily. She was hot, and a class apart—especially now when she stood to gain financially from the Air Force.

Too familiar with the inconsistencies of human character, he resolved to try again, perhaps after the usual mourning period, which in her case, he hoped, would not be too long, considering her less than favourable disposition towards the departed soul.

He left, but not without hope.

5

Soon after take-off on that fateful night, Mani reported control failure and switched off the RT. On reaching the target, he pulled up and lined his aircraft parallel to the seashore. After levelling, he cut off the engine to commence a controlled descent towards the ocean. His hands trembled as he gripped the ejection handle. He closed his eyes, took a deep breath, and ejected out of the cockpit.

A strong jet of wind hit him hard, but the drogue parachute that opened automatically, steadied the ejection seat. Ignoring a surge of pain in his neck caused due to ejection forces, he separated from the seat and opened his parachute. The aircraft dove straight into the sea, nose first, raising a huge splash and a deafening sound.

As Mani descended towards the ocean, he detached the parachute and inflated the dinghy. Wrapping his helmet, G-suit and heavy flying boots in the folds of his parachute, he dumped the bundle into the sea. The sack disappeared into the waters. He pulled out his compass to navigate the raft towards the shore. Now clad only in his inner clothing, he shivered in the cold wind. To keep warm, he paddled briskly, ignoring the pain in his neck.

It took him over an hour to hit the land near the rocky terrain he had seen during his last trip to the beach. He deflated the dinghy and ran in the direction of Digha, bracing himself against the chilly winds. When he saw the familiar figures of the Lovers' Rock, he heaved a sigh of relief.

The sudden, faint sound of a distant helicopter alarmed him. Gripped with fear, he sprinted towards the cluster of trees and collapsed from exhaustion. He lay dead-still until the sound of the rotors faded away.

Mani knew search and rescue operations were in place. However, the cover of trees reassured him. He reached for the camouflaged pit in which he had concealed his supplies during his last visit and extracted the sleeping bag and the haversack. It contained his clothes, a pair of shoes, a woollen shawl, a bottle of rum, cash and lots of dry fruits.

Discarding the wet inners and dinghy into the pit, he changed into fresh clothes. He pulled out the bottle of rum and drank it neat. Strangely, it felt as if nothing had happened that night. The bright moon and the stars, the sole witnesses, remained unmoved as ever. The rum and the dry fruits did him good. Before slipping into the sleeping bag and retiring for the night, he swallowed two aspirins to take care of the neck pain. The constant crackling noises of nocturnal creatures bothered him, but tired and exhausted, he dozed off.

❧

Mani awoke early in the morning and surveyed the area with his binoculars—not a single soul anywhere. After burying the sleeping bag and other refuse in the pit, he covered it with sand and foliage.

There was still an hour and a half to catch the seven o'clock bus, enough to cover the six mile distance. Throwing on a shawl and a cap, Mani took one last look at the Lovers' Rock before dashing off to Digha.

The sun, about to rise, tinted the sky with a burnished glow on the eastern horizon. He paused to capture the magnificent beauty of the orange ball slowly rising from the surface of the ocean, announcing the arrival of another day, and beginning of a new life for Mani. In less than an hour, he reached the outskirts of Digha town.

A handful of people strolled on the beach, or went about their morning chores. He must've looked like any other tourist enjoying a morning walk by the sea. He thought of Grace and hoped she would've acted her part well and prepared herself for his funeral.

The first sight of human activity that greeted him was people defecating around the rocks—a standard feature on most beaches in the country famous for open-air toilets. It reminded him of the nauseating sight of humans easing themselves shamelessly along the railway tracks, with their bare bottoms greeting you in the early hours of the morning. He turned away in disgust and headed straight for the bus stand.

The only shack open for business at that hour was a tiny tea stall near the bus stand. The dilapidated bus to Nurpur stood waiting for early morning passengers. He ordered tea and biscuits from the vendor and carried them into the empty bus. It departed twenty minutes late, after an unfruitful wait for passengers. Mani occupied the rear bench-seat and laid there resting his head against his haversack, covering himself with the shawl. The rocking motion of the rickety bus as it negotiated narrow pot-holed roads helped Mani doze off. He remained horizontal throughout, until the bus reached Nurpur, a little before noon.

Putting on his dark glasses, he alighted from the bus. The sweet aroma emanating from a Sardar Ji's dhaba revived his appetite. He settled down on a bench and ordered stuffed paronthas laced with a generous helping of home-made butter. He wolfed down three of them with curd and mango-pickle, finishing with a tall glass of buttermilk.

From Nurpur, Mani took another bus to Haldia and then crossed the river into Kantipura in a precariously overcrowded ferry which threatened to capsize any moment. Mani prayed to God for safe passage. Having survived a near-death ordeal, he had no desire to go down in the river in the company of Bangla Bandhus. By the time the boat arrived on the shore, darkness had settled. Too exhausted to go any further, he decided to check himself into a shabby joint, a ghastly place with pigeonholes for rooms.

❧

He dragged himself into one of these holes and dropped dead on the hard cot. After resting for an hour, he pulled out the bottle of rum and poured himself a stiff one. He'd polished off the remaining stock of dry fruits by the time he downed his second drink, and called for room service.

A lean, hungry-looking bloke with tired eyes and no visible sense of humour, wearing only a vest over his pajamas appeared at the door. 'Sir?' he scratched his thigh.

Mani was disgusted. 'Do you have any food?'

'Rice and fish curry,' he said, eying the bottle of rum.

'Whatever, bring it fast.'

The man produced Mani's order in a jiffy, this time with a broad smile, his gaze fixed on the bottle: a single piece of fish, or its distant cousin, floating in a pungent, watery grave. Mani could smell the bloke's intentions over and above the heavy smell of burnt mustard oil. He gave the remains of the bottle to him and asked for boiled eggs. The eggs came promptly, with finger chips thrown in as bonus.

'What's your name?' asked Mani, after he finished his meal.

'Partho.'

'All right, Partho, can you give me an omelette cooked in anything other than mustard oil for breakfast tomorrow?'

'Will do, sir.'

'Thanks, and tell me if there's a better place to stay?'

He scratched his armpits. 'No, no, sir, no chance. This the best, rest all dormitories—common latrine, open bath. Your type not stay there. Better here. Not worry, I make you happy... if only... if only you give me a little dose at night.' His mouth dropped to one side. 'This job very hard, sir.'

'I shall see about that but, first, you change the bed sheet and the pillow in my room before I catch virus.'

Partho disappeared and promptly returned with a pillow-cover and a sheet, a shade better, probably rinsed twice in the village pond.

'Don't forget about the omelette, and bring me tea at seven.'

Mani awoke in the morning with the pain in his neck aggravated. He felt the need to see a doctor. The omelette arrived cooked in fresh butter and the toast, done well. He summoned Partho to get him a bottle of rum and English newspapers from the market.

Partho's eyes brightened. 'Sure, as soon as the market opens.'

'By the way, is there any doctor available here?' Mani massaged his neck. 'I have a nagging pain in my neck.'

'No doctor, only compounder. But I give you good massage, sir, must try.'

Mani opted for Partho's offer. Partho fetched hot mustard oil and gave him a massage. While it did provide some relief to Mani's neck, his nostrils cried for mercy.

Partho turned out to be a useful man. He produced a bottle of rum and the morning copy of the *Statesman*. He couldn't believe it when he saw the front page. It was filled with the terrifying news of JFK's assassination. His own accident was covered briefly on the third page. The police and the Air Force authorities were still searching for the wreckage.

Mani remained indoors during the day and went out only after dark for fresh air, which was in short supply owing to the constant smell of fish that hung in the air. However, he found it better than the confines of his pigeonhole, which had a tiny window opening onto a garbage dump at the back that smelt of rotten eggs.

But for the services rendered by Mr Partho, inclusive of the regular massage twice a day, it would have been unthinkable for Mani to stay in that hole for another day. Thanks to the regular dose of rum, the curry contained enough fish, and the eggs invariably came with the complementary finger chips.

❧

When November turned to December, Mani checked out one morning and left for Calcutta, melting into the teeming crowds of the vast metropolis. To save on hotel bills, he took refuge in the railway trains for a few days, travelling third class to no place in particular, but to pass time. It worked out a lot cheaper.

Mani had grown a beard and a moustache by now. Looking into the mirror, he didn't see Mani Shankar Varadharajan, but someone else. He had to have a new name and new attire. He bought a couple of kurtas to wear over his trousers instead of shirts. For his name, he chose John Abraham, based on the names of two of his old schoolmates—John Cherian and Ebrahim Basha. He would've liked to inform Grace of his safety, but Flight Lieutenants didn't have telephones in their homes. Besides, they had agreed to make no contact whatsoever, until their scheduled meeting on 25 February at Hotel Blue Moon in Poona, for which a room had already been booked under the name of Miss Grace Wilson.

Drifting aimlessly for a couple of weeks, travelling long

distances and admiring the constantly changing countryside of the never-ending land, he found himself at Daman on the western coast. He liked the place and checked into a hotel. Later, on the recommendation of the room-service boy, he stood at the door of Mrs Lobo.

'Good morning, ma'am.' he said. 'I understand you have a room to let.'

Wearing a dressing gown over her stout figure and a smile on her round face, Mrs Lobo removed her glasses and looked him over. 'Yes, I do have a small room upstairs.'

'I need a room for a couple of months, if it suits you.'

'You are…?'

'I'm John Abraham, an artist. I've come here to paint seascapes.'

'Please come in. Would you like to see the room first?'

The narrow stairs led him to a small airy room with a single window that opened towards the ocean. A low cot, a table and a steel chair made up the furniture—enough to sustain him for two months. A tiny, open-air bathroom stood outside in the corner of the terrace.

'I'm afraid that's all we have,' Mrs Lobo said, when Mani came down.

'It will do for me,' he said. 'What's the rent like?'

'Well, you can have it for sixty a month.'

'Suits me fine.'

After they exchanged a few notes, the kind lady offered to include breakfast for a consideration of another thirty. He moved in the same day.

Mani had a great passion for painting, like his mother, who taught drawing in a school, and painted portraits in her spare time to earn some extra money. The artistic environment at home in the early years accounted for Mani's interest in art. But his headmaster father never approved of it. He wanted Mani to concentrate on science and math, to become an engineer. That was not to be, for Mani couldn't cope with the sciences and, instead, found an easy escape in joining the Air Force. The Headmaster didn't approve, but at least his son didn't become a drawing teacher.

Mani could have never imagined that one day he would abandon the Air Force in such a dishonourable manner. A sense of guilt troubled him, but having come so far, there was no going back.

After settling down at Mrs Lobo's he bought paints and canvas and decided to devote all his time to painting, rather than wasting time and money on aimless travels across the country. He had two months to go before his rendezvous with Grace.

He found his stay with Mrs Lobo, commonly addressed in the colony as 'Aunt Jane', most amiable. In no time, he too discarded the formal Mrs Lobo in favour of Aunt Jane. The affable woman seemed to have developed a liking for her tenant and the feeling was mutual. Mani would be gone for hours with his paints and canvas, producing half a dozen paintings in as many days. And Mrs Lobo would share a cup of tea with him when he returned.

'What do you do with all these paintings?' Mrs Lobo asked one day.

'I hope to sell them. It's my bread and butter.' He paused, and then added, 'Well, you may cut the part about the butter if you like, since there aren't too many buyers these days—bread alone might do.'

She chuckled. 'By the way, where do you eat your other meals?'

'Oh well, here and there, you know. One can fill the stomach quite cheap here in Daman. There's a nice joint in the market which serves good biryani. Besides, I'm not fussy about food. I can do without it sometimes and be quite happy with bananas; they're good for the system.'

'Why don't you join me tonight? I've made some fish. Not very fancy I'm afraid, but you are welcome.'

'That's very kind of you, Aunt Jane, but I'd rather not bother you too much.'

'Don't be silly, it's no bother, please feel at home.'

Dying for homemade food, Mani accepted the invitation. He relished the fish curry that tasted far better than what Grace produced at home occasionally. Even the most rudimentary knowledge of cooking was beyond Grace's grasp; she failed to profit from her mother's culinary talents.

'Tell me, Aunt Jane, how often do you cook fish?'

She smiled. 'Whenever Tanya leaves some extra dough.'

Tanya, her twenty-year-old daughter, worked at a resort near Silvassa, a few miles from Daman. Mani had met her briefly during her last visit.

'Suppose I give you another thirty a month, will you give me fish a few times at dinner?'

'I suppose I can, but you don't have to pay for it.'

'No, no, I insist.'

'Okay, you buy the fish, and I'll cook it for us.'

'It's a deal.'

The next time Aunt Jane served fish, Mani presented her a painting—a seascape.

'Oh no,' she protested. 'I can't accept your bread-and-butter.'

'The pleasure is entirely mine, Aunt Jane.'

'Thank you so much, but I don't think it's right.'

'I would be very pleased if you accept it as a token of my affection.'

'You're very generous,' she said, removing an old calendar from the wall to make room for the painting. It looked quite out of place in the company of Jesus and Mary, whose pictures adorned the walls amongst a few sepia-tinted family photographs.

'You have a family?' she asked.

He paused and looked out of the window, wondering what to say. 'Yes and no. I left home on my own accord. My father never approved of what I wanted to do in life. And my mother allowed me to pursue my goal.'

'Don't you think they would be worried about you?'

'I don't think so.' How could they worry about him now that he was dead and gone.

Tanya was visiting home when he arrived one evening.

'Your paintings are beautiful,' she said.

'Thank you, but I'm not quite satisfied with this,' he pointed to the one he had presented to Aunt Jane.

'Not just this one, I've seen them all.' She tossed a smile at Mani.

For a moment, Tanya's unsolicited intrusion into his privacy embarrassed him. Had it been anybody else, he would've taken offense. But Tanya's innocent smile weakened his defenses.

'You have?'

She nodded. 'I think you should show some of your paintings to the owners at my resort. They might like to buy some.'

'You really think so?'

'They are adding a new wing and might like to acquire some pictures to decorate the place.'

Mani thought for a few seconds and peered at Aunt Jane.

'I like her suggestion,' Aunt Jane said. 'There's no harm in trying.'

'Perhaps you could carry a few and see if they're interested,' he said.

'Why don't you accompany me?'

He rubbed his chin. 'It would be embarrassing to face rejection.'

'I'm sure there won't be any. Your paintings are far better than what they have.'

'Tastes can be very puzzling. I'd prefer it if you show them a few. We can meet them later if they like my work.'

'All right, if you so desire. But which ones should I carry?'

'I leave it to your choice.'

'You're making it difficult for me.'

'I trust your judgment.'

Tanya met his eyes. 'Do you?'

'I think so.'

Mani had discovered a cosy little place on the beach surrounded by rocks and a cluster of trees, with a spectacular view of the Arabian Sea. Isolated from the crowds, he enjoyed painting in that secluded spot. Composing a seascape one sunny day, he dreamt of settling down with Grace in a beautiful beach-side two-storey cottage with green shutters and a studio to call his own. He wished to do nothing but paint.

One more month and he would be rich enough to live his dream. Removing his eyes from the canvas, he imagined Grace emerging out of the rolling waves like a mermaid, and wondered if she was already blowing their money. But he didn't care—there would be enough to burn. At present, however, he had just enough to pay for his rent and his final passage to Poona.

A while later he had company. A few yards away sat a foreign couple on a rock.

'Hi, how you doing?' greeted the man with a Yankee accent and a broad grin on his sun-burnt face.

'I'm doing fine.'

Wearing baggy shorts, a Hawaiian shirt and an over-sized straw hat, the towering man approached him. 'I'm Sam Anderson, and this is my wife, Maggie.'

'Hello, I'm John Abraham.'

'That's a nice painting you've made,' Maggie remarked. 'Mind if we take a closer look?'

'You're welcome.'

Maggie removed her extra-large sunglasses. 'I hope we're not disturbing you?'

'Not at all, be my guest.'

'I like this painting,' she said, 'just right for my study back home.'

Sam nodded his approval. 'Do you sell your work?'

Mani had never sold a painting in his life. So far, his paintings had gone as free gifts to friends, often discarded in their basements, gathering dust. 'I wouldn't mind if the price is right.'

Sam removed his hat, exposing a bald pate. 'And what might that be for this painting?'

Mani glanced at the couple. 'Are you serious?'

'Yes,' he said.

Mani shrugged. 'Well, I'm open to an offer.'

'That wouldn't be right.' Maggie pursed her lips. 'What if our offer is far too short of your expectation?'

'Try me.'

The couple whispered to each other for a few seconds. 'How about a hundred dollars?' Maggie offered.

The brush almost fell from Mani's hand. A hundred dollars! About seven hundred rupees at the going rate! He didn't utter a word and continued to stare at his canvas.

With no answer forthcoming, Sam raised the offer to one-fifty.

'A hundred and fifty!' Mani raised his hands. 'You must be joking.'

The lady flushed when Mani faced her.

Even a modest frame, Mani guessed, would cost more than a hundred-fifty in their homeland. But it was good for him. 'A hundred-fifty would be just fine,' he said. 'I'm no Picasso.'

Maggie heaved a sigh of relief. 'That's very gracious of you, we appreciate it.'

'But it's still wet.'

'We'll take care of that,' she said.

Sam pulled out the dollar bills from his fat wallet.

Mani still didn't believe someone was actually buying his painting. 'I'd appreciate it if you pay me in Indian currency.'

'That's no problem,' said Maggie, reaching into her purse.

That evening, Mani returned home with a spring in his stride and nearly a thousand rupees in his pocket. On the way, he bought chocolates for Aunt Jane to surprise her, but what surprised him more was Tanya, who greeted him at the door, looking fresh as a peach.

'I've good news for you.' Her eyes sparkled.

'Really? When did you arrive?'

'This afternoon.'

'So what's the good news?'

'The owners at the resort like your paintings. They would like to meet you tomorrow.'

The coincidence intrigued Mani. He shook his head with disbelief. 'Young lady, you've brought me luck. I've just sold a painting to a foreign couple…a hundred-fifty dollars!'

'Wow!' Her eyes opened wide. 'Congratulations! This calls for a treat.'

'Absolutely.' He handed the chocolates to Aunt Jane.

'Thank you, John, I'm so happy for you.'

'We're going out for dinner.'

Aunt Jane cringed, 'Oh no, I don't have a decent thing to wear. I would rather—'

'Come on, Ma, be a sport,' coaxed Tanya. 'You haven't

been out of the house in ages. You could surely do with some fresh air.'

After some cajoling, Aunt Jane put on a sari, and the trio went out to dine at Roberios—a small open-air restaurant by the sea famous for seafood. The manager, the waiters and some of the diners came to their table to greet Aunt Jane in her rare appearance. Throughout the evening, she received more attention than her daughter or their escort did.

Tanya looked pretty in a purple gown. Mani felt drawn to her in a way that was quite different from his first encounter with Grace. One had been dynamite, a bomb, and the other, so demure and comforting. She blushed when he locked his eyes with hers a trifle longer.

The following day, Tanya took him to Silvassa and introduced him to the owners—Mr Nadir Shah and Mr Dara Shah—two elderly gentlemen of Parsi stock from Bombay.

'Well, Mr Abraham, we like your paintings,' said Mr Nadir Shah, the taller of the two.

Mani was elated. 'Thank you.'

'How much do you want for them?' he asked.

'I would prefer it if you made the offer.'

The tall man raised his eyebrows. 'Are you sure?'

'Absolutely.'

'All right, if you insist. How about three hundred each?'

Mani hesitated. He hadn't come to sell crockery or cutlery at wholesale rates. Each piece of canvas commanded a different price. At the same time, he knew he was not dealing with art lovers, but hoteliers who bought things by the dozen, like bed sheets, towels or toilet paper.

'Besides,' the man continued, 'we want you to do two large ones for our new wing.'

Mani accepted their offer without further vacillation. The Shah Brothers bought three of his paintings and paid cash.

'Now, about the large ones,' said the other Shah. 'Let's show you the new wing.'

They escorted Mani to an imposing hall with high ceilings and a winding staircase that led to the upper floor.

'We'd like one large painting here on the front wall and another across the landing on the first floor,' he explained. 'They should fill up the walls—at least four feet by eight feet or something.'

Overwhelmed by the dimensions, Mani barely managed to keep his composure. 'Have you any particular theme in mind? I mostly do landscapes.'

'That's exactly what we want, like the ones we have selected,' he said, flapping his hands in the air—the ocean, the rocks, the blue sky, and all that.'

'Perhaps you could throw in a boat or two,' added Mr Nadir Shah.

Mani raised an eyebrow and stared at him. 'To be frank, I've never done such a large canvas before. You may be taking a risk, Mr Shah.'

'We're ready to bet on you if you are willing.'

'It may take several weeks to finish one.'

The brothers conferred. Mr Nadir Shah, apparently the smarter of the two, made the offer. 'How about two-thousand each, if we provide all the materials you need?'

Mani did some mathematics in his head. The bloody thing came to just about sixty rupees a square foot. The Shah Brothers would have paid more for the tiles in their bathrooms. Doing a regular size was one thing, a four-by-eight, quite another. He was disappointed but didn't want to squander the chance to make some money, even if the offer didn't look too good.

Mani rubbed his chin. 'All right, it's a deal, but there are a few things.'

'Like what?' asked Mr. Nadir Shah.

'I'm afraid you'll have to put me up here for at least three weeks. I'll have to work for long hours, sometimes late into the nights.' That, he thought, should compensate for the shortfall in the offer.

The Bombay Brothers agreed.

Tanya scowled after they left. 'You should've demanded more.'

'I cannot be choosy. Thank God they didn't ask me to "throw-in" a few crocodiles.'

Tanya laughed so hard, her cheeks turned pink.

Back in Daman, he informed Aunt Jane about the project.

'That's great news,' she said.

Mani hesitated. He knew he'd have to part with her one day, but this was too soon. 'I'll have to move to Silvassa.'

Neither spoke for a few seconds. The news of his departure seemed to sadden her.

'I understand,' she said, turning away.

Mani searched for words to comfort her, but didn't find any. 'I hope you don't mind if I leave my paintings behind. I shall collect them later.'

'Not at all, you're welcome.'

'You're one of the kindest persons I've ever met, Aunt Jane. I feel sad going away so soon.'

Aunt Jane's eyes became moist. 'You've been like the son I never had. But you must do what you have to. I can only pray for your success.'

Mani took her hands in his. 'Thank you.'

6

The Steel Express stormed into Kharagpur Railway Station like a hurricane, blowing its whistle menacingly, until it slid onto the mile-long platform and exhaled its last breath. The crowds plunged forward into the unreserved compartments, ignoring those struggling to disembark. Travelling first class, Grace was in no hurry. With over fourteen-hundred-thousand rupees in her bank, and another two in her purse, thanks to the substantial insurance Mani had taken a few months earlier, she was now a rich woman, a very rich woman. Struggling to keep her excitement under wraps, she managed to present a gloomy face.

A small group of people, including the not-so-friendly Mrs Randhir, came to see her off at the station. Among them was George—perhaps to find out if there was any hope for him. Grace avoided him, suggesting none.

The hustle and bustle on the platform reminded Grace of her father, the towering Mr Robert Wilson, holding the green flag in his hand like a baton. He had ruled over this station for many years. As a little girl, Grace took pride in the fact that no train left the station without Mr Wilson waving the green flag. An imposing figure in his starched white uniform and black peak-cap, he would march up and down the platform like a general inspecting his troops. On this particular day, Grace was sure her dad would not have shown the green flag to allow his daughter to embark upon the dangerous journey, the consequences of which were largely uncertain. She became emotional and managed a few tears, which suited the occasion perfectly.

The women embraced Grace in turns since the train halted only for seven minutes. Sheila hugged her last. 'Keep in touch,' she said her eyes moist.

'Take care, Grace.' George tried to catch her eye. 'We'll miss you.'

Grace didn't oblige.

She rushed into the coach and waved from the window as the train started to move. Shooting past the suburban stations, the Express rapidly picked up speed and soon lush green paddy fields stretched over the horizon.

She closed her eyes and imagined she was riding a white horse, galloping towards the twinkling stars in the sky, reaching out to the moon. She wanted to erase the memories of Kkd as swiftly as the blurred images that rushed past her window.

❧

Three hours later, she arrived at the chaotic Howrah station, bustling with teeming crowds. Negotiating her passage through the surging mass of humanity, she came out of the terminal and hired a taxi to take her to the famous Park Street. Once there, she stopped at the imposing Park Hotel, once out of her league, to be admired only from a distance—but not anymore.

Grace checked in and settled into a spacious room on the top floor that afforded a grand view of Calcutta's skyline. Grace strode over to the balcony and watched the glamourous street below. The soft purr of the big limousines depositing elegantly dressed ladies and gentlemen in front of the famous restaurants gave her a high.

It wouldn't be long before she alighted from one of those beauties and stunned the crowds.

After a leisurely bath, she went down to the elite market and shopped like mad. The next day, she took an early morning flight to Bombay, the first time in her life and, to her dismay, found herself seated next to a burly sardar who stank of raw onion.

From Bombay she took a train to Pimpri. The Wilsons received her at the station. After settling in the upper room, Grace came down with the gifts she had brought for her parents.

'This is for you, Mom. I hope you like it.'

'Oh, thank you so much, Gracy,' said Mrs Wilson. 'But you shouldn't have bothered about gifts at a time like this.'

'And this one's for you, Dad.'

Mr Wilson's eyes lit up. 'Thank you, my dear, I'm overwhelmed. I always wanted to have one like this.'

'It has those leather patches on the elbows you so admire,' Grace said.

'Yes, I noticed. Just like what Clark Gable wore in *Gone with the Wind*.'

Mrs Wilson ran her fingers over the wool. 'It's so soft, Gracy. It must have cost you a fortune.'

'I'm glad you like it.'

'I shall treasure it.'

Dinner was a silent affair. Grace retired early. After her luxurious stay in Calcutta, Pimpri was quite a comedown. She resolved not to linger there any longer than necessary. Parental affection and care was no longer a priority. She wished to fly away to distant horizons with her golden wings and look for new pastures.

Over the next week, Mrs Wilson spent most of her time in the kitchen, cooking Grace's favourite dishes, or planning the next day's menu.

'Mom, enough is enough. Please don't pamper me,' Grace protested. 'I'm not on a holiday.'

'I don't know what else to do. My heart cries for you all the time.' Tears rolled down her cheeks as she lowered her head.

'Get a grip on yourself, mother,' Grace snapped. 'It won't help if you keep crying, especially when I am trying to get over it. I've other important issues to resolve.'

The old lady wiped her tears with her apron. Always so resilient and vibrant, Grace's mother now presented the picture of a broken woman. She was finding it hard to come to terms with Grace's loss.

That evening, Grace decided to disclose her plan after dinner.

'I've something important to tell you,' she said.

Mrs Wilson looked up.

'I'm not going to stay here for long.'

Mr Wilson raised his head. 'I understand, but what's the hurry?'

Grace rose from her chair and paced the floor. 'Dad, I've got to move on with my life. I'll go mad sitting here doing nothing. I've to look for a job in Bombay or someplace.'

The couple stared at each other. No one spoke for several seconds.

Mrs Wilson knitted her brows. 'But Gracy, you've hardly been here for a week.'

Mr Wilson narrowed his eyes. 'Surely you can rest for a couple of months, if not more.'

'Thanks, Dad. I'll rust here if I don't move out. I'm sure I'll find something worthwhile to do, which is hardly possible here in Pimpri.'

Mr Wilson shrugged. 'We know that, but—'

'No, Dad, the earlier the better. I'm sorry to disappoint you, but I must leave for my own good.'

Mr Wilson didn't press the matter further. Mrs Wilson quietly slipped away into the kitchen.

Grace followed her. 'Mother, you're not helping me.'

'Tell me what should I do to help you?'

Grace put her hands on her shoulders. 'If you really want to help me, have faith in your daughter and stop grieving. That chapter is over.'

'I will not stop you, but why can't you wait for a while?'

Grace thought for a moment and then announced, 'Another week, if you insist, and then I'm gone.'

❧

Grace arrived in Bombay just before Christmas and checked into a posh hotel in Colaba. In the evening, she went for a stroll in the market. Colourful decorations and fancy lights greeted her on the streets. Shops overflowed with merchandise spilling onto the sidewalks. Hungry shoppers looking for festival discounts flooded the stores. Excitement and gaiety filled the air. Grace wandered around, enjoying the festive crowds.

Taking a job was furthest from Grace's mind. She spent the next two days shopping with gay abandon. The magical transformation of a girl from the railway barracks of Kharagpur into a lady of considerable means was complete. The power of money intoxicated her. She wanted to travel and splurge. And the first place that came to her mind was Goa, the land of pleasure and exotic beaches she had heard so much about.

On day three, Grace left for the airport to board the afternoon flight to Goa. Dressed in a lavender bellbottom pantsuit, with a trail of Samsonite suitcases, she created a minor tremor as she arrived at the departure lounge. Eyes turned when she crossed over to collect her boarding pass. The airline staffer blinked when she removed her dark sunglasses and demanded a window seat, fluttering her eyelashes. She got what she wanted. Grace Wilson had arrived with a bang.

As Grace settled into her window seat, an elderly gentleman with thick curly hair and a disarming smile approached her.

'Good afternoon.' The voice that whispered in her ears was husky. He bowed his head courteously and sat next to her.

She nodded with a smile.

The suave, towering man appeared familiar to Grace. *Where have I seen him before?* As her nose picked up the man's musky cologne, she heaved a sigh of relief. This journey would be more pleasant than her flight from Calcutta.

The aircraft began to move. She glanced at him from the corner of her eyes, trying to place him. The man returned her gaze with a broad smile. Grace sighed and fumbled with the seat belt.

'May I?' he said, and helped her get the two ends right.

'Thank you.'

'You're welcome.'

The aircraft took off with a resounding roar. A sudden calm descended as the giant machine gained its cruising altitude. Seconds later, it banked into a smooth turn on Grace's side, constantly tilting the horizon. A spectacular view of the metropolis and the Arabian Sea unfolded before her eyes. The boats looked like tiny dots on a vast silver sheet, with long streaks of white trails in their wake. Moments later, the lush green forests took over. The streams and the tracks looked like thin ribbons crisscrossing the dense vegetation.

When the aircraft levelled off and the sound of engines eased, Grace stole a glance at her neighbour and realised why he looked so familiar. But she kept her thoughts to herself and did what most people do—she pulled out a magazine from the rack in front and turned the pages at random to kill time. When she got bored, she looked out of the window.

'Going on a holiday?' the gentleman asked.

'Sort of, yes.'

'Your first trip to Goa?'

She hesitated, unsure if she should start a conversation with a stranger. But the man exuded class and she saw no harm in being civil.

'Second. First was during a school trip many years ago. I hardly remember a thing.'

'Oh well, things have changed for the worse. The old-world charm has gone forever. Now it's the backpackers, drug peddlers and what have you.' He seemed lost in thought as the aircraft banked again.

'You remind me of Prithviraj Kapoor, the famous actor,' she said, after a long pause.

'So they say.' He smiled and peered at Grace. 'By the way, I am Eric Gomez. And you are?'

'Grace Wilson.'

'Nice to meet you.'

'Same here.'

'So, where are you from, if I'm not being too inquisitive?'

Grace was evasive. 'Well, I'm in the process of relocating. Right now I belong nowhere.'

An airhostess interrupted the conversation, serving coffee and snacks. Grace felt relieved and quickly changed the subject. 'You should've been in films.'

The man raised his eyebrows and looked into her eyes. 'It is you who should be in films, young lady, but not Hindi films—you don't look like the dancing-around-tree type.'

She chuckled. 'No way.'

'However, I've better things to do,' he said, pulling out a visiting card from his wallet and handing it to her. 'Besides, look-alikes have never been successful. They end up mimicking for the rest of their lives.'

She read the card.

Eric Gomez
ERIC ENTERPRISES
14 Cidade-De-Goa
Goa Tel: 1401

'You're a business person.'

'Real-Estate. And you?'

For a few seconds Grace didn't know what to say. She had to cook up a story, and fast. After an uneasy pause, she replied, 'Well…I…I'm a freelance writer, intending to cover the festivities of the New Year in and around Goa.'

'That's interesting. I'm sure you're going to have a jolly good time. I must warn you though, to keep away from those backpackers—they're spoiling the tranquility of Goa.'

'I will, thank you.'

'Where're you staying in Goa?'

'I really don't know. Some hotel I guess. Perhaps you could suggest some place decent.'

'Some place decent? I can surely recommend a decent place for you.'

'Where's that?'

A mischievous smile appeared on his face. 'It's not exactly a hotel, but there's a nice old lady who'll pamper you, and an old man who'll make you feel like a princess as long as you stay there.'

Grace tilted her head and tossed an inquisitive glance at the man.

He pulled out another card. 'Here's the address.'

Eric Mansion
14, Cidade-De-Goa
Goa Tel: 1402

Grace chuckled and shied away. 'That's very kind of you, Mr Gomez, but I shouldn't.'

'Not that it matters, but you can pay for it if that's what's bothering you,' he quipped. 'Perhaps you could leave a generous tip for the old man if you find the stay rewarding.'

Grace burst out laughing. This was the first time she had laughed heartily after Mani disappeared. 'It's very gracious of you, but I really must not, because I'm going to have a very erratic schedule. Thanks a lot anyway.'

'Very well then, if that's what you want, I recommend hotel Sea View. It's not a five-star facility, but a safe and comfortable place with a magnificent view of the ocean. I know the people there. If you like, I'll call them up to make sure you are looked after.'

'That would be very nice, thank you.'

'You're welcome.'

The airhostess came to collect the trays. Grace returned to gazing out of her window, enjoying the view of the clouds rushing by. A little later, the sound of the engines diminished and she felt a sense of floating in the clouds. Soon after, the captain announced landing.

'You know something, I'm glad you didn't accept my offer,' Mr Gomez said, fastening his seat belt. 'It makes sense not to trust strangers no matter how nice they seem outwardly, and that includes me.'

'Oh no, I can tell the difference.'

'Don't be too sure. There are all kinds of people out there. Give me a call if you need any help.'

'I will.'

The aircraft touched down and shuddered as the pilot applied brakes.

The arrival lounge bustled with tourists as Grace waited for her luggage. Her eyes searched for Mr Gomez, but he was gone.

As she came out of the airport, she saw Mr Gomez standing near the exit.

'May I drop you at the hotel?'

'Thank you so much, but I've already engaged this man,' she said, pointing to the taxi driver who had promptly taken charge of the Samsonites the moment she emerged out of the lounge.

Mr Gomez smiled. 'All right then, goodbye, and have a nice time. I hope we meet again.'

'Thank you for your help.'

He waved his hand and got into a big limousine.

❧

The Sea View was a cozy little hotel on the coastline. Christmas decorations greeted her when she arrived at the Reception.

'Miss Grace?' inquired the petite receptionist as Grace approached the desk.

Taken aback, Grace raised an eyebrow. 'Yes.'

'Welcome to Sea View.'

'I suppose Mr Gomez has contacted you already.'

'Yes indeed, please feel at home.'

She registered herself as Miss Grace Wilson and selected a room on the third floor with a large window opening out to the sea. She settled her things and soon the receptionist appeared with a small bowl full of fruits and pastries.

'I hope you're comfortable, Miss. Please let me know if you need anything.'

'Thank you.'

A small card in the tub caught her attention. It read, 'With compliments of Mr and Mrs Eric Gomez.' She was amused.

After changing, she slipped out of the hotel for a leisurely stroll in the market below. The strong breeze from the sea ruffled her skirt as she stepped out of the hotel. The shops were decorated and the streets full of tourists mingling with the locals. She noted in particular the relaxed, smiling faces all around her, unlike what she saw in the busy metros and other cities, where frowns were more common on the tired faces of harried commuters.

Goa had a laid-back charm. Grace noticed people greeting each other with warmth. Wearing trendy clothes, groups of young boys and girls roamed around, having fun. The general mood was festive. The cool evening breeze drifting in from the ocean and the cheerful atmosphere surrounding her lifted her spirits. Goans seemed happy and contented with their lives. She was glad she came to Goa. As darkness fell, she returned to her room and dialled the number on the visiting card Mr Gomez had given her. 'Hello, may I speak with Mr Eric Gomez?'

A baritone voice answered. 'Miss Grace?'

'Yes, Mr Gomez?'

'I hope you're comfortable?'

'Yes I am. I want to thank you for your help.'

'Not at all, it's a pleasure. Mrs Gomez and I would like to meet you while you're here.'

'It will be my pleasure.'

'Thank you for calling. Let me know if you need anything.'

She changed into a pink dress and came down to the restaurant on the second floor. The big hall was nearly full and a small band was playing on the stage at the far end.

'Sorry ma'am, we're already full,' said the door-man.

Grace stood motionless. Several pairs of eyes turned in their direction. 'I do notice some empty tables.'

'All are reserved, ma'am.'

A portly man in a black suit and bow tie, probably the head steward, approached her. He signalled to the door-man to back up and then addressed her courteously. 'Excuse me, ma'am, please come this way.'

He ushered her to a small table for two beside the window overlooking the sea and ordered a passing waiter to remove the 'Reserved' sign-plate from the table. 'Sorry, we have to resort to this practice to accommodate last minute guests—especially personal guests of Mr Gomez.'

She raised an eyebrow. 'Mr Gomez?'

'Mr Gomez is part-owner of the hotel.'

'Oh, I didn't know that.' Grace smiled, wondering what other surprises were in store.

'Is ma'am expecting somebody?'

'No, I'm alone.'

He shook his head. 'How sad.'

Grace smiled and picked up the wine menu. 'Which is the best wine you have?'

'Depends on what kind of food the lady would like to order.'

'Do you serve good prawns and shrimps?'

'Of course! Goan cooks are famous for seafood. You may like to try our crabs. You won't find them as tender and delicious anywhere else in the world.'

'Ah, you're already giving me an appetite.'

The man beamed. 'You can afford to indulge.'

Grace admired his easy, charming manner that reminded her of Mr Gomez. She wondered if all Goans were as chivalrous as these two elderly men she'd encountered so far. She studied the menu and blinked at the unfamiliar names listed under 'wines'.

'So which wine would you suggest?' she asked, to avoid revealing her ignorance.

'If you're feeling adventurous, I'd recommend a young German wine, or a Chenin Blanc that will set you up very well.'

'And set me back by a few hundred I suppose!' Grace chuckled.

'For a lovely lady on a beautiful evening like this, a-hundred-forty wouldn't sound too outlandish.'

Grace laughed softly and peered at him. 'All right, mister…'

'Charles DeCunha.' He bowed. 'But you may call me Charles.'

'Very well, Mr Charles, let's have Chinese Blank then.'

He raised his chin and blinked. 'Chenin Blanc, ma'am.'

'Yes, whatever.'

'Shit,' she said to herself, as soon as Charles left.

Grace glanced at the crowd. Women in colourful chiffons chatted away with balding men in lounge suits who smoked cigars and glanced at her furtively. A lacklustre band played a soft number, their trumpets sounding out of tune, the drums monotonous like a metronome. An elderly couple danced, if you could call it that, shifting their weight from one foot to the other, on the small dance floor. The atmosphere was subdued, unlike the boisterous evenings she was used to at Kkd.

She turned and gazed out of the window. Brightly lit restaurants lined the street below, bustling with revellers. The reflection of the moon danced over the shimmering waters of the dark ocean. In the distance floated a boat with its deck brightly lit and people partying.

She felt lonely and wondered what she would do in the coming days to distract herself. With no company, she was getting bored, and the crowd in the restaurant didn't inspire her as much as the crowds on the streets did. Briefly, she thought of George. She felt sorry for treating him the way she had. But it was the easiest way to disconnect from the past. She thought of Mani too, with a sense of guilt, but all her thoughts vanished as Charles brought the wine in a chiller and poured it into a long-stemmed glass.

'Would you like to order food now or later?'

Grace took a sip of wine and nodded with approval. This was better than anything she had tasted so far. She discussed the menu with Charles and ordered the delicacies he recommended. She finished half the bottle of wine by the time the food arrived.

Charles was right. She had never tasted such delicious crabs and prawns. She left a hefty tip and thanked Charles before leaving.

❧

The following day, Grace went sightseeing. The magnificent beaches, the ancient churches and the exquisite architecture enchanted her. She felt as though she had come to a foreign land, so very different from the other cities she had been to. By late evening, she was tired and was considering ordering food in her room when the phone rang.

'Excuse me, ma'am, there's a visitor for you,' informed the receptionist.

A visitor for me? In Goa? Slightly alarmed, she asked, 'Who is it?'

'Good evening, Miss Grace,' greeted a baritone from the other end. 'There's an old couple here to say hello to you, if it's not too inconvenient.'

'Mr Gomez?' she exclaimed.

'No, this is Prithviraj Kapoor.'

She chuckled. 'What a pleasant surprise.'

'Would you care to join us for dinner?'

Missing company, she accepted readily. 'Sure, I'll be delighted.'

'Good, we'll wait for you in the restaurant.'

'Give me a few minutes to dress.'

Grace changed into a beautiful peach-coloured evening gown she had picked up in Bombay. Mr Gomez, dressed in a blue pin-stripe suit came to greet her at the door when she appeared at the restaurant. He escorted her to his table and introduced his wife, Mrs Rosemary Gomez, a tall, good-looking woman, who carried her years gracefully on her sharp features.

'Hello, nice to meet you,' said the elegant lady.

'Nice to meet you, too.'

'That's a lovely dress.'

'Thank you,' Grace said, taking a seat across from her. 'I'm sorry I took so long to change.'

'You could've stayed with us,' said the gracious lady. 'We do have spare rooms, and I could use some company.'

'Maybe some other time; I'm constantly on the move right now.'

'I understand. Eric told me about your mission. I'd be interested in seeing what you write about Goa and its people.'

Grace kept her face expressionless and faced Mr Gomez. 'I was pleasantly surprised to discover that you own the place.'

'Only partly,' he said. 'But that's not the reason I recommended this hotel.'

'I find it quite hospitable.'

'I'm glad you approve.'

'Especially Mr Charles DeCunha, who made sure I enjoyed my first evening in Goa, even though I was alone and somewhat lost.'

Mrs Gomez smiled. 'He's a lovable character, been with us since the beginning.'

Mr Gomez picked up the menu and asked, 'So what shall we order?'

'Let the young lady decide,' Mrs Gomez suggested. 'Meanwhile, we should order something to drink.'

Mr Gomez turned to Grace. 'What would you like to have?'

Charles appeared with his customary smile. 'Good evening, ma'am.'

'Grace Wilson, if you please,' said Grace.

'Well, Miss Wilson, would it be Chenin Blanc or something else?' he asked.

'I'd love that.'

'Good choice,' Mrs Gomez approved. 'The same for me.'

Mr Gomez ordered scotch and soda for himself.

'So what have you written so far?' Mr Gomez inquired.

Grace shuffled in her seat. The only writing she had done was way back in school and a few hastily scribbled notes to her parents after they moved from Kharagpur. Before the old man pressed the matter further, she replied, 'I'm just floating around, taking notes. Writing will come later, I guess.'

'Did you find anything interesting?' asked the lady.

'Yes, of course! I liked the cheerful faces all around. One striking feature that sets Goans apart from the rest is their uninhibited and carefree disposition. That's something you don't find in other cities where people are always in a mad rush and with hardly a smile to spare. And of course, the magnificent churches and the wonderful beaches; it's simply mind-blowing.'

'That's the best part of the locals,' Mrs Gomez said. 'They're in celebratory mood all year round. I'm sure you'll get to see a lot more at this time of the year.'

The drinks arrived and, with it, a plate of fish fillets. Mr Gomez poured wine into two glasses and helped himself to some whiskey. 'By the way, what's your plan for the New Year? Would you like to join us at our club?'

'Thank you so much, but I'd rather move around a bit to grasp the essence of Goa and sample the delights of festivities about which one has heard so much.'

'The writer in you must be itching to capture the spirit of Goa during the festivities.' Mr Gomez said. 'However, be careful out there and keep away from strangers.'

'Come on, Eric, she's not a teenager,' scoffed Mrs Gomez. 'I'm sure she can take care of herself.'

'Of course, but a little caution won't do any harm,' he said.

'Don't worry, I'll be on my guard,' said Grace.

Mrs Gomez sipped her wine. 'All right, but do promise to spend an evening with us before you leave.'

'Yes, of course.'

The food was delicious. Grace adored the delightful couple. However, she was afraid of letting out more than what she would have liked them to hear. Grace thanked them profusely for the lovely evening, promising to meet again.

7

Mani was sad to leave Aunt Jane. The affable woman had treated him with the kind of warmth he had not experienced since he'd left home. He choked when he thought of his mother, who must be grieving over the tragic loss of her only son— the son who actually lived. But there was nothing he could do, at least at present.

Mani didn't feel the same way about his father. His old man was strong enough to bear pain, any pain. The son who defied him may as well be dead. Looking out of the window of the speeding bus, his vision blurred.

Tanya greeted him with a broad smile when he arrived at the resort and introduced him to her roommate Mehroo, a lean, pale-faced girl who offered a striking contrast to Tanya's tanned complexion and sturdy build. After they had tea, Tanya led him to his room on the upper floor in the new wing—a room that still needed a paint job. Two huge canvasses stood against the wall. He wondered if he should have asked for a six-inch brush and several litres of paint from a hardware store, instead of the usual stuff from the stationers.

'I'm afraid the room is not yet fully ready,' Tanya said. 'I hope you don't mind.'

'No, that's all right.'

She opened the door to the balcony to let in the fresh air. 'It's a nice place to sit out.'

'I like it. Perhaps I'll use this as my studio.'

'But it rains a lot and gets windy.'

He shrugged. 'I suppose I'll have to live with the paint smell.'

'Sorry about that.'

'Never mind, I'm used to it.'

'Would you like to join me for dinner?'

'I'd love that.'

'Shall we say eight o'clock?'

'That would be fine.'

After setting up his room, Mani put on a fresh kurta over his much used jeans. As darkness fell, he fixed double rum for himself and strode over to the balcony to admire the view. Tall eucalyptus trees swayed in the cool breeze and the moon played hide and seek behind a cluster of clouds. He longed to be with Grace, but that was still three weeks away. He wondered where they might be going after they met in Poona. Perhaps a tour down south to enjoy the scenic beauty of the virgin beaches or Munnar, to unwind in the tranquility of the lush green tea gardens covering the slopes?

But Grace might have different ideas. She might have already planned a cottage on a beach with a Jaguar parked in the garage… or a plush flat in Bombay's Marine drive that commanded a breathtaking view of the Arabian Sea. He glanced at his watch and gulped his drink before leaving for the dining hall.

Dressed in a blue sari, smelling of talcum powder, Tanya looked graceful. She greeted him in the dining hall filled with guests and led him to a corner table.

'I hope you're settled?' she asked, taking a seat across from him.

'Yes, thank you.'

'We would have given you a better room, but for the pressure of tourists. There's always a big rush around this time of the year.'

'It's all right. I would be more comfortable away from the crowds.'

'What would you like to have for dinner?'

'I'm comfortable with everything. Please, keep it simple.'

Tanya ordered Pork Vindaloo and naans. 'It's synonymous with Goan food. The "vin" is for the vinegar and the "ahlo" means garlic in Portuguese. It's the specialty of our resort'

'Quite a crowd,' he said. 'How long have you been working here?'

'Just completed three years.'

'You like it?'

'Of course, I do. Otherwise I wouldn't be here. You meet people from all over the world. It's interesting to learn how people behave so differently.'

Mani scanned the busy dining hall: a garrulous group of Bengalis at a table not far from theirs eating with their hands just like he had at home before mastering the knife and fork mess etiquette; a Guajarati family that chattered loudly as if sitting in their courtyard; a foreign couple who seemed lost in the cacophony.

Mehroo joined them. 'So what have you ordered?'

The girls shared an easy camaraderie and dinner was enjoyable, with Mehroo doing most of the talking.

The chatter-box left once they finished dinner to resume her duty at the reception desk.

Tanya led Mani to the far end of the garden and sat on a bench placed under the canopy of Bougainvillea. Neither spoke for a while. Eyes fixed to the ground and hands clasped in her lap, Tanya appeared nervous. Mani was drawn to her. He wondered if it was only a passing urge, but something in the air suggested that the attraction was mutual.

When the silence stretched too long, Mani gazed at her profile, 'I'll miss you after I'm gone.'

She blushed. A draft of wind tousled her hair. She shivered and hugged herself.

Seconds turned into minutes. 'Aunt Jane worries about you.'

She tilted her head to gaze at him.

'It's time you found a nice boy and settled down.'

She shook her head and lowered her eyes. 'She will have to worry for a long time.'

'Why?'

'I just know.'

'You have someone in mind?'

After a long pause she said, 'Maybe I have someone in my dreams—an illusion, which is going to haunt me for a long time.'

'And who is this Mr Illusion?'

'A ghost, who only shows up in the dark, and disappears when I open my eyes.'

Mani laughed. She sat motionless.

It started to drizzle, disrupting the moment. Mani returned to his room. As he lay in his bed, Tanya's image floated into his mind. Was it his hunger for love? Or a natural urge for female company? He wasn't sure. But that night, it was a different yearning from what he had felt when he first laid eyes on Grace's slender legs. He wanted to hold Tanya close to his heart, unlike the primal desire he felt for Grace. He was tormented between love and lust. But lust, combined with money, was a deadly combination he couldn't sacrifice for what he thought was a transitory diversion.

❧

Mani woke up early to paint, but a dark, chilly morning that was likely to end in rain presented him with a gloomy picture. He moved to the balcony to breathe in fresh air. A steady drizzle and mist turned the landscape into a hazy blur. With little natural light, it was not a good time to paint. He came into his room and gazed apprehensively at the empty canvases. The Shah Brothers should've engaged a bill-board painter instead of him.

The clouds cleared around noon. He stared at the large canvas for several minutes before deciding to paint the spectacular view of the sunset he had watched every evening at Daman. Starting with the huge orange ball of the sinking sun, he worked his way down to the blues of the ocean and the metallic browns of the rocks. He worked with his fingers, blending colours directly on the canvas in bold strokes. What he produced after two days of labour disappointed him. He found it difficult to handle the large canvas. It looked worse than the garish cinema posters one saw on every street corner.

The thought of failure haunted him. He wondered if he should pack his bags and leave. By daybreak, he switched off completely from his painting and decided to go for a long walk in the countryside. The unpolluted air and the earthy charm rejuvenated him. He returned to his canvas with fresh resolve and worked practically non-stop for four days, not even lifting his head away from the canvas when someone came to deliver meals. At last, satisfied with what he had produced, he decided to take a break.

Mani met Tanya in the afternoon. 'Would you care to go out with me tonight?'

Tanya blinked.

'I need a break. Perhaps we could eat out for a change.'

She raised her eyebrows. 'I didn't believe you could see beyond your canvas.'

'Well, I've a job to do, and it's a tough one.' He leant on the counter and waited.

Her eyes widened. 'I would be delighted.'

'Good. What time do you get off?'

'At eight.'

'Okay, I shall meet you in the lobby at half past eight.'

Later, Mani trimmed his beard and changed into fresh clothes. When he looked into the mirror, he was disappointed. The loose kurta over faded jeans went well with the image of an artist, but wasn't good enough to escort a young lady to dinner. He wished he had something better to wear.

Tanya was ready in her jeans and top when Mani appeared in the lobby. They walked along the tree-lined path leading to the main road in silence. An auto rickshaw took them to town, where they settled into a restaurant overlooking the street. Mani ordered a beer while Tanya opted for lemonade. She hardly lifted her eyes, which he attributed to her shy nature.

Tanya had an unpretentious, down-to-earth quality Mani had admired from day one. But today she looked a bit different— sweet and desirable. Or perhaps he looked at her in a different way.

Mani sipped his beer and lit a cigarette.

Tanya raised her head. 'How's your painting coming?'

'Not bad, I guess. Perhaps you should come over and have a look. A second opinion is always helpful.'

She fixed her gaze on her glass. 'I doubt if I could be of much help.'

'You'd be surprised. An independent opinion always puts things in proper perspective. An artist always thinks he's done a great job, but one has to see a work from different eyes.'

She didn't respond, turning her glass round and round in her hands.

'You're very quiet, today,' he said, after an uneasy pause. 'Is anything wrong?'

'No, why should there be?'

Mani tried to catch her eyes, but hers remained glued to the glass. 'Looks like I'm bad company.'

Tanya shook her head. 'No, no, it's not that. I'm sorry if I disappoint you.'

'You don't disappoint me at all. You intrigue me,' he took a swig of his beer. 'You're... so different.'

Tanya peered at him over the rim of her glass. 'I don't understand you.'

'I don't understand myself.' Mani shrugged. 'I'm sorry. I didn't bring you here to burden you with my own problems.'

'I don't mean much, but you're welcome.'

'You mean a lot, but sometimes, words get stuck in the throat.' He gulped his beer and signalled to the waiter. 'So, what shall we order?'

'Anything you like, but the distraction is not going to work.'

'There're things one can't share.'

'Yes of course; I know what you mean.'

They ordered food and ate in relative silence. The conversation remained peripheral and Mani allowed her to return to the resort with her reserve intact. As the auto raced through the darkened streets, the chilly winds sent Tanya's hair flying all over her face. Mani wanted to push her hair back and kiss her. But he didn't have the courage to frighten a girl ten years younger than he was. It didn't make sense to start something new when he already had a bigger picture planted permanently in his mind. Besides, he would be the last person to hurt Aunt Jane in any way by taking advantage of her innocent, vulnerable daughter—unless he had noble intentions, which unfortunately was not the case. The evening ended sooner than he would have liked.

Tanya came to his room in the morning to look at the canvas.

'It's wonderful!' she exclaimed.

'You think so?'

'Absolutely.'

Mani came and stood behind her. He breathed in her scent. She smelt fresh and sweet. 'You think it'll work?'

'I've no doubt it will.'

'I'm still not fully satisfied.'

Tanya moved closer to the painting. 'I'm not too sure, but this rock feature here...'

'Yes, please go on.'

'This large rock here,' she said, pointing to the canvas. 'It looks a bit flat to me.'

Mani stepped back to gaze at the canvas.

'I suppose rocks can be of any shape or size. I don't know if you need to meddle with it.'

'I appreciate a frank opinion. And I see what you mean.'

She turned to face him. 'Please don't take my view seriously. I know nothing about art.'

'You don't have to be an expert to appreciate art. How about the colours in general? I hope they're not too loud?'

'Of course not, especially the ones around the setting sun, and the sky above the ocean. I must say, the overall impact is wonderful.'

'You're being too generous.'

Tanya glanced at her watch and exclaimed, 'Oh, I'm late! I should be at the reception by now. See you later.'

She was gone like a whiff of air, leaving her pleasant fragrance behind.

Mani looked closer at the painting and wondered if he should work some more on the rocks. Unable to decide, he went out to the balcony. The room constantly stank of paint, and a break was in order.

The cool breeze and the view of swaying trees uplifted his mood. His thoughts moved from Tanya to Grace. Tanya was like the rocks he painted—strong, solid and at eternal peace. Grace, on the other hand, was more like the fierce waves of the ocean—eternally restless, full of fury and ready to destroy anything that came in the way. At present, however, he was unwilling to settle for the rocks—he was longing to embrace the ferocious waves.

In a couple of days, Mani finished the two canvases. The Shah Brothers were pleased with the results. It was time to say goodbye to Silvassa and to Tanya. Mani decided to pay a brief visit to Aunt Jane before leaving for Poona.

Tanya came to his room as he was preparing to leave for Daman. Mani would have liked Tanya to accompany him, but he chose not to ask her. Now that he was about to start a new life with Grace, he didn't want any distraction.

'You seem to be in a hurry to leave,' said Tanya.

Mani dumped the last of his belongings into his bag and looked up. 'I don't think I've a choice.'

'You could have stayed on for a couple of days.'

'I wouldn't like to overstretch the hospitality offered by the Shah Brothers.'

Tanya leant against the door and lowered her chin.

Mani's heart ached for her. He wanted to hug her, but checked himself. 'Tanya, I want you to know that you and Aunt Jane are the most compassionate human beings I've come across in my life, and I'll never forget the affection you showered on me throughout my stay.' He paused and then continued, 'Destiny is taking me away, but a part of me will always be with you. And I shall be there for you whenever you need me. I wish you all the happiness in the world.'

Tanya turned her face away. She did not exactly burst into tears, but her throat felt constricted. Standing before her was the man of her dreams, wishing her all the happiness in life, unaware that he was taking away all that he wished for her. What could she say? That she had built a dream around him? Admired him from day one? And hoped to raise a family with him? No, it was just an absurd dream—a figment of her imagination. It was time to abandon her dreams forever. John Abraham didn't belong in her life.

8

Mani arrived in Poona on the morning of 25 February, the appointed day, brimming with excitement and hope at the start of a new life with Grace. A chilly wind greeted him when he alighted from the train. He put on his jacket and went straight to Hotel Blue Moon, where a room in the name of Miss Grace Wilson had been booked three months ago.

After roughing it out in the railway trains and elsewhere, the grand ambience of the elite hotel overwhelmed him. He felt awkward approaching the smart receptionist.

She eyed him up and down, 'Yes?'

Mani knew at once that his pedestrian attire didn't go down well with the woman who was accustomed to dealing with gentlemen from the upper crust. He cleared his throat, 'I have an appointment with Miss Grace Wilson.'

She scanned through a register and shook her head. 'No one has checked in by this name.'

'Surely she must have a room booked?'

The woman checked her records and nodded. 'Yes, of course. Room 204 is booked for Miss Grace Wilson from 24th to 27th February, but she hasn't checked in as yet.'

Mani was stumped. 'That can't be. Please check again.'

The receptionist narrowed her eyes and raised her chin. 'May

I know who you are?'

Mani gathered his wits quickly and looked her in the eye. 'I…I'm John Abraham, an artist.' He leant forward and put his elbow on the counter, 'Miss Wilson had commissioned me to do a nude portrait of her.'

The woman's face flushed and she lowered her eyes. 'She is not here.'

'Has she not called or left any message?'

She replied in the negative.

Mani was puzzled. 'Perhaps she got held up or something. I'll wait for her in the lobby, if you don't mind. She might arrive any moment.'

'Suit yourself.'

Mani picked up his bag and settled into a sofa in the corner of the lounge. To avoid undue attention, he hid his face behind a newspaper and looked up at the new arrivals from time to time. He fidgeted and wondered why Grace hadn't arrived on the previous evening as planned. Has she fallen ill? Has her old man conked off or something?

He lit a cigarette and cursed himself for not having planned for such a contingency. He couldn't contact the Wilsons as they didn't have a telephone. But surely Grace should have called the hotel from somewhere and left a message.

After an hour, he picked up his bag and approached the receptionist again. 'Has she called?'

She pursed her lips and shook her head.

Dejected and confused, Mani left the hotel and entered a restaurant across the road. He hadn't eaten since morning, so he ordered breakfast and killed time over cups of coffee. He settled his bill and left his bag with the manager, saying he would collect it later when he returned for lunch.

To pass the time, Mani wandered into the market, going up and down several times, browsing through shop windows. Smartly dressed men and elegant women alighted from big imported cars. A blazing red sports car, parked across the road caught his attention. He smiled and knew Grace would have to make a choice pretty soon—perhaps a Jaguar if not a Rolls!

A mannequin in a shop window draped in a stunning turquoise gown caught his eye. The intricate golden work on the collar and sleeves glistened in the sunlight. It must cost a fortune, but did he care? Another day and he would be able to buy a dozen of those for Grace! He looked at the stony face of the mannequin, then to the pointed breasts jutting out from under the gown. Heat rose to his ears when he thought of Grace in that gown, his heart pounded against his chest in anticipation.

Across the road, he noticed an art gallery by the name of Anokhi. He went in and browsed through the paintings on display, examining each work with interest. He could do as well if not better. He picked up the brochure from a table and glanced through it. He gasped as he scanned through the prices. Not a single work was available for less than two-thousand rupees!

An attendant appeared before him. 'Does anything interest you, sir?'

'Some of them, yes.'

'They are collectors' items.'

'Is that so?'

'Prasoon Ghosh is an emerging artist of great promise. A couple of years from now, his works could fetch ten times more.'

Mani wasn't impressed by his sales pitch. 'God bless him, but I haven't come here to buy.'

Mani wandered around the streets for a few hours and made a mental list of things they would buy in Poona. He called Hotel

Blue Moon from a public booth to inquire about Grace. The answer was the same. Late in the evening, having lost his desire to eat, he returned to the restaurant to drink some more coffee. He collected his bag and returned to the hotel.

The reception hall glittered under a huge ornate chandelier. He approached the receptionist, this time a male. 'I'm here to meet with Miss Grace Wilson, room 204.'

The man checked his records and shook his head. 'Miss Wilson hasn't arrived.'

'Have you received any message from her?'

He consulted the logbook and replied in the negative.

'Can I help you with anything else, sir?'

'Yes, I'd like a room.'

The man smiled. 'Certainly.'

Mani selected room 209, the closest room available to 204. After showering, he returned to the lobby. Once again, he sat in a corner to keep a vigil on new arrivals. The imposing glass door swung many times over, but Miss Grace Wilson didn't show up. He stepped out of the hotel for some fresh air. Drifting with the tide of window-shoppers, he roamed the busy streets like a lost cow, until he found himself in front of a wine shop. The happy faces around him hardly inspired him. He bought a bottle of rum and returned to his room.

Pouring himself a stiff drink, he strolled over to the window and gazed at the star-studded sky. A distant aircraft on the eastern horizon reminded him of his last flight over Digha. What a pity, he would never fly again, but now he was on a different flight altogether. A flight that would take them places. Perhaps tomorrow he would be celebrating his reunion with Grace, not with rum, but with the best of champagnes and food… and fresh roses on her bed in room 204! He gulped his drink and poured another, and then another.

He finished half the bottle in less than an hour. But where the hell was Grace? What was keeping her from dazzling him? He ordered food and ate mechanically before retiring for the night.

Frustration turned into anger when Grace didn't show up the next day. He began to curse her. The bloody woman hadn't even bothered leaving a message! When darkness fell, his hopes dwindled and he began fearing the worst. *Was she up to some mischief? Was she planning to ditch him?* The thought sent shivers down his spine. His mouth felt dry, he broke out in a cold sweat.

No, this was not happening, not to him...he'd put his life at risk for her...she couldn't be doing this to him! He reached for his bottle and tried not to imagine the worst. He finished it, neat, and collapsed on his bed. He tossed and turned the whole night unable to sleep.

❧

On the morning of 27th, Mani woke up with a headache. After a quick wash he checked out of the hotel and went to the restaurant across the road to have breakfast. With no sign of Grace, he realized something was terribly wrong. He needed to unearth the truth, and so he took the afternoon bus to Pimpri, to pay a visit to the Wilsons. Arriving in Pimpri, he moved into a cheap hotel near the bus stand and decided to wait until dark.

A little after eight, he hovered around the Wilsons' house. The light was out in the upper room. He caught a fleeting glimpse of Mr Wilson through the window at the front. The old man wasn't dead after all. He knocked on their door.

Mrs Wilson opened the door. 'Yes?'

'Good evening, ma'am, I've come to visit Mrs Shankar.'

'I'm sorry, she isn't here. And you are?'

'I'm an old friend of Mani's.'

'Who is it?' inquired the old man from inside.

'A friend of Mani's.'

Mr Wilson appeared behind Mrs Wilson.

'Good evening, sir, I'm Squadron Leader John Abraham.'

'Come on in please, have a seat.'

Mani stepped in and sat down. The old man sat across from him, his eyes to the floor. Mrs Wilson stood by his side. They were all silent.

Mani cleared his throat. 'I couldn't believe it when I heard about the accident.'

Mr Wilson shook his head.

'I came to offer my condolences to Mrs Shankar.'

'She came here for a few days and then left for Bombay... said she'd look for a job,' muttered the old man without lifting his eyes from the floor. 'There's been no news from her since.'

Mani raised an eyebrow. 'You mean you don't know where she is now?'

'Not a clue.'

'It is worrisome,' added Mrs Wilson, wiping her brows with her apron.

Mani raked his hair and gaped at Mr Wilson. 'You haven't heard from her?'

'Not a word.'

'I don't understand... how could...?'

The room fell silent.

His worst fear had come true. Mani wiped the sweat from his forehead; frozen in the chair, he felt like a corpse. In fact, he was one, officially. Now he had just died a second time, and got dumped into a deep hole from which there was no escape. With Flight Lieutenant Mani Shankar buried in his grave in Kkd, the young, beautiful widow was free to do what she pleased with all the money. Her long legs could take her anywhere. She might even be with George the crook, getting off on Mani's grave…or on a bed of thousand-rupee notes. He clenched his fists with barely suppressed anger.

'Are you all right?' Mrs Wilson interrupted his thoughts. 'Can I get you a glass of water or something?'

'No, thank you, Sandra…' he blurted out, and instantly realised his mistake.

The colour drained from Mrs Wilson's face. She stared at the visitor wide-eyed and gasped for breath. 'Oh my God…it's you…Bob…don't you see, it's *him*,' she yelled, her body shaking uncontrollably. 'It's our Mani…Can you believe that?'

The old man lifted his head and dropped his jaw as though he were seeing a ghost, which was not far from the truth. 'What the hell are you saying? Mani is dead…he was…'

'Yes, Mr Wilson, she's right. I survived.'

'You what?'

'I ejected safely.'

'Then who the hell is buried in your grave, your twin?'

Before he could muster a suitable reply, the old woman came to his rescue. 'Thank God…thanks a million times, God.' Mrs Wilson hugged Mani. Tears rolled down her cheeks.

'I don't believe this. What the hell is happening here?' cried Mr Wilson. His glasses fell to the ground as he rose to confront the ghost who had suddenly appeared from his grave.

'It's a long story.'

'It better be good, dammit.' Mr Wilson paced the floor. 'Where the hell were you hiding all these months? How dare you cause so much pain to our Grace?'

'Calm down, Mr Wilson,' Mani snapped. 'You've no idea how much pain your Grace has caused me, and to both of you.'

Mr Wilson sank into his chair. 'What the hell are you talking about?'

Mani lit a cigarette. 'May I have something to drink?'

Mrs Wilson pulled out a bottle of rum from the cabinet and produced two glasses.

Mani poured a drink for himself and swallowed it neat, not bothering about the old man. He didn't have an explanation for having risen from his grave and presenting himself at the Wilsons' door unannounced.

Mr Wilson shook with rage. 'Will you bloody well utter something or shall I—'

'Calm down, Bob,' Mrs Wilson cut him short. 'Give him a chance to breathe.'

'Well I'm waiting, for God's sake,' yelled Mr Wilson and poured a drink for himself. 'Save the bloody dramatics.'

The ghost, now resurrected, told his story from the beginning. The Wilsons listened with rapt attention and trepidation. The old man gesticulated, grunted and paced up and down. By the time Mani ended the story, Mrs Wilson sat horrified, and Mr Wilson slumped into his sofa like a man hit by a freight train.

'I don't believe this. How could she do it?' Tears filled Mrs Wilson's eyes. 'He risked his life for Grace... and she simply vanishes! It's all because of you, Bob, you spoiled her...'

'Stop it, woman. That's enough. I seem to be responsible for every blessed thing that happens around here.' Mr Wilson screamed. 'Good Lord, I didn't have to live this long to hear this. They're both in this mess together... nothing short of criminals... and I refuse to have anything to do with this imposter.' He shouted at Mani. 'Leave us alone, will you, before I call the police.'

Mrs Wilson turned to the old man, her hands on her hips, 'Are you out of your mind? This man practically gave up his life for Grace, and you say you've nothing to do with him? Don't you see... don't you see what Grace has done to him? Ditching him just like that... and running away with all the money? Leaving him a dead man?'

Mr Wilson gasped for breath like a spent force. 'They've broken the law, dammit!' he mumbled and reached for his glass.

Mani rose from his chair. 'I should be leaving now. I'm sorry to have upset you.'

'Where do you think you're going at this hour?' Mrs Wilson asked.

Mani glanced at his watch. It was well past eleven. The late night show had ended, but his was only beginning. 'I'm staying at a hotel.'

'Not at this hour, you're not. You're staying here.' Mrs Wilson commanded.

Mr Wilson slipped out of the room without uttering a word.

'I don't think that's right.'

'Tomorrow, you're moving in here with your stuff.'

'You're too kind, Sandra, but I don't want to cause any more trouble for you. You can't be living with a corpse in the house.'

'Don't say that, for heaven's sake! You've suffered enough. I feel guilty for what Grace has done to you. But how could you... ?' Her face contorted in pain.

'You won't believe this, but I did it all for Grace. I wanted her to live like a queen.'

'By cheating the state?' She shook her head in desperation. 'I don't understand how you could do this. And look what you've done to yourself.'

Mani lowered his head.

'Now go upstairs. I'll bring some food.'

'I feel sorry for hurting Mr Wilson.'

'I'll handle him. He's a broken man today.'

❧

Mani climbed upstairs and took a deep breath, feeling a lot lighter after sharing the story with the Wilsons. But his life lay in ruins. He had lost everything: his identity, his wife, his job and all the money. And he could do nothing about it.

He ate his food and glanced at their wedding photograph on the shelf. He never could have imagined that behind those beautiful eyes lurked a poisonous snake, ready to bite the moment he turned his back. She was indeed the cruellest of the species that could be found on the planet. To have risked his life, and placed so much trust in the woman he adored, was a monumental mistake he would regret for the rest of his life.

He wondered if he should go back to Aunt Jane and Tanya. But with little money, and nothing to look forward to, he didn't have the heart to do so. Mentally drained and physically tired, he went to sleep, but not before resolving to hunt down the woman who walked out of his life in such a dastardly manner.

In the morning, Mani came downstairs and noticed Mr Wilson sitting in the backyard, his head in his hands, a newspaper folded by his side. The towering man appeared half his normal size, probably crushed under the weight of what his daughter had done. He left him alone and entered the front room.

Mrs Wilson sat on a chair, gazing at the floor. Grace seemed to have brought upon her parents so much misery and pain that his own hurt felt insignificant in comparison.

He pulled up a chair and sat beside her.

Neither spoke for several minutes.

Mani cleared his throat. 'I'm so sorry for what I've done.'

Mrs Wilson rose. 'Not for one moment do I approve of what

you did, but I'm terribly ashamed of what Grace did.' She wiped a tear and went into the kitchen to fetch sandwiches and tea. 'Now eat, and then go get your stuff from the hotel.'

'How can I move in here? What will you tell your neighbours? That your son-in-law has moved in from his grave?'

'We'll figure that out later, first you do as I say.'

With nowhere to go, Mani considered it wise to accept Mrs Wilson's offer. He moved in, with his self-respect bruised, and little else. To the outside world, he became John Abraham the artist, a paying guest with the Wilsons.

Mr Wilson didn't feel comfortable giving shelter to a criminal, but he did seem to entertain a modicum of sympathy for Mani and gave in. But for Mrs Wilson, Mani would have taken to the streets.

Mani devoted all his time to painting, working long hours at a stretch. Strangely, his frustration and misery brought out the best in him. Instead of the usual landscapes, he experimented with new themes, using bold strokes and vibrant colours. Perhaps they reflected his inner turmoil and deep-rooted anguish. The results fascinated him. He discovered new aspects of art hidden in his creative mind, which hadn't been explored before. Within weeks, he produced a few interesting pieces that he was satisfied with. It was time to test his skills in the market.

With great trepidation, Mani decided to take some of his paintings to Anokhi, the art gallery in Poona he'd visited before.

A skinny lady with a pointed nose sat behind a large table in a cabin at the back of the gallery. Another woman sat opposite her. Mani knocked at the glass door which displayed her name—Miss Shehnaz Dastoor.

Miss Dastoor, obviously in charge, removed her glasses and looked up. 'Yes?'

Mani cleared his throat. 'I'm an artist, and I wish to show you some of my works for an appraisal, if you have the time?'

'Have a seat.'

Mani pulled up a chair and bowed to the other woman.

'You are?' Miss Dastoor asked.

'I'm John Abraham.'

'Meet Mrs Naidu,' she gestured. 'Principal of the Sarojini Art College.'

The principal of an art college! Mani greeted her with an uncertain smile, feeling a bit jittery. 'My pleasure, ma'am.'

The woman, with a streak of white in her hair and a visible air of authority, nodded. 'Are you a professional?' she asked.

Mani ran his hand through his hair and said humbly, 'Not yet, but I'm aspiring to become one, if there's any room for a self-taught artist.'

The two women exchanged a quick glance. Mrs Naidu raised an eyebrow.

Miss Dastoor leant forward. 'Let's see what you've got.'

Mani placed his canvases on the table. The women examined them, one at a time.

Mrs Naidu's eyes widened. 'Interesting...very interesting. I like your sense of colour and perspective. And you have a distinctive style. What do you say, Shehnaz?'

'You should know better,' said Pointed-Nose. 'But I suspect a lack of direction. There's a perceptible mix of styles, a bit of this and a bit of that.'

'It may be due to lack of formal training,' the principal remarked, her eyes still on the canvas, 'but that's where the originality comes from.'

Pointed Nose picked up a canvas and gave it a second thought. 'I like this one—a bit overdone perhaps, but still engaging. She dropped her glasses and tapped her fingers on the table. 'What is your aim, Mr Abraham?'

Stupid Question. Mani interlaced his fingers and gazed at the woman. 'The aim is to put food on the table.'

The haughty woman rubbed her chin. 'I'm afraid it's not going to be easy in the art world. People like to buy established names. An unknown artist, especially one without credentials, is like a product without a trade mark, lying neglected at the back of the shelves.'

Mani pressed on, 'There are a whole lot of names that never went to a school to learn art and yet became very successful.'

Mrs Naidu stole a glance at him.

Miss Dastoor straightened in her chair. 'I don't deny it, but exceptions are one in a thousand.'

'I'm not suggesting that I am one, but you might like to put some of these at the back of shelves, as you put it, for a consideration, and give it a try.'

'I'm afraid it doesn't work that way. We don't work on commission basis. We only rent out the gallery space to established names or upcoming artists of recognisable merit.' She pursed her lips, 'I'd suggest you enter your work in competitions, or maybe join a group show to begin with. That's the only way to climb the ladder—one step at a time.'

Mani knew the interview was over. A John Abraham signature didn't amount to much. Rejection was difficult to swallow, but he was not unduly perturbed. 'Thank you for your time.'

Miss Dastoor reclined on her chair as he rose to leave, 'Sorry to disappoint you, we wish you luck.'

On the way out, he browsed through some of the paintings on display. Recognisable merit! The words echoed in his mind. As he came out of the gallery, someone tapped his shoulder. There stood the woman with white streaks in her hair—the Principal.

'Mr Abraham, don't be disheartened,' she said. 'You have it in you. Keep working hard, the harder the better.'

'Thank you.'

'Rejections are hard to take, but that's part of the game. Galleries are here to make money; they find it difficult to take risks.'

'You're very kind, ma'am, but do you think my work is good enough?'

The woman raised her eyebrows. 'It is better than good enough. You must believe in yourself. And keep working.'

'Thank you for the encouragement.'

'I think you would profit from a visit to Bombay, the Mecca of art lovers. Wish you all the best.' She disappeared into the crowds.

9

A few days later, Mani arrived at Victoria Terminus in Bombay. Like him, hoards of starry-eyed people came to the metropolis, big on hope but very little in their pockets. They slept on its footpaths or railway platforms. Some would eventually make it big, really big, while others would resign themselves to their fate and take whatever the city had to offer. Ordinary folk from remote corners of the land became big stars or mafia dons. And some, who came with a lot of money to make more, became paupers, plying auto rickshaws to feed their brood.

After visiting a few art galleries, Mani discovered that in Bombay too, the obsession with celebrated artists was so strong and widespread that no gallery had room for new talent. The stamp of a self-taught artist negated whatever merit his work had. He invited scorn, as though he were some kind of an untouchable whose entry into the holy temples of the art world was prohibited by its pundits. A few were not too dismissive of his work, but candid enough to admit their inability to take risks with an unknown artist.

An elderly gallery owner with an inflated ego told him quite plainly: 'I'm afraid you do deserve the position of an art teacher in a school, but you seem to have missed your vocation.'

But for the man's age, Mani would have liked to punch him in the nose even though he realised he was in no position to begin his career with an assault on the guardians of art.

Another cheeky one directed him to a derelict gallery in the suburbs, a two-hour journey in an over-crowded bus. The so-called 'art gallery' operated from a shed, where the bored housewives of the middle-class neighbourhood displayed their labour of love on a weekly rental basis. The collection, piled up against the walls, comprised Hindu gods and goddesses and a few landscapes, the likes of which one could buy on footpaths of Chowpati for rupees twenty a piece. The artist in John Abraham had never been so humiliated.

Mani decided to spend the night in the dormitory of a cheap hotel nearby. After dark, he carried a quart of rum to the open terrace to drown his sorrow. He cursed Grace for his miserable plight and wondered why the stars made it possible for a Robert Wilson to meet with a Sandra in the first place.

❧

Before catching the train back to Pimpri, Mani made one last attempt at the famous Jahangir Art Gallery.

'I like your work,' said the kind gentleman, 'but the earliest we can accommodate you in a group show would be sixteen months from now.' He shook his head, 'We're heavily booked for over a year.'

Tired and heartbroken, Mani sat dejectedly on the steps outside the gallery, his paintings by his side. He wondered if he should look elsewhere for his livelihood—selling milk in his uncle's dairy at Poddukkottai for example, or painting signboards in Bombay. He found it hard to believe that Flight Lieutenant Mani Shankar Varadharajan, a decorated fighter pilot, sat on the pavement not knowing where his next meal would come from. He was near to tears when he heard someone address him.

'Hello, young man, I liked your work.'

Mani turned to face the stranger. A middle-aged, stocky man, dressed in a crumpled safari-suit stood behind him.

'I'm Feroze Pestonji.' He extended his hand. 'And you are?'

'John Abraham.'

'Mind if I take a closer look?'

'You're welcome.'

The man sat on the steps and viewed his paintings. Mani feigned nonchalance and shifted his gaze towards the busy street.

'I must say you are talented!' Pestonji examined each canvas, nodding his head now and then. 'By the way, where did you learn to paint?'

'I'm self-taught, which is a huge disqualification.'

A thin smirk played on his lips. 'For all you know, it might be a blessing in disguise.'

Was he a conman trying to impress him for some ulterior motive? Mani had heard of dubious characters taking unsuspecting fools for a ride, especially in a place like Bombay. But he didn't have to worry, for he had nothing in his pocket to attract swindlers. All this man could squeeze out of him were his paintings. And Mani was not going to lose sleep even if he were to part with any of them.

'You know, putting colours on canvas is not good enough,' the man remarked rather authoritatively. 'I know you have the gift, but it takes more than that to succeed. It's a vicious circle out there, especially for one without any credentials.'

Mani wanted to tell him to mind his own business, but he saw no harm in listening to his blabber.

'It's all about how you sell your name and build your brand.' He flapped his hands in the air. 'Marketing is the name of the game. That, my friend, is more important today than the content on the canvas.'

Mani tilted his head and gazed at the stranger.

'Take Iqbal Hussain, for example. If he shits on a canvas, it becomes a piece of art, and buyers would shell out loads of money for his unique creation.'

Mani gave a hearty laugh, his first in a long time.

Pestonji continued, 'Once a brand is established, even the most bizarre stuff becomes the work of a genius, and no one dare challenge the greatness of it. After all, it is not difficult to keep the critics and the media in good humour. You-scratch-mine-and-I-yours—that is how the system works.'

Mani knew what he meant, but he couldn't be sure of his intent.

'Tell me, how much do you want for these paintings?'

Mani was taken aback. 'Are you offering to buy?'

Pestonji nodded. 'If the price is right.'

'I'm open to an offer.'

He knitted his eyebrows together, 'Three hundred...four hundred apiece maybe?'

The offer reminded Mani of the Shah Brothers. It seemed Bombayites knew how to strike a good bargain. 'I suppose so.'

Pestonji shook his head. 'The trouble with young artists is that they are ready to settle for peanuts. Even a peg or two of rum, or a meal for that matter, would be enough.' He chuckled, 'because you do not know the value of your own work and have no clue how to launch yourself in the world of art.'

The man sounded a bit conceited, but what he said made sense.

Pestonji rose from the steps. 'Let's move to the café and have a chat over a cup of coffee if you have the time.'

Hungry and tired, Mani was tempted. A cup of coffee, and perhaps a bite, might help sooth his nerves. But he could hardly afford to foot the bill, if that was Pestonji's intention. Nonetheless, he picked up his wares and followed him to an open-air café nearby that was bustling with the evening crowd. Pestonji chose a corner table and signalled for the waiter.

'Coffee or tea?' the man asked.

'Coffee would be fine.'

'They serve excellent mutton patties.'

The tantalising aroma from the adjoining tables sent Mani's stomach churning with hunger. But he had no intention whatsoever of washing the dishes if the old man didn't pick up the tab.

'I'm sorry, Mr Pestonji, I can hardly pay for coffee, unless of course the owner is ready to accept one of my paintings to cover the bill.'

Pestonji laughed. 'I understand. Please don't worry, it's on me.'

Mani let out a sigh.

'Two coffees with lots of cream, and two plates of mutton patties.' Pestonji placed the order with the waiter. 'And make it quick.'

Pestonji waved at a passing acquaintance. 'You know, not too long ago, another struggling artist sat on that chair, just like you. He also couldn't pay for the coffee. Today, he commands astronomical prices for a whole lot of rubbish he produces by the dozen every month.'

'I don't get it,' Mani said. 'Are you a buyer, a collector or what?'

'I'm what you might say, a three-in-one—a buyer, collector and a promoter.'

'Promoter?'

'A salesman if you like, who knows how to package talent into a marketable product.'

'For a handsome consideration, I suppose.'

'Of course; nothing comes free in this world, including death.'

Mani gazed apprehensively at the unusual character. He had a thick moustache that was turned upwards like an ancient warrior's. His hawk-like eyes were set close to the bridge of his nose. Pestonji's narrow face reminded Mani of a dubious character in a movie. He hoped the offer of coffee and patties was not prompted by nefarious motives.

Pestonji threw his hands in the air. 'I did everything for him to be recognised in the right circles. He made a lot of money, bought a big car, the works, and then forgot about me.'

The patties arrived with the steaming cups of coffee. Mani attacked the patties as Pestonji continued his story. 'And now, he doesn't care to acknowledge me.'

Mani swallowed a mouthful and looked up. 'That's a dastardly thing to do.'

Pestonji shrugged, 'Good gestures are seldom rewarded, bad ones always. And he isn't alone. There've been others who came to Bombay with their sling-bags, had coffee and the works on me, made money and then disappeared from my life as though they never met me.'

The note of bitterness didn't escape Mani's notice. 'I'm sorry to hear that.'

'You won't be sorry when you come into money.'

'I doubt that very much.'

Pestonji raised his eyebrows. 'I've never failed in my judgment. And I smell success in you.'

Mani wondered if the build-up was aimed at selling a dream to him at a cost.

Pestonji took a bite and continued, 'You know, there are a whole lot of chaps floating around on the streets of Bombay, holding their art degrees and peddling their wares without success. And then some who did cinema posters for a living, and are now much sought after and toasted in high society. Degrees or artistic merit alone never provided a safe route to success in the art world. One has to establish a brand to sell a name.'

After a long discourse on how things worked in Bombay, Pestonji made an offer that revived Mani's belief in his self-worth which had suffered a serious blow during the last couple of days.

'Here's the deal,' he said. 'I'll provide all financial support and necessary backing to launch you in a professional manner. In return, I'll take a thirty percent cut on all future sales. You'll have to work diligently and produce at least fifty paintings to make a selection before we put up a show.'

Mani gazed at the man in disbelief. How could he afford to take such a risk! 'What if I don't sell?'

'You leave that to me. Your job is to paint, marketing is mine.'

Mani couldn't have asked for more. Pestonji was not a conman any more.

After fixing their next meeting, Pestonji asked, 'So how much do I pay you for these five paintings?'

That put Mani in a spot. Was it a calculated manoeuvre by the crafty old man to take him for a ride? It would've looked very odd if he were to accept money from the man who had offered to promote him. But what if it was a clever ploy to acquire his paintings for free? After all, he might also disappear from his life, like Grace did.

Before Mani could think of a suitable response, Pestonji put his doubts to rest. 'How about five hundred each?'

Mani felt relieved, but now the situation became more complicated. He shuffled in his chair and decided to be upfront with him instead of being evasive. 'Mr Pestonji, I shouldn't be accepting any money from you...but I wouldn't be honest if I said I don't need the money. Fact is I'm going through hard times and...'

Before Mani completed his sentence, the man pulled out crisp currency notes from his wallet and shoved them into Mani's hand.

'No, no...that's too much really...I'

'Young man, I'm not doing you any favour. Before long, I will be selling them for twice the amount or more. It makes good business sense, and I'm willing to bet my money on you, provided you follow the course I chart out for you.'

Mani was grateful. 'I don't know how to thank you…'

Pestonji raised his hand, 'Save the words.'

10

By day three, Grace had had enough of Sea View. It didn't offer the kind of action she craved. She scanned the local newspapers to see what New Year entertainment packages other establishments were offering. A half-page advertisement about a place called Paradise Resort caught her attention. It boasted of idyllic surroundings, a private beach and an all-night band especially brought in from Bombay.

'Oh, that's a very popular joint,' said the receptionist, when Grace inquired about it. 'A bit expensive, but worth the money.'

'I was thinking of going there for New Year eve,' said Grace.

'But we too have a special dance session with lots of prizes.'

Grace thought about the aging band and the matching crowds. She decided to call the Paradise Resort from her room.

'Good morning, Paradise Resort,' the man answered.

'I wish to book a room for a few days, starting tomorrow. And make it the best you have.'

'I'm afraid we are fully booked until the second of January. But there's an outside chance of some cancellations. We can place you on the wait list, if you like.'

'How long is your wait list?'

'You would be third, if you book right away.'

'What would it take to make it to the top?'

The answer came, but after a pause. 'Well... it'd be difficult, Ma'am... but let me see...'

Grace waited for a few seconds and said, 'Would a hundred rupee note do the trick?'

'I... I suppose so,' said the man, now in a much softer tone. 'However, if you double the offer, I should be able to confirm straight away.'

'Great, double it.'

'Your good name, Ma'am?'

'Grace Wilson.'

'Yes ma'am, and by the way, my name's Rego.'

'I'll remember that, thank you.'

Grace called Mrs Gomez in the morning to inform her that she would be going away for a few days.

'Where are you going?' Mrs Gomez asked.

'A place called Paradise Resort. I hear it's one of the best around.'

An uneasy pause ensued before the lady responded, 'Oh... well, I hope you enjoy it there.'

'I shall look you up when I return.'

'Sure, we'd be delighted.'

'Please convey my thanks to Mr Gomez for making my stay memorable.'

❧

Grace arrived at the resort on the afternoon of 29th December. The exclusive resort overwhelmed her. Surrounded by thick jungles on one side and the sea on the other, Grace couldn't help but feel that she had come to an exciting place.

A young lad at the reception greeted her. 'Good afternoon, Ma'am. Welcome to Paradise Resort.' His voice sounded familiar.

'Do you have a booking?'

Grace removed her dark glasses. 'Grace Wilson.'

'Yes, of course. I've arranged the best suite for you, ma'am. I'm Rego.'

Grace slipped two hundred rupee notes to him in an envelope and signed the register.

Suite number fifteen on the first floor enchanted her. The door opened to a cozy little sitting area that led to a well-appointed sleeping room at the back. A peep into the spacious bathroom, the size of her bedroom at Kkd, delighted her. The white marble flooring, the colourful tiles and the antique vanity mirrors took her breath away. Fresh carnations stood in a vase by the side of the huge tub, and layers of white towels hung on the brass railing.

The huge double-bed faced a large window that opened onto the lush green lawn below. She leant over the window ledge to get a better view.

Rows of cottages lined both sides of the lawn. Small groups of people lazed under colourful garden umbrellas. In the distance, people frolicked in the rolling waves of the magnificent Arabian Sea, their bodies shining in the sun. She was thrilled.

After a luxurious bath in the evening, Grace changed into cream-coloured slacks and a form-fitting green top. She left her hair loose and went for a stroll on the beach. Curious eyes followed her everywhere, conversation ceased when she passed by. Traversing the cobbled path, her peripheral vision noted the spell she cast with satisfaction. Grace enjoyed the attention, but never returned their gazes, as if she was a Grace Kelly. In fact, she was no less. She went and sat on a rock, admiring the brilliant orange glow of the setting sun and the strong breeze of the ocean.

But she longed for company. Being alone in exotic surroundings made her lonely. She folded her long legs and clasped her hands across them, thinking of the rollicking times she'd had in Kkd. The money had given her a new high, but the zing was missing.

When the stars covered the skies, Grace changed into a silk dress and entered the lively lounge. She ordered wine and moved towards the dining hall. A suave gentleman, with the looks of a movie star, stared at her when she arrived at the door. She settled down at a corner table across from him. Dressed in grey trousers and maroon jacket, with a colorful scarf thrown around his neck, the man looked classy. He sat talking to a lady in a red sari.

Grace ignored him at first, but his persistent gaze unnerved her. She couldn't help but return his gaze over the rim of her glass as she sipped her drink. She held his gaze for several seconds and then picked up the menu.

A waiter arrived to take her order. 'By the way,' she asked without lifting her head, 'who's that gentleman near the door, sitting with the lady in red?'

'Oh, he's our boss, Mr Mark Braganza, the owner of the resort.'

'And that would be his wife, I suppose?'

'No, she's a cousin from Bangalore who visits occasionally. Mrs Braganza died a few years ago. Boss never married again.'

'I'm sorry to hear that.'

Grace glanced in the direction of the couple and caught the lady in red watching her. She sipped her wine and turned towards the window. It was dark outside. Grace could see their reflections in the window panes. The man was constantly gazing at her. The lady in red had turned away. Grace placed her order and carried her glass into the verandah. The sensuous scent of the exotic flowers and the heady fragrance of the forest enveloped her. She knew the effect she had on the man. Owner of the resort! And single! It excited her.

The waiter appeared at the door. 'Excuse me, ma'am. May I serve dinner?'

'Can you serve it here in the open? I'd like that very much if you don't mind.'

'Certainly.'

Grace ate her meal under the canopy of a thousand stars, with wind blowing through the trees, producing its own music. The atmosphere enthralled her, but the loneliness haunted her. She signed the bill and threw a fleeting glance at the man before leaving. He gave her a smile. The game had begun. This was going to be one hell of a trip.

❧

The scent of the mysterious beauty and the rustle of her skirt sent Mark's blood racing as she passed by. He couldn't resist gazing at her receding figure. Mark had enjoyed the favours of the best looking women in town, but the siren who just left a whiff of her fragrance behind posed a new challenge.

'Maaark?' The woman in red winced. 'Here you go again.'

Mark sighed and lit his cigar.

'It's time you settled down, instead of running around like a dog, chasing every new car that passes by.'

He smiled. 'I'm waiting for the right woman.'

'You're an incorrigible flirt.' She raised an eyebrow and looked him in the eye. 'I thought the one who just passed by may fit well into your specifications.'

Mark blew smoke in the air and narrowed his eyes. 'The dimensions are pretty impressive, but more often than not, beautiful women suffer from intellectual bankruptcy. They might be good in bed, but are hollow in head.'

'If you're looking for some high-class snob, I doubt if you'll find it in a nice package.' She smirked.

'Maybe not, but I'm wondering what a beautiful woman like

her is doing in this remote corner, all by herself.'

'I think she's looking for a mate, but I doubt she'll allow you to scratch her fenders that easily.'

He leant forward. 'You want to bet?'

'Don't be too sure.'

'Is that a challenge?'

'No, I'm aware of your skills in handling beautiful women, but for heaven's sake, settle down, Mark. It's time you raised a family.'

'I know you mean well, Sherry, you always have. Give me some more time.'

Sherry gave him a stern look. 'That's what you said last year, and the year before.'

Mark took a long drag on his cigar and closed his eyes.

'I won't visit you again, unless it's to witness your marriage.'

Mark took her hand in his and nodded. 'I won't disappoint you, I promise. You're the only family I have.'

Mark found out more about the mysterious woman from the booking details. Miss Grace Wilson had arrived from Bombay, destination unknown, permanent address: B/11, Railway Colony, Kharagpur. The woman had deposited thirty-thousand rupees in safe custody and paid ten-thousand as advance to cover her stay—an amount sufficient to see her through comfortably for a whole year! Something was not right. A single woman travelling alone with so much money made him suspicious.

When he saw the Wilson woman going towards the beach, he withdrew the duplicate key of room fifteen from the safe in his office and quietly sneaked into her suite. A familiar fragrance greeted him. Two suitcases, both locked, lay on the sideboard. An assortment of exotic perfumes and colognes graced the dressing table. He walked to the window and, through the gaps in the curtains, saw her frolicking in the sea.

It didn't take him long to find the keys in a purse that lay under the pillow. He hurriedly opened the suitcases. At the bottom of the larger one lay a portfolio that contained an assortment of documents. In an inner pocket he found two cheque books and two passbooks of bank accounts at Kharagpur and Pimpri in the name of Mrs Grace Shankar! Mark knit his brows. Mrs Grace Shankar?

The entries in one book suggested a single withdrawal of rupees two lakhs and a balance of over twelve lakhs. The other showed a deposit of one lakh and no withdrawals. The woman, he estimated roughly, was sitting pretty over fifteen hundred thousand rupees, not accounting for the cash deposit at the resort! Another side pocket revealed a thick wad of currency notes he didn't bother to count. It wasn't exactly a gold mine, but it was enough to keep him in good humour for a few more years. Mark scurried back to the window. Mrs Grace Shankar was blissfully rolling in the giant waves.

He replaced everything in exactly the same order he had found them and slipped out of the room.

Back in his cottage, Mark ambled to the sea-side window of the living room and focused his powerful binoculars on the captivating beauty emerging out of the waters. Clad in a yellow bikini, she displayed a figure such as never before seen by Mark Braganza in his entire life—a figure that would've launched a war in the medieval times! The lethal combination of beauty and a hefty bank balance sent his heart racing.

Cousin Sherry was right—Miss Grace Wilson fit Mark's specifications perfectly, and to hell with the intellect. Sherry wouldn't be disappointed on her next visit. From that moment, Mark followed Grace's movements discreetly. How could a phenomenal beauty like her, with all the money in the world, isolate herself he wondered? He promised to change that forever.

On New Year's Eve, Grace noticed the arrival of big limousines bringing in loads of young revellers for the dinner and dance night. She dressed for the occasion in a powder-blue gown with elaborate silver work and matching accessories that complemented the tan she'd acquired from her long stint in the sea. When the noise level from below reached a sufficient high, she dabbed a Nina Ricci perfume, touched up her makeup and made her way to the main venue.

Festive lights and garden-fresh flowers greeted her when she descended the stairs. The scent of lilac filled the air. Huddled in small groups, people engaged in light banter. A pianist played a soft melody to set the mood. The loud guffaws melted into soft murmurs the moment Grace appeared at the arched entrance. She stood for a few moments, surveying the scene. Eyes turned towards her. Immaculate in a dark blue suit, Mr Braganza approached her. She pretended not to notice.

A musky fragrance with a hint of tobacco filled her nostrils. 'Good evening. I hope you're comfortable?'

'Do I know you?'

Mark looked her over from top to bottom. 'Perhaps not, but I'm in the business of knowing people who visit the resort.'

Grace raised an eyebrow.

'Especially beautiful people, who come with a certain aura and mystery surrounding them.'

Notwithstanding the flattery, Grace was suspicious about his reference to the aura and mystery. She gazed into his eyes…oh those deep blue eyes in which she could drown!

'By the way, I'm Mark Braganza. Now, if you allow me, may I have the pleasure of escorting the evening's singular sensation to the bar?' His eyes twinkled as he offered his arm.

Her cheeks felt hot as she took his arm. 'You flatter me.'

'You enthral me, and I wouldn't be surprised if I make more enemies today.'

She blushed.

'What would you like to drink?'

'I shall look after myself, thank you.'

'Not tonight.' He ordered pink champagne and thrust a long-stemmed glass into her hand.

Grace was amused. 'Thank you.'

'My pleasure,' he said, raising his glass of scotch.

'You seem to own the place,' she quipped.

'As a matter of fact, I do. I hope we don't disappoint you.'

Grace turned to look at the crowds and asked, 'To what do I owe this unusual gesture?'

'To the creators, who brought you into this world.'

Grace caught his eyes. 'Do you always charm your guests with such extravagance?'

'Only when there's someone special, which is rare.'

'I'm flattered.'

'I mean what I say.'

'Hello, handsome,' a tall, swarthy woman dressed in a black sari and a low-cut blouse accosted them. 'How are you?' she asked, as Mark turned to face her.

'Hi, Kaveri, I'm doing fine, thank you.'

The Black-Cat tilted her head and ran her brown eyes over Grace's figure rather patronisingly. 'So I see.'

Mark cringed.

'Are you going to introduce us, or shall I do it myself?'

Mark obliged and lit a cigar.

The woman turned to Grace. 'Your first visit?'

'Second; the first was during a school trip,' Grace said. 'Things have changed a lot since.'

She rolled her eyes and glanced at Mark. 'Indeed, haven't they?'

'Can I get you a drink?' Mark asked.

'I never refuse a good offer,' she said, her eyes on Grace. 'The usual please.'

Mark ordered rum and coke for the intruder.

'Excuse me,' Grace said, and slipped away, carrying her drink with her.

'Well, well, well, there goes the latest siren.' Kaveri licked her lips. 'So, what's the scene?'

Mark stiffened. 'Bright as ever.'

'Yes, of course, I should know better.'

'Good for you. And now if you'll excuse me, I've a lot on my hands.'

'You sure do, I can see that.'

'Why don't you join the crowds and mingle?'

Her thick lips curled into an involuntary smile. 'Don't you worry, darling. I won't hang around if that's what's bothering you.'

'Look, Kaveri, it's long over. Surely you don't want us to discuss the weather?'

Kaveri swallowed her drink and gazed at Grace. 'Quite a piece of meat isn't she?'

Mark cursed the bitch.

And the Bitch went on. 'Indeed, I envy her... and pity her at the same time. The lamb doesn't know the slaughter house is round the corner.'

'For God's sake, Kaveri, leave me alone.'

'Come on, lover boy. I'm not a spoilsport. Won't you allow me to finish my drink?'

Mark blew smoke in her face.

Kaveri wasn't one to give up so easily. 'By the way, where has this ravishing bird come from? I hope she is of the migratory type.'

'You don't have to be so bitchy.'

'No, of course not, I wish you good luck.' She emptied her glass and slipped away.

Mark sighed with relief.

❧

Grace ran into the lady who had shared the table with Mark the previous night—Mark's cousin.

'Hello, I'm Sherry,' the lady said. 'That's a lovely dress you're wearing.'

'Thank you. I'm Grace, Grace Wilson.'

'Are you visiting alone?'

'Yes.'

'So am I,' she said and gazed at the crowds. 'How do you find it here?'

'Oh, it's a marvellous place, and I'm going to stay here for a while.'

'I'm sure you will. But keep away from that bimbo,' she said, eyeing the woman in black. 'My brother has a knack for getting into bad company.'

'Your brother?'

'My dearest cousin and an incorrigible flirt.'

Grace chuckled. 'I'm thoroughly amused.'

'I notice you've already made his acquaintance,' she said, as Mark approached them.

'So the two of you have already met,' Mark remarked.

Sherry winked at Mark. 'Why don't you ask the lady for a dance?'

Mark looked at Grace. 'Shall we?'

They danced to a slow number. After the band stopped, people demanded fast music. Mark and Grace returned to join Sherry.

'You two look great together,' Sherry said.

Grace blushed.

'Let's go for a refill,' said Mark.

'You go ahead,' Sherry said, stealing a glance at a middle-aged man who sat alone, smiling at her from the other end. 'I think I can use some company.'

Mark pursed his lips and nodded.

Sherry faced Grace. 'Pleasure meeting you.'

'Same here.'

Mark led Grace to the bar and filled her glass.

Grace gazed at Sherry and her companion. 'An old friend?'

'Her ex-husband, divorced, but they meet here every year around this time. Neither of them married again.'

'How interesting.'

'Let's go sit on the deck outside.'

'Aren't you going to say hello to him?'

'We're not on talking terms.'

Grace sat on a cushioned chair and sighed. 'It's wonderful out here.'

Mark sat beside her.

The cool breeze laden with the scent of the forest and that of Mark enchanted her.

He sipped his drink and peered at her. 'I wonder what brings a mysterious beauty to this isolated resort, all alone and unescorted.'

'Destiny,' she said.

'You haven't told me anything about yourself.'

She lapsed into silence.

'I'm sorry if I'm being too inquisitive.'

'No, no, it's just that… there's nothing much to tell.'

'Of course there is. I can see it in your eyes.'

Grace tilted her head and gazed at him. 'What do you see in my eyes?'

'That you're hugely mysterious, hauntingly beautiful, terribly engaging, and alone.'

She laughed. 'How many times have you used this line?'

Mark exhaled a breath. 'I wouldn't deny it, but there's a big difference in what you say and what you really mean.'

Grace sipped her drink. 'And what do you really mean?'

'That I've never in my life met anyone as beautiful and fascinating as you are.'

'You amuse me.'

'I'd consider it a dishonour if I fail to amuse you.'

The wind had become strong and the noise level from the lounge louder. Grace swept her hair back and gazed at the horizon.

'A few months ago, I lost my husband in an air crash.'

'Oh, I'm so sorry to hear that. How did it happen?'

'He was a fighter pilot...crashed into the sea...just vanished without leaving a trace.'

'Good gracious no. It must've been terrible. I shouldn't have brought this up.'

'It's okay. I'm trying to get over it. One has to move on in life, and that's what I'm doing.'

'How strange! I lost my wife at sea too.'

'What?'

'A couple of years ago, my wife, Irene, drowned right in front of my eyes, swallowed by strong currents. I couldn't do a thing to save her.'

Grace sat up. 'I'm sorry.'

A bunch of revellers spilled over onto the deck.

'Come, let's move in,' said Mark, annoyed at the interruption. 'Let's have another dance.'

The dance floor was packed to capacity. Mark held her close and Grace rested her head on his chest.

When the music stopped, Mark glanced at his watch. 'I think we should eat our dinner before it gets too rowdy.'

'I'd like that, too.'

After a sumptuous dinner, they moved back into the hall. Uproarious merrymaking and blaring music greeted them. Mark led her to the floor packed with frenzied couples gyrating to the beats. Grace plugged her ears with her hands. Mark pulled her closer into his arms. The lights went out and shouts of 'Happy-New-Year' reverberated in the hall. He lifted her chin and kissed her lightly. When the lights came back on, they broke apart.

'Happy New Year,' he said.

'Same to you.'

Firecrackers burst outside the hall.

Grace looked up into his eyes. 'I want to retire if you don't mind.'

Mark escorted her to her room.

'Thank you for a lovely evening,' she said. 'I had a wonderful time.'

'Pleasure was entirely mine.'

At the door, Grace turned to face him. 'Good night.'

'Sweet dreams,' he said and waited until she closed the door.

Had it been any other woman, Mark would have carried her into her bed. But Grace Wilson was special—like a rare wine which must be sipped slowly and not gulped.

11

Grace woke up to the soothing rumble of the ocean. She hugged the soft pillow, thinking of last night's kiss. It had taken enormous will power to leave it at that. She didn't want to give the impression of being too easy. Mark was different from all others she had encountered before. Sophisticated and charming, he was a class apart, but she wanted to go slow.

She rose a little after nine and blinked at the bright, sunny day. Mesmerised by the grand view of the ocean, she stood motionless at the window. The lawn was practically empty and the beach nearly deserted. Perhaps people still slept in their rooms after the all-night party. It felt like a lazy morning, a lull after the storm of last night's frenzied celebrations. But for her it was the beginning of a new life, a life full of promise. She took a deep breath and decided to go for a swim.

Arriving at the beach, she dropped her robe on a rock and plunged into the inviting waters. After half an hour, she found herself too far out into the sea and decided to turn back. A man in dark glasses stood near the rock where she had left her robe and towels. It infuriated her. As she came closer, she gasped. There stood Mark Braganza, holding her robe in his hand.

At first, she became conscious of her semi-nakedness. But her instincts told her to display her assets to advantage. She emerged from the waters and presented a vision lethal enough to demolish her latest victim.

'Good morning, and a very happy New Year to you once again,' Mark said, his eyes on her cleavage.

She snatched the robe and wrapped it around her body. 'Thank you and same to you.'

Mark passed her the towels. 'You shouldn't be swimming so far out into the sea at this time of the day. It could be dangerous.'

'I didn't encounter any sharks,' she said, knowing that one stood so close to her, ready to swallow her whole.

He chuckled. 'Not a shark, but the ocean has bigger teeth.'

'I'm a good swimmer.'

Mark bent down and placed his foot on a rock, folding his arms over on his knee. 'So was Irene.' He gazed at the horizon with a hint of sadness in his eyes.

Both fell silent, watching a flock of flamingos dive at the breakers.

Mark pelted a stone into the waters and glanced at her. 'Isn't it strange that both of us lost our spouses to the sea?'

Grace pondered over it. One was an accident, and the other by design—a design that suited her well. Even if Mani survived it didn't matter, for officially he was dead and buried for good.

He tilted his head and looked into her eyes. 'I want you to promise me something.'

'What?'

'That you'll never go that far out into the sea all by yourself.'

Pleased by his macho protectiveness, she met his gaze. 'Alright.'

'Do you have plans for this afternoon?'

Grace knew it was coming. 'I'm a bit groggy—didn't sleep well last night. I think I should take a long nap to recover from the fatigue.'

'Well, in that case, how about dinner with me tonight, at my place?'

My place! She skimmed her tongue across her lips and fought to keep her composure. 'I can manage that.'

'Good. I'll meet you at eight.'

Back in her room, Grace disrobed and admired herself in the mirror, turning to one side and then another. The extended swim in the ocean, and the brief encounter with Mark had turned her cheeks a lovely shade of pink.

In the evening, Grace tried on a number of dresses for the occasion. A fawn-coloured dress with a low-cut neckline suited her. It blended well with the tone of her skin. She let her hair fall free all the way down to her waist. With a touch of lip gloss and eyeliner, she looked her seductive best, ready for the kill.

Dressed in a brown polo-neck jersey and beige-coloured trousers, Mark Braganza stood at her door with a yellow rose in his hand and a captivating smile. He handed her the rose and escorted her to his cottage.

The large cottage perched high on the small hillock at the far end of the property presented an impressive picture. Covered on all sides by morning-glory, it was picture-postcard perfect. A set of zigzag stone steps lead to the front verandah. As they entered the spacious living room, Grace sighed. 'Wow, this is wonderful!'

'Thank you.'

Grace's eyes travelled the length and breadth of the room. A large window at one end commanded a spectacular view of the ocean. The logwood furniture, deep settees piled high with cushions and other aspects of the cottage interior clearly reflected the rugged taste of its occupant. An assorted collection of guns stood on a stand in one corner. Several animal trophies mounted on the walls suggested a hunter's retreat in the jungle. The elaborate bar put together with rocks and rough stones in the centre of the room and bar stools carved out of tree trunks completed the picture. A piano stood near the window. The black-and-white photograph on it caught her attention.

'That's Irene,' Mark said. 'Just before we married.'

'She's so lovely and serene,' said Grace, eyes glued to the picture. 'Why does God take away such angels?'

Mark turned to the bar, ignoring the question. 'What's your poison?'

'I'll have wine.'

'I've saved a bottle of French Bordeaux just for an occasion like this.'

Mark poured wine for her and scotch for him.

Grace settled into a chair. 'Do you play the piano?'

'No, I'm not the gifted one. Irene used to play on it, quite beautifully in fact. I can play the gramophone if you like.'

Grace chuckled. 'You must be a keen hunter, what with all these trophies.'

Mark lit a cigar. A pleasant aroma of musk and tobacco filled the room. 'I was, at one point in time, but right now I'm the one who is being hunted, ready to be mounted on the wall.'

'What do you mean?'

Mark narrowed his eyes and looked into hers. 'Some people kill with guns, others with their sheer beauty—like you.'

Like all men, Mark started with the watery soup of flattery. Grace sent him a coquettish look over the rim of her glass. 'You don't cease to flatter me.'

'I mean it from the bottom of my heart.' He gave her a look that would have melted even the most resolute mother superior on the planet. 'I've never met anyone like you before.'

Grace sighed, delighted at the pampering. If Mark were to take her in his arms at that moment, Grace would have dissolved into his embrace without the slightest protest. However, the practical side of her nature compelled her to dangle the carrot a little longer, to make him want her more. The tactic never failed her.

Grace strolled across to a cluster of pictures on a sideboard, showing Mark in the company of beautiful women. 'Judging from these pictures, you seem to have met many.'

Mark came and stood behind her, engulfing her in his heady aroma. 'I'm not a hypocrite to deny it, but no one ever dazzled me as much as you do. You've struck me like a bolt of lightning, electrifying me.'

Grace felt a surge of heat rising through her body. She swallowed her wine and gazed at a large photograph that showed Mark in his Jodhpurs, standing over his trophy on the floor—a deer. For a second, she felt herself in a somewhat similar position, with Mark towering over her —except she would be gasping for breath, unlike the deer. She wondered why no one, not even George, and least of all Mani, had ever thrilled her in this way.

Mark put his hand on her shoulder.

The touch sent a thousand watt current flowing through her body, but she controlled herself. 'I see many Kaveris in these pictures.'

'Ah, they are mostly family, except for a few that represent the transitory phases of my life. As I said before, I'm no saint. And I can tell that you must have ruined the lives of many a man with your beauty.'

Ruined the lives of many! Mark's words echoed in her mind, reminding her of her past suitors. She emptied her glass and faced her latest, ready to surrender.

Mark pulled her into his arms and kissed her full on the mouth. Their lips parted only to deepen the kiss.

Gasping for breath, she withdrew and returned to her chair. She knew when to stop, even though she went limp in his arms.

'I want you in my life, Grace,' Mark demanded, 'forever.'

Although the first part of his speech suggested an invitation to bed, the second inspired some hope of permanency. Grace wanted him as much as he desired her, but Mark would have to do better than that to claim her.

Mark hesitated. 'Did I upset you?'

'No.'

'Then what is holding you back?'

She flushed. 'Things are happening too fast…I don't know if I should get involved so soon after…'

Mark lifted her chin. 'Either you want me in your life or you don't.'

It was too much to hold back. 'God knows I want to be in your life forever, but…'

Mark put his finger on her lips. 'Will you marry me?'

Grace wanted to melt into his arms, but hesitated. She gazed at him in a daze. 'Are you serious?'

'I've never been more serious in my entire life.'

'We hardly know each other, Mark.'

'Grace Wilson, I know all that I need to know about you.'

She bit her lip and hoped her secret would remain buried, but she needed to make Mark wait a little longer. 'I don't think we should rush into something as serious as marriage. I need more time.'

Mark took her face in his hands. 'I'd allow you to test my patience for as long as you want, but I know both of us are ideally placed to be united.'

Grace retreated to the large window and gazed at the stars. Mark put on the music—Nat King Cole's *Unforgettable*.

She shuddered as the cool breeze sent a chill down her body.

Mark wrapped a shawl around her shoulders. This thoughtful gesture reassured her that she had met the right man.

Mark placed his hands on her shoulders. 'I'd have succumbed to half a dozen proposals in the last two years, but didn't. Because I was waiting for the right person–and that person has come into my life only now, to fill the void in my life.'

Grace stood still. Am I dreaming? Is this really happening? God let his words be true. She turned and slipped into his arms.

The soft music and the soothing roar of the ocean made her dizzy. Locked in each others' arms they danced. It was truly an unforgettable evening.

❧

Mark Braganza came into Grace's life like a Greek God and revived her hope for an exciting, fulfilling future. Grace carried the lingering sweetness of his kiss on her lips that night, and into the morning when she woke up. A wonderfully charming man, an exotic resort, a life full of glamour and, above all, long-term security—what more could she ask for?

Mark invited Grace to visit his new projects coming up at the rear of the property. Wearing a straw hat, Grace turned up in white shorts and a light-blue sleeveless silk shirt. He led her down a dirt track flanked by tall trees, to a secluded area surrounded by rocks. A handful of workers were laying bricks.

'I'm planning to put up a swimming pool between these rocks, and a few cottages scattered around the pool in the wooded area. This will be an exclusive retreat for high-paying guests who like their privacy.'

Grace could have never imagined that she would one day lord over such a fantastic property. 'Splendid idea, but all this is going to take a lot of time.'

'Ten months at most.'

'Ten months!' Grace glanced at him, 'But I don't see very many people working.'

'The contractors are bound to complete the project in time. Otherwise they don't get paid. I've already taken bookings for next season.'

Grace removed her glasses. 'I'd be surprised if they complete the task in such a short time.'

'These are the best contractors in the area. They'll be here in full strength soon.'

'I hope so.'

'Let me show you something else.' Mark guided her to the top of the rocks. 'Here, I'm going to build an artificial fall with water flowing down the slopes into the pool to give the place a natural feel.'

'That's a marvellous idea, Mark. I can visualize the whole project. It's going to be a dreamy place.'

'Let me take you to the terrace to give you a bird's eye view of the property.'

Mark led her up the stairs to the large terrace. The terrace led to a raised platform covered by a canopy of multi-coloured bougainvilleas. An antique wrought iron bench that must have once graced a public park was placed under it.

Grace stepped onto the platform and gasped at the magnificent view of the sea disappearing into the horizon. She removed her hat and glasses. 'This is the best view so far.'

'My father used to sit on this bench for hours and watch the sun go down into the sea.'

'Everything looks so beautiful from here.' Grace stepped off the platform and strolled towards the other side of the terrace.

Mark followed her. 'How long are you going to torture me?' he asked, almost breathing down her neck.

She turned slowly and gazed into his eyes. The wind ruffled her hair, partially covering her eyes, like the passing clouds over a bright moon. He brushed the strands aside and caressed her cheek.

Grace felt weak in her knees. 'It's been only two days since we met.'

'Two long and agonising days.'

'I don't need to tell you how I feel about you, Mark, but…'

'But what?'

'I don't know…'

Mark put his finger on her lips.

Grace closed her eyes.

Mark took her into his arms and kissed her softly.

Grace returned the kiss, but not as passionately as she would've liked. That, she thought, could wait.

When they parted, Mark summoned a waiter to place his order.

'I think it would be a great idea to keep an open-air bar over here,' Grace suggested. 'It would be a fantastic place to unwind with a drink.'

'That's a good idea.'

A waiter appeared with the drinks. Mark poured champagne for both of them. Glass in hand, Grace leant over the parapet and gazed at Mark's cottage. Flocks of birds flew in delightful formations in the sky. Trees swayed in the afternoon breeze.

'Your cottage reminds me of paintings by the old masters.'

'Yes, a lifeless canvas, in which resides a lonely man, waiting for somebody to fill the void.' Mark tossed a glance at her.

Grace peeked at him from the corner of her eyes.

'Destiny has brought us together, Grace. We belong to each other.'

'I guess so.'

'By the way, I'm flying to Bombay this evening. I hope you're not leaving in a hurry.'

'Of course not. How long will you be gone?'

'Three or four days at most. That should give you enough time to think seriously about us.'

They moved to the antique bench. Grace sat cross-legged, showing off her lovely feet strapped in white sandals.

'I like your idea of the bar. We may set up the counter here under this canopy.'

'I'd rather have it in that corner, against the backdrop of the big tree over there.' Grace pointed to the spot. 'And the tree lit up at night for effect.'

'I'll have to commission you to do this.'

'I'd love to!'

'I hope I can afford your fee.'

She laughed. 'I didn't ask for one.'

'Meaning you're going to stay here longer?'

Grace flushed a little. 'I hope so.'

Moments later, a waiter served them steaming Mutton Biryani.

'I'm famished,' said Grace, her appetite aroused by the aroma of exotic spices.

After lunch, Mark escorted Grace to her room.

Grace leant against the door. 'Have a nice flight.'

'Thanks. But remember, I want an answer when I return.'

At night, Grace realised that the time to play games was over. Tactics, if overdone, would have just the opposite effect. She didn't want to put off Mark. She decided to call the Gomezes the following morning.

'I've some good news to share with you,' she announced when Mr Gomez answered the phone.

'You do?'

'I'm planning to get married soon.'

'Great! Who's the lucky man?'

'Mr Mark Braganza of Paradise resort.'

The line went silent.

'Hello… Mr Gomez… you there?'

'Are you serious?' he asked. The uneasiness in his voice came loud and clear across the phone line.

'Of course I am.'

No response.

Grace wondered why. She waited.

'Just a second, Rose wants to talk to you.'

'Hello, Grace. Good to hear from you. I'm sure you must be very happy. How about paying us a visit before you get busy with your plans?'

'I would love it. Mark's gone to Bombay, and I might as well do some shopping.'

'Good. Should we send the car to pick you up?'

'I'd hate to bother you.'

'No bother at all. How about tomorrow morning? Perhaps you could stay with us for a couple of days?'

'I'd appreciate that very much.'

'The car will pick you at around ten o'clock.'

'Suits me fine, thank you.'

Grace looked forward to meeting the couple. They were the only two people she wanted by her side at her wedding. She had no one to share her happiness with. She couldn't think of informing her parents, let alone inviting them. Mani, if alive, might have contacted them already. After all, she didn't commit any crime in the eyes of the law, Grace reasoned with herself. Yes, she had deserted him… but that was nobody's business. And Mani couldn't rise from his grave to claim his share. He was dead and gone as far as she was concerned, and she, a widow, had every right to marry anyone she liked.

12

Mani arrived at Mr Pestonji's flat in an old dilapidated building on Warden Road that looked as if it could do with some repairs. He climbed the worn-out stairs to the third floor and rang the bell. Pestonji opened the door, dressed in typical Parsi-style payjama and a sleeveless muslin-shirt.

'John, it is good to see you! Come on in.' He ushered Mani into a moderately furnished drawing room in which the sofas appeared to have been used for generations. 'I hope it wasn't difficult for you to find this place?'

'No, I had no problem.'

Pestonji gestured towards a ratty old sofa. 'Make yourself comfortable.'

Mani propped his paintings against the wall and sat down. Several sepia-tinted family pictures stood on the mantelpiece and a large painting of a castle adorned the pale green wall. Light filtered into the room through multi-coloured window panels, drawing interesting patterns on the white terrazzo floor.

'Let's see what you've got.'

For the next half hour, Pestonji devoted his attention to the paintings, not uttering so much as a word. He would squint at each canvas, step back to study it from a distance and mutter to himself. Mani kept his fingers crossed, wondering if his work would pass the old man's scrutiny.

'Can I get you something cold to drink?' Pestonji asked at last.

'That would be nice, thank you.'

Pestonji disappeared into the kitchen and returned with two glasses.

'Here, have some lemonade.'

The cool breeze from the ocean coupled with the soothing drink eased Mani's trepidation.

Pestonji announced his verdict. 'Excellent work, John, I'm impressed.'

Mani took a deep breath and relaxed. 'You really think so?'

'I see a lot of potential,' he said. 'Let's move to the balcony to view these in a better light.'

Pestonji discussed the finer points of perspective, depth and colour in each painting with Mani late into the evening.

'But this is not enough. You've to produce another dozen or so to have a wider choice, before we go public,' Pestonji said. 'The art world is very discerning and averse to self-taught artists. I suggest you move in here with me and concentrate on your work, instead of commuting between Poona and Bombay. 'I'm afraid there's not much to offer except this balcony, if you're willing to rough it.'

Mani was reluctant. 'That's indeed very nice of you, Mr Pestonji, but I don't wish to cause any inconvenience to you and your family.'

'You're not the first one here, John. There have been others before you. It'll be easier for us to interact on a regular basis. Don't think I'm doing you a favour. I'm looking after my own interests. Besides, I could do with some company.'

Pestonji, a bachelor, lived with his niece, Shehnaz, and her husband. Both worked in a bank. When Pestonji introduced them to Mani, the couple didn't seem pleased at the prospect of putting up with an unwanted guest in the house. But the old man had the last word.

The balcony, though small, had a wonderful view of the ocean. Covered with windows on all sides, it provided additional living space. To have a roof over one's head in a posh area such as Warden Road excited Mani.

Before the end of the week, Mani moved in and set up home in the balcony. He awoke to the chirping of birds and a cool breeze from the ocean and looked forward to a new beginning. A knock on the door startled him.

Mr Pestonji appeared with a smile and two mugs of tea. 'Good morning.'

'Oh, thank you. You shouldn't have bothered.'

'No bother at all. I've company for a change.'

'But you have your niece and...'

He shook his head. 'No way, and I suspect they don't enjoy each other's company either.' He sipped his tea. 'You know, in this city most people live under one roof not out of love, but compulsion. Shehnaz, and that husband of hers, live with me because it provides a roof over their heads—and I get food put on the table in return. That's it.'

Mani felt awkward. He himself was there not out of love for the old man, but need.

'Believe me I'm doing them a great favour. Otherwise, they would be living in faraway suburbs, commuting by overcrowded trains or buses all their lives.'

Mani kept quiet and wondered if he could ever repay him for his generosity.

Pestonji pointed to the rocky beach that lay about two-hundred yards from his building. 'You see that place over there? It's called "Scandal Point". The name comes from the notorious stories associated with it. I'd advise you to keep your distance.' He chuckled and turned to leave. 'Let me know if you need anything.'

'You're so kind, Mr Pestonji, no wonder people took advantage of your generosity.'

During the day, Mani set up his studio. In the evening, he strolled towards Scandal Point. It reminded him of Lovers' Rock at Digha, except here, real people cuddled together in pairs. He thought of Grace and a sword of bitterness pierced his heart. He sauntered to the market on Warden Road, famous for its lustre and glamour. After loitering for a while, he returned to the house and dined with Pestonji, in the company of Shehnaz and Navroz, her long-faced husband, who remained uncommunicative throughout.

While Mani worked on his paintings, Pestonji revived his contacts in the art world and booked a prestigious gallery in advance. Some of the well-known art critics visited his home to select the best works. The man took care of everything: the framing, the catalogues, the invitation cards and the customary cocktails without which nothing was possible in Bombay. He fixed up with a famous industrialist to inaugurate the show. To add to the glamour, he arranged to have the presence of a few socialites and starlets from the film world.

Mani confronted him one morning. 'Mr Pestonji, I'm afraid you're taking a big risk, investing so much on an unknown entity.'

'Trust me, John. I know what I'm doing. You've no idea what it takes to make it big. We have to blow our trumpet loud enough to announce your arrival, otherwise nobody will notice.'

Mani avoided his eyes. 'I don't wish to let you down.'

'I'm not a fool to have picked up a John Abraham from the footpaths of Bombay for nothing. I know the game inside out.'

Mani ran his hand through his hair and fidgeted. 'What if you don't recover the costs?'

Pestonji narrowed his eyes. 'Let me tell you something, John Abraham. In this game, a few paintings are labelled as "sold" beforehand. A couple of them are gifted to a select few who represent known collectors and the corporate world, with the explicit understanding of future acquisitions of the artist's works. These people play an important role in the success of an artist.'

Pestonji filled in Mani further. 'Bombay is known for its filthy rich who are willing to invest in art as a status symbol. The art world provides a unique platform, where they get to hobnob with the elite, the culture-vultures and the cream of society. They are not there to appreciate art, but to be seen and photographed among glamorous people. And once your canvas reaches their living rooms, you're made.'

Pestonji's strategy didn't appeal to Mani much, even though he was the best example of deception. However, he was in no position to argue with his mentor.

❧

John Abraham's show opened at the famous Akbar Art Gallery at Marine Drive, on a cool winter evening. The crowd comprised a few titans of the industry, a couple of second-rung film stars and art collectors. Pestonji had also invited socialites. Decked up in their best silks and chiffons, they added colour to the opening night. The cocktails ensured good attendance of the press and those who mattered in the art world.

Two dozen elegantly framed paintings were on display, including the ones that Pestonji had acquired for a princely sum of five hundred each. The response was astounding. Pestonji introduced John to only a select few, saying that the artist avoided press and fiercely guarded his privacy.

By the time the cocktails finished, half the paintings displayed the 'SOLD' label—some genuine, and some to create an artificial impact. With highly favourable reviews in the press, people flocked to the show in large numbers. Within a week, almost the entire exhibition was sold out, the paintings fetching three to five thousand rupees apiece. The ones that Pestonji had bought went for three thousand each!

After the show concluded, Mani shook his head. 'I don't believe this.'

Pestonji beamed. 'Didn't I tell you I wasn't doing you any favour? And now you'll see what I do with the rest of your paintings in a few months from now.'

❧

For the next ten months, Mani immersed himself in studying modern art from the Impressionists to Post-Impressionists and experimented with new techniques. When the whole of Bombay slept and the dogs barked in the streets, Mani painted. Consumed by his passion to create new works, he lost track of date and time. The hustle and bustle of Warden Road didn't interest him anymore.

The only concession he permitted himself was a brief break on the rocks in the evenings at Scandal Point. Even there, he would think and smell paintings, occasionally allowing his thoughts to drift back to Tanya. He longed to meet her, but he had no time for personal pursuits. Besides, Pestonji wouldn't allow any distractions at this stage of his career, and Mani didn't want to displease the man who had invested so much in him.

After two more shows, one in Delhi and another in Bangalore, John Abraham's name began to be discussed in the art circles in hushed tones. His shows received excellent reviews in the press and his paintings sold for amounts far exceeding their creator's expectations and those of his mentor too. Mani had talent and

Pestonji knew how to market it.

With enough money in the bank, Mani decided to ask for a break. 'I want to take some time off, if you don't mind,' he requested Pestonji during their morning tea. 'I need to get away for a while.'

'Sure, you deserve it. You've done extremely well, my friend, and there's plenty of time before your next show in Calcutta.'

'Not *my* show, Mr Pestonji, it'll always be *our show*... or no show at all.'

'You really mean it?'

'Absolutely.'

'Aren't you going to ditch me, like the others?'

'On the contrary, I hope you don't ditch me, for I'm nobody without your guidance and support.'

'By the way, where do you plan to go?'

'I have some folks in Daman I haven't seen for a long time.'

Pestonji gave him an inquisitive look. 'We've been together for so long and yet you haven't told me anything about yourself. I hardly know you, other than as John Abraham, the painter.'

Mani wanted to be just that—John Abraham, the painter. The rest was buried in his grave at Kkd, and he saw no reason to dig it up.

'There's nothing much to tell.'

'Of course there is. I see it in your eyes all the time, and in your paintings.' He gazed at Mani's latest canvas and went on, 'The contrasts, the sweeping strokes and strange mix of colours... they reflect conflict... perhaps the turmoil in your mind.'

'I don't know. I just do what comes to mind.'

'You express with your paints what you cannot with words. There's a hidden energy in your work, something you don't see, but I sense.'

Mani laughed. 'You ought to have been a professor of art, or a mind reader.'

'You're wrong on both counts. I'm neither a professor nor a mind reader, but I can read the merit of a painting.'

Mani shrugged. 'You haven't told me much about yourself either.'

'What shall I say? I lived and worked in art galleries since the age of sixteen, and never failed to spot a winner? Which is why people take notice when I launch someone. Nothing excites me more than picking up raw talent and nurturing it to its logical conclusion. But in you, I see more than an artist, the human side of which is hidden behind the layers of paints on your canvas.'

Mani thought for a moment. 'In fact, the human side of me is buried under the weight of guilt I carry for the wrongs I've done in the past. Painting provides me an escape—a reason to live.'

'You hide more than you tell.'

'Someday I will tell all, but right now I need a break.'

'Of course you do, and I guess somebody's waiting for you on the shores of Daman.'

That is exactly what he wanted to find out. With Grace out of his life, he needed an emotional anchor; someone he could trust and share his life with. 'I should be back by Tuesday.'

'Take your time, John,' Pestonji said, with a twinkle in his eyes. 'Before you go, however, I suggest you visit the barber shop and buy some fresh clothes. You don't have a single piece that doesn't stink of paint.'

In the evening, Mani walked down Warden Road and did some window shopping. This was a posh market where the likes of Flight Lieutenant Mani Shankar wouldn't have fit in, but John Abraham was a different customer altogether. He strode into a big store and proceeded to the men's section. No one attended to him for a couple of minutes. Feeling awkward, he wondered if he should've gone to the suburbs where common people shopped for their needs. As he was about to leave, a salesman approached him.

'Yes?' he asked in a condescending tone. Dressed meticulously and smelling of strong cologne, the dashing fellow intimidated Mani.

'I'm looking for jeans, size thirty-four.'

The man pulled out a few pairs and placed them on the counter. 'Hundred-five apiece,' he said, as if it was enough to send Mani back to the streets.

Mani had never bought a pair for more than sixty or seventy bucks at most, but today he wanted to test the man's patience. 'Got anything better?'

He raised his eyebrows. 'Excuse me?'

'I want top-end stuff.'

The salesman looked dismissively at Mani and pulled out two more samples. 'Hundred ninety-nine each.'

Mani turned them over and stroked his beard. 'Can you do better than this?'

Face flushed, the man retreated into an inner chamber and emerged with two more pairs on hangers. 'Two fifty each, imported.'

Mani selected two pairs of jeans and asked, 'Do you also stock kurtas?'

'Yes, sir,' deferred the salesman, this time with a slight bow. 'Please come this way.' He ushered Mani to another counter manned by an attractive girl with high cheek bones and a pleasant smile. 'Please show the gentleman the very best we have.'

Three kurtas and many smiles later, Mani walked to the ladies' section. A portly gentleman, probably the owner of the store, emerged from behind his desk. 'May I help you, sir?'

'I'm looking for something special for a young lady.'

'You're at the right place. We stock one of the best collections you can find in Bombay.'

Browsing through a wide range of dresses, Mani bought a soft pink gown for Tanya, and a Pashmina shawl for Aunt Jane.

'Perhaps you may like to sample some of the best perfumes we imported recently from Paris.'

Mani sniffed several samples in dainty little bottles and bought two. The bill came to a staggering three-thousand-fifty, but he knew another canvas of his would cover the cost.

'Thank you, sir. We hope you visit us again.'

The next morning, he hired a taxi and set course for Daman.

13

Thick clouds hovered in the sky when Mani arrived at Daman. A strong gust of wind blew in his face as he got out of the taxi. He shuddered and hesitated before walking the distance to Aunt Jane's door. He waited for a few moments and then knocked.

Aunt Jane opened the door. '*John*!' she cried out wide-eyed 'I don't believe this.'

Mani grinned.

'What a pleasant surprise! Come on in.' She dusted the chair with the ends of her sari.

Mani placed his suitcase on the floor. 'So how are you, Aunt Jane?'

'Same as before—nothing ever changes in Daman. She closed the door to keep out the wind. 'Where have you been all this while? I thought you'd forgotten us.'

'How can I ever forget you, Aunt Jane? Work kept me extremely busy, with little time to do anything but paint.'

'Let me make a cup of tea for you.'

Mani took a long breath and looked around. Nothing had changed in the modest but warm home. The same pictures of gods and deities greeted him from the faded yellow walls. A small black-and-white picture of Tanya stood on the shelf alongside a vase containing plastic flowers. Everything was in its place, except the painting he had gifted to Aunt Jane. He wondered if Tanya trashed it for good.

'I feel like I'm home.'

'Yes, you are. But what took you so long?'

Mani avoided the question. 'The wind is very strong today.'

'It's been like this since morning.'

'How is Tanya?' he asked when she brought him tea.

'She's getting along. Is sugar okay?'

'Yes, thank you.'

'You just disappeared from our lives,' reproached Aunt Jane, with a hint of sadness in her eyes. 'Without leaving a trace.'

'I had to make something out of my art before showing up. Besides, I wanted to give you a surprise.' He couldn't think of a better excuse.

'You just did. Tanya should be here tomorrow.'

Mani hoped so too. He knew Tanya visited on Sundays and had planned to reach before she came. 'I hope she's doing well.'

'She's doing all right, the same old routine, but I'm worried about her.'

'Why?'

'It's time she settled down with someone nice and caring.'

'I'm sure things should work out well for her.'

'There's a proposal from this nice boy in the merchant navy based at Cochin, a distant cousin on her father's side. But she's not considering it as seriously as she ought to.'

Mani was gripped by a sudden sense of anger at the faceless man in Cochin who threatened to jeopardise his own plans. That Tanya didn't consider it seriously came as a relief.

'I don't think you should worry too much about Tanya. She's mature enough to know what's good for her.'

'Poor girl is working hard when most girls her age have already started families.'

'Destiny will take care of everything.'

'I'd like to believe you.'

In the brief silence that ensued, they could hear the howling wind outside.

'Is the spare room rented out?'

'It was, for a short period after you left, but not anymore. Tanya uses it now whenever she visits.'

'In that case I should book a room at…'

'Absolutely not, you're welcome to use her room. But I wouldn't know in what shape Tanya has left it. I can hardly climb the stairs because of my knees.'

'I don't want to cause any inconvenience to Tanya. I would rather…'

'You're at home, remember? Tanya would be quite okay in my room. Please go ahead, make yourself comfortable.'

The first thing Mani noticed upon entering the room was his painting, nicely framed and mounted on the wall. His faith in Tanya was momentarily restored. Mani felt the room was suffused with her scent. A gown and a dress hung from the two pegs on the wall. This strong sense of her presence overwhelmed him. He wanted to open the window to let in fresh air but stopped just short of doing so as he didn't want the winds to sweep away Tanya's scent from the room. Instead, he lay down on the bed and thought about how he would face her.

Aunt Jane was frying fish in the kitchen when Mani came down with the gifts he had bought in Bombay.

'Ah, it smells so good,' he said. 'Looks like I'm in for a treat.'

'I know it's your favourite.' She covered the pan and joined him.

Mani handed her the gift.

'Thank you, John, but it wasn't necessary at all.' Her eyes

brightened when she opened it. 'It's beautiful.'

'And this is for Tanya.' He handed her the other box.

'You shouldn't have bothered, John. I wouldn't know how to return your kind gesture.'

'Your love and affection are the greatest gift I could ever ask for.'

'That's all I can offer. But tell me about yourself.'

Mani gazed out of the window. 'It's a long story that nearly ruined me. But the hand of God came into my life, quite by chance, in the form of a good man, who saw some potential in my work and took me under his wings. He gave me shelter and organised my shows at his expense. The rest is unbelievable. I was nobody before I met him. And now I'm somebody in the art circles. But for him, I would've been on the streets.'

'Tanya did tell me she'd read about your shows in the papers.'

'She did?'

'Yes, and she was very excited. She wanted to congratulate you on your success, but didn't know where to reach you.'

'I was so consumed by my work that I lost track of everything else in my life.'

'I don't know much about art but I knew you'd succeed.'

Aunt Jane's fish-fry served with French-fries satiated Mani. 'I haven't eaten such a wonderful meal in a long time. Does Tanya also cook as well?'

'She's catching up, but she does the pork very well.'

'Oh, so let it be pork tomorrow.'

In the morning, Mani went for a stroll on the beach and visited the spot he had called his studio. Nothing had changed. He sat on a rock, thinking about his first sale. He couldn't believe the dramatic change Pestonji had brought in his life and hoped Tanya would do the same.

After breakfast, Mani settled into a chair and browsed through an old magazine while waiting for Tanya. He remembered his torturous wait for Grace in Poona. Today was different, although the thought of facing Tanya after such a long time gave him the jitters.

At nearly half past eleven he heard a knock. He braced himself and opened the door. Tanya stood like a statue, her eyes wide. The strong wind ruffled her hair, covering her face.

'Hello, Tanya, how are you?'

She swept back her hair. Her expression changed from shock to a frown. 'Am I at the wrong house?'

Taken aback, Mani said, 'No.'

She narrowed her eyes and gave him a cold stare as if he was a stray dog who appeared at her door, wagging his tail. 'Then you must've lost your way.'

For a moment he didn't know what to say. She had every reason to be upset with him, but her response unnerved him. 'I had, but not anymore,' he mumbled.

'I doubt it very much.'

'Tanya,' came the sharp voice of Aunt Jane from behind him.

'Excuse me,' Tanya said and slipped away into the house without even a glance in his direction.

❧

Tanya's words, *You must have lost your way,* echoed in Mani's mind as he sat on the steps outside Aunt Jane's abode, his heart wounded and hopes bruised. He had never expected such a cold reception from Tanya.

Was it a sign of rejection? He hoped not. He wondered if it had been a mistake to visit Daman after such a long time, unannounced and perhaps unwelcome.

Aunt Jane joined him and sat next to him. 'I'm sorry, John. I don't know what came over her. I've never seen her like this before.

I must apologise for her behaviour.'

'You don't have to. Perhaps I shouldn't have taken things for granted.'

'No, it's nothing like that. You're always welcome here. It's just that…Tanya was a little…'

'I don't blame her.'

She placed a hand on his shoulder. 'Please forgive her. Tanya has been upset about not hearing from you at all for so long.'

'I feel bad about it myself. I must apologise to her.'

Thunder rumbled in the distance. Aunt Jane looked up at the sky and rose. 'Come inside before it starts raining.'

Tanya's clothes were gone when Mani returned to her room. He lay on the cot and closed his eyes, thinking about their last meeting at Silvassa. How sweet she had looked! He wished he had taken her into his arms then and claimed her forever. But his obsession with Grace had driven him to near insanity. He had been chasing a dream without knowing that a disaster awaited him. Footsteps outside the room brought him back to the present.

Tanya stood at the door, her hair loose and face devoid of expression. 'Are you ready for lunch?'

Mani rose and tried to catch her eye.

She turned away.

'I'm sorry to have upset you so much. I'd appreciate it if you would hear me out.'

'I don't think it matters.'

'It matters more than anything else to me.'

'You expect me to believe that?'

Mani fell silent. After more than a year, he couldn't be sure of her feelings for him, but her anger suggested something deeper than what appeared on the surface. Why would she be angry if it didn't matter, he reasoned with himself.

'I was so consumed by my work that I lost track of everything.'

Tanya tossed a glace in his direction. 'I was very happy to learn about your success, but you vanished from our lives…as if we never existed.'

'Believe me, Tanya. I was going through some very rough times. I suffered from betrayal, humiliation and was haunted by failure. It took me time to achieve something worthwhile in life before I could think of anything else.'

Tanya narrowed her eyes. 'The fact is we're far removed from your world, and I don't know what brought you here.'

'You want to know what brought me here?' Mani asked, turning towards the window. 'I was floating like a fragile boat caught up in a storm in the ocean, searching for an anchor, without realising that it lay here in Daman. What brought me here is the love and affection I didn't receive anywhere else since I left home ten years ago.'

'That is history…we don't belong to your world anymore.'

Mani choked. 'I wouldn't have come here if you didn't belong to my world. I came here to find out if that love and affection still exists.'

Tanya entered the room and pulled out a folder from a drawer. She placed it on the table and walked out of the room.

For several seconds Mani stood motionless and then opened the folder. Inside, he found newspaper cuttings of his press reviews pasted neatly on each page, starting from his first show to the last in Bangalore. Stunned, he felt guilty for not sharing his success with one who cared so much—someone so far and yet so close. He longed for her in a way he hadn't before.

Aunt Jane and Tanya were setting the table for lunch when he came down. Tanya avoided his gaze throughout and ate her meal in silence. Aunt Jane breached the silence with her stories.

Mani cornered Tanya after they finished their meal. 'Would

you like to come for a walk on the beach?'

Tanya glanced at Mani and then at her mother. 'It might rain.'

'Take your umbrella,' said Aunt Jane.

After a moment's hesitation, Tanya slipped into a raincoat and handed the umbrella to Mani.

The threat of a storm kept people away from the beach. Mani struggled to keep the storm in his heart from erupting. He had so much to say and yet, the words didn't come easily. They walked on the beach in silence, feeling the sand on their bare feet.

Tanya shivered against the strong winds and walked with her head down, her hands inside her coat pockets.

Mani gazed at the sea. 'I love the ocean, the swaying trees and the constant roaring of the waves crashing against the rocks.'

'I thought you didn't see or hear anything beyond your paintings.'

'For all these months, I did not. I worked like a man possessed and didn't register how time flew by. There was so much happening, I didn't have time for myself. It was nothing but painting and running between one show and the next, beating the deadlines.'

'I prayed for your success each day.'

'I knew you would, but I need more than your prayers.'

The clouds darkened. She folded her arms across her chest.

Mani pointed to the familiar cluster of trees. 'There's my studio.' He led her to the cozy little place hidden behind huge rocks sheltered under a cluster of trees. 'This is where I composed my first painting.'

'Ah, we used to play hide-and-seek around these rocks as children,' she said and sat down on a rock.

It started to rain. Mani sat next to her, holding the umbrella over their heads.

After a long stretch of silence as they watched rain drops falling on the rocks, Mani couldn't hold back any more. 'I want you in my life, Tanya.'

She blushed.

'I never realised how deeply I wanted you.'

She closed her eyes.

Mani lifted her face and kissed her eyes. 'Will you marry me?'

She burst into tears. 'Oh God, yes! I worshipped you from day one... and you didn't care... just disappeared from my life.'

Mani wiped her tears with his lips and kissed her deep on her mouth. She kissed him back. He held her tight. They remained locked in each others' arms for a long time without exchanging another word.

Tanya was glowing by the time they returned home.

'Aunt Jane, this time I've come with a purpose,' Mani said, as she sat in the verandah. 'I hope you won't disappoint me.'

'What is it?' she asked.

Tanya slipped into her mother's room.

Mani sat by her side. 'I seek the most precious gift you can ever offer.'

'What can I offer you, other than my blessings?'

'That I already have.'

She looked at Mani, perplexed.

'I've come to ask you for Tanya's hand in marriage.'

'Am I dreaming?'

'I've nursed this desire for a long time, but first I wanted to become worthy of her.'

'Are you sure of what you're saying?'

'Absolutely.'

Her eyes turned moist. 'Did you hear this, Tanya?'

Tanya came and stood behind her mother, placing her hands on Aunt Jane's shoulders.

'Did you hear this?' she repeated.

Tanya hugged her mother. 'Yes.'

'Oh John, what do you want me to say…I think I could die of happiness!' She took Tanya's hands into hers. 'This is the happiest moment of my life. Nothing will please me more than giving my daughter away to you.' She kissed Tanya's hands. 'You're blessed my child. I'm so happy for you.'

'I hope I live up to your expectations,' Mani said.

Aunt Jane took Mani's hand into hers. 'You're way beyond our expectations, John, the son I never had. God has smiled on us, at last. Tanya's papa must be smiling from the heavens.'

'I'm afraid we'll have to wait for a while, until I find a place of my own in Bombay.' He glanced at Tanya. 'It shouldn't take more than a couple of months I guess.'

'I shall wait for you as long as you wish.' Tanya reassured him.

'What about your parents?' Aunt Jane inquired. 'Have you taken them into your confidence?'

Mani looked away, not knowing what to say. He had no doubt his parents would welcome Tanya with open arms, even though they might not welcome him. He resolved to confide everything in Tanya someday, and send her to inform his parents that their Mani was alive as John Abraham—in shame, if not in glory.

14

It had already started pouring when Mani returned to Bombay, a happy man with hopes to set up a new home. The heavy downpour flooded the streets. He released the taxi and landed in a pool of water rushing down the slopes of Pedar Road. But on this day he didn't care and enjoyed getting wet as he walked to Pestonji's house, splashing and kicking the water like a young boy returning from school.

'Goodness, man, couldn't you hire a taxi?' Pestonji exclaimed when Mani arrived at his door, completely drenched.

Mani grinned. 'I wanted to enjoy the rain.'

By the time Mani changed into dry clothes, Pestonji appeared with a cup of hot tea. 'So, how was your trip?'

'It was good.'

Pestonji sat on a chair. 'I've some good news for you.'

Mani wondered if his own should wait. 'What news?'

'We're having a show in Goa.'

Calcutta, and now Goa? 'We aren't even ready for Calcutta, Mr Pestonji, how can we…'

'Calcutta is cancelled because they're renovating the gallery. So I booked a show in Goa.'

'How much time do we have?'

'Three months. And you have to finish those two landscapes

for the Continental Hotel by the end of this month.'

'Three months?' Mani was exasperated. 'How am I going to cope with that? I'm not a machine.'

The old man gave him a stern look. 'You can do it. We already have a substantial collection, and there is time to add a few more. I'm trying to rope in the Governor of Goa to inaugurate your show, which should matter a lot.'

Mani slumped onto his cot. It was not the best time to disclose his plan. He knew he would have to live with the paints and canvas for the next three months without entertaining any thoughts of Tanya or a new home. Even though he had more than a dozen paintings in stock, he needed to do more.

'You don't seem happy.' Pestonji said.

He hesitated. 'I thought I could take a break for a while… and think of…'

'Take a break?' Pestonji snapped. 'I don't understand. You're about to reach the pinnacle of glory and you want a break?'

The look of disbelief on Pestonji's face told Mani he had said the wrong thing. He couldn't afford to displease the man. He sipped his tea and kept quiet.

'Such opportunities do not knock at one's door every day.' Pestonji waved his hand impatiently. 'Public memory is too short, my friend. If you don't cash in now, you will be forgotten as just another bloke who had his moment of success and then vanished from the scene. A sustained effort is required before you can relax and hibernate like most successful artists do, but only after they've made a lot of noise in the press.'

Mani lit a cigarette and saw his dream vanish in the clouds of smoke.

'Besides,' Pestonji continued, 'the governor's wife is a great connoisseur of art. I'm sure we'll see some of your works in the

Government House, which will be good for publicity.'

'I suppose I cannot let you down.'

'Not me. You cannot let *John Abraham* down—not after having come this far.'

Mani almost choked over the phone when he informed Tanya about the impending delay.

'I'm sorry, but we can wait,' said Tanya. 'You must do what is best for you. Another three or four months is not going to make any difference.'

'I'll miss you.'

'Me too.'

❧

Despite his success, Mani's work did not garner much respect from the established masters of the time. Gradually, however, the sheer strength of his mounting sales, the single most important factor that separated the successful from the gifted, won them over. That talent alone did not guarantee success, was demonstrated by the genius of Pestonji, time and again. Mani knew that some of the most outstanding works of art commanded high regard only long after their creators died. He was lucky to enjoy the fruits of his labour in his lifetime, thanks to Pestonji.

Inspired by the rocks at Breech Candy, he decided to do a large painting of Lovers' Rock at Digha from memory. After several days of work, the result fascinated him. It revived old memories of Grace, and some bitterness.

'This one's come out very well, John.' Pestonji said, his eyes bright. 'I must get an ornate frame for this painting to enhance its overall appeal.'

'Thank you, but I won't sell it.'

Pestonji shifted his gaze from the canvas to Mani. 'Why not?'

'I want to keep it for myself.'

'All right, but we must include it in the show. This will be a big draw.'

Mani now lived two different lives: One, as John Abraham—the successful artist who lived away from the glare of publicity, and two, as Mani—hiding from the law. He found it difficult to cope with both, because success and publicity went together. Although he kept a low profile, the fear of discovery constantly haunted him.

One day Pestonji suggested something he feared most. 'John, I'm aware of your aversion to the press, but there are two scribes I cannot deny an interview with you.'

Mani nearly dropped his brush.

'Mr Abbas Ali of *Life Times* and Shefali Rajdan of *Art & Kraft* played a big role in getting you the best reviews in the press. Shefali has a formidable reputation in art circles, and her pen carries a lot of weight.'

Mani cleaned his brush and hesitated. 'I've nothing to tell the press.'

'The press has an insatiable appetite for news, and you are the news.'

'I do not wish to feel like a dumb ass amongst the bulls and the holy cows of the art fraternity. I don't understand their language. I'm not yet ready for them. Maybe we could do it some other time.'

'You can't keep them away for too long.' Pestonji shook his head and left it at that.

Mani heaved a sigh of relief.

15

Eric Mansion turned out far more opulent than Grace had imagined. A short driveway from the wrought-iron gate led to a large porch covered on all sides with lush green creepers and the porch in turn led into the colonial building. Meticulously manicured lawns flanked the cobbled path. The car halted in the porch. Two magnificent marble statues of fairies stood on each side of the broad steps that led into a vast verandah, the size of a cricket pitch.

Mrs Gomez, dressed in a floral gown, appeared on the verandah. 'Hello, Grace, good to see you,' she welcomed Grace. 'I hope you had a comfortable ride?'

'Yes, thank you.'

Grace's breath caught in her throat as Mrs Gomez led her into the main hall filled with florid eloquence. The tall arched windows filtered soft morning light onto the rich carpet and antique furniture. A crystal chandelier hanging from the high ceiling added to the grandeur. Exquisite artefacts decorated every nook and corner of the hall. Huge paintings and family portraits in ornate frames adorned the walls. Separated by lace curtains, a grand piano stood on a platform in one corner. A winding staircase with a carved wooden banister completed the picture.

'Is this place a museum?' Grace wondered. 'It is simply breathtaking.'

Mrs Gomez smiled. 'Thank you. Come, let's sit. Would you like some tea?'

'I'd like that.' Grace sank into a deep sofa.

'So, tell me about your stay at Paradise Resort.'

'Oh, I'm enjoying every minute of it. Have you been there?'

'A few times, yes. But that was long ago.'

'Mr Gomez must be away on work.'

'He'll join us later.'

After tea, Mrs Gomez escorted Grace to a tastefully furnished room on the first floor.

'This is wonderful,' Grace said, looking out of the rear window that opened onto a small swimming pool on the grounds below. Tall trees shielded the pool from the outside world. 'I made a terrible mistake not coming here earlier.'

'You're welcome. Let me know if you need anything.'

Grace rested for a while and then changed into a pale green dress for the evening. The Gomezes were waiting in the hall when she descended the majestic stairway.

Mr Gomez greeted her warmly. 'You look gorgeous.'

'Thank you. How are you?'

'I'm fine.'

Mrs Gomez invited Grace to sit with her on the long sofa.

'Let me fix you a drink,' Mr Gomez said. 'What's your preference?'

'I'd like some wine.'

'What about you, Rose?'

'The same for me.'

Mrs Gomez turned to Grace. 'So, you met your man at the resort?'

'Mark Braganza is a charming man. We hit it off very well.'

Mrs Gomez glanced at her husband. 'When are you planning the wedding?'

'We'll decide after Mark returns from Bombay, but it won't be long. I'd like you both to be present by my side.'

Mr Gomez didn't utter a word, which was unusual considering his exuberant nature. Given their phone exchange, while Grace wasn't exactly expecting him to jump with joy, the least she expected was the customary congratulatory gesture, which was not forthcoming.

'Is anything wrong, Mr Gomez? You don't seem happy.'

Mr Gomez cringed. 'Are you really serious about this man?'

Grace stiffened. He spoke as if 'this man' was a janitor or something. For the first time since their acquaintance, Mr Gomez seemed less civilised than she thought him to be. She tilted her head. 'Excuse me?'

'You seem in great haste.'

Grace looked askance at Mrs Gomez.

'What do you know about Mark Braganza?' Mr Gomez asked, without lifting his head.

'Everything I need to know.'

Mr Gomez raised his head. 'Look, young lady, it's none of my business to question your judgment. But sometimes, decisions made in a hurry can get one into a lot of trouble.'

'What are you trying to say?'

'I'm afraid you've no idea what you're getting into.'

'Eric...! Must you?' Mrs Gomez interjected.

Mr Gomez rose from his chair. 'Come with me.' He led Grace towards the piano. A large portrait of a gorgeous girl with a Mona Lisa smile greeted her from the wall.

Grace gasped for breath. It was Irene—an exact replica of the small photograph she had seen on the piano in Mark's cottage. Irene? Mark's ex-wife? Here in the Gomez residence?

'This is our daughter, Irene.'

Grace's mouth opened. 'I don't believe this!'

Mr Gomez gazed at the portrait with sad eyes. 'She used to play the piano for hours, turning the place into a concert hall. No one has touched the piano since she was taken away from us.'

'I'm sorry... I didn't know...' Grace's voice cracked.

'Have you any idea how she died?' His sonorous voice quavered.

'Mark told me about the accident.'

He faced her. 'I'm sure he did. But trust me, it wasn't an accident.'

Grace froze, her eyes on the portrait. There was something sad about Irene's smile.

'Mark Braganza made it look like one.'

Grace shuddered, her throat felt dry. 'What?'

'You know very little about Mark.'

Grace refused to believe what she heard. Was the old man jealous of her liaison with his daughter's ex? How was Mark roaming free if he was involved? Irene's eyes in the portrait intimidated her... as if trying to warn her.

'I'm sorry to disappoint you, but I thought you should know.'

Grace shook her head. 'You must be mistaken.'

'The only mistake we made was to allow Irene to have her own way. Mark married her not for love, but money.'

Grace returned to her seat, her head spinning and legs heavy.

Mrs Gomez dabbed her eyes with her handkerchief. No one spoke for a couple of minutes. The silence added to the tension.

'I could've never imagined Irene was your daughter,' Grace said. 'Losing her must have been terrible indeed. But I cannot believe anyone would have harmed her, least of all Mark.'

'Strange things happen in life.' Mr Gomez said. 'One gets

blinded by love and that's what happened to Irene. We didn't know what she was getting into, and neither did she.'

Glass in hand, Mr Gomez hovered around Grace. 'Look, Grace, we have no intention whatsoever to upset you in any way. You're wise enough to know what's good for you. However, I would be failing if I didn't warn you.'

Grace crossed her legs nervously and reached for her glass.

Mrs Gomez faced Grace. 'I must apologise. We shouldn't have brought this up. It's your life, and we've no business to interfere. If you're happy, you have our best wishes.'

The dinner that night was a quiet affair with no further mention of Mark Braganza. Grace's stay at the Eric Mansion came to an abrupt end. She returned to Paradise Resort the next morning.

❧

Grace wanted to find out more about Mark, but at the same time, she did not. She had no doubt Mark proposed to her for love. He couldn't have known about her money. Nonetheless, she decided to visit Mark's cottage to have a chat with the maid.

The maid greeted Grace at the door and invited her in for a cup of tea. She was gripped by a sudden surge of fear when she saw the animal trophies mounted on the walls, their eyeballs glaring ominously. Grace walked across to Irene's photograph on the piano. Her beautiful, sad eyes haunted her. She wiped the beads of sweat from her forehead and settled into a sofa as the maid appeared with tea.

'What's your name?' Grace asked.

'Saira Banu.' She poured tea for Grace.

'How long have you been working here, Saira?'

'Six years. I came here to join my husband,' she said, sitting down on the carpet beside her. 'He is the gardener.'

Grace stirred sugar into her tea. 'You must've known Irene very well.'

'Yes, a very generous and compassionate human being.'

'I believe she came from Goa?'

'Her parents live in Goa. They never visited after ma'am passed away.'

'Why is that?'

'I don't know. Sahib and madam's father were very close once. But later things became sour between them and he stopped coming. Only Irene ma'am used to visit them, always alone.'

'That's sad.'

The maid hesitated and then spoke in a hushed tone. 'Money matters. It's the greatest of ills that can destroy relationships.'

Grace managed to keep a straight face.

'Tell me about the accident?'

Saira took a deep breath. 'God only knows what happened there. Sahib managed to survive, but ma'am couldn't make it due to strong currents.'

Grace sipped her tea. 'Some people talk of foul play.'

The maid covered her mouth with her hand. 'That's absurd! Who would've thought of hurting such a good soul? She was an angel and everybody loved her.'

'Including Mr Mark?'

Saira turned her face and sighed.

'Thank you for the tea.' Grace left without pressing her further.

Later that afternoon, she visited the nearby colony of fishermen. A fish-eyed, sallow-faced old man sat hunched near a boat, working with the nets. He looked up when Grace approached.

'Hello, are you going fishing?'

'No, not at this time. You a tourist?'

'Err... I'm a writer. I write stories.'

After exchanging notes about fishing, his family and the weather, Grace broached the subject of Irene's accident.

His eyes narrowed. 'Ah well, God alone knows what happened. We're poor souls, cut-off from their world, except for a couple of lads from hereabouts who are employed there. We heard about the accident. The police came... got entertained for a couple of days... and then went away. We never saw them again. She was a kind lady... distributed sweets during festivals, gave medicines to the sick, even money at times. God bless her soul.'

'Some say it wasn't an accident.'

Deep lines etched his forehead. 'Who knows, the tale never ended conclusively. Perhaps you can write a story on it.'

A flock of seagulls flew overhead, flapping their wings in unison. A couple of urchins, naked under their shirts, came running and stood at a distance, gaping at her.

Grace peered at the old man. 'How do you think I should end the story?'

'Only God can give you the answer for that.'

'I'm talking about a story. I can twist it any way I like. God has no role to play in it.'

'God has a role to play in everything. He will tell you what to write.'

'You believe in God?'

'Yes, and also the ocean, which provides us means to live, and sometimes takes away lives when it's time to depart from this world.'

'And sometimes when it's not the time to leave?'

'More often than not, there's always the hand of a devil behind untimely demise.'

'Do you suspect the hand of a devil in Irene's demise?'

'Could be, who knows.'

'Thank you for your thoughts. I hope you live long.'

'I don't care. I've done no wrong in my life. Afraid are those who do wrong. I'll embrace death willingly when my time comes.'

16

Grace beat a hasty retreat and returned to her room. Her expedition to Goa had not been very rewarding and her encounters with the maid and the fisherman had been discomfiting. She was apprehensive, but not for long.

Grace forgot all about Irene when Mark returned from Bombay with an electric-blue dress and imported perfumes in dainty little bottles for her.

'Thank you, Mark, so thoughtful of you.'

He handed her another little box from his pocket.

'A diamond ring!' She gasped.

Mark lifted her chin and looked into her eyes. 'Do you accept?'

'Yes.'

Mark took her into his arms and kissed her. She kissed him back, this time passionately.

Before the week ended, they settled for a quick court marriage without any fanfare. Only a handful of close friends attended the beach party to celebrate their union. They proceeded to Ooty, in the pristine hills of the Nilgiris, for their honeymoon. Grace returned a very happy and contented woman.

A colourful envelope addressed to Grace awaited her. She opened it and was surprised to find a beautiful greeting card from the Gomezes. The footnote read:

Wishing you and Mark, all success and happiness in life.
Eric and Rose Gomez.

Their warm gesture moved her.

'What is it, darling?' Mark asked.

Grace hesitated. 'A greeting card,' she said, avoiding his eyes, 'from some people I met in Goa.'

'I didn't know you had friends in Goa.'

'There's something I must tell you.'

'What?'

'I came to know Mr and Mrs Gomez in Goa, but I was absolutely shocked to discover that Irene was their daughter.'

Mark cocked his head. 'How interesting; I thought such things happened only in the movies.'

'I'd met them quite by chance before I came here, and visited them when you were away in Bombay. I nearly lost my breath when I saw Irene's portrait.'

Mark lit his cigar. 'A strange coincidence.'

'I couldn't believe it.'

'Eric still feels I was responsible for not having saved Irene.' He gave Grace a piercing look. 'I wouldn't see them again if I were you.'

❧

Mark Braganza celebrated his latest catch with great fanfare. He threw lavish parties and pampered Grace. She acquired a permanent glow on her face and a sparkle in her eyes. Much sought after in Goa's high society, Mark paraded Grace in social gatherings with an exaggerated sense of pride. He spared nothing to make her feel like a queen. Indeed, she looked and behaved like one.

When he took her to the races in Bombay, Grace caused a minor riot amongst the gentry turned out in their Sunday best.

Dressed in a yellow strapless blouse and knee-length skirt and wearing an elaborate hat, she drew more attention than the horses. Wearing a red-and-white striped jacket and flannel slacks, Mark too stood out in the elite crowd. He had won many a heart at the race course, but hardly ever a race.

An old friend of Mark's, famous for sporting beautiful cars and equally beautiful women, approached them. 'Hi, old chap, haven't seen you around,' he said, running his eyes over Grace's body.

Mark shrugged. 'Been busy.'

'Yes, of course,' he said, with a naughty smile and tried to catch Grace's eyes that were camouflaged behind dark glasses. 'May I have the pleasure of gaining your acquaintance, Miss ... ?'

'Mrs Braganza,' Mark corrected and turned to Grace. 'Meet Prince Zaved Hussain of Junagarh, who never loses a race.'

'Pleasure meeting you,' he bowed slightly.

Feeling no less than royalty herself, Grace acknowledged him with a nod and turned away to gaze at the crowds.

The prince raised an eyebrow, his eyes still on Grace's behind. 'Congratulations Mark. I must say you've done pretty well for yourself.'

'Thank you.'

'I may be lucky with the horses, but never lucky in love.'

'Come on, beat it.'

'How about joining me tonight for dinner at the Taj? I would be delighted to have your company.'

Having been in the same league, Mark knew the tactics of the philanderer well. He was in no mood to take chances with the man known to have destroyed many a marriage in the past. 'I'm afraid that won't be possible. We have other engagements.'

'No wonder. Perhaps some other time then.'

The prince of Junagarh was not the only one to invite

them. There were others who liked the company of glamorous women, and Grace Braganza fit the scene very well. Selective in his pickings, Mark made sure they obliged only the very best. Grace excelled in the company of the elite of Bombay. They spared nothing to pamper her and Grace enjoyed every minute of it. Mark Braganza, however, returned home much poorer, but richer in social ratings.

One day, as they were having breakfast, the phone rang. Mark answered. 'Yes, Mr Jain, how are you? Yes, yes... I know... I'm sorry. Give me some more time... I... no, no... it wouldn't take long... maybe another week... yes, I promise.'

'What was that about?' Grace asked.

Mark brushed it off with a wave of a hand. 'Never mind, just a business associate.'

A couple of days later a Mr Victor called. Grace picked up the phone.

'I'm not available,' Mark whispered.

Grace answered, 'Mark is not available at the moment. I'll ask him to call you later.'

Mark didn't bother to call back. An hour later the phone rang again, but he didn't pick up and signalled Grace not to.

'What's the matter?' she asked.

'He's always asking for free rooms for his bosses from Delhi and I'm in no mood to oblige.'

'The free-loaders, you mean.'

'Exactly.' Mark had no problem staring someone in the eyes and telling lies.

A week later, Mr Jain came on the line as Grace picked up the phone. 'Mr Jain,' she announced, holding the receiver out to Mark.

'Tell him I'll call back.'

Grace hesitated. 'He'll call you back.' Grace heard him for a few seconds more before hanging up. 'He said to tell you he might visit you next week.'

Mark turned his back.

'What's going on, Mark?'

'Don't answer the phone when you hear unfamiliar names at the other end, including Victor, Jain or whoever.'

'I don't understand.'

'Relax, darling. It's just some money matters I have to sort out, no big deal.'

❧

Intoxicated with glitz and glamour, Grace was far removed from the ground realities. Mark had borrowed heavily to maintain a lifestyle of extravagance, leading to a financial crisis. People turned their backs on him when he sought fresh loans. What remained of his friends was a handful of parasites with empty pockets and a great appetite for free food and wine. But Mark knew where his funds would eventually come from—they lay safe in the bank at Kharagpur. He had everything worked out. The script was ready, and it was time to roll out the cameras.

To begin with, he stopped entertaining people at the resort and, much to Grace's discomfiture, went out of circulation. He became less communicative and aloof.

'What's the matter, Mark? You don't seem yourself these days.' Grace asked while having their morning tea.

Mark turned a page of the newspaper. 'Nothing, why?'

'You're hiding something. Tell me what's bothering you?'

'Not something that should concern you, my dear.'

'What do you mean not concern me?' She tilted her head and gazed at him. 'Don't you think I've a right to know what's going on?'

Mark sighed and sipped his tea. 'I'm going through a bad patch that's all.'

'What bad patch?'

Folding the papers by his side, he looked up. 'Must you know everything?' He rose and walked to the edge of the garden, cup in hand, gazing at the dark clouds hovering in the sky. 'I'm sure it's going to rain today.'

'Maaaark...you don't have to be evasive.'

'These projects, you know, they're getting delayed. And I've taken a few group bookings for the coming season. If I do not finish the bloody pool and the cottages in time, there's going to be trouble, big trouble.'

'Weren't the contractors supposed to complete the work before the next season?'

'The blighters want payment in advance before they resume work.'

'So, what's the problem?'

'The problem is, I've some loans to clear, and a lot of money is blocked with the travel agents. They take months to clear their dues.' He threw his hands in the air. 'And the bloody contractors are just not prepared to wait that long.'

Grace narrowed her eyes, her face drawn.

'But I'll find ways to tide over the situation, I always have.'

'How much do they want to start with?' Grace asked, after a long stretch of silence.

'Come on, darling, you don't have to worry about that. Leave it to me. I'll cancel the bookings if required.'

'I don't think that's such a good idea.'

'I know, but there's no way out.'

'Aren't you worried about your reputation, having committed once?'

Mark's faith in Grace's limited intelligence was momentarily restored. 'You're right, but I'm not unduly worried. You lose some and gain some—that's how it is.'

She lapsed into silence.

Mark returned to the papers. The premature termination of the dialogue didn't please Mark, but he knew he had made the first move smartly.

Grace brought up the subject the next morning. Common sense was returning, but in small measures. 'Mark, you didn't tell me how much is needed to get things started.'

'It's a beautiful morning, Grace, no time to discuss finances.'

'I'm your wife, in case you didn't know. For God's sake, tell me how much?'

'How's that going to help?'

Grace cleared her throat. 'I have some funds.'

Now she was talking! Mark locked his fingers and lowered his voice. 'It's in lakhs, if you must know.'

'Lakhs!' she exclaimed. 'What do you mean?'

'Two lakhs, minimum.'

'Two Lakhs?' Her voice quivered. 'I don't get it.'

'There're some old dues which need to be settled.'

Grace lit one of her thin filters and puffed deeply a few times.

In the uneasy silence that ensued, Mark wondered if he had messed up. Perhaps he shouldn't have alarmed her by quoting a large figure.

After a long pause Grace uttered the sweetest words Mark had heard in a long time. 'I can raise it.'

He could barely suppress his exhilaration. 'Raise it, how? It's not a small amount, Grace. It's a hell of a lot of money.'

'I know, but I have some to start with.'

He chuckled. 'Where do you think you can lay your hands on

that kind of money? Unless you belong to the Birlas or the Tatas?'

'I'm not joking, Mark. I do have sufficient funds in my bank at Kharagpur.'

Mark feigned surprise. 'You have?'

'Yes.'

Mark gazed at her with mock revelation. 'That's great, but no thanks. I shouldn't bother you at all…I…'

'What's the use of having money in the bank if it can't be put to use?'

Mark held his breath, trying hard not to look too excited.

Grace disappeared inside and returned with her cheque book.

The dark clouds of uncertainty, hovering over Mark's head for so long, seemed ready to pour rain and fill his empty coffers.

She signed a cheque for two lakhs and placed it on the table.

Mark recoiled. 'What're you doing?'

'I'm doing what I would have done earlier, if only you had confided in me.'

Mark shook his head. 'I appreciate your offer greatly, I do. But this isn't right. I won't feel comfortable about this.'

'You don't need to feel that way at all.'

Mark jumped from his chair. 'It's your money, Grace, how can I…'

'All right, if you feel uncomfortable about it, you can pay me back when you get your dues. I don't think it would make any difference though.'

Even in a crumpled dressing gown, her hair tied in a careless knot and face devoid of make-up, Mark thought Grace had never looked more desirable. Mark ran his hand through his hair. 'That's very generous of you, Grace, but…'

'No ifs and buts,' she snapped. 'It's time to transfer my accounts to Goa.'

Mark wanted to get horizontal with her right then, but common sense prevailed upon him to remain composed.

A fortnight later, Grace's money was transferred into a joint account in the local branch in Goa. It took less than a couple of months before Mark literally assumed full control over her account. The Victors and Jains never called again. Work began at the pool, but at a slower pace. Grace never questioned him as long as the fast pace of her social life went uninterrupted.

Within days, a shining black Mercedes—second-hand but in great shape—stood in their porch and a liveried chauffeur waited to transport Mrs Grace Braganza to town in style. The old friends were back in circulation and so were the parties. While Mrs Braganza reclaimed her prime position in the social circles, Mark did likewise at the Mahalaxmi Race Course in Bombay, chasing trailing horses.

❧

Grace maintained a very busy social calendar. She didn't have the time or inclination to notice what was happening elsewhere. Life went on as usual, until one day when she chanced upon a bank statement lying on Mark's table.

She couldn't believe her eyes, her hands trembled with rage. The document showed a balance of less than a lakh in her account. She collapsed into a chair and cursed herself for trusting Mark so blindly. She realised, albeit too late, that a little common sense would've enabled her to enjoy a rather comfortable life instead of playing into Mark's hands. She had no one but herself to blame for her plight.

Grace confronted Mark with the bank statement. 'What's the meaning of this?'

Mark cleared his throat. 'What do you mean?'

Grace placed her hands on her hips and glared at him. 'Ten

lakhs down the drain in less than a year, and you want me to tell you what it means?'

'Look who's talking. Do I need to give explanations?'

She cocked her head. 'You mean you've nothing to say?'

'I didn't go to town in a chauffeur driven Merc to your endless parties and shopping expeditions,' he said, flapping his hands in the air. 'Look at your wardrobe and see where your money has gone.'

Grace shook with rage. 'You did better than that at the races and God knows where else?'

'I didn't ask for your money in the first place, remember?'

'You manipulated and squeezed me dry. I trusted you, and this is what you do to me?'

'As if you've no role to play in it.'

'Don't give me that crap.' Grace threw the statement in his face and stormed out of the room.

When funds dried up, creditors began knocking at their door with annoying frequency, threatening legal action. The Mercedes was the first to go, followed by other assets. In the days to come, Mark had to relieve half the staff at the resort and install Grace to look after the reception and housekeeping. The occupancy went down due to rapid deterioration of standards. The existing cottages were abandoned and business activity restricted to the rooms in the main building. The so-called pool remained dry. Mark sold his arms and trophies in order to maintain appearances in society. They still turned up at social dos dressed well, except now they arrived in a dilapidated old Ambassador, instead of the black Mercedes.

17

John Abraham's show in Goa opened in a blaze of publicity. Pestonji beamed with satisfaction, welcoming the guests at the entrance. Anybody who was somebody in Goa was there, if not to appreciate art, then to make a statement.

The crowds gathered well before the arrival of the guest of honour, Mr Akhtar Habib, the Governor of Goa. The street was filled with gleaming Buicks and Cadillacs. Men turned out in their lounge suits and women in their best silks and the air was a heady potpourri of exotic perfumes. Classical music playing softly in the background completed the ambience.

The Governor's retinue of escort cars, flashing red lights, arrived half an hour late. The Governor's wife, the statuesque Mrs Tara Habib, created more flutter than her husband. According to the grapevine, her overwhelming charm and proximity to the woman who ruled the nation at the time had made Mr Akhtar Habib's entry into the Governor's house rather easy.

Mrs Habib, famous for her regal looks and impeccable taste, had a great appetite for collecting art. Her presence alone drew a sizeable gathering of local luminaries.

Pestonji escorted the first lady and the Governor into the gallery and introduced John Abraham to them.

The Governor greeted Mani with a casual nod and turned to

scan the gathering for familiar faces.

'Nice to meet you, Mr Abraham,' said the gracious lady. 'I've read about your work and looked forward to meeting you.'

'I'm honoured, Ma'am,' Mani said.

A bunch of socialites surrounded Mrs Habib for reasons far removed from art. 'Hello, Tara,' twittered a portly woman bedecked with several rows of pearls. 'It's been months since we last met at the Rotary Club musical.'

Mani slipped away to a cabin at the back, away from the crowds.

As the ladies tittered about the musical, Pestonji made his excuses and joined the group trailing behind the Governor.

While receiving the normal courtesies from the audience, Mr Habib took a round of the exhibits, as if looking for his mother-in-law arriving in a train from Timbuktu. He didn't seem to have an eye for art—not a single work on the wall captured his interest—but anything beautiful draped in a sari or skirt engaged his attention. There were plenty of saris to keep him enthralled.

Falling back, Pestonji returned to Mrs Habib, who stood in front of a landscape with her followers in tow. 'Isn't this beautiful?' The rest nodded with agreement.

'This is fascinating. The artist seems to have drawn inspiration from the French Masters of Impressionism.' Unlike her husband, she devoted considerable time to each painting. As she came in front of the *Lovers' Rock,* her eyes widened. 'This is a masterpiece,' she pronounced.

'Yes, absolutely... marvellous... exquisite... perhaps the best...' the collective voices echoed from behind her.

Pestonji approached her. '*Lovers' Rock* is the artist's favourite, and he wishes to keep it for himself.'

Mrs Habib shook her head. 'What a pity. This should have graced the lounge at the Government House. The colours would've gone well with the ambience.'

'That would have been a great honour,' Pestonji said.

Mrs Habib stood spellbound in front of the large canvas. 'I'd like to have a word with Mr John Abraham.'

'I'll bring him to you in a while.'

Mrs Habib selected a couple of paintings for the Government House and an abstract work for her personal collection.

Mr Pestonji returned with Mani.

'Your works are fascinating, especially *Lovers' Rock*,' she gushed, 'I think we should invite you over to the Government House one of these days. Perhaps you could suggest a few works for the library.'

Pestonji smiled. 'It would be an honour, ma'am.'

She faced Mani. 'I can't believe you're entirely self-taught. I wish you all success.'

Mani thanked her and once more slipped away as soon as someone else claimed her attention.

❧

Not ones to miss an opportunity to be noticed, the Braganzas attended the John Abraham show in Goa. Arriving fashionably late, they stood at the entrance for a few seconds, in the manner of royalty overseeing their subjects before granting an audience. Grace in a black dress, and Mark in a dark, pin-striped suit, commanded attention and adulation in equal measure.

'Look who's here,' Grace nudged Mark.

Mark raised an eyebrow. 'Who?'

'The Gomezes.'

Showing not the least bit of interest, Mark turned to acknowledge the greeting of a passing acquaintance.

'The least we can do is say hello.'

Mark smiled at a lady passing by. 'I don't think it's a good idea.'

'I don't see any harm in exchanging greetings.'

'Go ahead, but don't drag me along, when you know the meeting won't be pleasant for both sides.'

'No way, you've got to come with me. It would be very embarrassing otherwise.'

'It will be a big mistake.'

'No, it won't.'

Grace approached the Gomezes as they stood admiring a painting.

'Hello, Mr Gomez... Rose...'

'Oh hello, Grace, what a pleasant surprise,' Mrs Gomez said. 'It's so good to see you.'

Mr Gomez faced Grace, ignoring Mark. 'You're looking great.'

'Thank you.'

Mark turned to Mrs Gomez. 'How are you, Rose?'

'I'm fine, thank you.'

'It's been so long,' Mark said. 'You look younger by the day.'

She smiled and turned to Grace. 'So, how are you, my dear? You look stunning in this dress.'

Grace blushed.

Mr Gomez turned back to the wall. 'Nice paintings, aren't they?'

'We've yet to go round.' Grace said.

'You must. John Abraham is an upcoming artist who has risen rapidly. I strongly recommend that you invest some of your money in his art.' He turned around and shot a glance at Mark. 'If he has any.'

Mrs Gomez's face flushed.

The sarcasm hurt Grace. She had never been able to reconcile such rude behaviour with the suave gentleman she had first known.

Mark cocked his head and looked the old man in the eye. 'You've some nerve, Eric. But thanks, we don't need your advice on where to invest.'

'Perhaps not,' said the older man with a patronising smile. 'Maybe I should've learned a thing or two from you.'

'It's never too late,' Mark retorted.

Mr Gomez glanced at Grace. 'I hope she learns faster than Irene did.'

Mrs Gomez glared at her husband. 'Eric, please.' She turned to Grace, 'It was nice seeing you. Perhaps we should get together some other time.'

Grace understood the situation. 'Yes, of course.'

Mr Gomez turned back to the paintings.

'See you around,' Mrs Gomez said. 'Take care.'

Grace nodded.

'Are you happy now?' Mark seethed.

Grace was embarrassed. 'I'm sorry. I never expected him to be…'

'So mean?'

She didn't reply.

'And you wanted me to say hello to the bloody man. Don't you ever ask me to see that man again.' He grit his teeth and joined his friends.

Somewhat rattled, Grace moved slowly from one canvas to another, her mind still on the brief encounter that had left a bad taste in her mouth. Then she came in front of *Lovers' Rock*.

She froze. Her stomach churned and her heart began to pound against her chest. *Lovers' Rock? Lovers' Rock of Digha?* The same rocks…the same ocean…the same rising sun! How could it be possible? Only two people in the entire world knew about Lovers' Rock: She and Mani. But this painting carried the signature of a 'John Abraham'. It didn't make sense. A sudden chill ran down her spine. She stepped back and gazed with foreboding at the familiar scene, still so vivid in her memory.

Pestonji approached her. 'May I help you, ma'am? You seem to like this painting very much.'

Grace managed to mutter, 'Yes... it is... incredible.'

Pestonji handed her a brochure. 'I'm the artist's manager.'

Grace withdrew to the bench across from the painting. She studied the brochure with trembling hands. It carried a small picture of the artist—a bearded man with long hair and dark glasses. Her eyes strained to make out the features. And when she did, Grace uttered a soundless gasp. There was a scar above the left eyebrow! Goose bumps sprang up on her arms. She couldn't shake off the ominous feeling that someone was watching her. He was alive... and kicking... as John Abraham... lurking in some dark corner. Grace didn't have the guts to turn around and look. She sat glued to the bench.

'You don't look well.' Pestonji was concerned, 'May I get you some water?'

'Yes, please.'

❧

From his cabin, Mani had noticed the slender woman in black standing in front of *Lovers' Rock*, her hair falling free, almost touching her waist. She reminded him of Grace—the same height and the same posture. When she turned, Mani thought his eyes were playing tricks on him. But there was no denying it: she was Grace, as stunning and elegant as ever.

Grace? In Goa? For a fleeting moment, Mani forgot all about her betrayal and the subsequent hatred towards her that his anguish had hardened into. He wanted to run and take her into his arms. It surprised him. He couldn't believe he still had feelings for the woman who had deserted him not too long ago. He went rigid in his chair. Seconds later, he saw her examining the brochure. He didn't have to guess what she was going through and he relished it.

Pestonji entered the cabin and filled a glass of water from the pitcher. 'A lady is feeling sick.'

'Not surprising.'

'What?'

'I have to ask you for a favour. Please find out all you can about the lady in black you just met. And don't ask me why.'

Pestonji raised his eyebrows.

'I've some old scores to settle.'

'Old scores…?'

'Please, I'll tell you about it later.'

❧

Grace drank the water. She had broken out into a sweat.

Mark approached her. 'Are you all right?'

'I don't feel well,' she mumbled, gazing at the painting in a daze. 'Let's go home.'

'You sure?'

She nodded and handed the empty glass to Pestonji.

'I can arrange for a room if she would like to rest for a while,' Pestonji offered.

'I don't think that will be necessary,' Mark said. 'You are…?'

'Feroze Pestonji, John Abraham's manager.'

'Thank you for your help.'

'You're welcome. May I have the pleasure of your acquaintance?'

'I'm Mark Braganza.' He pulled out a card and handed it to Pestonji. 'Nice meeting you.'

Grace rose from the bench.

Mark took her by the arm and escorted her out of the hall.

Pestonji followed. 'I'm so sorry you have to leave. I wish you could've stayed on for the cocktails.'

'Perhaps some other time,' Mark said, getting into the driver's seat of his car.

Pestonji glanced at the card and wondered why the owners of a resort, dressed like royalty, would come in such a dilapidated car. The old Ambassador pulled away from the curb, discharging thick clouds of smoke from its exhaust, indicating the poor health of the engine ... and perhaps that of its occupants.

Pestonji also wondered about scores John had to settle with the lady in black. He could hardly see any connection between John Abraham and the stunning woman. He sought out his friend, Richard DeCosta, the owner of the gallery, to find out more about the couple. They had worked together in Bombay for several years before DeCosta converted his ancestral home into an art gallery.

'I met an interesting couple, Dickey,' Pestonji said, showing him the card Mr Braganza had given him.

DeCosta flinched. 'Mark Braganza!'

'You know him?'

'Yes.'

'His wife seemed keen on the *Lovers' Rock*.'

'His second wife.'

'Really?'

DeCosta lowered his voice. 'There's a nasty story doing the rounds about the man.'

Pestonji's antennae shot up. 'What kind of story?'

'Mark's first wife drowned in mysterious circumstances a couple of years ago.' He paused and smiled at a passing guest. 'The man is capable of doing anything for money.'

'What do you mean?'

'Braganza gained a substantial amount from his wife's insurance. People suspected foul play.'

'You believe that?'

'At first, I didn't. But the manner in which his stock rose and fell so dramatically raised doubts in my mind. One moment he was indulging like a prince and the next he was borrowing from all and sundry. I believe he's down in the dumps again.'

'How's that related to his wife's death?' asked Pestonji.

'You never know what that man is capable of doing—especially when it comes to money.'

'But he owns a resort.'

DeCosta shook his head. 'Some people live way beyond their means. Mark is famous for squandering money and flaunting women, a lethal combination that can ruin a man. Come, let's join the others. The Governor has already moved out onto the lawn.'

The image of the battered Ambassador and that of the mysterious woman puzzled Pestonji. What a woman indeed! He took a deep breath and followed his friend.

Select invitees had started trickling onto the lush lawn behind the gallery for cocktails. DeCosta had made good use of the space to display his collection of stone and terracotta sculptures. A bar under the canopy of a thatched roof gave a rustic appeal to the setting. The sweet fragrance of a Jasmine tree added to the heady ambiance of the evening.

Holding a drink, the Governor held court in one corner of the lawn and, at another corner, people flocked around the charismatic Mrs Habib.

'Let me introduce you to the Gomezes,' said DeCosta. 'Mr Gomez is a leading real estate agent and Irene's father.'

'Irene?'

'Braganza's first wife.'

'You don't say...'

DeCosta introduced Pestonji to the Gomezes.

Pestonji greeted Mrs Gomez. 'I hope you liked some of the paintings.'

'Of course we did. John Abraham is brilliant! We've already booked one and seriously considering another.'

'Which one is that?'

'There's a small one in the corner titled *The Sun*. I like the swirling colours and the sense of movement. It would fit well in our study.'

'You know, Mrs Gomez,' DeCosta interjected, 'John Abraham owes much of his success to my friend, Feroze. He has quite a reputation for picking winners.'

A waiter brought their drinks. DeCosta excused himself to attend to the Governor.

Mrs Gomez sipped her wine. 'We would very much like to meet the artist.'

Pestonji saw a good opportunity. 'Of course, I'll be back in a minute, if you'll excuse me.'

'John, you've got to meet this couple,' said Pestonji as soon as he entered the cabin.

'I'm not in a mood to meet people.' Mani had a faraway look in his eyes.

'This is not just *people,* but those closely connected with the husband of the lady you want to know more about.'

Mani furrowed his eyebrows. 'What do you mean?'

'Come with me.'

Mani followed Pestonji and met the couple.

'We're fascinated with your work, Mr Abraham,' Mrs Gomez said, 'especially your landscapes. It's hard to believe you never went to an art school. Is this your first visit to Goa?'

Mani nodded. 'Yes, it's a beautiful place.'

Mrs Gomez whispered something in her husband's ear.

Mr Gomez nodded and turned to Mani. 'How long are you staying in Goa?'

'Another week or so I guess.'

'We'd like it very much if you would consider spending an evening with us.'

Pestonji didn't wait for Mani's response. 'It would be a pleasure.'

Mrs Gomez faced Mani. 'Would you consider having dinner with us tomorrow evening?'

Pestonji knew Mani never accepted such invitations. But if he wanted to learn more about the Braganza woman, there couldn't be a better chance. He nudged Mani. 'That would be fine, thank you.'

After exchanging a few notes about his paintings, Mani returned to his cabin and Pestonji to the Governor's corner.

The noise level increased gradually as the intake of alcohol grew. It was the kind of evening where everybody had a great time discussing politics, the tourist scene, the hippies and little about art. Having sold a dozen paintings, however, it didn't matter whether the honourable Governor discussed the possible reshuffle in the cabinet or the weather. What mattered to Pestonji were sales, and the response was overwhelming.

After a while, the Governor made his way to the exit with a large tail of followers.

'Thank you very much, sir,' Pestonji bowed as Mr Habib entered his limousine. 'It has been a great honour to have you, and ma'am, grace the occasion.'

Mrs Habib peeped out of the window. 'You'll hear from the Social Secretary in a day or two. Keep an evening free.'

'We'll look forward to it, thank you.'

The Governor's contingent of cars departed, their sirens disturbing the quiet of the night.

After the guests left, Pestonji and Mani joined Mr DeCosta at the bar.

DeCosta turned to Mani. 'I'm curious to know why you're not keen to sell the *Lovers' Rock*. It has been the singular most favourite of the evening and would've easily fetched anything from twenty to thirty thousand!'

Mani swung around on his bar stool. 'It's not about money, Mr DeCosta. I just want to keep it for myself.'

'Even Mrs Braganza seemed enamoured by it.' Pestonji remarked.

Mani cringed. 'I'm intrigued by that couple.'

DeCosta took a deep breath. 'Mark Braganza is known to attract women, especially those loaded with money. First it was Irene, Gomezes' daughter, and now this ravishing beauty. God alone knows where she came from, but I can bet she must've come with a lot of money.'

Mani shifted on his stool.

DeCosta continued, 'Poor Irene; she was such a good soul. I feel so sad for the Gomezes.'

'By the way, we're having dinner with the Gomezes tomorrow,' said Pestonji.

DeCosta raised his glass. 'They are the best hosts you can find in Goa. I'm sure you're going to enjoy the evening.'

❧

The strong winds accompanied by occasional showers that lashed the city during the day died down to a gentle breeze that was laced with the pleasant aroma of wet earth. A portly maid escorted Mani and Pestonji when they arrived at Eric Mansion. Mrs Gomez greeted them warmly and led them into their living room, the size of a basketball court.

Mani was amazed by the opulence and grandeur. The tall imposing figure of Mr Gomez emerged from a side door.

'Hello Mr Pestonji, Mr Abraham,' he shook hands with them. 'Please make yourselves comfortable.'

Mani and Pestonji sat on the long sofa opposite Mrs Gomez.

'So, how is the show going?' Mr Gomez asked as he took his seat.

Pestonji smiled. 'The response has been overwhelming.'

Mani's eyes travelled from one corner of the hall to another, admiring the artefacts and paintings on the walls. 'You have a marvellous collection of paintings.'

'Thank you,' Mrs Gomez said. 'And now I've added to it—a John Abraham!'

While Mr Gomez busied himself in fixing drinks for everyone, Mrs Gomez chatted with Mani. 'I'm impressed by the variety of your work. I wonder how you manage to shift from the contemporary to abstract with such flourish. Artists usually confine themselves to one school of thought.'

Mani rubbed his chin. 'I do like to experiment sometimes. And the results are interesting.'

'Somehow I find it difficult to appreciate modern art.' Mr Gomez opined.

'What you perceive as weird may be another man's treasure,' said Mrs Gomez. 'I believe one has to develop a taste for it.'

Pestonji crossed his legs. 'Tastes are changing rapidly, Mr Gomez. There's a huge demand for modern art, especially if a canvas has a famous signature.'

The old man shook his head. 'Perhaps I'm getting a bit rusty.'

Mani surveyed the hall. 'Mind if I have a look around?'

'Sure, you're welcome,' said the lady.

Mr Gomez and Pestonji followed him.

'That's my grandfather in his hunting gear, the breeches and the famous Jodhpurs—almost a must those days.'

'That's my father,' Mr Gomez pointed to the next portrait.

Mani examined the portrait closely. 'Exquisitely done I must say. Who painted this?'

'This was done by a German artist, a Mr Miller, who stayed in Goa for a couple of years during my father's time.'

'We don't have very many portrait painters these days.' Pestonji said ruefully. 'Photography has overshadowed that line of art.'

Mani stopped in front of a huge landscape. 'This is simply awesome!'

'It's close to your style,' remarked Mrs Gomez.

'I'm nowhere near this masterpiece.'

After viewing several paintings and photographs they walked over to the piano. Mani noticed the large portrait on the wall.

'That's Irene, our daughter.' A pall of gloom crept over Mr Gomez's face.

Mani couldn't remove his eyes from her.

'We're truly saddened to learn about the unfortunate accident.' Pestonji said.

'A cruel act of God,' Mani added.

'Had it been an act of God, cruel or otherwise, we would have accepted it,' Mr Gomez said, with a hint of recrimination in his eyes. 'But it was not.'

No one spoke for a few seconds.

Mr Gomez ran his hand on the polished surface of the grand piano. 'The piano has remained silent ever since she went away. Its soothing notes died with Irene.'

Pestonji shook his head. 'I can't figure out why a flower must blossom, if it must wither before its time?'

Mr Gomez clenched his fists. 'It didn't wither. It was plucked, not by the hand of God, but by the hand of a demon, her husband, Mark Braganza.'

Pestonji stared at him. 'Mark Braganza of Paradise Resort?'

'You seem to have met the devil already.'

'Mrs Braganza seemed keen on *Lovers' Rock*,' Pestonji slipped in.

'Braganza can't even pay for the frame, let alone the painting.'

Mani still gazed at the portrait. 'Only a cruel man would bring harm to such an angel.'

Mrs Gomez wiped her moist eyes as they returned to their seats. 'I'm sorry, gentlemen, we shouldn't have brought this up. Eric hasn't gotten over it.'

Mr Gomez paused. 'I'm worried about Grace, his present wife. She doesn't know what she's gotten into.'

Mani shuffled in his chair. 'You seem to know her.'

'We met briefly; a charming girl who succumbed to the evil designs of a cunning man. I wish to God she doesn't come to any harm.'

The room fell silent.

Mr Gomez cleared his throat. 'Irene fell victim to Braganza's dubious designs. I've no doubt he was after Irene's insurance money.'

Mrs Gomez excused herself and left the room.

'Mark gained a substantial amount of money from her death and burnt it all in no time. Surprisingly, the man bounced back after his marriage to Grace. God alone knows where he got his money from.'

Mani had no doubt where the money came from. Grace couldn't have rested her shapely bottom on that hot money for too long. 'Does she belong here?'

'No, she was visiting. A freelance journalist she told me. We were on the same flight from Bombay and got to know each other. Guess that's where she came from.'

Mani fought to suppress a grin. *Freelance journalist?* The woman could hardly compose a letter to her mother.

After another round of drinks, with the Braganzas for snacks, they settled down to dinner. It was a sumptuous spread, the like of which Mani had never savoured before.

As they repaired to the vast verandah for coffee, Mani went out to fetch a painting from the car. He handed it to Mrs Gomez. 'This is for you, ma'am.'

She let out a breath. '*The Sun!* This is too much, I can't accept it.'

'Please don't disappoint me.'

Mrs Gomez blushed. 'You're extravagantly generous, John. Thank you for this kind gesture. We shall cherish it.'

'Do visit us again when in town,' Mr Gomez said.

'I might like to settle down here by the sea.'

'Sure,' said Mr Gomez. 'I'll get you the best deal in town.'

❧

After returning from Eric Mansion, John strolled onto the balcony and gazed at the stars. Pestonji knew something was bothering him. 'Mind telling me what's going on?'

John hesitated and then turned slowly to face him. 'I'm afraid you'll find it difficult to come to terms with my past.'

'What do you mean your past?'

'I have sinned.'

'I don't believe you.'

'I'll tell you everything, but first I've to ask you to do me a favour.'

Pestonji sat down on a chair. 'Go on.'

'I want you to visit Paradise Resort after we wind up the show.'

Pestonji cringed. 'What's the story, John?'

'Can you keep a secret?'

'Of course, you can trust me.'

'That woman in black...was my wife.'

Pestonji blinked. '*What?*'

'She ditched me.'

Pestonji couldn't believe that a phenomenal beauty like Grace Braganza was once married to an artist struggling on the streets of Bombay. Surely there was more to the tale. He looked questioningly at John.

'She dumped me for the money.'

'What money are you talking about? I don't understand!'

'I'll tell you the whole story later, if you don't mind.'

'What do you expect me to do without knowing anything?'

'I want you to find out everything about the Braganzas.'

'So you want me to do a Sherlock Holmes. What is your motive?'

'You'll be the first to know, but not now.'

Pestonji rose from his chair and pondered over it for a few moments. 'All right, if that's what you want. I wouldn't mind a holiday at Paradise Resort.'

18

On the drive back to the resort, Grace shrunk into her seat like a frightened cat. *Mani? John Abraham? Lovers' Rock?* Grace couldn't believe it. She had a growing suspicion that she'd been watched by the man she never expected to encounter again. The constant rattle of the battered car and the clatter of the aging engine did nothing to sooth her troubled nerves.

Mark stole a glance at her. 'You don't seem well at all.'

Grace reclined in her seat without responding and covered her face with her hands. The image of the bearded man with the familiar scar on the eyebrow haunted her.

Mark eased off the accelerator. 'Shouldn't you see a doctor?'

'No, let's go home.'

She shut her eyes and felt like a lifeless dummy. With all her money gone, and dreams of a luxurious life shattered, she felt miserable. Especially when the man she dumped so mercilessly had risen like a shining star, while she ended up behind a reception desk. She knew of Mani's interest in art, but the fame of a John Abraham astounded her. Tears rolled down her cheeks and a lump formed in her throat.

'I liked that painting, the *Lovers' Rock,*' Mark said, as he turned on to the hilly road. 'It would've looked great in our lounge.'

Grace recoiled at the very mention of the painting. She

would've hated to see it anywhere. The thought of viewing the damn thing every blessed day at the resort mocked her. She opened her eyes and gazed at the winding road. The dark rocks and the dense trees rushing past her vision seemed like demons.

Mark struggled with the sluggish gears. 'You liked that painting didn't you?'

'Fuck the painting for heaven's sake.'

Mark shot a glance at Grace. 'Why are you so cranky?'

'Just get me home, will you?'

The ups and downs on the rough road reminded Grace of her own life. The dark, ominous hollow that loomed large ahead where the car's headlight beams couldn't reach suggested that her life headed towards a similar doom. She closed her eyes again. With not a word spoken, the drive felt longer than it ever had.

Once they reached home, Grace stumbled up the steps leading to the cottage. Mark vanished in the dark. She hurried over to the bar and poured herself a large drink of rum before settling down on the sofa. She lit a cigarette and puffed nervously, gazing at the floor.

Saira came out from the kitchen. 'May I get you something?'

'No.'

'You don't look well.'

Grace dismissed her with a wave of her hand, her thoughts back to the gallery. She rose and paced the floor. John Abraham, a successful artist? And she? A lowly receptionist stuck with a man who had milked her dry... and was steering her towards disaster. Her throat tightened and tears welled in her eyes. She wallowed in self-pity and cursed Mark under her breath. But, in the end, she could only blame herself.

By the time Mark arrived, she was already on her second rum. Mark went to the bar and fixed himself a drink. Leaning on the counter, he faced her. 'What's bothering you, honey?'

'Honey' sounded like poison. Grace crushed her cigarette in the ashtray. 'Leave me alone, will you?'

'Excuse me?'

Grace stomped out of the room and settled into a chair in the dark end of the verandah.

Mark followed her. 'Have I done anything wrong?'

'No, you've done wonderfully well for yourself,' she said, sarcastically.

'What do you mean?'

'Ten lakhs down the drain in less than a year, do I really have to remind you?' she said acidly. 'And nothing to show for it except false vanity.'

Mark stared at her. 'Ah, look who's talking? You didn't feel that way when you were gallivanting around in a chauffeur-driven limousine, buying fancy costumes by the dozen each month and partying like crazy. I've yet to clear your bills.'

She winced. 'What I did with *my* money is none of your business. It was nothing compared to what *you* did with *my* money at the races and God alone knows where else.'

'Ah, so now it's your money versus my money. You didn't feel that way earlier.'

'I shouldn't have trusted you,' she muttered.

'Trust does not figure in my vocabulary.'

'I've sufficient reasons to believe so,' she said, knowing full well that she'd herself abused the trust of a man who had risked his life for her. However, this was no time to think of her own guilt, but to confront the man who turned out far smarter than she believed he was.

'I gave you everything you ever dreamt of, dammit.' Mark punched the air. 'Treated you like a queen, and now you've the cheek to accuse me of everything that's gone bad, as if you had no part in it?'

'Treated me like a queen, only to dump me at the reception.'

'Stop complaining, holy cow,' he retorted. 'I'm not sitting on the throne either.'

Grace sat in the dark, fretting and sulking long after Mark disappeared. She retired to her room and switched off the lights.

❧

The following day, Grace surfaced well after Mark had left for his office. She retrieved her cheque book from Mark's desk and without informing anybody, left for her bank in Goa.

The bank manager rose from his chair. 'Good morning, Mrs Braganza. What can I do for you?'

'I wish to withdraw some money.'

'Certainly, please be seated.' He gestured and sat back in his chair. 'Is Mr Braganza out of town?'

Grace removed her glasses and pulled out her cheque book. 'What's my balance?'

The manager summoned the dealing clerk. 'Would you like a cup of tea?'

'No, thanks.'

When the clerk announced the balance, Grace's jaw dropped. 'Only thirty-seven thousand?' She gaped at the clerk and then the manager. 'How could that be? There must be some mistake. I should have about a lakh.'

The clerk brought the ledger and showed her the recent withdrawals. A chill ran down her spine. More than seventy thousand rupees had been withdrawn in the last week alone.

Damn! Why hadn't she visited the bank before? She left in a state of turmoil, with thirty-seven thousand in cash and nothing but contempt for Mark Braganza. She drove towards the seafront and sat in the car, gazing at the sea for a long time. There was no one she could talk to. She put on her dark glasses to hide her tears from the urchins who knocked on the car window for alms. She considered visiting the Gomezes to seek solace in her moments of distress, but dropped the idea. Having ignored their advice, she found it difficult to face them.

She returned home with a broken heart and shattered dreams.

19

A week later, Pestonji checked into the Paradise Resort at sundown and fell in love with the place. He welcomed the opportunity to spend a few days away from the hustle and bustle of Bombay in the quiet, serene environs of the isolated resort.

A smart young lad greeted him at the Reception. 'Good evening, sir, may I help you?'

'I would like a room with a view.'

'Certainly.' He placed the check-in register on the counter. 'How long do you intend to stay, sir?'

Before Pestonji could answer, someone called out to him.

As he turned around, he came face to face with Mark Braganza. 'Welcome to Paradise Resort.'

'Hello, Mr Braganza, good to see you. I must say you've a great place out here. I'm sure going to enjoy my stay.'

'I hope so, too. Are you visiting alone?'

'Yes.'

'You should've come with Mr Abraham. I'm sure he would've liked it.'

'He's a bit tied up right now, but I'll definitely recommend this place to him.'

'Do feel at home.' Mark turned to the receptionist. 'Make sure Mr Pestonji is well looked after.'

'How is Mrs Braganza?' Pestonji was solicitous. 'It's a pity she fell ill.'

'She is a bit under the weather. Should be fine in a day or two, I guess. See you around.'

Pestonji admired the view of the ocean from his window and listened to the soothing roar of the surf. Over to his right, perched on a hillock, stood a magnificent cottage, the likes of which he'd seen only in the movies. How nice it would be to live in a place like that. He looked forward to meeting the mysterious woman.

When he visited the bar in the evening, no one stood behind the counter. Minutes later the same lad appeared from the reception desk.

'Drink, sir?' he asked.

Pestonji ordered an ice-cream soda.

'What's your name?'

'Raju.'

'I don't see very many visitors around here. Is this normal at this time of the year?'

'These are bad times, sir,' he said, opening the bottle of soda. 'It used to be nearly full in winters, but not anymore. This was a favourite haunt of film crews from Bombay. The famous film, *Raat Ki Raani,* was shot here extensively. I appeared in one scene.' The actor in him beamed.

'How interesting.' Pestonji sat on the bar stool and rested his elbows on the counter. 'So you're a receptionist, a barman, and an actor—all in one.'

'Those were good days,' he said ruefully. 'I could easily make around ten rupees every day in tips alone. We made more in tips than in wages. Now I make that much in a week or longer, if I'm lucky.'

'That's sad. But what happened to the crowds?'

The young lad pursed his lips and shrugged.

A telephone rang nearby.

'Excuse me, sir; I'll be back in a minute.'

Pestonji sauntered into the lounge and noticed faded carpets, soiled curtains and sagging sofas—a sure sign of decay. He decided to have a chat with Raju at the reception desk. There's always much to learn from the lowest in the food chain. The higher you go, the stiffer the lips.

'How do you manage things all on your own?'

'Actually, Mrs Braganza is the one in charge. I assist her.'

'You mean Mrs Braganza herself looks after the reception? Don't you have other staff to stand in?'

'We're short of staff.'

'Why is that?'

He hesitated.

A giant of a woman charged the desk, huffing and puffing like an angry bull. 'Are you in charge here?' she asked Raju, none too politely. Pestonji shifted to one side to allow her more room to manoeuvre her bulk.

Raju flushed. 'Yes, ma'am, may I help you?'

She folded her arms over her ample bosom and squared her hips. 'I placed an order for food at eight and now it is nine,' she fumed, pointing to her wrist watch. 'Are you getting it from Goa or what?'

'I'm sorry, ma'am. I'll check on it.'

'What kind of place is this? Don't you clean the bathrooms or bother about changing the soiled linen?'

'I'll look into it straight away.'

'Please do, or else we're out of here first thing in the morning.' She stormed out of the hall, leaving a vacuum in her wake.

The woman reminded him of the Braganzas' Ambassador car

leaving the gallery on the opening night, except this one didn't emit smoke. Poor Raju disappeared into the interior. Pestonji waited.

'Sorry, I had to leave.'

'Your kitchen staff is letting you down?'

'Only a part-time cook and a lone helper, which is why all the problems, sir.'

'If she comes back, she'll mow you down.'

He grinned.

Pestonji left him at his post and strolled into the dining hall.

An elderly man sat alone at a corner table, eating his food and reading a book at the same time. With thick sideburns, a balding pate and bifocals perched on the bridge of his nose, he looked more like a professor, preparing for his next lecture than a tourist. Pestonji opted for a table at the other end. It took quite some time before a waiter appeared with a dirty menu. Half the things listed were not available. He settled for chicken curry and rice, which came half an hour later.

The 'professor' didn't lift his head even once, until after finishing his meal. He rose and rewarded him with a brief smile. Pestonji smiled back. When crowds are thin, strangers tend to become friendly. He hoped to have some company after all.

Pestonji woke up to a chilly morning and decided to go for a walk on the deserted beach. A lone man sat on a rock at a distance. As he got nearer, he recognised him—the professor!

Pestonji greeted him. 'Good morning.'

'Morning,' acknowledged the man, his hands tucked in the side-pockets of his jerkin.

Pestonji shivered against the cold wind and rubbed his hands in front of his chest. 'Mind if I sit here?'

'Be my guest,' he said turning to face Pestonji. 'I don't own the place.'

Pestonji extended his hand in greeting. 'I'm Pestonji, Feroze Pestonji from Bombay.'

The hand that shook his felt like that of a plumber's. 'Fernandez,' he said.

'Are you on a holiday?' Pestonji asked.

'Not exactly; it's business mixed with pleasure. And you?'

'I'm on a short vacation.'

'I thought you might also be one of us who come here routinely to recover their dues and return empty-handed. There are more creditors visiting this place than tourists.'

'Creditors?'

The man nodded. 'Yes, the suckers who got taken in by the smooth talking Braganza and the allure of that beautiful wife of his.'

Pestonji feigned ignorance. 'Braganza?'

'The owner of the resort, Mark Braganza.'

The chance meeting with this man was a surprise bonus.

'I'm not the only one, you know. There are a whole lot of others like me who come knocking at his door and leave with nothing but false promises. He's a shameless scoundrel. When it comes to honouring his dues, it's one-way traffic.'

'I'm sorry to hear that,' Pestonji said, meaning just the opposite. He was more than happy to get some first-hand information.

'This is the third time I've been here in as many months. I park myself here for a few days each time—a good excuse to get away from the wife,' he chuckled. 'The old girl has a good chunk of her money blocked with Braganza. I've less reason to complain since I thoroughly enjoy my stay here, with all expenses on the house. That's one way to recover something out of the rascal.'

Pestonji was getting closer to the truth earlier than he had expected.

Fernandez's eyes brightened. 'An enchanting beach, blissful

solitude, plenty of booze on the house and a mystery novel to read; what more could I ask?' He grinned.

'I envy you.'

'You won't, if you get your money blocked with the devil.'

'I don't have that kind of money.'

'Good for you.' Fernandez gazed at the sea. 'But then you have that ravishing beauty,' he sneered, 'real food for the eyes and a compensating factor.'

Pestonji realised he was in dubious company, but he was not one to complain if the end result was promising. 'I haven't met the lady.'

'Quite a piece of meat, I tell you; makes me feel young again. I wouldn't mind sharing a thing or two with her—and write off the loan, if you know what I mean.' A cheeky smile appeared on the corner of his pouty lips. 'The lucky bastard,' he hissed through his teeth. 'They don't make them like her anymore.'

Pestonji could only gape at the old man.

'Haven't seen the bloody female for three days in a row. I'm beginning to miss her. The whisky doesn't taste as good, you know.'

'Does he owe you a large amount?'

'It's not small, but that woman should be worth every penny.' He laughed, showing his yellowing teeth. 'Fifty grand, no less.'

A long pause ensued. The morning stars faded into the grey sky. Pestonji was in no hurry, he wanted to engage him further. 'I don't understand. With such a wonderful resort, Mr Braganza should be swinging.'

Fernandez scoffed. 'He isn't swinging but sinking. I wouldn't be surprised if he shuts down the resort and declares bankruptcy, unless, of course, he finds another sucker to bail him out.'

'He must owe a large amount to people?'

'Not less than three or four lakhs, maybe more. Mark is a

compulsive punter, a habitual loser at the races and the woman a huge spender.'

Pestonji picked up a shell from the sands. 'It's a colossal amount. How does he raise that kind of money?'

'He has a knack for finding some joker or other to come to his rescue. I hope he finds his next fool pretty soon and pass on a few bucks to us. Otherwise, I'll extend my visits for longer periods and enjoy the hospitality.' He glanced at his watch and rose. 'I must be going now. Why don't you join me over a couple of beers at noon? I could use some company.'

'That's very generous of you. I'll see if I can.'

'It's all on the house, which is why it is more enjoyable.'

Pestonji had learnt much from his brief encounter with Fernandez. He knew there was more to come. After breakfast in his room, he sauntered out with his camera to take a tour of the premises.

Raju greeted him as he stepped out on to the deck.

'I hope there's no objection to my taking photographs?'

'Not at all.'

Pestonji gazed at the quaint little cottage on the hillock. 'That's a beautiful cottage up there.'

'That's Mr Braganza's home.'

'Oh, I see.' He focused his camera and took a few shots of the cottage. 'I think I should go to the terrace and take some aerial shots.'

The view from the terrace excited Pestonji. He snapped several shots and spotted Mark Braganza walking towards the far end of the garden with newspapers in hand. He took a shot and decided to join him.

'Good morning, Mr Braganza.'

Mark lifted his head from the papers. 'Mr Pestonji. Good morning to you.'

'I hope I'm not disturbing you.'

'Not at all, please sit.'

Mark unfolded the papers on the table. 'Another mutilated body of a woman found floating in the surf, a foreigner.' He spoke as if it were a common occurrence.

Pestonji picked up the papers and glanced at the ghastly picture on the front page. 'That's horrendous.'

Mark shook his head. 'Third such case in the last ten months. Goa is becoming notorious since the hippies started arriving with their drugs and free sex.'

'It's going to ruin the image of Goa,' Pestonji said.

'So, how was your exhibition?'

'It was great. We should be planning our next in Goa, since the response was overwhelming.'

'That's good.'

Pestonji placed the camera on the table. 'How's Mrs Braganza today? I hope she's better now?'

'Yes, I think she should be up and around soon.'

'It'll be a pleasure meeting her again. Mrs Braganza does have an eye for quality art. She liked that painting, *Lovers' Rock,* which John was not keen to sell. But then...everything has a price.' He leant forward in the manner of a seasoned salesman. 'I should be able to swing it for twenty, twenty-five thousand, with ten percent commission for me, if you're interested.'

Mark flinched. 'Twenty-five grand! You must be joking? I'd rather spend that money on doing up things.'

'It's no big deal for a *John Abraham*. That painting is a rare specimen, Mr Braganza. One year from now, it'll go for double the amount.'

'Perhaps it will, but I'm not interested.'

Pestonji cleared his throat. 'I can forgo my commission if you think it might please Mrs Braganza.'

Mark brushed off his suggestion with a wave of his hand. 'I don't think so. You might as well drop the idea altogether and enjoy the scenery. I have other things to worry about.'

One of Mark's 'worries', Mr Fernandez, was already enjoying his hospitality in room number six. He looked forward to meeting him later in the day and discovering more about the Braganzas.

Pestonji gazed at the row of cottages. 'I wonder why all these cottages are not in use?'

'They need extensive repairs. Besides, there aren't many takers these days,' he said, ruefully. 'No point adding to the overheads.'

'What a pity, I would've loved to stay in one of those.'

'Not in the near future.'

Pestonji rose from his chair. 'I should be going now. Please convey my regards to Mrs Braganza. I'll see if I can bring the price of that painting down…just in case.'

❧

At noon, Pestonji knocked on the door of room six.

With a glass of beer in his hand and a grin on his face, Fernandez opened it. 'Ah, Mr Pestonji, come on in, I was expecting you.'

The stink of beer mixed with tobacco greeted Pestonji as he entered the untidy room: clothes lay all over, towels hung on the backs of the chairs and empty beer bottles littered the floor under the table. Fernandez emptied a chair and offered it to him.

'Let me pour some beer for you.'

'No, thanks, Mr Fernandez, I just came to say hello as I plan to leave tomorrow morning.'

'Come on, it's all on the house, and some delicious kebabs

to go with it.'

'Please, I don't think I should—doctor's orders.'

'To hell with the doctors,' Fernandez frowned. 'Your date of departure is already fixed, beer or no beer. So why bother? Look at me, I'm a chronic diabetic and I have a heart condition. But I'm not going to quit this world in a hurry.'

'Thanks. But I'd rather not drink.'

'All right, as you wish.' He threw his hands in the air and sat down. 'So you took some pictures of the rascal from the terrace. Pity you couldn't capture his wife in your camera—your film would've burnt, I tell you.'

'She's not well, I gather.'

Fernandez knit his brows. 'Bullshit, all she needs is a good lay, and she'll be basking in the sun like a contented hen.' He burst out laughing, wiping his mouth with the back of his hand.

Pestonji felt awkward sitting with a man with such depraved manners. But he had a mission. 'By the way, have you any idea where she came from?'

Fernandez poured more beer in his glass. 'Nobody knows. But she must've come loaded with money. The couple spent lavishly after their wedding—Mercedes with a chauffeur, imported dresses, gala parties and the works. And Braganza, who had been missing from the party scene for quite a while, returned in great style. He paraded his new wife with great pride.' He gulped his beer and shook his head. 'I really envy the bastard.'

'She must come from a wealthy background.'

'Who knows, but this man can smell money from miles. Especially when it comes packed with a good pair of legs. First, it was that poor girl, Irene, from one of the richest families of Goa, and then this angel. The man attracts them like bees to the honey pot.'

'I believe his first wife perished in a drowning accident.'

'It wasn't an accident, believe me. He must have made it up to look like one. The scoundrel collected a lot of money from her insurance.'

'What about the police? They must've investigated him.'

Fernandez laughed. 'The police can be bought in Goa for a case of scotch or less.'

'Don't you think it would be difficult to hide the truth for long?'

'Not when you're Mark Braganza. And now that he is back in the red, one doesn't know what future awaits his present wife.'

20

After dispatching Pestonji to Paradise Resort, Mani returned to Bombay with mixed feelings. Grace's chance appearance at the gallery excited him more than the success of the show. It was a treat to see her crumbling in front of *Lovers' Rock*. Nothing could quell the rush from seeing her like that. He could not have imagined a better way to punish the woman without actually facing her.

Mani felt uncomfortable coming back to the house without Pestonji. Facing Shehnaz and Navroz in the absence of the old man didn't appeal to him. They never made him feel at home and treated him like an unwanted burden. He arrived at Warden Road well after the couple had left for work. He booked a call to Tanya's resort, but it didn't materialise.

Disappointed, Mani dozed off until he heard voices in the living room. The constipated couple was back. 'Oh shit,' he said to himself and looked at his watch—seven-thirty. He decided to sneak out, but Shehnaz caught him in the living room.

'You're back alone?'

'Yup.'

She raised her chin, pointing her sharp nose somewhere between Mani's eyes like a double-barrel gun. 'Where's Uncle Feroze?'

Mani picked up his umbrella. 'In Goa.'

'An agent called in your absence about a flat you wanted to hire. Here's the card.'

'Change of plan. I'm staying put.'

Shehnaz's face lost colour. '*What?*'

Her husband showed up, adjusting his thick glasses on his parrot-like nose. 'Oh, so the paint-smell is back again.'

She grimaced. 'Yeah, it was nice to smell fresh air for a change.'

The sarcasm didn't ruffle Mani. 'You better get used to it. I'm not going to leave in a hurry.' He turned to leave.

'It's time you made your own arrangements, mister,' she snapped. 'I'm not going to cook for you forever.'

Mani turned back. 'Thank God for sparing me the agony. You may save your culinary talents for your mate,' he said, and slipped out of the door. He could be nasty when he wanted to.

After wandering around Scandal Point and later, the market, he ate his dinner and returned to the house very late. He didn't use the spare key on purpose and pressed the bell—once, twice and a third time, before a bare-chested Navroz opened the door, rubbing his eyes.

'Couldn't you use the key, mister?' he hollered. 'It's well past eleven, for heaven's sake.'

Mani grinned, 'I lost the key.'

'Damn you.'

In the morning, Mani went for a walk and sat on the rocks, thinking about Tanya. He didn't wish to keep her in the dark anymore and wondered if he should reveal his true identity. After pondering over the matter for over an hour, he thought it prudent to come clean instead of postponing the inevitable.

Back home alone, he booked a call to Tanya's resort. While waiting, he worked on an unfinished painting—to reward Shehnaz with the smell of paint she'd missed over a week. The call came through late in the afternoon. He shuddered.

'John! I was dying to hear your voice.'

'How are you?' he asked.

'I'm fine, what about you? Tell me about your show. How did it go?'

'It went off very well, but I missed you.'

'Me, too.'

'There's something I want to tell you, Tanya.'

'What?'

He lapsed into silence.

'What is it, John?'

'I'm afraid I'm going to disappoint you.'

'What are you talking about?'

Mani cleared his throat and braced himself. 'I'm not who you think I am...John Abraham is not my real name.'

The reply came, but after an uneasy pause. 'What do you mean?'

'I'm somebody else...who's sinned in the past.'

'Don't frighten me, John.' The alarm in her voice came loud and clear over the phone.

'I've cheated the state.'

'No!' she breathed.

'It's a fact.'

'Listen, John, for me there's only one John Abraham, and I do not wish to know anything about the other you.'

'Tanya, you don't understand.'

'I don't want to understand.'

'I was married to somebody else...who ditched me for money.'

'Stop it, John. I don't want to hear it.'

'You must know the truth.'

She cried over the phone. 'I don't want to lose you.'

'Me neither, but I can't to keep you in the dark.'

'I've nothing to do with your past.'

'I'm afraid the past may catch up. I wouldn't want you to suffer because of me.'

'I'm ready to face anything in life with you, better or worse. If you have done wrong, let God take care of that.'

'Are you prepared to spend the rest of your life with a man who has committed a felony?'

'Yes, as long as you haven't killed somebody or robbed a bank?'

Mani shrugged. 'No, but...'

'When are you coming to Daman?'

'As soon as I can, believe me.'

'Leave your past behind when you visit me, or don't come.'

'Tanya...'

'I love you and it's not going to change, ever.'

'I love you, too.'

❧

Pestonji returned to Bombay armed with information about the Braganzas. After hearing the story, Mani went into deep thought. This was his chance to strike at Grace where it would hurt most. He was so obsessed with revenge that he didn't want to let go of the opportunity.

'What now?'asked Pestonji.

Mani picked up the photographs of the resort.

'The place looks promising to me,' he said, gazing at the picture of Mark's cottage.

'But woefully neglected. Braganza doesn't have the funds to undertake even the routine maintenance.'

Mani rubbed his chin. 'Perhaps we could help him out.'

'I beg your pardon?'

'I'm tempted to invest in the property.'

'Are you crazy?'

'I'm not, Pestonji. This is something I have to do.'

Pestonji rose from his chair in a huff and paced the floor.

'I see a good opportunity.'

'You want to get back at your ex-wife?'

'That's the general idea. Besides, the photographs present a promising picture of the resort, an ideal place to settle down and paint in the midst of nature.'

Pestonji stared at him. 'You're not serious, are you?'

'Yes, I am.'

'I think it would be a foolish idea to dump your hard-earned money into a sinking ship, even though you have a hidden agenda.'

'I won't deny the motive is important, but more than that, I'm excited about the place.'

'Mark Braganza is not the kind of person you can trust,' Pestonji said. 'He has taken many a people for a ride. I can't just sit around and watch you go down the same path.'

'I appreciate your concern, but I'm prepared to take the risk, and I'm counting on you to help me in my mission.'

'I'm always there for you, John, but this doesn't make sense.'

'This is not just a business proposition. I must teach that woman a few lessons.'

'My friend, women are known to have destroyed many a man in history. You're chasing a lost cause for whatever reason, but you'll be a lot happier if you forget the past and move on.'

'Move on, I will, but not before punishing her for what she did to me.'

'Your anguish is understandable, but the intent is fraught with disaster.' Pestonji shook his head and sat down. 'You're a prisoner of your pride, consumed by a passion for revenge that could ruin everything you've achieved in your life.'

'I'm prepared for the worst, but I wouldn't let her rest in peace.'

A long silence ensued before Pestonji asked, 'What exactly happened between the two of you? It's time you told me the whole story.'

Mani turned to the window and gazed at the sky. It was just like when he last flew over Digha. He shuddered to think of the horrendous thing he had done for the sake of his fatal obsession—a woman who didn't care whether he lived or died. For Grace, Mani Shankar was dead and gone, but his ghost in John Abraham was alive and coming to haunt her. He turned slowly to face Pestonji.

'A couple of years ago, it was a similar night, a dreadful night that was to change my life forever—the night I ditched my fighter plane in the ocean.'

'*Fighter plane? Ditched it?*' Pestonji's eyes turned wide. 'What in hell are you talking about?'

'It's a long story.' Mani turned back to the window. 'I was a fighter pilot before I met you...'

Pestonji jumped from his chair. 'What nonsense!'

'I ditched my aircraft into the ocean and disappeared.'

The old man's face turned many shades, from shock to anger and then dismay as Mani went on to narrate his story.

❧

Pestonji found it hard to believe that this humble soul from Timbuktu could ever have been a decorated fighter pilot with the stupendous audacity to do what he had. And all for a woman who, by any stretch of imagination, didn't look the type to build a good home. No wonder she ditched him for the money that belonged to neither of them.

No sensible person would've liked to associate with such an absconder whose rightful place belonged not in the premier art galleries, but behind bars. As a law abiding citizen, it was his duty to report the man to the police. But Pestonji was not a ditcher like Grace Braganza. He didn't have the heart to abandon John when he needed him the most.

That night, the two of them huddled together in a long debate, until the newspaper boys started making their rounds in the early hours of the morning.

The following day, they met one of Pestonji's trusted acquaintances, an attorney.

21

A new guest arrived at Paradise Resort one afternoon. Wearing a long coat, a baseball cap and dark glasses, he stood not less than six-foot-plus. A frail looking woman, half his size in length and breadth, accompanied him. She came with three rows of pearls and a sullen face.

Sitting in the lounge, Mark lifted his eyes from the newspapers. With his dark moustache and thick sideburns the new arrival would nevertheless have been noticed.

'I would like a double room,' he said to Grace at the reception.

'Certainly.' Grace forced a smile and presented the check-in register to the visitor.

Apparently in his mid fifties, the tall man removed his glasses and ogled at Grace's figure. He held the pen in his hand for a moment too long, his face red and his eyes refusing to leave the vicinity of her cleavage. Grace stared at him disapprovingly and folded her hands across her chest.

Used to seeing such spectacles, Mark winked at Grace.

The frail woman glanced at Grace and turned away, covering whatever little assets she possessed, under a shawl.

Mark approached and greeted them. 'Welcome to Paradise Resort. I'm Mark Braganza, your host.'

Mr Patel shook his hand. 'Jayant Patel, real estate agent from Bombay.'

The towering man entered their names—Mr and Mrs Jayant Patel.

'How long do you plan to stay, Mr Patel?' Grace asked in a business-like tone.

'A couple of days, maybe more.'

'By the way,' interjected Mrs Patel, her tone demanding, 'I'm a strict vegetarian. Do you have separate cooking arrangements for vegetarians?'

Mark stole a quick glance at Grace. 'Yes, ma'am, we do. I'm aware of how particular and discerning our guests are.'

Mr Patel smiled—he must have known about the drill.

'I hope so,' said the wafer-thin lady, her sharp nose pointing in the air.

Built like a tanker, Mr Patel looked like a basketball coach than a real estate agent. Mark wondered how the frail woman had managed to endure this giant of a man for God knows how long and still remain in one piece!

Grace instructed Raju to escort the couple to their room.

Mark glimpsed at the extra-large behind of the lady, quite disproportionate to the rest of her frame. 'That woman spells trouble,' Mark whispered. 'I know one when I see one.'

Grace looked at him sharply. 'You seem to know more about women than anything else.'

Mark smiled. After all, what man would know more about women than him? He studied Grace. Despite all her charm, Grace had almost outlived her utility in his scheme of things. But there was a time for everything… and her time had not yet come.

'Are they settled?' Grace asked when Raju returned.

'Not before inspecting several rooms and making a lot of fuss, demanding a change of linen.'

'I knew it,' Mark said.

Later, in the evening, Mark saw Mr Patel sitting alone in the lounge, browsing through a magazine.

Mark approached. 'Good evening, Mr Patel. I hope you're comfortable?'

Patel looked up. 'Yes, thank you.'

'Mind if I join you?'

'Not at all, I could use some company.'

Mark took a seat across from him. 'May I buy you a drink?'

'Thank you, I've already ordered.'

Mark ordered whiskey for himself. 'So, how was your day?'

'It was good. I intend going for a survey of the area tomorrow morning. A client of mine is interested in buying a piece of land here. Perhaps you could suggest something?'

'May I ask for what purpose your client requires the land?'

'He wants to build a hotel.'

Mark raised an eyebrow. 'A hotel?'

'Not a very wise decision, would you say, judging from the situation here?'

'I don't know about that, but the occupancy is not so encouraging. Which is why I've locked some of my cottages.'

'Well, who cares whether he builds a hotel or a zoo for that matter, as long as I earn my commission.' Mr Patel chuckled. 'The man is loaded and has to park his money somewhere.'

Mark certainly didn't relish the idea of someone else fishing in his territory. As it was, he was going through a rough patch. A new player in his area would hurt more. 'I wonder what attracted your client to this place.'

Mr Patel sipped his drink. 'Goa, Mr Braganza, is on the world map of tourism. People are looking for properties in the area. This is going to be *the* happening place in the coming years. All you need is a skilled craftsman to turn this wilderness into a jewel.'

'You really think so?'

'I do. And this man knows how to sell his product. Otherwise he wouldn't be rich today. I'm sure if a place like yours was managed professionally, there would be a lot of potential. People are travelling a lot more than they did a couple of years ago. I saw huge crowds in Goa and wonder why they're not coming your way. Perhaps you have to revamp the whole place and advertise extensively. I, for one, didn't even know that Paradise Resort existed.'

Mark was in no mood to learn his craft from a real-estate agent. He would have liked to tell the bloke to mind his own business, but he knew he wasn't doing a very good job of running the show himself. He hesitated and then went on.

'I know what you mean, Mr Patel. But it's easier said than done. The overheads are onerous and the returns quite uncertain. Things are not all that rosy in this business.'

'The returns will come if you invested and marketed the product more aggressively.' Mr Patel paused, scanned the surroundings and grimaced. 'One cannot expect results without making investments where they're due. And then you've to make a lot of noise about it in the media for people to take notice.'

'I've always believed in word-of-mouth publicity.'

'Word-of-mouth publicity is fine, but not good enough. For all you know it may be doing you more harm than good.'

Mark knew his resort was losing its draw, with more and more of his regulars patronising other places mushrooming all over Goa. With the possibility of another hotel coming up in the area, his days seemed numbered. With no funds at his disposal, he could hardly think of a turnaround.

'I'm sorry to disappoint you, Mr Braganza, but this place needs a complete overhaul.'

Mark pursed his lips. 'Funds, Mr Patel, funds. Eventually it boils down to money, which is hard to come by. Let me order another drink for you.'

'Only if you allow me to sign for it.'

Mark shrugged. 'All right, if you insist.' It was a tactic he often employed with unsuspecting guests.

'Mr Braganza, money should not be a problem as long as the end result is promising. There is no dearth of investors. A whole lot of people out there are waiting, loaded with cash not knowing where to park their funds.'

Mark's antenna went up. His instincts told him he could use Mr Patel's services to tap the right sources for money. He thought for a moment and asked, 'You said you're looking for a piece of land for your client?'

'Yes, that's why I'm here.'

'And you do see a lot of potential?'

'Of course, I do.'

Mark gazed at him. 'How about your client investing in Paradise Resort, instead of starting from scratch and taking a risk?'

Mr Patel's eyes brightened. 'That's not a bad idea, Mr Braganza. I think it should appeal to my client. After all, who wouldn't want to invest in a sailing ship rather than assemble one in this jungle? Besides, it would make my job much simpler.'

'Makes good business sense to me.'

'We'll have to see if my client will approve of a partnership.'

'I'd be grateful if you could sell the idea to your client. And, of course, I'll take care of your commission.'

'Let me first explore the possibility. We can discuss the nitty-gritty later.'

'Why not put our cards on the table right now so we understand each other better?'

Mr Patel considered the point, running his hand over his bald pate. 'The usual rate is four percent. But in this case, I would say five or six, since this involves extra effort in convincing the client without jeopardising his own interests.'

'Five percent would be fine with me.'

Mrs Patel showed up in the lounge with a scowl on her face, interrupting their chat.

Mark rose from his chair to greet her.

'Do you know what time it is, Jayant?' She ignored Mark. 'Ten-thirty, for God's sake, and you're still going strong!'

Mr Patel sank back in his chair.

'I'm so sorry, Ma'am,' said Mark. 'I shouldn't have detained your husband for so long. We lost track of time.'

'Relax, woman,' snapped Mr Patel. 'We're talking business here, not discussing movies.'

'You can do that tomorrow. I've already ordered dinner in the room.'

He raised his hands in mock defense. 'Okay, I'll be there in a minute.'

Mrs Patel walked off, without looking back.

'Ah, dinner in the room means vegetarian fare served in the steel utensils she carries with her religiously, like her herbal toothpaste and that foul smelling medicated soap. I should've ordered some kebabs with our drinks.'

'Oh, I'm so sorry,' said Mark. 'I didn't know you fancy non-veg. Should I order now?'

Mr Patel gulped his drink hurriedly. 'You've got to be kidding. I should run before the roof starts crumbling. See you tomorrow.'

'Good night, Mr Patel.'

The man raised his hand in acknowledgement without turning back.

❧

That night, Mark briefed Grace about the possibility of arranging finances through Mr Patel and suggested they invite the couple to dinner the following evening.

Grace screwed up her face. 'Ugh! I hate the look of that man and that long-faced woman.'

Mark grinned. 'You'll like the look of this man when the money starts rolling in, and perhaps show him a little more of your cleavage without complaining.'

Grace rolled her eyes. 'Perhaps you would like to bed that skeleton of a woman, if the money starts rolling in.'

'Come on, Grace, be serious. I'm sure you won't like the look of this man if his client puts up a hotel around here.'

'I wouldn't read too much into this after just a brief exchange over drinks. He'll probably enjoy the free treats and then vanish from the scene, making a fool of you.'

'I don't think he's the type.'

'Don't be too sure.'

'He hasn't promised the moon, said he'll try, and I've offered to pay for his services.'

Grace arched her eyebrows. 'I hope not in advance?'

'What do you take me for? You think I'm a fool?'

'Okay, wise man, but dinner and all can wait. I'm in no mood to entertain the odd couple just because he sold you an idea.'

'It was not his idea but mine.'

'Well, then go ahead, feed them at the restaurant, but leave me out of it.'

Infuriated with Grace's attitude, Mark retired after a quiet dinner.

❧

Mark often enjoyed a glass of beer under the huge banyan tree.

Waiting for his breakfast, he browsed through the morning papers.

'Good morning, Mr Braganza,' Mr Patel appeared in his track suit. 'Nothing like a morning jog on the beach.'

'Good morning, please join me for a glass of beer.'

'I never refuse a good offer.'

Mark signalled the waiter and ordered beer for his guest and sausages for good measure.

Mr Patel settled into a garden chair. 'I had a long talk with my client last night.'

'*You did?*' Mark sat upright.

'He seemed interested.'

'That's good news.'

'Yes, and now I don't have to tire my bones hunting for that piece of land in this jungle. I must warn you that this man is very shrewd when it comes to business. However, I know how to tackle the likes of him. I'm sure he'll melt when he sees the place.'

'You think so?'

'I'm absolutely certain, especially when he finds that Mrs Braganza and you run the show. It makes all the difference who is in command on the ground.'

'Is he likely to visit?'

'Not yet. I would rather work on him a bit before I bring him here. Of course, you'll have to put up a good show and spruce up things to charm him.'

Mark poured beer for the guest and extended the plate of sausages that just arrived.

Mr Patel mouthed a big chunk of sausage. 'How delicious! My wife doesn't even allow eggs in the house.'

'You're welcome.'

The cool breeze from the ocean had become strong. Mr Patel leant across the table. 'Look Mr Braganza, let me be frank with you. You must appreciate that nobody will invest in a venture without control over management and finances. I can visualise the possibility of an investment with some kind of partnership or a long-term lease with dual control. If you're open to such an arrangement, we can proceed with the matter seriously.'

Mark saw an opportunity to escape from the clutches of his creditors and was prepared to compromise as long as the arrangement was reasonably favourable for him. 'I'm open to an offer, if you can take good care of my interests.'

'Of course I will, if only…'

'What?'

Mr Patel smiled. 'If only you raise the bar to six percent. I see a difficult task on my hands.'

'All right, six percent it is, but let it be good.'

'I shall try my best to get you a favourable deal, but let me make it clear that this client of mine will want a top class facility with no compromises on quality, and that would mean heavy expenditure.' He paused and then went on. 'Therefore, don't be too put out if you find him demanding. I'll make sure he is reasonable enough.'

Mark shuffled in his chair. 'I don't know what's on your mind, Mr Patel, but all I have right now is this ship, and if your client wishes to refurbish it, he'll have to finance it. Believe me, I would've done it myself if I had that kind of money.'

'I understand. I've already talked to him about that.'

'Some more beer?' asked Mark.

Mr Patel raised his half empty glass. 'Okay, but make it fast before the woman starts howling.'

'Why don't you have lunch with me?'

'No, no, you don't understand, I've to apply for express permission from the home ministry.' He chuckled. 'Perhaps I could join you for drinks this evening.'

'You're most welcome. Let's meet in the lounge at eight.'

'That would be fine.'

Mr Six-Percent drank like a long-distance trucker while debating issues with Mark that evening, eyeing Grace at the reception desk every now and then. Mark saw Grace leave after a while.

Six-Percent's eyes followed her glorious behind until she disappeared.

'Mrs Patel must be cursing me already for keeping you away from her for so long,' Mark tried to distract him.

'Oh, not to worry. She's a hard nut on the outside, but quite soft otherwise.'

All bones and no meat, Mark wondered where the man found the softness on his wife's skeleton. Nevertheless, he glanced at his watch and rose. 'I think you're right. It's getting late. I shall let you know how things turn out. And then you could come over to Bombay for detailed discussions. My client has a cosy little place by the sea. It would be a good idea if you could bring Mrs Braganza along... combine business with pleasure.'

The spark in his eyes did not escape Mark's notice.

22

After waiting anxiously for two weeks, Mark received a letter from Mr Patel. He ripped it open and began to read it.

Dear Mr Braganza,

I am pleased to inform you that my client is impressed with what he saw at your resort during a secret visit about which I had no previous knowledge. In a way, it is better he got a true picture. The good news is that he is serious about the proposal.

I have had detailed discussions with him and his attorney and negotiated a favourable deal that should satisfy both parties.

My client has offered to invest an amount equal to fifty percent of the current value of your property for a long-term partnership with dual control, and equal share in profit and loss. A rough estimate of the value of your property is about ten lakhs. Therefore, he proposes to invest five lakhs. We estimate an initial expenditure of about two to three lakhs to revamp the place, the rest being the working capital.

I am afraid one specific demand that is central to the whole proposal may go against your interest: he wants your living quarters, your cottage, to be placed at his disposal for his personal use. He has proposed to do up two cottages on the grounds, at his cost, and convert them into decent accommodation for you. Further, my client is willing to pay one lakh as compensation.

To maintain status quo, he proposes that you and Mrs Braganza continue to manage the affairs of the resort in conjunction with his representative. He is offering an annual package of twenty-four thousand rupees for you and twelve thousand for Mrs Braganza, with ten per cent increase per year. Judging from the going rates, it sounds pretty good to me.

If you are not keen on a long-term arrangement, he will agree to a minimum seven-year term with the provision that you return fifty per cent of his initial investment, if you terminate the contract before the completion of this period.

By the way, I tried my best to persuade him not to press for your cottage, but that, he insists, is paramount and not negotiable. If it is not acceptable to you, he is out of this. I trust you will give the matter serious thought.

If you are inclined, I would advise you to come over to Bombay for a detailed discussion. Let me know so that I may make necessary arrangements for you and Mrs Braganza. Please convey my regards to Mrs Braganza.

Sincerely,
Jayant Patel

Mark went out to the deck and gazed at the cottage where he had spent the best years of his life. He could never dream of giving up his home for anyone even if it was for the Duke of Edinburg.

Several thoughts flashed across his mind: How dare Patel's client make such an outrageous demand? Who does he think he is? Next, the bloody man might demand to bed Grace, though that would be less painful. But five lakhs! And one lakh to move out of the cottage sounded too good. He looked at the dilapidated cottages and wondered how Grace would adapt. No, that would be too much of a sacrifice. But one lakh could take care of some of the irritating creditors who were getting more insistent. If the cottage was not negotiable, Mark had to find ways to squeeze the bugger elsewhere.

His mind focused on the money that would come in, Mark began to relax and made his peace with the decision to part with his cottage. It was a tough decision, sure to provoke Grace.

Back in his office, he read the letter again, pausing to examine each aspect. Twenty-four grand for him didn't leave much ground for further negotiations; even ministers in the government didn't earn that much. Grace would be pocketing twelve grand to just relax her shapely bottom at the reception. One of his ex-flames, Yasmin, made as much flying five days a week on the Goa-Bombay route, serving coffee and putting up with the endless tantrums of the passengers. Except for the cottage, the offer seemed too good. But a hundred thousand for shifting your luggage was no joke. He pocketed the letter and made his way to the reception desk.

'Grace, show me the check-in register. I want to see who stayed with us.'

'Sure. There aren't very many names though. Who are you looking for?'

'No one in particular, I just want to see—'

'There weren't any pretty women with slender legs who would interest you, if that's what you're looking for.'

'Cut the crap,' he said, and scanned the register. He didn't find anyone who could fit the profile of a possible investor. The register indicated only a handful of visitors: A young couple recently married, a Bengali family with their rowdy brood, two elderly ladies who chatted all the time over dozens of cups of tea, a French national who kept to himself, and a priest who spent most of his time in the fishers' colony for God knows what—none fitting the description of someone who wanted him out of his cottage for a consideration of a lakh of rupees.

'Darling, there's a letter from Patel,' Mark said over drinks that evening. Grace had settled into her favourite sofa with a glass of wine as Mark took his usual position at the bar.

Grace scrunched her nose. 'Ugh, that creep? What does he say?'

Mark took out the letter from his pocket and gave it to her.

As Grace read it, her face changed colour, from pink to white and then red. 'This is ridiculous!' she exploded. 'Why the hell do you entertain such rogues? This is nothing short of daylight robbery.'

Mark had prepared for the onslaught. He sipped his drink and tried to maintain his composure. 'What other choice do we have?'

Grace reacted sharply. 'Don't tell me…'

'You think I want to leave the cottage just like that?'

She narrowed her eyes and gave him a hard look. 'You mean you're ready to give up our home and invite some invisible joker from nowhere to lord it over us?'

'So what do you suggest we do?'

'We tell them to go to hell, that's what we do.'

'And how do you think we will clear our debt?' he lost his cool. 'Put your ass on the line?'

Grace's face turned purple. 'You've some nerve to speak to me like that. Aren't you ashamed of what you did with my money? And now you're ready to give up all that your father built?'

'I'm not giving-it-all-up, holy cow. I know how to handle the moneybags, and you will bloody well do what I tell you to, whether you like it or not.'

'You've gone nuts.'

'I'm trying to put some sense into your brain.'

'So you want us to pack our bags and spread the red carpet for some jokers to throw us out of our home?'

He clenched his jaw. 'If you don't want to spread the red carpet, then be prepared to spread your legs. Or else…'

Grace shook with rage. 'Else what?'

'You might like to join Irene at the bottom of the sea.'

Grace's jaw dropped and her stomach turned over. She stared at Mark in horror. 'You killed her, didn't you?' She whispered.

The look on his face answered her question—a menacing look that sent a shiver down her spine.

Mark, who had come into her life like a Greek God, now looked like a monster she had to guard against with all her might. This was the lowest point in her life. But Grace Wilson was no Irene. She wasn't going to be pushed around by the evil man she had begun to hate.

'I know how clever and cunning you are, Mr Mark Braganza, but you can't be a winner all the time. Your luck will run out sooner than you realise.'

He laughed. 'You've no idea whom you're talking to.'

'I'm talking to a mad man who is ready to become an employee in his own shop. I won't be surprised if they kick out your butt in the long run.'

Mark's brow puckered. 'What do you take me for? I'm not a fool to allow any such thing to happen to me.'

'Do what you like, but I'm not prepared to leave the cottage.'

'You will not only leave the cottage, but me too, if you want to depart in one piece.'

Grace couldn't leave Mark even if she wanted to. The lack of intimacy in their relationship over the last few months clearly suggested that the party was over. But she had nowhere to go, not even Pimpri. She'd rather take her chances with the devil than face her parents. Grace stayed up late into the night, her mind churning as she planned her next move. Grace Wilson was not the kind of woman to give up easily. She had lost everything to Mark, but still possessed one commodity that never failed her—her sex-appeal. And who but she knew how to use it to her advantage?

❧

Once Mark left for Bombay, Grace stood naked in front of the full-length mirror in their bathroom and marvelled at her image. Even after two marriages, and a few indiscretions, her breasts were youthful and body supple. Had she been born in the US, she would have easily made it to the centrefold of *Playboy,* and stormed into Hollywood.

She might as well spread her legs to get back at Mark and turn the table on him. You wait, Mark Braganza, Grace laid down the gauntlet, see how Grace Wilson uses her charms on this faceless man... and reduces you to a mere dog on a leash. You used me, robbed me of everything... and now it's your turn!

Mark arrived at Mr Patel's swanky office on the fifth floor of a tall, imposing building. The vast picture-window behind his desk commanded a spectacular view of the famous Marine Drive—the pearl necklace around the business district of the mega city and the magnificent Arabian Sea.

'I was hoping Mrs Braganza would have come with you,' said Mr Patel while motioning across his large desk for Mark to take a chair. 'I had fixed up a nice place for you in Juhu.'

'She had to stay behind at the resort since we have a group

arriving in a couple of days.'

'Yes, of course, I understand,' said Mr Patel with a laboured smile. 'The personal touch is very important after all.'

Mark surveyed the office and admired the décor. Six-Percent obviously did very well to maintain such a plush office on Marine Drive. Real estate agents in Bombay were making a lot of money, rapidly turning into builders of repute. He had little doubt Mr. Patel was following the same route to prosperity.

'What would you like, Mr Braganza, coffee or something cold?'

'Coffee will do, thanks.'

Mr Patel pressed the intercom and ordered coffee.

'Have you studied the proposal?'

'Yes, I have.'

'How do you feel about it?'

Mark thought about Grace. 'I have to admit, I'm interested but not very excited.'

'Why is that?'

'Perhaps I should meet your client and discuss the matter face to face.'

Patel drummed his fingers on the table. 'I'm afraid that won't be possible. The gentleman is presently out of the country. Besides, it's an established norm in my line of work to introduce the two parties only after preliminary negotiations are over. He has left the final decision with his attorney, whom we shall meet in the evening. My client's absence should not matter at all.'

'Still, we should know who we are dealing with.'

'You will, soon enough, after we've sorted out the details.'

Mark gazed out of the window. The afternoon sun shone brightly, turning the surface of the ocean into a glaring sheet of chrome that almost blinded him. He sipped his coffee and faced the realtor. 'This demand for the cottage sounds outrageous to me.

Mrs Braganza is terribly upset about it. After all, sentiment is more important than money. It's too much of a sacrifice.'

'For the kind of money he's offering, I would consider it a bonanza.'

'But why would he want to uproot us from our home?' Mark said puzzled. 'He could've just built a castle for himself anywhere on the property.'

'I know, but he's sold on your cottage.'

Mark flinched. 'It doesn't make sense.'

'It doesn't make sense to me either, but he is unrelenting. I've already exhausted my energy in trying to persuade him not to press for it. He seemed so charmed by your cottage that he refuses to listen.'

Mark tilted his head. 'When did he visit the resort?'

Mr Patel shrugged. 'I don't know either, but he did.'

'I don't think we can part with our cottage for what you're offering.'

'He's giving you a lakh just to shift your luggage to an alternate accommodation, which I think is quite generous.'

Mark crossed his legs and stared at the giant. 'I'm not too sure which side you are on, Mr Patel, but surely you could have gotten us a more favourable deal? If your client is so adamant about the cottage, he'll have to pay a substantial amount for me to move out of my ancestral home.'

Mr Patel leant back in his swivel chair and rolled the paperweight on his table. 'If you think I didn't try, let's call it a day. I like to represent a person who trusts me.'

Grace would surely have walked out of the room at this point. But the lure of money acted like a leash around Mark's neck. Common sense told him to bargain hard if he wanted to keep out of trouble that waited for him back home.

'It's not lack of trust, Mr Patel. I know your primary loyalty is to your client, but surely the six percent should account for something more. After all, I'm offering a running show, not selling a dream. Besides, there's the question of the goodwill built over the years.'

Mr Patel rose from his chair and paced the floor. 'Let me tell you something, Mr Braganza. This man is crazy, offering to invest so much money into your resort with no guarantee of returns. He's taking a huge risk. As for your goodwill, you should know better than I do. It will take a lot of effort and money to rebuild the goodwill from scratch. I'm not suggesting it's the end of it. There's always room for negotiation. Which is why, I've arranged this meeting with his attorney. You should know that part of your six percent will go into his pocket, which would be icing on the cake.'

Mark swallowed hard, hoping for a better offer to take back home.

Mr Patel pulled a file from the drawer and placed it on the table. 'I'd like you to have a look at this report compiled by professionals of repute. You will see that it would take a minimum of five years to break even, keeping the best scenario in mind.'

Mark glanced at the concluding portion of the report that showed the graphical representation of the inflows and outflows that converged at the end of the five-year period.

'This is all hypothetical.'

'Yes, but it is based on sound logic, and fifty percent average occupancy, which is hard to expect considering your present state of affairs.'

Mark rose from his chair and walked to the window. The room was silent except for the distant roar of the sea and the continuous honking of horns on the street below. In the last four years, the best occupancy figure he had achieved was thirty-three percent. The offer seemed generous. Not that it mattered, but it wasn't good enough to broker peace with Grace. He admired the big imported cars passing on the street below and wondered when he would be able to afford one of those beauties again.

'I suggest we wait for the meeting with the attorney,' Mr Patel broke the silence. 'I'm not charging you for thin air, trust me.'

Mark turned. 'Are you sure this attorney has the power to negotiate?'

'Of course he does, except the cottage clause.'

The meeting with the attorney, a short man with a large head, lasted three hours. Mr Patel didn't have to bargain hard and finally managed to clinch a deal that didn't leave a bad taste in Mark's mouth. In short, a firm commitment for a six-year term instead of the seven proposed initially, and fifteen percent annual increase in their emoluments against the offered ten. But he wanted more for vacating the cottage.

'Mr Braganza,' said Mr Shah, the attorney, eyeing Mark through the top half of his thick bifocals, 'I've never before drafted a deal such as this, which is so grossly in favour of one party. In this case, that's you. My client seems to have lost his mind on this. Surely, you don't mean to rob him?' The attorney's eyeballs looked larger than those of a bull when he lifted his head.

Notwithstanding the merit of his argument, Mark saw no harm in making one last attempt to squeeze him further. 'Certainly not, Mr Shah, but it is too much of a sacrifice to part with one's home just because your client has taken a fancy to it.'

Mr Shah pulled out an envelope from his briefcase and placed it in on the table. 'This, Mr Braganza, is the best we can do.'

The size of the envelope suggested a handsome amount. Mark glanced at Mr Shah.

'There's twenty thousand in it.' Mr Patel said. 'Do we have a deal?'

Mark barely managed to suppress a smile. 'Icing on the cake,' he said while pocketing the envelope.

'I'll have the draft agreement delivered to you tomorrow morning,' said the attorney, before parting. 'We should be able to visit you in about a week's time to sign all the papers and register the deed at Goa.'

Mark rose from his chair and gazed at Mr Shah. 'By the way, who is your client?'

Six Percent and Mr Shah exchanged a quick glance. 'You'll meet him next week.'

'Does he have a name?'

Mr Patel chuckled. 'Mr Braganza, does it matter whether he is Tom, Dick or Harry? I can assure you that you will find this man most accommodating.'

'You're a lucky man, Mr Braganza.' Mr Shah reassured him, 'Take my word for it.'

'But why all the secrecy?'

Mr Patel shrugged. 'That's the way he wanted it, and we are paid to follow his instructions.'

Mark decided to forget about the elusive man who was mad enough to place so much money at his disposal. But the thought of moving out of his cottage still disturbed him. He considered it prudent to reduce the bulge in his pocket and buy Grace some gifts before telling her to pack her suitcases.

23

It had rained heavily the previous night. The driveway was strewn with leaves and flowers. The tall trees, washed fresh by the rain, looked greener than the brightest of greens. Dark clouds hovered in the sky threatening them with another downpour any moment. A couple of children played on the lawns. Their bursts of laughter could be heard well above the sound of the waves.

Grace leant back in the deck chair as the gentle breeze, laden with the scent of pine and magnolia, wafted and tugged at her hair. The soft rumble of the sea soothed her nerves. She wondered if all the glamour and glitter of the material world that had so consumed her could ever match the profound joy nature provided in such abundance, something she had started noticing only now when she was troubled. Perhaps one is closer to nature only after losing all the material wealth one possessed.

Mark paced up and down nearby, glancing at his watch, waiting for Mr Patel and his mysterious client to arrive from Bombay.

'It's a beautiful day,' he said, gazing at the horizon.

'It is, but who knows what's it going to be like tomorrow?'

Mark stopped and threw up his hands in exasperation. 'There you go again. Why can't you be a little optimistic?'

Seeing the abandoned cottages on the grounds, Grace grimaced. 'I dread to imagine how we're going to live in those shacks.'

'Woman, you have to reconcile to the situation, the earlier the better. You don't have a choice.'

She threw a contemptuous smile at Mark and smiled inwardly. *It'll be you, Mr Mark Braganza, who will have to reconcile to the situation, not me.* Dressed in a low-cut blouse and a figure-hugging knee-length skirt that showed her body to advantage, Grace was ready for the kill. She knew how to demolish men with her assets and a Mr Faceless could hardly pose a challenge. Grace waited for a few seconds and then walked back to her desk.

A swanky red Chevrolet Impala splattered with mud pulled into the driveway. Mark scrambled to the portico. Grace touched up her make-up, flipped her hair back and braced herself to face the man destined to call the shots at Paradise Resort—her next prey!

As the car doors flew open, Mr Patel emerged, accompanied by Pestonji.

Grace shrank back. *Pestonji? And Patel?* What in the hell was happening here? Something inside her snapped.

What she saw next, swept the ground from under her feet. The man with the beard, whose picture on the brochure at the art exhibition had nearly given her a heart attack, was shaking hands with Mark! Her knees trembled. *Mani? John Abraham?* What the fuck…!

Mark escorted Mani into the hallway that led to the reception area.

'Darling, you won't believe this.' Mark grinned. 'Meet Mr John Abraham, our new partner. Mr Abraham, my wife, Grace.'

Grace's mouth fell open but no words came out. She turned her face and barely managed to keep her balance. Mani moved on without even a nod, as if she didn't exist.

Before she could recover, Pestonji stopped at her desk, greeting her with a broad smile. 'Hello, Mrs Braganza, nice to see you.'

Grace ignored him and summoned a bellboy. 'Show these guests to their rooms.'

Mr Patel, his eyes on her cleavage, lingered long enough to infuriate Grace even further. 'I wish you had come to Bombay with Mr Braganza. I'm sure you would've enjoyed your stay.'

She fixed the obnoxious man with a steely stare. 'Get lost.'

His face lost its humour. He rubbed his chin and moved away.

Grace took a deep breath and collapsed in her chair and covered her face with her hands.

'Are you all right, Ma'am?' Raju asked. 'You don't seem well.'

'Please mind the desk. I've got to go.' It took a while before she mustered enough strength to rise and make her way to her cottage. The short distance that felt like a mile.

Grace staggered to the bar and poured herself a double whiskey. *Mani, a partner?* This couldn't be happening. Never in her worst nightmares could she have imagined that she would end up in such a calamitous situation. She lit a filter and took a long, deep drag. Mani and his crony breathing down her neck for six bloody years was unthinkable. And to vacate her cottage for Mani was most humiliating.

Her days at Paradise Resort, she thought, were numbered. She sank into the nearest sofa and stared out of the open window. She didn't know what to do. Even the tears seemed to have dried up, depriving her of any relief from her agony.

Mark returned late in the evening. 'What's the matter? Are you all right?'

Grace closed her eyes, not responding.

'This is no time to switch off. We have to attend the meeting scheduled at eight. You cannot afford to mess it up. Pull yourself together, for God's sake.'

'I'm not attending any bloody meeting. I don't feel well.'

'No wonder you aren't feeling well. Drinking like a trucker, you can't be expected to think straight anyway.'

'What do you want me for, an ornamental piece?'

'Maybe, yes. At least you could put your equipment to good use, if nothing else.'

Had it been anybody other than Mani, Grace would have certainly liked to contribute her charm all the way down to the basics, and teach Mark the lesson of his life. Now, with destiny taking an ugly turn, her deadly charm seemed impotent. She swallowed her drink and, with it, her pride.

❧

The meeting in the lounge lasted nearly two hours. Discussions centered around immediate renovation plans and the working arrangement between the two parties under the joint control of Mark Braganza and Pestonji, with the latter functioning on John Abraham's behalf.

'I take it that both parties are fully satisfied with the terms of agreement,' declared Mr Patel, after they concluded their negotiations. There being no dissent, he proceeded further. 'Very well then, we shall all meet at the Registrar's office at Goa tomorrow morning to seal the deal.'

Mani rose from his chair. 'That suits me. I can return to Bombay by the afternoon flight.'

Mark raised an eyebrow. 'Why leave so soon?'

'I've some urgent business to attend to. However, Mr Pestonji has total authority to function on my behalf. He will have full access to the funds I'm placing at his disposal for all the renovation projects. The work must be completed by the end of next month.'

The overbearing tone of his partner didn't please Mark. But money always talked the loudest. He suspected his word would carry less weight in times to come.

Mr Pestonji congratulated Mark. 'I've no doubt this partnership will flourish and last longer than you may have anticipated.'

Mark shook hands with Pestonji and then with Mani.

Mr Patel beamed.

Mani and Mr Patel moved to view the photographs displayed on the walls.

Seeing him alone, Mark cornered Pestonji. 'You never really came here to sell that painting, or for a holiday, did you?'

Pestonji pursed his lips. 'Not really. John would never have parted with it. I'd have been in great trouble if you had agreed to buy.'

'Then why the pretence?'

'You'll appreciate that a certain amount of groundwork is required before taking big decisions.'

'I still don't understand the need for all the secrecy around Mr Abraham. It wouldn't have made any difference.'

'You never know.'

'And Mr Patel didn't come for a holiday either.'

Pestonji nodded. 'As I said, discretion was necessary to assess the overall situation. After all, a lot of money is involved.'

Mark padded across to Mani, who stood in front of a large photograph. 'This is one of our hunting photographs dating back to my father's time.'

'Are you the young boy in the knickers?' Mani asked.

'Yes, that's me.'

'I see. Hunting seems to have been a family passion.'

'Not anymore.'

'Perhaps some other sport engages your attention these days.' Mani commented obliquely.

Mark didn't quite know what Mani meant, but he smiled inwardly. True, he didn't hunt for animals anymore. Women with beauty and money were his consuming passion. Mark then asked Mani the one question that intrigued him. 'Mr Abraham, I'm curious to know how you became interested in the resort.'

'I'd much prefer if you call me John. As for your question, I find this place ideal to pursue my interests. I hate the hustle and bustle of Bombay.' He sauntered across to the window and gazed at the cottage that had, until moments ago, belonged to Mark. 'Besides, I'm captivated by your cottage atop that hillock. It is simply breathtaking. I can't imagine a better place to live in. I would love to paint in the midst of nature, with a magnificent view of the ocean.'

'And for that you are willing to move us out of our home?'

'Well... Mr Braganza, I...'

'Please, call me Mark.'

'All right, Mark, I'm truly sorry for the inconvenience. But please go ahead and modify the two cottages according to your taste. I do not wish to disappoint Mrs Braganza.'

Mark pulled out a cigar box from his coat pocket and offered one to John, who declined. 'I'm afraid you've already done that.' He tapped the business-end of the cigar on the box and lit it with a lighter.

Mani shrugged. 'I think I've made a fair offer.'

'Mrs Braganza isn't too pleased with it.'

'I'm ready to call off the deal,' Mani said, 'if it so displeases Mrs Braganza.'

Mark nervously ran his other hand through his hair. 'No, no, I didn't mean it that way. I don't think we should bother too much about women. There're other ways to please them.'

Mani shifted his gaze towards the cottage. 'It's easier said than done. There are some who are difficult to please, even if you lay down your life for them.'

❧

It took more than an hour, and a few bribes, to rouse the lazy staff at the Registry to get things moving. The Registrar, a pot-bellied Goan, reeking of feni, finally showed up at noon. By the time the formalities were over, Mani had missed his flight and had to return to the resort.

Pestonji and Mani went for a walk on the beach in the evening. Later, they enjoyed the bird's eye view of the premises from the terrace. The photographs hadn't prepared Mani for how breathtaking it all was.

Mani gazed at the verdant forest that surrounded the resort. 'It's awesome,' he uttered quietly. The sun had already set, turning the whole sky into an artist's palette of myriad colours. A narrow road cut through the forest like a thin ribbon and disappeared into the distant horizon. He gazed at the picturesque cottage and longed to see Grace move out of it. He sat on the wrought-iron bench under the bougainvillea canopy and took in the magnificent landscape that lay before him—an ideal subject for his next painting.

Pestonji sat down next to Mani. 'Now that you've got what you wanted, what next?'

Mani watched a flock of birds flying high in the sky in the typical V-formation and reflected how it could be a symbol of victory. But the real victory was still far away. 'This is just the beginning.'

'And a very expensive one.'

'I want that woman to suffer...silently but surely, with no shoulder to cry upon.'

'Revenge is not the best way to seek redress. Reconciliation is a better recourse to find peace.'

'You expect me to reconcile with a woman who literally buried me alive, leaving me for dead? I want her to feel that pain with every single breath of her life.'

'Revenge may cause more pain to you than you realise.'

'I was consumed by passion, a passion that has now turned into hatred. Having come this far, I'm not going to walk away and forget the whole thing.'

'I admit you suffered, but not entirely due to Grace. You suffered because you did something wrong to escape from reality. And I believe that, eventually, Grace will suffer too, with or without your intervention. Some way or another, we all pay for our sins, like you paid by losing your identity and everything else with it.'

'I promise I won't harm her physically. She deserves more than just physical pain.'

Pestonji furrowed his eyebrows. 'Don't tell me you've no feelings left for her?'

'To be honest, I do, but they are buried under layers of hatred.'

Pestonji shook his head. 'I wonder how this is going to end.'

Mani opened his mouth to respond, but the sound of approaching footsteps distracted them.

Mark appeared on the terrace. 'Ah, there you are. Sorry to interrupt you. I wondered where the two of you had disappeared to.'

'We're enjoying the view from the top,' Pestonji said.

Mani faced Mark. 'Indeed, it looks incredibly beautiful from here. I like the expansive feeling.'

'Grace had once suggested putting up a bar in that corner.'

'That's a brilliant idea,' Mani said. 'I'm sure we'll make good use of Mrs Braganza's talents and rich tastes.'

'Actually I came to ask if you would like to dine with me.'

'Thank you, but not tonight. I would rather have a quiet dinner with Mr Pestonji and retire early.'

'We can wind up early if you so desire.'

'I need to sort out a few things with Mr Pestonji before I leave.'

'Of course. See you in the morning then. Enjoy yourselves.'

Once back in his suite, Mani disclosed his marriage plans.

Pestonji's eyes widened in surprise. 'Congratulations! That's great news. Who's the lucky girl?'

'You'll have to come to Silvassa to meet her.'

'Of course, I would love to. Have you fixed the date?'

'I'll let you know soon. I wish to have the wedding reception here and combine that with the re-opening of the resort.'

'I'll go along with this plan if that's what you want, but I do expect some fireworks.'

'I'm afraid you'll have to take care of everything. Invitation cards, publicity, the works. And please make sure the Braganzas move out of the cottage by then, or else they will have to move into one of the rooms.'

'I'll take care of that. But I'm worried about you, John. What if the law catches up with you?'

Mani walked to the window and gazed at the horizon. 'Flight Lieutenant Mani Shankar Varadharajan lies buried in Kkd and long forgotten by now. John Abraham is a different entity.'

'I think I'd better pull some strings to get you the necessary papers, before you get into any trouble with the law.'

'I trust you'll do what's best for me.'

Pestonji rose and paced the floor. 'What if Grace goes to the police to spite you?'

Mani smiled. 'You're forgetting she was my partner-in-crime. Do you think she has the nerve to spend even a single night behind bars?'

Pestonji didn't respond.

'Not even in her worst nightmare,' Mani answered his own

question. 'She'd rather jump into a well. As for me, I can endure it.'

'Perhaps you can, but what happens to the girl you wish to marry? Does she know?'

'I told Tanya I'm not John Abraham, but she refused to hear anything about the other me that didn't exist for her. I confessed to her that I've done wrong in the past, but she isn't ready to listen beyond that and says she's prepared to face what comes.'

'I don't think you're being fair to her.'

'I'm prepared to bare it all, provided she's ready to listen. I tried. She says she wants nothing to do with my past. So what can I do? I wouldn't mind at all if you told her everything.'

'She must be one hell of a girl or blindly in love with you. Now, I don't know whether to call you John or Mani!'

'I killed Mani long ago. I am John Abraham and will remain so for the rest of my life.'

'It is difficult to understand how you can harbour so much hatred for someone you once loved.'

'You cannot imagine the agony of being deserted by the only person I risked my life for. It felt like my insides were being eaten up by ants, little by little, day after day. That's exactly how I want Grace to feel.'

'I dread to imagine how Grace is going to take all this.'

'Grace not only ditched me, but also her parents. They have no clue about her whereabouts, their only daughter. I feel so sad for them.'

Pestonji was shocked. 'You mean they don't know?'

'They don't know whether she's alive or dead. But they do know about how she ran away with all the money and disappeared without a trace after dumping me into my grave.'

'How sad.'

Mani let out a deep breath. 'Destiny brought me to Grace

not out of love, but lust. I discovered the difference when I met Tanya.' He raised his fist in the air. 'But Grace's destiny is now in my hands. I would rather see her employed as a maid, scrubbing the toilets, instead of decorating the Reception.'

24

Within days, two dozen workers arrived at the resort. Work began round the clock, in double shifts. Not to be left out of the loop, Grace gave her own directions, often changing her mind, confusing the workers. And she constantly sulked and complained about everything.

Pestonji privately instructed the contractor to ignore her and get on with the job to complete the project in time. To keep her occupied, he assigned Grace the responsibility of furnishing the resort, hoping it would keep her away from the work areas. He cautioned Mark to keep a watch on the budget.

When Grace brought back the first supplies of curtain material and a couple of rugs, Pestonji complimented her. 'You've excellent taste, Mrs Braganza. These will be wonderful in the lounge.'

'They're not for the lounge, Mr Pestonji,' she smirked. 'These are for our cottage.'

Pestonji swallowed hard and wondered if the woman intended to cover all the walls in her new home with drapes. 'You mean the whole lot?'

Grace looked him in the eye. 'Do you mind?'

Pestonji realised humour was not part of the agenda. The lady meant business. He also realised that the earlier she was divested of marketing responsibilities, the better. He turned to Mark for his reaction.

Mark recoiled. 'For heaven's sake, Grace, we don't need a truck load of supplies for just three rooms. Besides, what's wrong with our old curtains and carpets?'

'They won't fit,' she said. 'And it would be too rude to leave the house bare for Mr Abraham.'

'Come on, Grace, let's not—'

'You leave this to me,' she snapped. 'I know what I'm doing.'

'You've gone nuts.'

'It's all right, Mark,' Pestonji intervened. 'Let Mrs Braganza have it her way.'

Grace sneered. 'Thank you very much.'

A few days later, as Grace sat browsing through a fashion magazine, Mark came up to her. 'The tailors have messed up the curtains. I suggest you attend to them before they do any further damage?'

Grace continued flipping through the magazine, not looking up as she asked, 'What happened?'

'They've used the wrong material for the dining hall. And now we're running short for the rooms. You should've spent more time with them yesterday, instead of lazing around.'

'Excuse me?' Grace put down her magazine. 'You better mind your own business.'

'It's time you minded yours. Or take a break to visit your folks, if you have any.'

Grace glared at Mark. 'What's that supposed to mean?'

'I'm not speaking Greek.'

Blood rushed to her cheeks, but she kept quiet.

Just then, Pestonji came in. 'Ah Grace, there you are! I hope you've made some selections for the lounge because...,' He didn't get the chance to finish.

'No, I didn't have the time.' Grace raised her chin.

Pestonji gaped at her. Holy cow! Didn't have the time? The bloody woman had already made two extended trips to town, and she didn't have the time? An immediate change in the strategy was needed.

'I think we should give you a break and do the rest of the shopping ourselves.'

Grace's face flushed. She stomped out of the room without uttering a word.

Mark sighed. 'I'm sorry, Mr Pestonji. Grace is too damn upset these days.'

Pestonji refrained from commenting but made sure Grace never went shopping unsupervised.

❧

Despite these teething troubles, the renovation work proceeded on schedule and all the cottages and rooms were refurbished. Some of Mani's paintings decorated the walls, *Lovers' Rock* taking the prime position in the lounge. Four additional cottages were built at the rear. Paradise Resort was transformed on time.

Pestonji surveyed the progress with satisfaction. 'I think it's time to invite John.'

Mark nodded. 'I'm sure he'll be pleased. The place has returned to its original glory.'

'I hope Mrs Braganza is satisfied with your new home.'

Mark sighed, 'She's not complaining much.'

'It's come out quite well as I noticed.'

Mark hesitated and rubbed his chin. 'Not quite, but a lakh-plus in the bank feels better.'

Pestonji chuckled. 'Now we've got to furnish the cottage for John and his bride.'

'Yes, of course.'

The following day, Pestonji rang up Mani and informed him of the progress. He advised him to come over.

'Have the Braganzas moved out of the cottage?' Mani asked.

'Yes, they have. So when should we expect you?'

'By this weekend.'

'We're doing up your cottage now. It should be ready before you arrive.'

'Keep it simple.'

That evening, Pestonji found Grace sitting glumly in the lounge, lost in thought, gazing at *Lovers' Rock*. He came and stood behind her. The whiff of her scent reminded him of his childhood when heavenly-scented ladies dressed in their georgettes constantly hovered around his rich and flamboyant uncle. He was then too young to understand their games but old enough to delight in being smothered in their perfumed embraces.

'Isn't that beautiful?' he said.

Grace gasped and turned around. 'You startled me.'

'Sorry, I didn't mean to. May I join you?'

Pestonji didn't wait for her sanction and sat down on a chair. 'I hope you're comfortable in your new home?'

She snorted. 'As if that matters to you?'

'I would be the last person to see you unhappy,' Pestonji kept his voice civil. 'Please feel free to ask if you need anything.'

'Thank you for your concern.'

'We're doing up the cottage for John and his wife. I'm wondering if you could give us some of your brilliant ideas.'

Grace paled visibly. 'Don't play games with me, Mr Pestonji.'

He cleared his throat. 'You don't seem in a good mood.'

She didn't respond and turned back to the painting.

Pestonji admired the picture she presented with her youthful figure and long tresses falling freely over her shoulders. Despite the permanent frown Grace wore, she still looked stunning. No wonder John risked his life for the deadly woman.

'John Abraham is arriving this weekend.'

'So I hear.' A hint of a smile appeared at the corner of her mouth. 'By the way, who's the lucky dame?'

'Sorry?'

'The female your master is marrying.'

The venom in her voice didn't escape Pestonji's notice. He let it go. There was ample time to deflate her ego.

'John is not a master, but a good friend. And he's gone past the age of getting infatuated with "dames" as you put it.'

'I'm curious, nonetheless, to know who this female is.'

'I haven't met the lady yet. But I can tell she truly loves John Abraham for his qualities as a human being, not for his money or fame. There's no dearth of *dames* throwing their charms at John, but he has no time for such bimbos.' He glanced pointedly at her tapered calves and smooth legs.

Grace pulled her skirt down a couple of inches, giving him an eyeful of her cleavage and folded her arms across her chest.

'I'm sure they'll be thrilled living in that lovely cottage up on the hill.' Pestonji ignored the provocation.

Grace crossed her legs. 'I hope she knows what she's getting into. She better be prepared for some surprises.'

'Like what?'

A sinister smile split her face. 'You'll see.'

'On the contrary, there might be more surprises for you than anybody else.'

'What do you mean?'

Pestonji grinned. 'You'll see.'

Grace rose from her chair and walked away with a sensual swagger, affecting a confidence she didn't feel.

ぁ

Mani arrived in his red Chevy, its boot packed with paintings. Pestonji and Mark escorted him to his new home.

Mani's eyes brightened as he entered the living room. 'I'm impressed.'

'You should thank Mark. He's been very helpful in doing up the place.'

'Thank you, Mark. I look forward to your support in every way.'

'Sure, any time.'

Mani walked to the picture window and admired the view. 'I'm sure Tanya would be delighted.'

'Would you like to take a round of the premises?' Pestonji asked.

'Let's do it tomorrow morning. I'm too tired right now. Besides, it's getting dark.'

After Mark left, Mani inquired about Grace. 'How did she take it?'

'She's still fuming, like her car, but a trifle less lately. Made a lot of noise in the beginning, created quite a ruckus with the workers, but she seems to have run out of steam.'

'And Mark?'

'Money is more important to Mark than anything else, including Grace. He seems reconciled to the situation and has, surprisingly, been very cooperative.'

'I'm glad to hear that.'

Taking stock of the finances over dinner, they retired for the night.

The next morning, Pestonji and Mark escorted Mani on an extended tour of the property. Mani was pleased. 'You people have done a marvellous job,' he said, as they returned to the lounge. 'I'm sure our guests will be happy.'

'I've already sent feelers to travel agents abroad,' Mark said. 'I'm sure of getting some group bookings.'

Pestonji faced Mani. 'When do you think we should announce the opening?'

'Give me another day or two to decide, if it's okay with you?'

'We'll need time to organise the show,' Mark said.

Business took up most of the leisurely breakfast that followed. Pestonji looked at his watch and then at Mark. 'Oh, it's almost lunch time. Mrs Braganza will be annoyed with us for having kept you for so long.'

❧

Pestonji and Mani went for a long stroll on the beach and admired the rapidly changing colours of the horizon as the sun prepared to sink into the Arabian Sea.

Mani gazed at the sky washed in various hues of orange, pink and blue. 'I've fixed the wedding date tentatively for the eighteenth.'

'That's great.'

'I plan to leave here soon, and would like you to accompany me to Silvassa. I hope that's all right with you?'

'Of course, I'd love that.'

'After the wedding, Tanya and I plan to visit Lonavala for a couple of days before returning in time for the opening.'

Pestonji jumped. 'Ah, I know a nice place to stay in Lonavala—Cactus Villa—run by a distant aunt of mine. I'm sure you'll love it.'

Mani raised an eyebrow. 'Cactus Villa? That's an interesting name.'

'Aw, well, it's a long story. I haven't spoken to her in ages, but I'll book it for you if you like.'

'I'd like that very much, thank you.'

'We could plan the reception on the twenty-fourth, which is a Saturday. It would be convenient for our overnight guests.'

'That suits me fine. I would be grateful if you and Mark took care of all the arrangements.'

'We will.'

Neither spoke for a while as they stopped to watch the surf continually, untiringly, pounding the rocks.

'Grace seems to have gone underground,' Pestonji broke the silence. 'I'm wondering what the face-off will be like when you two finally meet each other.'

Mani's mouth puckered as though he'd bitten into a sour grape. 'If we get within close range, things might turn nasty. I'd prefer it if she remains in hiding for some more time.'

'How long can either of you postpone the inevitable?'

'I intend to keep away from her to prolong her agony.'

Pestonji picked up a shell from the sands and pocketed it. 'So the lady gets what she deserves.'

They resumed walking and covered quite a distance before they came upon a cluster of large rocks huddled under dense trees.

Mani took a deep breath, enjoying the scent of the forest mixed with the salty tinge of the sea. 'This should be a nice place to set up my studio.'

'But it does rain often?'

Mani surveyed the area and discovered an ideal spot that was sheltered by a huge rock where he could park his equipment safely. 'That shelter should work even in rains.'

When it became dark, they returned to their rooms. As Mani came out into the verandah after his dinner, he noticed a figure in white sitting on a bench in the backyard of what Pestonji had told him was Mark's new home. It was Grace—she always liked to wear white at night. He strode over to the edge of the verandah to get a clearer view. It was indeed Grace, a figure of grief—a marble statue washed by the moonlight.

25

As she came out of her house the next day, Grace watched Mani heading towards the beach carrying a sling bag, a canvas and an umbrella tucked under his arm. It was time to come out of hiding. The devil had arrived and she needed to sharpen her claws to saw off his horns. She composed herself and went to join Pestonji and Mark.

Dressed in white bell-bottoms and a sky-blue sleeveless blouse with the top button undone, Grace sneaked into the lounge and approached the duo bent over a stack of paintings.

'Ah, there you are,' Pestonji said as soon as he caught her scent. 'We could use your help. John has left these paintings. You might like to suggest where to display them.'

She scoffed. 'As if my views matter.'

'Of course they do.'

Grace glanced through the paintings as if they were a stack of trash. Given the choice, she would've liked to dump them all into the Arabian Sea. She turned up her nose. 'I think some of them could fit into the staircase, or maybe in the bathrooms to add some colour.'

'Are you out of your mind?' Mark snapped. 'These are not some ordinary posters! John Abraham has been more than generous to spare them for the resort, instead of selling them for huge sums of money.'

Grace twisted her lips awkwardly. 'You asked for my opinion. Take it or leave it.'

Pestonji swallowed hard. 'That's it?'

'That's it,' she repeated, without blinking an eye.

'In that case, you better take care of the plumbers. They've yet to fix the leaks in the Gent's washroom.'

Mark didn't utter a word. She hadn't expected him to. 'I care a damn about the Gent's washroom.' She stomped out and returned to her cottage.

Grace poured herself a stiff one to calm her nerves that evening and settled into a corner of the empty lounge, once again gazing at *Lovers' Rock* and contemplating the havoc it had wreaked in her life. Mani had captured the scene masterfully. The blighter seemed to have improved a lot since those early days. Grace felt sorry for herself. She desperately needed a life buoy. She wondered how she could corner Mani, who had been avoiding her ever since that fateful night.

Mani appeared in the hall just after Grace downed her second whisky. She tensed, preparing to confront him. But Mani didn't even glance in her direction as he disappeared into the bar. This was clearly not the right time. She had to catch him alone. Thwarted, Grace returned to her cottage. It was a relief that Mark had not yet returned from wherever he was, not that she cared anymore. She ate her dinner and retired for the night.

The next day, on her way to the Reception, Grace noticed Mani and Pestonji sitting under a tree in the garden. She sauntered into Mark's office and dropped into a chair. He didn't even raise his head from the papers on his desk, as if engrossed in serious matters of the state.

She waited for a minute, then asked, 'What's keeping you so damned occupied?'

'Do you mind?' he said, without lifting his head.

'As a matter of fact, I do.'

He looked up. 'What do you expect me to do, get up from my chair and lay down a red carpet for you?'

'At least you could lift your empty head.'

'And do what?' he smirked, 'Admire your boobs?'

Grace clenched her fists on the arm rests. 'What's troubling you?'

'I should address the same question to you.'

She furrowed her brows. 'I'm wondering how swiftly you've been taken in by these moneybags. You don't even care how much it upsets me each time I see these jokers.'

'I don't understand what your problem is, Grace. Can't you be a little more cooperative instead of sulking and complaining all the time?'

Grace frowned. 'I'm not going to be a pawn in their hands like you are.'

'Come on, woman, we've got to work as a team, for heaven's sake. No use throwing tantrums all the time. These people are staying, and you better…' He trailed off when Pestonji appeared at the door.

Grace straightened up.

'Sorry, am I interrupting something?' Pestonji asked.

'No, no, please come in,' said Mark. 'We were just discussing the weather.'

Pestonji pulled up a chair and sat down. 'It is a lovely day.'

An involuntary smile curled Grace's lips. 'I'm tempted to go on a long drive along the beach, preferably in the red convertible.'

'You're most welcome,' Pestonji said. 'I don't think John would mind lending the car to you.'

Grace would've loved to take the Chevy and smash the damn

thing into the nearest rock or, better still, push it into the sea. The thought of Mani and his bride driving in that beauty made her nauseous. All Mani had given her at Kkd was that good for nothing rattle-trap, the bloody Standard Herald. How she missed her black Mercedes! She could see the Chevy parked where the black Merc once stood. A lump formed in her throat as she declined Pestonji's offer with a flippant wave of her hand.

Pestonji placed a sample card on the table. 'John wants us to check this invitation card. He wants to use it for both the resort's opening and his reception.'

Mark studied the card. The front carried a picture of *Lovers' Rock*. He turned the page to read the content inside and went back again to the front page. 'I like this.'

'How about you, Mrs Braganza?'

Grace took one look at the card and pushed it back on the table. 'I don't think my views matter, but if you want a frank opinion, this is a vulgar display of vanity. You might as well put a picture of Mr Abraham and his mate on the card.'

Her suggestion laced with sarcasm brought a flush of colour to Pestonji's cheeks. After an uneasy pause, he cleared his throat and muttered, 'She has a point, Mark. We should think of something better.'

'I'm inclined to agree with John's choice.' Mark said. 'This is quite an original idea.'

Grace knew that Mark's 'inclination' had more to do with being on the right side of the boss. He never failed to agree with Mani or Pestonji. She despised him for his subservience, but it was better than having an assertive Mark—when it came to her long-term plan.

Pestonji leant back in his chair. 'We would certainly like your suggestions, Mrs Braganza.'

'Why should I bother when the three of you have all the bright ideas?'

'I'm sorry you feel that way,' Pestonji said. 'But let's put our heads together and think of something appropriate.'

'I'd rather have a picture of the resort on the cover,' Grace said. 'And a simple message inside to announce the opening and whatever.'

Pestonji peered at Mark. 'What do you say?'

'Better ask John.'

Pestonji rose from his chair. 'I think we should give this matter more thought before going to the printers.'

After Pestonji left the office, Mark lit a cigarette.

'You amaze me,' said Grace scornfully. 'You conduct yourself as if they are our masters, not partners.'

'I'm trying to cooperate and I expect you to do the same.'

Grace threw her hands in the air. 'You're a gone case.'

'That applies more to you than me. You're still living in a fool's paradise.'

'Yes, indeed. I didn't know that a *fool* presided over this paradise—until now.'

Mark's face contorted. 'Why don't you move your ass out of my office and do something useful for a change?'

Rising from her chair, Grace offered a thin smile. 'I will, Mark Braganza. But it won't be long before they kick your ass out of this office.' She didn't wait for his reaction. She whirled around and, nose in the air, strutted out of the room.

❧

A slight drizzle greeted Grace when she woke up in the morning and peeped out the rear window. Morning fog covered the cottage that had been her home until recently. She sighed deeply as she recalled the hours she spent in her verandah, admiring the magnificent view and enjoying the soft breeze laced with the scents of the forest. What she smelt now was the paint that had not fully dried.

Seconds later, a figure emerged from the cottage, holding an umbrella. It was Mani. Her eyes followed him until he disappeared from her vision. She went to the west-side window and saw the umbrella moving southward. This was a good opportunity. She quickly changed into her jeans and a top and decided to pursue.

Mark was at the breakfast table.

'I'm going for a swim,' she said, putting on a raincoat.

'Aren't you having breakfast?'

'Later.'

'It might rain.'

'Don't worry, I won't drown. I may not be a great swimmer like Irene was, but I know how to guard myself.'

Mark dug his fork into the sausage. 'Don't be so sure.' She stopped at the door. 'As if you care.'

Grace scampered after the lone figure that was moving towards the rocks. Keeping a safe distance, she raised her hood over her head and followed him discreetly until he disappeared behind the rocks. She climbed atop a mound and spotted him sitting in a cave like feature, gazing at the sea.

The clouds opened up and she took cover under a tree.

Mani now sat in front of a canvas. The man had already set up a studio. Grace shivered as the wind became strong. One look at the swelling waves told her this was not her day. Having seen Mani's retreat in the jungle, she returned home, vowing to visit the place again.

'Pestonji and I are going to Goa,' Mark said, as Grace removed her raincoat. 'Got to see the printers, do some shopping and meet a whole lot of people. We'll be spending the night at DeCosta's.'

'When will you be back?' she asked, drying her hair with a towel.

'By tomorrow evening, I guess.'

Grace couldn't have hoped for better news. By late afternoon, the rain clouds were gone. Mani hadn't shown up the whole day. When darkness fell, Grace changed into a green dress, Mani's favourite colour, and made her way to the deserted lounge. She ordered wine and browsed through old issues of magazines, waiting for her opportunity.

Half an hour later, Mani appeared and went straight into the bar. She froze in her chair and knew she would have to make the first move. Minutes later, she noticed him going up the stairs that led to the terrace with a drink in his hand. This was her chance. She gulped down her wine and followed him.

Strong winds greeted her as she stepped onto the terrace. Leaning on the parapet, Mani stood gazing at the horizon. The surf crashing on the rocks matched the turmoil in her heart. The wind blew strands of hair across her face as she stepped closer. For several seconds, she stood behind Mani.

'I'm sorry, Shanks,' she mumbled, with all the sadness she could feign. 'Please forgive me.'

Mani turned, his mouth open.

Grace tried to engage his eyes, but they were on her figure, each curve visible as her dress was moulded to her body on that windy terrace. And who but Grace Wilson knew that look on his face. She smiled—a smile that had melted him way back at the railway club—and hoped it would do the same again.

Alas, Mani turned away, without uttering a word.

She swallowed hard but recovered quickly. 'I'm glad you made it big.'

Mani lit a cigarette. Grace took a step forward and stopped just short of touching his shoulder with her hand. 'I know you must be very angry with me...for what I've done to you in my weaker moments,' she muttered, her voice cracking. 'But I'm prepared to do anything...to make it up to you.'

'Like what?'

'Anything in the world,' she replied promptly, '*anything*.'

Mani turned slowly and glared at her. 'You have some nerve, Mrs Braganza. Believe me, you've done me a great favour. And you will do another, if you leave me alone and get lost.' He crushed his cigarette under his foot and left her standing in a daze.

Grace Wilson had never been treated with such disdain. While she hadn't expected Mani to embrace her, the manner in which he rejected her left her trembling. She felt like the cigarette butt that just got crushed under his foot. Tears welled in her eyes. She slumped on the bench, feeling lost, but not defeated. She wiped her tears and resolved to confront the only man in her life who had the temerity to insult her on her own ground.

There were other ways to humble a man, especially Mani Shankar Varadharajan from Poddukkottai. She smiled to herself, a sinister smile, and vowed to draw out Mani from his cave, with his tongue hanging and pride between his legs.

26

Mani woke up to a clear day, a welcome change from the intermittent rain that had kept him from his canvas. In his total isolation, all he had done for the last few days was walk in the rain, breathe in the unmatched scents of the forest and enjoy the incredible beauty of nature. He looked forward to finishing the seascape he had been painting.

He collected his binoculars and reached the beach well before sunrise. The early morning breeze intoxicated him. The sloping hillocks to his left, and the verdant forest, elated his soul. It took him half an hour to reach his natural 'studio'.

He scanned the horizon through his binoculars. There was not a soul visible anywhere. Perhaps he was the first man to have set foot on this isolated patch of land. The spectacular view stimulated his creative juices. When the first rays of the sun filtered through the tall trees on the hillocks behind him, he set up his canvas and began to paint.

An hour later, he rose and studied his painting from a distance. It was turning out well, but he needed to work more on the rocks, always a challenge to capture the sharp features, the crevices and the contrasting tones. He removed his slippers and walked barefoot into the cool waves. He reflected on his brief encounter with Grace the previous night. The evil woman had some nerve to seek forgiveness!

But Grace still looked as ravishing as when he had first seen her at the Railway Club. The enticing image of her sheathed in the green dress that clung to her body danced in front of him.

It unnerved him that he could still desire the woman. No, Grace should get what she deserves he resolved. After splashing water with his feet for a while, he returned to his cave and worked on his canvas.

A while later, the distant sound of splashing distracted him. He lifted his head to peep over his canvas, but saw nothing. A big fish perhaps, or a shark. He hadn't heard of sharks in the region, but one never knew. He brushed off the thought and resumed scraping the paint off the edges of the rocks he had painted on his canvas—a technique he had discovered quite accidentally, with amazing results.

He heard the sound again, this time a little closer. He got up with a start and noticed a lone figure swimming in the distance. Who could that be? He looked through his binoculars. A mermaid-like figure, splashing in the surf, filled his lenses. As she emerged from the waters, Mani's heart pounded against his chest.

It was Grace!

He removed the binoculars and stood motionless, gawking at the advancing figure. This was one shark he had never expected to encounter in those waters. What in the hell was she up to? But now she was here, alone, and advancing towards him, in a skin-coloured bikini that left nothing to the imagination. The goddess stopped just a few feet from him, water running down her curves. She parted her lips and gave him a look that had melted his heart many a time before. Seeing her near naked after so many years sent the blood rushing through his whole body.

That man was not yet born who wouldn't desire to bed the heavenly beauty who stood before him. Eyes riveted on her youthful body, he was tempted to give in to his primal instincts. He wanted to drag her by her hair behind the rocks, pin her down on the sand and ravish her. It required a herculean effort for his mind to suppress his lust and for him to return to his senses.

Lips parted suggestively, Grace reached for the bikini straps at her back and started unfastening them, slowly. Mani's heart leapt into his throat as Grace let her top drop to the sands, revealing her pert, firm breasts, her hard nipples pointing at him, challenging his senses.

Holy shit. Mani couldn't take it anymore. 'Stop it, woman.' He forced cold steel into his voice. 'Take your act somewhere else.'

Grace stepped forward, breathing hard. 'Please forgive me, Shanks...I need you like never before,' she pleaded, stroking her thighs. 'We belong to each other...you know that.'

Mani turned his face away and struck out his hand as one does to ward off evil. 'Go away, you bitch!' he cried. His voice echoed in the rocks. 'You belong to no one but money—not me, not Mark, not even your parents. Even money has disowned you for good. God will never forgive you.'

'I'm s-sorry, Shanks...I...'

'And now you have the audacity to offer the only thing you're left with, your body, to pay for your sins?' He pointed a finger at her. 'Grace Wilson, you might as well hang yourself in a meat shop. There will be plenty of takers.'

Grace's face turned ugly, her lips quivered with anger. She folded her arms over her breasts and shouted back. 'Don't do this to me, Shanks, I warn you. I can crumble your empire in a minute.' Her expression changed dramatically from that of a purring cat to a snarling tigress ready to attack.

'Oh, really? Well, go ahead, call the police. It'll make sensational news. I would love to see you behind bars in the company of whores, scrubbing filthy toilets every single day with your own hands...and servicing the hungry guards by turns, every other night.'

Grace ground her teeth, her eyes blazing. 'Like hell, I will. You must be out of your mind to challenge me. I've done no wrong, Flight Lieutenant. It is you who has committed a crime, not me.'

'You have lost your grip on reality. No jury in the world would believe that you were not involved.'

Grace bent down to pick up her bikini top.

Mani went on, 'Woman, you not only ditched me, but abandoned your parents so brazenly and ran off with all the money. You cannot escape the long, painful tenure in prison if you ever open your mouth.'

Grace glared. 'Don't threaten me. Or you'll rot behind bars for life.'

'No, I won't. You should know by now that I can rough it out, like I did after you ditched me. I'll get out of prison earlier than you would like to believe. And you, Mrs Grace Braganza, will come out mercilessly bruised and scarred for the rest of your life, with nobody out there to engage you even as a maid.'

Grace shook with mounting rage. ' How dare you…you son of a—'

'Or maybe the inmates might provide you shelter out of pity, in one of those whorehouses to rot forever. Go call the police. I won't stop you.'

Grace froze. Having her merchandise slighted, she threw a steely glance at her tormentor. 'I'll see you in the courts.'

'Any time you say.'

Grace walked away, her legs wobbling.

Mani gazed at her receding figure with pity. He wondered if she would do something stupid to harm herself. One couldn't be sure of what she might do in her fury and desperation. Mani didn't wish to jeopardise his second shot at life, at any cost. He had sinned once, and he could sin again… if required.

27

A week later, Mani and Pestonji drove to Bombay and after a night halt, on to Silvassa. Bombay never seemed to end. Its boundaries spread in all directions. It took them almost two hours to hit the countryside.

Mani didn't wish to tell Pestonji about how Grace had employed her tactics to make peace with him. He didn't think she would dare open her mouth. After all, she had nothing to gain and much to lose. Brushing aside her threats, he looked forward to starting his new life with Tanya.

'John, you haven't told me anything about Tanya,' Pestonji reminded him.

'Tanya is simple, understanding and a down to earth soul who will make a good home. She has no pretensions whatsoever, and knows nothing about my involvement in Paradise Resort.'

Pestonji raised an eyebrow. 'You haven't told her?'

'No. I want to surprise her.'

'Some surprise! I dread to imagine how many more await her.'

'She doesn't even know where we're going to live after we're married.'

Pestonji was puzzled. 'You mean she hasn't even asked?'

'She knows I live in a cozy little balcony with a view, thanks to a kind-hearted man who goes by the name of Feroze Pestonji.'

Pestonji chuckled. 'Come on, John, that balcony will always be yours, even if you start living in that dream cottage.'

Mani nodded. 'It would be our second home.'

'You're welcome.'

Mani negotiated a curve at high speed and, suddenly noticing a herd of sheep ahead, he had to slam down hard on the brakes.

Pestonji gasped, as the car came to a stop. 'That was close.'

Mani honked a few times. The shepherd took his own time to give way as if doing them a great favour, but not before throwing a dirty look at them. Mani cursed and floored the accelerator as soon as the road cleared. The car lurched forward.

Pestonji admonished Mani. 'You aren't flying an aircraft, are you?'

'I wish I were.' Mani's thoughts strayed back to his days at Kkd. The thrill of flying the sleek Hunters, the exciting dog fights, the crew-room banter and the wild parties in the officers' mess—all gone with one disastrous move he made for the lure of a pair of legs. The near-death experience sent a shiver down his spine. He thanked God for saving him, and for bringing Aunt Jane, Tanya and Pestonji into his life.

Neither spoke for a while. Mani stopped at a road-side stall to buy cigarettes. He noticed a heavy build up of clouds on the distant horizon. Expecting rain, he raised the canvas hood of the car. Silvassa lay another fifty miles ahead. He wanted to reach before dark.

'I wonder how Grace is going to cope with the situation,' Pestonji remarked once they resumed their journey.

Mani eased the accelerator and rested his elbow on the edge of the window. 'I get a nagging feeling that Grace is not going to last long in her position. She's too proud a woman to put up with humiliation and is capable of surprises.' He shifted gears and let the car glide down a long slope.

Pestonji shook his head. 'I pity her, but then she's herself responsible for her predicament.'

'She'll give up sooner than we realise.'

Pestonji pursed his lips. 'I wonder if she is left with any choice.'

'She is left with a good pair of legs that can take her places. She might even ditch Mark and run away with some other joker with a fat pocket.'

'I hate to hear you speaking like that. After all, she was once your wife.'

'She was not worthy of being my wife and deserves no respect. She was a false delusion that consumed me, body and soul.'

'I hope Tanya, with her experience, would like to take an active part in running the show at Paradise Resort.'

'Absolutely. I've no doubt she would be delighted.'

It started to rain. Mani raised the windows and further reduced their speed.

'What if Grace decides to tell all?' Pestonji cautioned.

'Grace would never risk going to prison.'

'I wouldn't be so sure if I were you.'

'I know Grace better than you do.'

'Perhaps not.'

Mani threw a questioning glance at his companion.

'If you had known her, you wouldn't have ditched your aircraft in the sea.'

Mani didn't have the answer for that one.

They arrived at the resort in pouring rain. Tanya greeted them at the reception desk. Her eyes sparkled and her cheeks turned pink.

Dressed in simple salwar-kameez, she presented a startling contrast to the sexy siren they'd left behind.

'I'm so pleased to meet you,' Pestonji said, when introduced.

'Me too,' she said, escorting them to the far end of the verandah.

'I didn't know John was hiding a precious jewel in Silvassa,' Pestonji remarked as they settled into the cane chairs.

'You embarrass me, sir.'

'Not at all; I know when I see one.'

Tanya blushed.

'John should know better, because not too long ago I saw one in him.'

Mani tilted his head. 'Don't believe him. He picked up a piece of broken glass from the street and sold it to unsuspecting buyers as a diamond.'

Tanya chuckled. 'I don't know about that, but he's certainly mistaken about me.'

Pestonji smiled. 'I usually never err in my judgment.'

Tanya thought for a moment and gazed at Pestonji. 'I'm just an ordinary shell John picked up from the shores of Daman.'

'Perhaps a shell that houses a pearl in its core,' Pestonji retorted.

Tanya lowered her eyes. 'I've nothing in the core but gratitude for God to have brought so much happiness into my life.'

Pestonji tossed a glance at Mani. 'God always rewards the virtuous. I'm sure John would be very lucky to have you in his life.'

Mani shuffled in his chair. 'I don't think I qualify for God's favours, but to have Tanya in my life is the biggest reward I can dream of, despite all the wrongs I've done in my life.'

Tanya gazed into Mani's eyes. 'We should leave the wrongs and rights in the hands of God.'

Mani leant forward in his chair. 'Perhaps Pestonji should tell you more about me than you care to know.'

'I'd rather listen to my own voice.'

Pestonji was visibly moved. 'I admire you, young lady, for your unflinching trust in this man. He may have done wrong in the past, but he's done right in choosing you as his partner in life.'

Tanya lowered her eyes.

'However,' Pestonji continued after a pause, 'it is better to know the facts before one ties the knot, rather than postponing the truth.'

'I tied the knot with him long before he ever cared to know,' she said. 'And I'm not going to untie that even if he did something wrong in the past. The present is more relevant to me than the past I choose not to know.'

Mani's eyes filled with pride. The contrast between the two women in his life was so glaring that he wondered how he came to love them at different times.

'You're gifted with noble thoughts,' Pestonji remarked. 'I'm enchanted.'

'Humble would be more appropriate to describe my thoughts,' she said. 'Nobility mainly resides in higher places.'

Impressed by her modesty and presence of mind, Pestonji found himself lost for words. He had known many a woman in 'higher places' who had lost their 'nobility' in the back seat of their limousines. And here was this small-town girl who displayed a wisdom not easily found behind velvet curtains.

'You amaze me, dear girl,' he said at length. 'But then, lotus blooms best in marshlands.'

'And so does cactus in the desert,' she said.

Mani too marvelled at the brilliance of her insightful rejoinders and wondered if he could ever match hers. He realised how hollow his first love was, if one could call it that, against the richness of his second.

Pestonji gazed at Tanya. 'You ought to have been a poet. I'm touched by the depth and purity of your thoughts.' He faced Mani, 'John, you're blessed, my friend. I hope you treasure this jewel through the rest of your life.'

Tanya and Mani opted for a brief wedding ceremony, devoid of any pomp and show. Only a handful of Aunt Jane's close relatives and Tanya's friends, including the staff at the resort, attended.

Aunt Jane couldn't control her tears when Mani led Tanya to his red Chevy decked with flowers. The small crowd cheered as they set course for their long journey to the pristine hills of Lonavala.

Pestonji returned to Goa to take charge of the last minute preparations. The morning after his arrival, he spotted Grace sitting alone at the far end of the garden.

He greeted her and sat on a chair across from her. The dark circles around her eyes suggested she hadn't been sleeping well.

'You don't look too well.'

No response.

'I'm sorry if this is not the best time, but I came to ask you for a favour. Here's a list of guests who are expected to stay for the night after the reception. I hope you don't mind taking charge of the allotments. Just make sure that those marked in red are accommodated in the deluxe rooms.'

Grace hesitated before picking up the list.

Pestonji looked on as she read the names.

Suddenly, her face turned white as if she had seen a ghost. The list trembled in her hand.

'Is there a problem?' he asked.

Grace didn't answer, her eyes riveted to the paper.

Pestonji rose and slipped away quietly without waiting for an answer.

❧

Grace couldn't believe her eyes when she read the whole list. A lump formed in her throat. She tried to get to her feet but couldn't. Her body felt like a mass of stone anchored to earth.

At the bottom of the list she found the names of Mr & Mrs Robert Wilson encircled in red. She balked at the prospect of meeting them.

The bloody man was determined to shame her and she couldn't do a thing about it! Mani's words, 'hang yourself in a meat shop', echoed in her mind and pierced her heart. And now this! Somehow, she dragged herself to her cottage, her legs heavy as lead. She dropped onto her bed and buried her face into the pillow.

For the first time in her life, Grace experienced a profound sense of guilt. She realised that in her mad pursuit of glamour, she had forgotten all about her roots and about those who mattered and cared for her. She felt like jumping into the nearest well to put an end to her misery.

Somehow, she gathered enough strength to confront Pestonji the next day. He was sitting in the lounge, alone, browsing through some papers.

'Mr Pestonji, may I ask you a question?'

'Yes, of course.'

Grace took a seat across from him. 'Do you mind telling me what you know about Mr and Mrs Wilson?'

Pestonji paused for a minute, prolonging her agony. The first dose had been effectively administered, and it was now time to inject some more. 'Not much, really, except that they are personal guests of John.'

'I see, and about me?'

'About you?'

'Yes, about me. And I hope you'll give me a straight answer.'

Pestonji smiled from the corner of his mouth. 'I'm afraid a straight answer might not please you.'

'Spit it out, I'm listening.'

'Are you sure you're ready for this?'

'What makes you think otherwise?'

Pestonji looked into her eyes. 'Very well, to give you a straight answer: what little I know of you is that God gifted you with enormous beauty, sculpted you with his own hands, but he went to sleep when your brain was being assembled.'

Grace gave him a steely stare. 'What's that supposed to mean?'

'I'm sorry to say this, but you won't understand. Because somewhere up there, your screws are loose,' he said, pointing to his head. 'Now if you will excuse me, I have work to do, and I suggest you do likewise.'

'Mr Pestonji, if your mother did not teach you manners, it's too bad for you. But let me make one thing clear right away: I'm not going to take any bullshit from a gutter-born like you. If you have any fancy notions, you bloody well get the hell out of here along with your master.' Grace was spitting fire like a steam engine negotiating a steep climb. 'And don't you ever dare speak to me like that again, or I'll have you thrown off the premises.'

Pestonji forced a grin. The audacious woman needed to be put in her place.

'You're asking for it, lady, and I have no desire to deny you the pleasure. Coming from your foul mouth, a sermon about manners sounds blasphemous. It confirms the little I've learnt about your past deeds.'

Grace shifted in her chair.

'My mother's teachings might not have been the best, but she never taught me to abandon or betray loved ones. The disgusting way in which you rewarded your mother for teaching you good manners should fetch you a gold medal in treachery.'

Her face red, Grace trembled with mounting rage.

Pestonji went on, 'As regards throwing us out of your premises, get your brain examined and recover whatever is left of it. You've lived in a fool's paradise far too long. It's time to face the realities of life.'

Her hate-filled stare did not flicker, but the message seemed to have gone home. The temptress lost all her sheen. Pestonji gathered his papers and walked away.

28

The drive through the verdant terrain lifted Tanya's mood as the red convertible raced towards Goa. Tall pines and cedar trees dotted the landscape and gaps in the tree cover presented occasional glimpses of the sea in the distance. Fresh from the misty meadows of Lonavala and brimming with joy, she wondered about the place John was driving her to.

She must have dozed off, for when she woke up next, the setting sun's reflection from the ocean dazzled her. She rubbed her eyes and gave John a smile.

'Another ten miles,' he said.

John had told her little, except that her new home would be on a beach, which was heartening since she always wanted to live near the ocean. 'Let it be a surprise,' he had said, and Tanya didn't pester him for more.

After negotiating numerous rough patches on the weather-beaten road, they arrived at Paradise Resort. She thought she was dreaming when the car stopped in the porch of a massive colonial building in the thick of a forest. Colourful creepers adorned the exterior walls and arched windows peeped out from behind the sweet-smelling climbers. Chirping birds greeted her as she stepped out of the car.

Pestonji handed her a bouquet of fresh flowers. 'Welcome home.'

She blushed. 'Thank you.'

'Did you enjoy the trip?'

'Yes, it was very exciting.' She noticed someone approaching from the other side of the car with a thin smile.

'Welcome to Paradise Resort, Mrs Abraham,' said the stranger with a polite bow.

John introduced him to Tanya. 'Meet Mr Braganza. He has been kind to offer me partnership in his resort.'

Tanya gaped at Mani and then at Pestonji. Partnership? Resort? She was confused. She stole a glance at the stranger in a maroon blazer who had a colourful scarf thrown around his neck. His piercing gaze made her uneasy.

'Pleased to meet you,' she said.

'I'm sorry my wife couldn't be here to welcome you; she's not been keeping well.'

'I hope she recovers in time,' John said, 'to receive our guests tomorrow evening.'

Pestonji and Mark escorted the couple into the lounge. Impressed by the opulence, Tanya nudged John. 'What is all this?'

'I've invested in this property and we are partners.'

While the men discussed the arrangements for the forthcoming event, Tanya's gaze travelled from one end of the hall to the other, taking it all in. She could hardly believe this was theirs. She left the men and walked across to view the pictures on display. A large painting on the opposite wall caught her eye. She moved closer and found John's signature at the bottom. Her thoughts strayed back to the day she had first discovered John's paintings scattered in the small room at Daman. John Abraham seemed to have come a long way since then.

'Like it?'

She turned and saw John standing behind her. 'This is

wonderful, John. When did you do this?'

'A couple of months ago.'

Tanya turned back to the painting.

'You see those rocks? Don't they look like lovers?' he asked.

'Oh, yes, they do.'

'I call it *Lovers' Rock*. This one is a favourite of mine.'

'You always underestimated the value of your art.'

'You may not like to believe it, but the opposite is closer to the truth.'

Mark approached them. 'Mrs Abraham, I must say your husband is being too modest. He's been very generous to spare so many of his priceless paintings to adorn the walls of the resort. I would've gone bankrupt if I were to buy them.'

Mani shrugged. 'The pleasure is mine. Sometimes I wonder why people pay so much for my work.'

'Your signature, John,' Mark responded. 'People would pay anything for a "John Abraham". I wouldn't be complaining if I were you.'

'I'm not complaining, Mark, just wondering.'

'I'm sure even if you put your signature on something trivial on a canvas, it will fetch a high price.'

'That, my friend, is the hallmark of a genius.' Pestonji butted in from the other end. 'But I can tell you John Abraham will never put his signature on some trash.'

Mark cleared his throat. 'I didn't mean it that way.'

'Perhaps not. Shall we have tea?'

After a while, Tanya slipped away onto the deck. The breathtaking view of the sunset enthralled her. Never in her life could she have imagined that her destiny would take such a wonderful turn. She was excited.

❧

Mark was not particularly impressed when he saw Tanya alight from the car in her crumpled sari and her hair in a mess. Not the kind of woman he would give a second glance. Nevertheless, he knew too well that many of the 'Plain-Janes' could be surprisingly hot in bed. Like Saira, the maid, who came to offer her services to run the household—and, occasionally, had extended her services to him when Irene visited her parents in Goa, which had been often.

Mark could use his charm on Tanya to get even with John Abraham and see the man leave his property forever. After all, despite the lure of money, having to vacate his beloved cottage had been humiliating. He had to move cautiously and wait for the right time. Judging from his past conquests, the small-town girl from Daman wouldn't be much of a challenge.

While Pestonji and John discussed the guest list, Mark followed Tanya to the deck. He paused by the door. Tanya's slender back, her exposed waist and rounded hips made him reconsider his first impression of her. The blazing red sari complimented her tanned, youthful skin, and defined her contours to her advantage. He moved closer to catch the scent of his prey. Tanya recoiled.

'I'm sorry. I didn't mean to startle you, Mrs Abraham.' Mark moved away and gazed at the horizon. 'I hope you like the view.'

'Yes, I do.'

'It's even more beautiful when viewed from the top.' Mark lit his cigar. 'Perhaps I should escort you to the terrace for you to enjoy the grand panorama.'

Tanya folded her hands across her chest without responding.

A subtle hint of uneasiness in her body language didn't escape his notice. Nine times out of ten, women would blush and follow him to the terrace, like puppies trailing a scent, but this girl from Daman happened to be the tenth. He knew the species from small towns were a different breed altogether— they hid more than they revealed. But when they did, they beat their cousins in their best silks and chiffons. He smiled to himself. The red sari, flapping in the wind, would soon be kissing the floor.

'And there on that hillock,' he pointed towards the cottage, 'is your new home.'

Tanya raised her hand to her mouth in awe. 'I don't believe it!'

From where she came, it must've been a wild dream thought Mark. 'I lived there all my life. And now it's yours.'

'What do you mean?'

'Your husband took a fancy to it.'

'I don't understand…'

'He paid for us to vacate,' Mark gazed into her eyes, 'I would've given it for free, if I had known it was for you.'

Tanya tilted her head in his direction. 'And why is that, may I ask?'

Mark blinked and offered a weak smile.

'Mr Braganza, I am not fully aware of the situation here, but I'd appreciate it very much if you shared your generosity with someone else.'

Mark liked women with gumption and a sharp tongue—the sharper the better. He changed his tone. 'Oh, I'm sorry; I didn't mean to offend you.'

'You just did,' she said and returned to the lounge.

Mark gazed at her receding posterior with a condescending smile. He always liked the excitement of a challenge and clearly saw one in that red sari. He took a long drag on his cigar and hurled it into the air.

❧

Mani rose from his chair as Tanya appeared at the door. 'Ah, there you are. What do you think of this place?'

'I'm overwhelmed.'

'Get ready to play an important role in running the show.'

'I would be pleased to do my bit.'

'I've no doubt you'll do more than your bit,' said Pestonji. 'That would allow John to concentrate on his painting.'

Nothing would have pleased Tanya more than taking an active part in the management of the resort. Her stint at Silvassa would come in handy. The brief encounter with Mark had ruffled her nerves, but she knew how to keep male chauvinist pigs and Lotharios at bay. She could've put him down brutally, but considering he was a partner, she didn't wish to start on a sour note.

Tanya was elated as she arrived at her new home with a beaming John. 'You didn't tell me anything about the resort.'

'I wanted to give you a surprise.'

'It's like a fairy tale…a dream…something I could've never imagined possible.' Tanya's eyes misted. 'I wonder if I deserved all this in my life.'

'On the contrary, I'm not sure if I deserve you…but I'll try to live up to your expectations, despite my inglorious past.'

'Please, don't mention your past again.'

After an express tour of the cottage, Tanya came to the large window in the living room and admired the delightful view of the ocean.

'Isn't this beautiful?' asked John, as he came up from behind.

They remained locked in each other's arms for a long time.

John was still asleep when Tanya woke up to the soothing sound of the surf. She wrapped herself in her dressing gown and strolled into the front verandah. She closed her eyes and said a prayer, thanking God for bestowing so much so soon in her life. When she opened her eyes, John stood in front of her, wrapped in a shawl.

'Isn't this heavenly?' He smiled.

'Absolutely… a dream I do not wish to end.'

'It won't, I promise.'

They settled into garden chairs and a waiter brought their morning tea.

Tanya poured tea into two cups. 'I believe the Braganzas lived in this cottage before us?'

'Yes, they did.'

'You made them move out of here?'

'I offered good money for the cottage, and they agreed to move into a newly refurbished cottage down below.'

'I'm not sure if it was the right thing to do.'

'Nobody forced them. They needed money, and I made an offer—that's it. And I paid for modifying the new cottages to their taste.'

'Somehow, I don't feel very comfortable about it.'

'Believe me, I've done them a great favour.'

A pair of white doves landed on the tiled roof of the verandah. Tanya took it as a sign of welcome and didn't pursue the matter further. Her gaze followed the flight of a flock of birds that flew over their heads and compared it to her own—from a modest home in Daman to this heavenly paradise, and a dream-like cottage she could call her home. But the image of Mark shadowed her happiness.

'Mr Braganza doesn't seem happy about this.'

'Well, he couldn't have asked for more.'

'I don't think I'm going to like that man.'

'What makes you think so? He's been very cooperative so far, and I see no reason why he wouldn't be in future.'

'That remains to be seen.'

29

Grace's tender body ached on the hard bunk assigned to her in a stinking hole, the size of a matchbox. Three sleazy looking females, her cellmates, laughed and jeered at her with their filthy teeth. Their hungry, lusting eyes made her nauseous. She shuddered when the strong iron door opened with a screech in the middle of the night. At the door loomed the half-naked figure of a huge, pot-bellied giant, his eyes bulging out of their sockets. The foul-smelling guard leered like a hungry street dog, saliva dripping from his swollen lips and hands reaching down the front buttons of his trousers. Grace struggled to get up and run, but her cellmates kept her pinned down on her cot, calling her a bitch, a whore and other names she had never heard before. She tried to shout for help, but all the air had gone out of her lungs; and she found, to her horror, she could no longer breathe.

She woke up with a start, bathed in sweat, her mouth dry and heart pounding against her chest. It took a minute before she realized she had been dreaming. For several seconds she couldn't move. After regaining her senses, she drank some water from the glass kept on her bedside table and then tiptoed into the toilet trying not wake up Mark, who was sleeping like a log next to her. She buried her face in her hands and sat on the commode.

After a while, she splashed cold water on her face and looked into the mirror. No, she couldn't possibly go to jail...not in the company of whores … and face those hungry bastards at night! Her whole body shook with fright and she popped two sleeping pills into her mouth. She returned to her bed and lay there, staring at the ceiling through what was left of the night

The last tactic she had employed to broker peace with Mani had failed miserably. Although she still possessed the trump card that could send her tormentor to prison, Grace was apprehensive. She realised it was a double-edged sword that could slash Mani's neck but also her own, on the rebound.

❧

Grace was groggy in the morning, but her devious mind was still ticking over her predicament. Nobody on earth could claim she knew about Mani's plan in advance. As far as she was concerned, Mani died in a fatal accident, and she could jolly well do what she pleased with the insurance money. Mani would find it very hard to prove her involvement in the plot. But the night time visitation of the hungry whores sent a thousand watt current flowing through her veins. She couldn't take the risk.

Grace hobbled to the rear window and gazed at her old cottage. She saw the new occupant moving about in the lovely garden that she had nurtured so fondly, and vowed to make the woman's life miserable. And that of her husband. She turned when she heard Saira at the door with a cup of tea.

'Saab wants you to join him in his office,' she said.

Grace ignored her and glanced at her watch. It was well past ten. 'I'm feeling drowsy. Maybe I should catch some sleep after breakfast.'

Around noon, Grace arrived in the reception area wearing a loose shirt over a pair of battered jeans. She noticed Mark supervising the staff working on the deck. Raju stood at the reception desk with the guest list.

'Have you seen Pestonji?'

'He's taken some of the guests from Bombay to their rooms.'

'Which ones?'

Raju read out the names. 'Mr and Mrs Patel, Mr Shah, and another couple not listed here.'

She hesitated. 'What about Mr and Mrs Wilson?'

Raju pursed his lips. 'They haven't arrived yet.'

She heaved a sigh of relief, but knew it was only temporary. She felt like running away from everything and not showing up at all.

Pestonji appeared in the hallway. 'Good to see you taking charge, finally.'

She shot a glance at the old man. 'I think I should handover to the woman who arrived yesterday. A new mug-face might do better at the reception desk.'

Pestonji couldn't take Grace's pugnacious remark lying down. 'You're right; she would be better than the face of a pregnant cow in labour to greet the guests.'

Grace maintained her composure. She knew how to respond to his verbal assault. 'Then why not summon the holy cow to receive the likes of Patels and Shahs, the bloody schemers and fixers? I'm not exactly dying to see the faces of such loathsome characters, let alone receive them.'

Pestonji waited for a few seconds before serving her with an ace of spades. 'Maybe not, but you might like to receive the Wilsons when they arrive.'

A surge of anger mixed with despair hit her hard. For several seconds she sat motionless, her eyes on the floor. 'When are they expected to arrive?' she asked dully after a while.

'They're arriving in Goa by bus, I'm told.'

'And how do they come here from Goa?'

Pestonji raised an eyebrow. 'I'm touched by your concern for John's personal guests. Do you know them by any chance?'

She kept her hands clasped in a white knuckled grip and didn't look at him directly as she spoke. 'That doesn't answer my question.'

'I've requested Mr DeCosta to pick them up, unless you wish to go and receive them yourself at the bus stand?'

Grace fidgeted. Her defenses weak and spirits at an all-time low, she softened a bit. 'Why are you doing this to me?' she mumbled.

'Who is doing what to you?'

'Why did you have to invite them?'

'Surely John has the right to invite his loved ones on such an occasion, even though you don't seem to believe in such gestures?'

Colour drained from her face. She bit her lip to stop them from trembling. 'I'd like to be informed when they arrive.'

'Yes, ma'am, and now if you'll excuse me, I've work to do.'

With tears in her eyes, Grace staggered into Mark's office. It seemed that her living nightmare was growing worse each day.

'What's wrong?' Mark asked when she entered his office.

She slumped into a chair and dabbed her eyes with a hanky.

'What happened now?'

Grace blew her nose. 'As if you care.'

'Frankly, I don't... the way you've been behaving lately...'

'I can't stand that conceited, low-born bastard who's been insulting me from day one. I fail to understand why you give so much importance to that minion.'

'He's no minion, in case you haven't registered. You've got to give him his due.'

Grace glared at him. 'What do you expect me to do, kiss his ass?'

'Don't start again, for heaven's sake. We have jobs to do, and you're supposed to take care of the guests, instead of wrangling for no damn reason.'

Her frustration flamed into anger. 'To hell with your guests,' she screamed. 'I'm not a bum-sucker like you are.'

Hearing the commotion, Raju peeped into the door.

Mark clenched his fist and banged the table hard. 'Shut up and get off your haunches... and do what you're told to do.'

Grace jumped from her chair. 'I'm not going to live here anymore to serve these jokers.'

'Nobody's stopping you.'

Grace stomped out of the room, slamming the door behind her.

❧

As darkness fell, Grace heard the cars arriving. She peeped out of her living room window and saw fancy lights illuminating the lawn. The deck had been cleared to make room for the dance floor. A group of musicians milled in a corner, setting up their equipment and testing their mikes. A makeshift bar had been set up below the deck and chairs arranged on the lawn.

Dressed in a dark, pin-striped suit and smelling of musk, Mark left without saying another word.

Grace poured herself a stiff drink of whisky. The festive atmosphere depressed her. Rejected by Mani, humiliated by Pestonji and ignored by Mark, she felt utterly defeated. She took a long swallow of her drink and coughed as it burned her throat. The prospect of facing her parents sent goose pimples through her body. By inviting them, Mani had played the cruellest of his cards. She wanted to run away, but where could she go? Besides, she'd no money.

A gentle knock distracted her from her thoughts. She turned and saw Raju standing at the door.

'What is it?'

'Mrs Gomez is inquiring about you.'

'Tell her I'm not well.'

'Yes, Ma'am.'

'Have the Wilsons arrived?'

'No.'

Grace glanced at her watch. 'What about Mr DeCosta? Has he arrived?'

'Yes, an hour ago.'

Grace frowned. 'Ask Pestonji what happened to the Wilsons. They were supposed to come with DeCosta. And get me a pack of cigarettes on the double.'

She slumped into the sofa and wondered about her parents. Raju didn't show up even after a quarter of an hour. She paced up and down, smashed her cigarette into the ashtray and came onto the verandah. A distance away, guests mingled with each other and soft music played in the background.

'Dammit, where the hell did you disappear to?' she yelled at Raju when he returned.

Raju placed the cigarette packet on the table. 'Mr Pestonji sent me on an errand.'

'Fuck Mr Pestonji, you understand?'

Raju dropped his gaze to the floor.

'What's the news of the Wilsons?'

'Mr Pestonji said they might come on their own as Mr DeCosta couldn't pick them up.'

Dread and anger knotted up her insides. Grace dismissed Raju and grit her teeth.

True, she didn't wish to face her parents at this juncture. She had deserted them, treated them badly, but she couldn't tolerate anybody else treating them shabbily. She wanted to demand an explanation from Pestonji, but didn't have the strength to confront him. Instead, she sank into the sofa and cursed.

An hour and two more glasses of whiskey later, she heard a tentative knock at her door. Who could it be this time? God, not her parents! She couldn't face them. Her heart began to thump against her chest. She stubbed her cigarette in the ashtray and staggered to the door with her heart in her mouth.

30

A cool breeze blew over the resort, gradually becoming stronger as the evening progressed. Soon it was dark. A million stars covered the deep-blue sky. Pestonji and Mark received the guests as they started arriving for the double celebration.

'Ah, you two look great together.' Pestonji complimented Tanya and Mani when they joined them.

Dressed in a glittering turquoise sari and sporting a yellow rose in her hair, Tanya glowed. Wearing a black kurta-pajama suit, with a shawl draped over his shoulders, Mani complemented her.

Mr and Mrs Gomez came with a bouquet for the young couple. Mr DeCosta arrived with his wife and two daughters, minus the Wilsons. The Wilsons had never been invited. John didn't wish to cause more pain to Grace's parents than they had already suffered. It was Pestonji's idea to put their names on the guest list to spite her.

The chief guest for the evening, Mrs Tara Habib, arrived without the screaming sirens and escort cars as the Governor was out of town. Wearing a golden sari and a matching shawl, her hair done in a Jacqueline Kennedy style, she looked a class apart. A whiff of herbal scent filled the air as she stepped out of the car.

Mani and Tanya greeted the tall lady and escorted her to the main venue. Pestonji followed, leaving Mark behind to receive other invitees.

'You've a wonderful place out here,' Mrs Habib remarked, gazing at the imposing building. 'I don't know why we didn't visit the resort before. Perhaps I should bring Akhtar Mian to spend a weekend in this place.'

'You're most welcome, Ma'am,' said Pestonji graciously even though he was a bit rattled at the prospect of putting up with the Governor's retinue. 'It would be a great honour.'

As the evening progressed, more guests arrived, the band played soft tunes, people mingled and waiters circled the lawn with trays laden with drinks and snacks.

Mark took the mike. 'Ladies and gentlemen, may I have your attention, please.' He waited for a few seconds for the crowd to become silent. 'It gives me great pleasure to welcome you all this evening to celebrate a new beginning at the Paradise Resort.' His baritone filled the air. 'My special thanks to Mrs Tara Habib, who took time out from her busy schedule to grace the occasion. We are honoured by your presence, ma'am.'

Mrs Habib smiled.

Mark continued, 'I must acknowledge, with gratitude, the enormous contribution made by Mr John Abraham, now my partner, who needs no introduction. We have joined hands to return the Paradise Resort to its former glory and position it as one of the best destinations on the west coast.'

Mani acknowledged the applause with a slight bow.

'We are here this evening to also welcome Mrs Tanya Abraham, Mr Abraham's new bride. We wish the couple a long and blessed marriage.' He glanced in Tanya's direction. 'I'm sure, with her past experience in hospitality, Mrs Abraham will prove to be an asset for the resort.'

The crowd clapped.

'The evening is young and the atmosphere just right. May I

invite the newlyweds to the dance floor? Thank you.'

The band began to play a romantic number. After a few moments of hesitation, Mani and Tanya took the floor. More couples joined.

Pestonji invited Mrs Habib and the Gomezes to take a tour of the premises. His friend DeCosta also followed.

Mrs Gomez's eyes widened as they made their way into the lounge. 'The place is completely transformed.'

Mrs Habib seemed pleased. 'Very tastefully done, and I can see John Abraham's paintings everywhere!'

'John is very excited about the place,' said Pestonji. 'He's looking forward to capturing the beauty that surrounds the resort in abundance on his canvas.'

Mrs Habib turned to Pestonji. 'I wouldn't be surprised if he produces a few masterpieces. And there's the *Lovers' Rock*. It looks just right over there.'

'I must say, Braganza is very lucky to have found a generous partner in John Abraham,' said Mr Gomez. 'He could never have acquired any of John's works, not to mention such a heavy investment in the resort, which needed a facelift badly.'

Mrs Gomez nudged her husband to restrain him.

DeCosta suppressed a smile.

'I'm sure the partnership will be good for the resort,' said Mrs Habib, 'and bring in more tourists to the state.'

Mr Gomez tossed a glance at DeCosta. 'I hope so, too.'

After a quick round of the refurbished dining hall, Pestonji escorted them back to their seats and joined Mark, who stood near the bar, talking to a couple.

Pestonji tapped his shoulder. 'That was a good speech.'

Mark smiled. 'Thank you.'

'Hello, handsome,' a husky voice called out from behind Mark.

'Since when have you become short of dancing partners?'

Mark turned around. 'Hello, Kaveri, how are you?'

'I'm fine, thank you, but where's your better half?' asked the tease dressed in a hip-hugging purple sari and a low cut blouse, with a cleavage as deep as that of Gina Lollobrigida.

'She's not well.'

Kaveri rolled her eyes. 'Is she in the family way?'

'Not that I know of,' he said, dropping his gaze on her bulging belly. 'But you seem to be well on the way. Is this your third... or fourth?'

'Third; I can gift it to you if you're having problems.'

Mark recoiled and turned his back towards her.

Pestonji barely managed to suppress a smile and slipped away.

'Hello there, Mr Pestonji,' Fernandez waved to him from across the bar. 'How are you, my friend?'

'I'm fine, thank you.'

Fernandez came closer. 'What the hell are you doing in this place, for God's sake?'

'Well, we saw a good opportunity and decided to grab it.'

'My dear fellow, you've just grabbed a poisonous snake that will bite you sooner than you realise.'

'We've taken good care of our interests.'

Fernandez raised his eyebrows. 'I'm beginning to suspect your interests run deeper than just financial ones.'

Pestonji gazed at the crafty fellow but said nothing.

'Is that bomb also part of the deal?'

Pestonji considered it wise to get rid of him.

'By the way, I don't see that siren anywhere,' Fernandez said, scanning the gathering. 'Where the hell is she hiding on a day like this?'

'She's not well, and now, if you'll excuse me, I've got to go.'

'Sure, but watch your tail.'

As Pestonji moved away from the obnoxious fellow, Tanya approached him. 'Uncle Feroze, what is wrong with Mrs Braganza?'

'There's nothing right with that woman. I haven't seen a smile on her face since the day we arrived.'

'Why is that?'

'She's not worth the bother, and I would advise you to keep a safe distance from her. She can be very nasty and uncivilised.'

'She must be very upset having to give up her cottage for us.'

'She is, but Mark didn't complain.'

'I'm not too happy about this.'

'Think no more of it, and enjoy your evening.'

Tanya paused for a while, gazing at the dancing pairs. 'The least I can do is to visit her if she's not well.'

Pestonji cringed. 'I don't think it's such a good idea.'

'I don't see any harm in it.'

Pestonji knew it was asking for trouble, but he gave in to her insistence.

❧

When Grace managed to open the door with her shaking hands, Pestonji stood outside with the woman she hadn't met before but guessed who she was. Her eyes shifted back and forth between the two.

'Yes?' she said.

'Mrs Abraham wanted to say hello to you,' Pestonji said.

Grace put on a blank expression as if visited by a door-to-door salesgirl.

'Hello, Mrs Braganza, I'm Tanya. I'm sorry to learn you aren't well. I came to inquire if I could be of any help.'

Grace gave her an intimidating look. She didn't want Mani's

wife at her door, but now that she was there, she didn't have much choice. *Could be of any help. Yes, she could be a good replacement for Saira.*

'May we come in?' asked Pestonji.

Grace smirked. 'I'm not in the mood to receive visitors.'

'I thought so, too,' he said. 'But it wouldn't cost a dime in extending basic courtesy to someone who is decent enough to call on you, leaving her own reception party.'

'Thanks, but I'd rather be left alone.'

Tanya stepped back.

Pestonji tilted his head. 'Oh, I forgot. Civility is not one of your virtues. I regret having given in to Tanya's insistence to call on you. Let's go, Tanya. She's not worthy of your concern.'

'I don't need anybody's sympathy.'

'No, you don't. And I doubt if you'll find any.'

'Get lost. I didn't invite you.'

Tanya's face paled.

Pestonji smiled. 'You can say that again to your parents when they arrive later tonight.'

Grace grit her teeth but said nothing.

'I'm sorry to have upset you, Mrs Braganza,' Tanya said. 'Believe me, I didn't mean to hurt you. I apologise for the inconvenience.'

Pestonji and Tanya turned and left Grace standing at the door.

Tanya's gentility moved her. In the last few months, no one had spoken to her with such compassion, let alone inquired about her. She felt a faint twinge of guilt for having been rude to the woman who meant no harm.

Pestonji's parting words had hit her hard. She dreaded the thought of having to face her parents. After finishing her drink, she pulled herself together and made her way to a dark corner of the lawn without changing out of her battered jeans and loose shirt. Nobody noticed her. The party was in full swing. Grace sat on a chair next to a lone elderly gentleman with a thick moustache who sat enjoying his drink.

'Good evening,' he said, rising a little from his chair.

Grace acknowledged him with a forced smile.

The man caressed his moustache and shot a glance at her. 'I'm General Rodriguez, and who might you be, if I may?'

Grace didn't care if he was a General Montgomery or John F. Kennedy. To cut him short she answered, 'Marshal Goebbels from Gestapo Headquarters.'

He burst out laughing. 'That's a good one, lady. I'm floored. Now I'm more than curious to know what your real name is.'

'I'd appreciate very much if you'd leave me alone.'

The general rose from his chair and saluted her. 'Nice meeting you, Marshal. Your guns are loaded. I better move out of the line of fire.'

Despite her troubled state of mind, Grace found a reason to smile. Had it been any other occasion, she would've liked to engage him. But this was not her day.

'In any case,' said the general before moving away, 'I needed to replenish the fuel tank.'

Grace chuckled. 'Would you be kind enough to send a glass of whisky my way?'

'Sure, what's your poison?'

'Single malt, and make it large.'

'You got it.'

A waiter brought her a glass of single malt.

Grace had managed to shake off the general, but what she saw next coming her way nauseated her.

Fernandez approached her with a swagger. 'Hello, Mrs Braganza. It's good to see you.'

Grace crossed her legs and ignored the creep.

'I don't believe this,' he said. 'Why are you hiding in a corner when you should be dazzling the audience like a star and setting the place on fire?'

She sipped her drink without responding.

He sat on the chair vacated by the general. 'What's the matter? You don't look yourself tonight,' he said, feasting his eyes on her cleavage revealed by her loose shirt. 'Although, I must say you look as ravishing and desirable as you would in a formal gown.'

Grace tilted her head. 'Excuse me?'

The man met her gaze with a leer. 'After all, the contents are more important than the packaging.'

Grace's cheeks turned crimson. 'Why don't you flush your filthy mouth in a commode?'

'You seem in your worst mood tonight. Is something wrong?'

Grace shot him a venomous look.

'Braganza seems to have made good use of your charm to win these blokes. I wish you had given us locals a chance.'

Shaking with anger, Grace got up from her chair and threw her glass at Fernandez. 'You bastard,' she shouted at the top of her voice. 'You sewer rat…how dare you talk to me like that?'

The chatter of the crowds sank into a hushed murmur. Heads turned towards Fernandez, his face drenched and mouth open in shock, with a cut on his lip.

Pestonji came running.

Someone caught hold of Grace just when she was removing her sandal.

Fernandez wiped his face with his hand and muttered through clenched teeth, 'You fuckin' whore…you…'

'Stop it, man,' Pestonji yelled.

A couple of guests dragged Fernandez away from the scene.

Grace still shook with rage. 'Son of a bitch...'

Mrs Gomez dashed to her side. 'Get hold of yourself, Grace. Let me take you home.'

Mark appeared on the scene, looking dazed. 'What happened?'

Grace fumed. 'Ask that gutter-born friend of yours what happened.'

Mark grabbed her hand. 'You're drunk and creating quite a scene. For heaven's sake, go home and don't show up again in these rags.'

Grace jerked her hand free and pushed him away. 'Leave me alone.'

Mrs Gomez slid her arm around Grace's waist. 'Come with me.'

'Where're you taking me?' Grace asked when she realised they were heading towards her old cottage.

'Home.'

'That's not my home anymore,' her voice cracked.

Mrs Gomez stopped. 'What do you mean not your home?'

'I've lost everything... my home... my money... my honour... everything.' Tears welled in her eyes. She stumbled and leant on Mrs Gomez's shoulder. 'I'm ruined.'

'Oh dear, you've taken one too many.'

Grace wiped her tears and turned around, pointing to her new home. 'I live there now. Mark has sold himself to these jokers, giving it all up.'

Mrs Gomez took her home and settled her into a sofa. 'You need to rest.'

Grace let out a deep breath. 'You were so right about Mark. I should've listened to you... he killed Irene... and will do the same to me... just like her.' Her voice cracked and she sobbed.

'Don't say that, Grace! Calm down, everything will be all right.'

'I need a drink.'

Mr Gomez appeared at the door. 'No, you don't.'

Grace sank further down into the sofa and hid her face in her hands.

'What you need is not another drink, but the courage to fight evil,' he said.

The hint of retribution in his voice didn't escape Grace's notice. But the good man didn't have a clue about her real story. 'You'll never know what I'm going through. I made a grave mistake, not once but twice, and no one but I alone am to blame for it.'

'Irene said the same thing to me once and look what happened to her. I'd hate to see you going the same way. This is no time to drown yourself in alcohol, but to stand up and face the challenge.'

'Stop it, Eric,' Mrs Gomez snapped. 'This is not the time for all this. Please leave her alone.'

Mr Gomez walked to the door and turned back. 'I'm sorry, Grace. I didn't mean to hurt you. But I never expected Grace Wilson to give in to the whims and fancies of Mark Braganza.'

Grace closed her eyes. The past had come back to haunt her. The distant roar of the surf reminded her of the Lovers' Rock at Digha where it had all begun.

Mrs Gomez ran her hand over Grace's head. 'Would you like to lie down?'

'I appreciate your concern, Mrs Gomez. You're very kind, but no one can help me now.'

Mrs Gomez took Grace's hands in hers. 'I'll stay with you if you want.'

She opened her eyes. 'I need to be alone.'

'I'd rather not leave you alone in this state.'

'No, I'll be all right.'

'No more drinks, you understand.'

Grace nodded.

After hesitating for a minute, Mrs Gomez left.

❧

Grace closed the door and poured herself another drink. She hobbled up to the window and, like a statue, stared into the darkness for a long time. Her life was as dark as the world outside, with not even a flicker of light in sight, except for the wobbling image of the sinking moon on the surface of the ocean, so much like herself. The howling winds through the gaps in the trees sounded ominous, sending a shiver down her body. She had never felt so low in her life. Glamour, money, fame—she had tasted all in good measure, but to what end? Everything was fake, an illusion, a transitory euphoria that had driven her to greed, deceit and personal gratification.

She could not face the past without remorse, the present with dignity or handle the future without fear. Hers was a self-inflicted pain and suffering was inevitable. Her anger turned into severe depression. No, she could never live like a crippled soul for the rest of her life.

A strong gust of wind sent the curtains flapping against her face. She lost her grip and her glass dropped on the floor, shattering into pieces—like the remains of her own life.

She staggered into her bedroom and stared at her reflection in the mirror with horror: her face was haggard and eyes looked like the ones she had seen on the animal trophies that once adorned the walls of Mark's living room. She stumbled into the bathroom to throw up. No, she wouldn't allow Grace Wilson to be seen in such a pathetic state, ever.

She showered and changed into a peach-coloured gown, her favourite. She brushed her long tresses, applied make-up and stood in front of the mirror for several minutes, admiring her image.

Then, she picked up a pen.

31

A persistent knock on his door jolted Mark out of his sleep. After returning from the party, he had slept in the spare room. He glanced at the wall clock with bleary eyes and cursed. Six-thirty in the morning? He had slept only for four hours! Damn, who could it be at this hour?

The unwanted visitor knocked urgently. Mark slipped into his dressing gown and staggered to the door.

Shaking uncontrollably, face drained of colour, Saira stood at the door. She gasped for breath, barely managing to speak. 'Hurry up... Grace ma'am... at the beach...'

'What?'

'She's... she's dead... come quick,' she said, panting for breath.

Mark's jaw tightened. 'Are you mad?'

Tears welled up in Saira's eyes. 'Please sa'ab, hurry,' she said, and left him gaping after her.

Mark dashed back to get into his trousers and throw on a shirt. He rushed towards the door and stopped. Grace? At the beach? Puzzled, he ran back to their bedroom. The bed was empty, the sheets unruffled. Grace's jeans and shirt lay on a chair, her robe on the bathroom floor.

As he was about to leave, he noticed the corner of a blue envelope under her pillow. He ripped it open and pulled out the note from inside. His heart leapt to his throat. The constriction in his gut eased after he read the full note.

If there was one thing in his entire life that astounded him beyond his wildest imagination, this was it. Grace had not left a suicide note in his hand, but a million dollar note! Perhaps, the piece of paper was worth more. He slipped the note back into the envelope and stuffed it deep down his pocket. A hundred questions raced through his mind as he flew out of the cottage.

A handful of people had gathered around a mermaid-like figure washed up on the wet sands. As he rushed, the crowd parted. Grace, the epitome of beauty, lay at the edge of the water, drenched in her peach-coloured dress, her long tresses swaying in the gentle waves.

Kaveri and her husband, Dr Swamy, stood by her side, looking dazed.

The doctor removed his glasses and nodded solemnly. 'I'm sorry, Mark. She's gone.'

'This can't be happening… she was… she was so full of life!' His voice cracked as he dropped on his knees. Leaning forward, he caressed her face and wondered if there ever would be another Grace in his life.

'This is so tragic, Mark,' said Kaveri. 'I just can't understand.'

The doctor placed his hand on Mark's shoulder.

Sitting on the other side, Saira covered Grace's upper body with her shawl.

The small crowd whispered to each other, shaking their heads in disbelief.

The thought of the departed soul troubled Mark. This was not what he would've wanted, but the note in his pocket acted like a balm that took care of his transitory pain. He went and sat on a rock a little distance away and gazing at the remains of his wife. The morning stars were the only ones in mourning, and perhaps the flock of birds that hovered above. Someone brought a white sheet and covered Grace's body. Mark buried his face in his hands as more people arrived at the scene—some out of curiosity and others to offer condolences that hardly registered.

'Good Lord, this is unthinkable,' said Pestonji.

'This was no way to go,' muttered Kaveri, pretending to wipe a tear Mark knew didn't exist.

Mrs Gomez came and stood shaking near the body, covering her mouth with her palm, while Mark struggled to maintain a solemn exterior.

Mr Gomez stood grim-faced at a distance.

Mani and Tanya approached Mark, their faces drawn. 'I'm so sorry for your loss,' said Mani. 'I just cannot believe this.'

Mark rejected all the crap and said nothing.

❧

Mark had nothing to worry about this time. Everything was straightforward. Grace committed suicide and he'd played no part in it.

The police came and searched for possible clues in Grace's bedroom. They found nothing. Mark had carefully hidden the note inside his socks. After making preliminary inquiries of the staff, the lawmen assembled everybody in the lounge.

Mrs Gomez, the last person to have seen Grace alive, was the first to be questioned.

'Ma'am, can you tell us what happened last night?' asked Inspector Dara.

'I was standing with my husband when we heard a commotion at the other end of the lawn. I saw Grace shouting at somebody. I rushed to her side to restrain her. This man appeared drunk. Somebody whisked him away before things got worse, and I brought her home.'

'You brought her home alone?'

'Yes. My husband joined us later.'

The inspector turned his gaze towards Mark. 'You mean to say Mr Braganza didn't come to the house with his wife?'

'Not at the time,' Mrs Gomez said. 'She seemed agitated and wanted to be left alone.'

'Mr Braganza, I find it hard to believe you didn't accompany your wife when she was so upset and needed your support.'

'Grace had great regard for Mrs Gomez, and I thought she would be in a better position to handle her,' replied Mark.

'Handle her? You mean she was out of control?'

'Mr Dara, I do not wish to tarnish the image of the deceased, but Grace could be very hostile when angry. Knowing her temperament, it made sense to leave her under Mrs Gomez's supervision.'

'Most husbands that I know of would try to console an agitated wife.'

Mark stared at him. 'I wanted her to return to sobriety. Besides, I had too much going on last night, with the governor's wife on our hands and all the guests.'

The inspector returned to Mrs Gomez. 'Ma'am, did you inquire about what happened?'

Mrs Gomez hesitated and sat upright in her chair. 'Well, she was not in a proper frame of mind to talk.'

'Was she drunk?'

Mrs Gomez's mouth twitched. 'I suppose she was, yes.'

The inspector paced the floor. 'What time did you take her home?'

'I'm not sure... maybe ten-thirty, eleven.'

'So you brought her home and then what?'

'I told her not to drink anymore and go to sleep. I offered to stay with her, but she declined.' She tossed a glance at her husband, 'I wish I had.'

'Know anything about the man she had this quarrel with?'

'I've seen him around, but I don't know who he is.'

The inspector waited for a few seconds and turned to Pestonji. 'Can you describe, sir, what happened?'

'I saw the two of them hurling abuses at each other.'

'You know this man?'

'I've met this man, Fernandez, a couple of times here at the resort—a moneylender, I believe.'

'Is he here?'

'No, I sent him packing last night.'

'What caused the showdown?'

'I can't be sure, but Mr Fernandez is not the kind of person to exercise discretion, especially after a few drinks. He might have offended Mrs Braganza in some way or another.'

'Didn't you ask him what happened?'

'He was too drunk and abusive. I thought it wise to bundle him into his car and instruct his driver to take him home.'

'Mmm...' muttered the inspector as if he had already caught the culprit by his balls. Then he stepped on Pestonji's toes by adding, 'Is there a chance he didn't go home and, instead, lurked around?'

Mark gazed at the nincompoop with disbelief.

Pestonji gaped at the hawk-eyed inspector. 'Pardon my saying so, but are you suggesting that Fernandez sneaked into the cottage at night, ordered Mrs Braganza to change into a formal gown and then invited her for a walk on the beach before knocking her down into the sea?'

Despite the solemn occasion, Mark could barely suppress a smile. The inspector's face turned a notch redder. His two subordinates exchanged smiles.

A thin smirk curled the inspector's lips. He tapped his baton on his palm a couple of times. 'Mr...'

'Pestonji, Feroze Pestonji,' he said.

'Well, Mr Pustoon ji, I would appreciate it if you stick to answering the questions.'

'Yes, sir, and the answer is *no*.'

The inspector turned to the doctor. 'I believe you were among the first to discover the body.'

'Yes, my wife and I had gone for a stroll on the beach when we noticed a couple of locals bent over the body. We were shocked to find it was Mrs Braganza. She had no pulse.'

'Did you see any sign of injury?'

He shook his head. 'No, I didn't see any visible sign of injury.'

The inspector faced Kaveri. 'Ma'am, how long have you known Mrs Braganza?'

'I met her socially a couple of times. I didn't see her in the crowds last night, not until much later when this thing happened.'

The inspector arched an eyebrow and dropped his gaze at her cleavage. 'How well do you know Mr Braganza?'

Kaveri drew a sigh and crossed her legs. 'We've been friends long enough.'

'Would you know anyone who could have harmed Mrs Braganza?'

Kaveri glanced at Mark and pursed her lips.

Mark tugged at his shirt collar and wondered if the jilted woman would take advantage of the situation and point a finger at him.

'How would I know?' she answered, glancing once more at Mark. 'I hardly knew her.'

Mark shuffled in his chair, avoiding her gaze.

'Mr Gomez, how would you describe Mrs Braganza's condition when you saw her last?'

'She seemed terribly depressed and none too happy with what was happening around her.'

'Can you explain that, sir?'

'Well, she was thrown out of her house for one. The rest has to come from the gentlemen present here.'

'I see.'

Mark entertained the notion of pretending he hadn't heard, but resigned himself to responding when the inspector turned to him and asked, 'Can you tell us why, Mr Braganza?'

'She wasn't exactly thrown out. We offered our cottage to my new partner for a substantial consideration.'

'And what might that be?'

Mark loosened his shirt collar. 'I don't think I'm obliged to give you financial details.'

With a scowl on his face, the inspector went on. 'Mr Braganza,' he asked in a tone normally heard in a court room when the prosecutor confronts a confirmed scoundrel. 'What time did you come home last night?'

'One, one-thirty in the morning, I guess.'

'Can you be more specific?'

'I didn't exactly check my watch. I was tired and went to sleep in the guest room.'

The inspector raised an eyebrow. 'You didn't sleep in your own bedroom?'

'No, I didn't want to disturb my wife at that late hour.'

'Did you see Mrs Braganza in her bed?'

'No, I didn't even enter the bedroom.'

'All right, so you come home late and go straight to the guest room without bothering about Mrs Braganza?'

'As I said before, I did not want to disturb her at that late hour.'

The inspector flipped his notepad over, reading back his notes. 'According to my information, you had a heated altercation with your wife earlier in the day?'

Mark wondered what else the bloke had discovered. 'Yes, we had a little argument. No big deal. Show me one married couple who doesn't, including you.'

The inspector rubbed his chin and lowered his head. 'What did you argue about?'

Mark glanced at Mrs Gomez before replying, 'It was a private matter I can't discuss in the presence of the respectable lady.'

'Excuse me, inspector,' Mr Gomez said, rising from his chair, 'I suppose we can leave now since we've nothing more to contribute?'

'Yes, sir, you may go for now. If we need you again, we'll call you.'

The inspector gazed at Mark after the couple departed, waiting for an answer.

Mark looked him in the eye and replied, 'Grace was complaining about my nocturnal duties... if you must know.'

Inspector Dara's face flushed. One of his deputies coughed to muffle his laughter. Kaveri covered her mouth to suppress a giggle. Tanya looked the other way. Pestonji chuckled.

'Mr Braganza, I'd appreciate it if you could refrain from being evasive,' said the inspector. 'I'm only doing my duty.'

'I understand, Inspector, but you're wasting your time if you think I'm in any way responsible for this tragic event. I've lost my wife, for God's sake, and you're questioning me as though I'm the one who pushed her into the ocean.'

'I'm sorry to say this, but no one can be ruled out.' The inspector turned to the large window, opening on to the deck. 'I believe this is the second time you've lost your spouse to the sea. Seems like a strange coincidence.'

Mark regarded the inspector with contempt. He lit his cigar and exhaled smoke before responding. 'Is that a question or a suggestion?'

An uneasy calm descended on the lounge, with only the muted rumble of the surf filling the hall. Mark knew what the man was getting at, but he maintained his cool. The note hidden in his socks was enough to shut up the inspector. But Mark was not about to squander the 'million dollar' note on a rotten policeman.

'I'm sorry if I offend you, but it will make my job simpler if you cooperate.'

'Well, what do you want me to say?' Mark flared. 'That I pushed my wife into the sea?'

The uniforms exchanged a couple of glances before the inspector continued. 'I understand Mrs Braganza was not present during most of the celebrations. Any particular reason?'

'She wasn't feeling well.'

'But she did consume a lot of liquor?'

'Perhaps she did.'

'Was she an alcoholic?'

'Not an alcoholic, but she liked her drink.'

Inspector Dara grabbed a glass of water from the table and took a sip. 'Did you know a Mr Fernandez?'

'He lent me some money at one time and took the liberty of using the services at the resort for free, as if he owned the bloody place.'

'Still, you invited him, didn't you?'

'No, I didn't. Fernandez is a compulsive gate-crasher, a shameless freeloader if you know what I mean.'

'Looks like he was not on his best behaviour with Mrs Braganza last night.'

'Apparently not, but Grace knew how to handle such rogues.'

The inspector called his deputy and instructed him to summon Mr Fernandez to the police lines first thing in the morning.

'Mr Braganza, I'd like to know if you ever noticed any suicidal tendency in your wife?'

Mark took a long drag on his cigar. At last the bugger was on the right track. 'No, Grace was always full of life. She liked to entertain and be entertained. She was the life of any party.'

'But not this time?'

'She had been a little upset lately after I got into partnership with Mr Abraham. Grace always wanted to dominate and didn't feel at ease in the altered situation. But I cannot believe she would've taken such an extreme step because of that.'

'We are policemen who are taught to examine even the most absurd in a given situation, no matter how bizarre it may sound. We don't have any definite clues as of now, but things will be clearer after the post-mortem.'

'I hope so,' Mark muttered.

The inspector sat on a chair, flipped his notepad shut and drummed his fingers on the armrest. 'What bothers me, however, is the dress she was found in. Everybody had seen her wearing jeans and a shirt. I can't imagine her changing into a fancy gown after all she had gone through, and then ending up like that.'

The dress had puzzled Mark, too. But he knew the woman better than the rest. Grace wouldn't have liked to be seen in a pair of battered jeans in her last appearance. She must have chosen to go in style, one last time.

The inspector turned his gaze to Mani. 'Mr Abraham, I believe you moved into the cottage that belonged to the Braganzas.'

'Yes I did, and paid good money for it,' he shifted in his chair. 'But I don't see what that has got to do with this.'

'Perhaps that is the reason Mrs Braganza was so upset.'

'Look, inspector, I'm very sad about this tragic event so soon after our arrival. It has left me and my wife terribly shaken. As regards the cottage, I didn't force anybody. I settled the issue with Mr Braganza quite amicably. I wouldn't have known if she was indeed so upset with the arrangement. Besides, Mr Pestonji functions on my behalf to handle the affairs of the resort. I'm here to concentrate on my work, which is painting.'

The inspector turned to Tanya. 'Perhaps Mrs Abraham could've interacted with her?'

'I tried to meet her when I learnt she was ill,' said Tanya truthfully, 'but she seemed very disturbed, and unwelcoming.'

A long pause ensued before the inspector rose from his chair. 'I'm sorry for your loss, Mr Braganza. That will be all for now. I'll let you know if I want more information.' He put on his cap and left the hall, followed by his deputies.

That night, Mark poured a stiff drink of scotch as Saira cooked dinner for him. He lit a cigar, perched his feet on the coffee table and read the note several times. He still couldn't believe in his luck. He was excited and ecstatic. Grace had left damaging remarks about him in her note, but she wasn't to know that she'd left behind a jackpot by exposing the truth behind John Abraham. He hid the note in a black, empty bottle of wine and placed it on the topmost shelf of his bar.

'Dinner is ready,' announced Saira, as she came into the room. 'Shall I put it in the hot case?'

Mark sipped her drink and gazed at her.

Saira tensed and lowered her eyes.

Even after giving birth to two brats, Saira maintained a trim figure, her brown body contrasting with her white blouse. He emptied his glass and reached for her.

Saira hesitated but didn't protest.

Mark pushed her into the bedroom and switched off the lights.

❧

When the police closed the case as a suicide, a deep sense of guilt overwhelmed Mani. Despite all his hatred for her, he hadn't wished for such a disastrous outcome. He couldn't escape his share of the blame and didn't know how to cope with it. After hearing the result of the police's investigation, he went to meet Pestonji, the one person he could share his thoughts with.

Pestonji opened the door, letting him in without saying a word. Mani dropped into a chair. Neither spoke for a few minutes. A growing look of anguish crept over Pestonji's face. 'I feel so sad, the way it all ended.' He waited for a few seconds and then walked over to the window.

'I could never have dreamt Grace would take such an extreme step,' said Mani. 'I feel responsible.'

'I share the guilt too. But who would've imagined Grace ending her life like that?'

Wrestling with his conscience, Mani joined Pestonji at the window. The surf crashing on the rocks sounded as if Grace was calling out to him from the depths of the sea, accusing him of her tragic end. He shivered.

Pestonji shook his head. 'Perhaps God didn't want to prolong her agony.'

Mani sighed, but it came out more as a moan. 'This is a lame excuse to cover the guilt, an easy way to console ourselves. The truth is that we drove her to her death.'

Pestonji raised his finger to his lips as he heard footsteps outside his room. He waited for a few seconds and then said softly, 'We can't do anything about it now, can we?'

Mani returned to his chair. 'I suppose not…but I feel sick to my stomach.'

'It's all over, John. The sooner you get over it, the better.'

'What will I tell the Wilsons?'

'You won't say anything to anyone. You never met Grace, and that's it. Perhaps Tanya and you could visit them one of these days.'

'I would like to, but how can I take Tanya with me?'

Pestonji paced the floor. 'I think it's time you bring Tanya into your confidence and tell your story before she hears it from someone else.'

'There's nobody else other than you…now that Grace is gone.'

'As of now, yes, but who can tell about tomorrow? You can never be sure of that. It is very difficult to hide the truth for long.' He switched on the lights and paused for a few seconds. 'I won't be too surprised if some snoopy character hungry for news digs out your past and reveals all.'

Mani shuddered and ran his hands over his face. He couldn't rule out the possibility. The fear of discovery constantly haunted him.

Pestonji continued. 'I'm sure Tanya will be more understanding and provide you with the support you need to get on with your life.'

Mani always had faith in Pestonji's judgment. 'No, I won't allow that to happen. I should tell Tanya before someone else catches up with my past.'

However, the fear of losing Tanya sent an icy chill coursing through his veins, despite her resolve to stick with him.

'I would even suggest that Tanya visit your mother and tell her secretly that her son is alive. Your mother should not leave this world without seeing the face of her only son, even if it is masked.'

The thought of his mother formed a lump in Mani's throat, his eyes turned moist.

Pestonji poured a drink for Mani. 'You have to come clean and face the situation with courage. I might sound a bit old-fashioned, but I do believe in giving something back to humanity. God has given you enough. You should invest in charity and be honest with Tanya. The first will give you some peace, and the second might help you get over the huge burden of guilt you are carrying.'

Mani gazed at the dark clouds rushing past the moon. He hoped the dark clouds in his life would disappear over time, and Mani Shankar Varadharajan would remain safely buried in his grave, never to surface again.

Pestonji continued, 'Sealing the wound now would be better than concealing it with the bandage of untruth. It will never heal and the pain will prick your conscience for the rest of your life.'

'I cannot take the risk,' Mani said, without facing Pestonji. 'Mani is dead and gone, and so is Grace. That chapter is closed forever.'

'That chapter is not closed, my friend. Somebody is going to stumble upon it sooner or later, and then it will be too late.'

'I'll take my chances.'

'And risk ruining what you cherish most?'

He turned to face his mentor—his friend, philosopher and guide. 'I took the biggest risk of my life to save a marriage which didn't really exist, and I'm now prepared to take another to save the one which is real.'

32

Mark marvelled at the way in which Tanya took control of things that Grace had neglected for quite some time. Within the first week, everyone came to know she meant business. Charming and yet demanding, Tanya had a way of getting work done without being harsh. Both with the staff and with guests, she dealt in a manner that won their hearts, unlike Grace, who'd routinely offended them.

Mark was unable to charm her and it rankled. He sauntered into the hall one day and, spotting her sitting alone at the reception desk, decided to redouble his efforts with her.

'Hello, Tanya. I must say you're managing things remarkably well.'

Tanya didn't look up from her papers.

'We've greatly benefited from your past experience.'

'Thank you.'

'Except for one thing.'

She looked up.

He leant over the desk, almost breathing down her face. 'Your sari.'

Tanya recoiled. 'Excuse me?'

'Saris don't look presentable at the Reception,' he said, gazing down at her blouse. 'A skirt would be more appropriate, although, you look hot in saris...especially that red one.'

Blood rushed to Tanya's face. 'Mr Braganza, I'd appreciate very much if you'd mind your own business. If you're looking for some cheap thrills, try your stunts somewhere else.'

Mark stood up and puckered his lips. 'Yes, Ma'am, but I only meant it as a compliment.'

She rose from her chair and glared at him, 'I know exactly what you meant, and I would advise you to refrain from making such comments in the future.'

Mark quirked an eyebrow.

'And by the way,' she went on, 'I don't appreciate being addressed by my first name.'

Mark had never before encountered a woman who had put him down so bluntly. But then, he was not particularly desperate to undress this cheeky woman who didn't have much merchandise to show anyway. It was only a matter of time before someone else would walk into his life with long, slender legs—and much more. The smell of money never failed to excite women; he knew he would be coming into a lot of it. In any case, Tanya would be packing her bags soon, along with the rest.

'I admire your spunk, but you're forgetting who the real boss around here is.' He left for his office without waiting for her reaction.

A couple of days later, Raju entered his office. 'Sir, a couple wants to see you.'

'Who?'

'An Air Force officer and his wife. They checked in last night.'

An Air Force officer! This could get interesting. Mark arched an eyebrow and glanced at Pestonji. The old man shuffled in his chair.

Mark leant back, rolling the paperweight on his desk. 'Show them in.'

'Good afternoon,' said the officer as the couple entered. 'I'm

Squadron Leader Pratap and this is my wife, Simran.'

The lady with smoky eyes arrived with a pair of extra large earrings and an equally large smile, her lips parted in a luscious manner. A rosy fragrance filled the room. Mark greeted them, 'Please, be seated.'

He gave the smoky-eyed lady a once-over and noted her luscious lips.

'You have a lovely resort,' she said removing her Panama hat as she sat down. 'I wish we could stay here a little longer.'

The officer came to the point. 'Actually, we came to inquire if you offer any discount to defense personnel like many others do.'

Mark thought for a moment and then addressed Smoky Eyes, 'Well, we never thought of it before. But now that you mention it, we wouldn't mind offering a discount to officers who fight for the nation.' He turned to Pestonji. 'What do you say, Mr Pestonji?'

Pestonji rubbed his chin and gaped at the couple.

Mark knew what was going on in his mind. The last thing Pestonji would want is to see men in blue visiting the resort and jeopardise Mani's cover. 'I suppose a twenty percent cut on the room tariff wouldn't hurt us?' Mark asked Pestonji.

Pestonji nodded.

The officer smiled. 'Thank you, we appreciate that very much.'

Mark gazed at Smoky Eyes and wondered how Air Force chaps managed to hook the best looking females. Perhaps it was the blue uniform that made even the ordinary look smart, like Mani.

'Simran is very impressed by the art works on display,' the officer said.

'Oh, they're absolutely breathtaking,' she said, 'I'm particularly intrigued by a painting in the upper lobby. It's remarkably similar to what we have at home. The trees... the rocks... even the colours are the same. I cannot believe it's done by two different artists.'

Pestonji sat up in his chair.

'A fellow officer had painted it for us,' the squadron leader explained.

Mark tossed a glance at Pestonji.

'Well...John Abraham's paintings have appeared in the press,' Pestonji said levelly. 'Perhaps you should ask your friend if it was a copy.'

Smoky Eyes shook her head sadly. 'We can't.'

The officer shrugged. 'Poor chap died in an air crash.'

'Oh, I'm sorry to hear that,' Mark affected surprise, 'Was he a pilot?'

'Yes, and as good an artist as he was a pilot,' he said. 'We were in the same squadron.'

Pestonji stiffened.

'By the way, who is this artist...John Abraham?' Simran asked. 'We see his works all over.'

Pestonji cleared his throat. 'John Abraham is a reputed artist and a partner in the resort.'

'Oh, that's great,' her eyes shone. 'I would love to meet him.'

Mark leant back in his chair apprehensively. Several thoughts flashed through his mind. If the couple were to discover the truth, he would stand to lose everything—and perhaps part of his property in the event the state initiated recovery procedures. John Abraham's identity had to be protected at any cost. He knew Pestonji's mind would be working feverishly to keep his protégé under wraps.

Sure enough, the old man showed his skill. 'I'm afraid that won't be possible,' he said. 'John disappears into the woods to paint and seldom shows his face around here. He has left the business part entirely to us in order to concentrate on his paintings. No one knows when he comes and goes.'

Mark's fears were put to rest, but nevertheless he decided to take a dig at the crafty old man. After all, he deserved to be rewarded for his brilliant act when he first came to the resort, masquerading as an agent to sell *Lovers' Rock*.

'Perhaps they could catch him later in the evening,' Mark suggested and noted a flicker of annoyance in Pestonji's eyes with pleasure. 'He could do with some company.'

Pestonji recovered fast. 'John is a very private person and doesn't like to be disturbed after his day's work. However, I'll find out if he is available in the morning.'

Smoky Eyes flashed a smile that could disarm an enemy. 'That would be very kind of you, mister…'

'Oh, I'm sorry,' Mark said, 'Mr Pestonji represents Mr John Abraham, who is my partner.'

'We'd be grateful if you could fix a meeting,' said the Squadron Leader. 'Simran is mad about art.'

The officer rose to leave. 'Thank you for your time.'

Pestonji hesitated. 'By the way, when are you leaving?'

Mark smiled. He knew why the old man didn't ask 'how long are you staying'. Pestonji wanted them out as much as he did.

'We plan to leave tomorrow evening.'

' Enjoy your stay,' Pestonji said.

Mark's gaze followed her shapely behind as Smoky Eyes left with a tantalising swagger.

❧

Although Mark succeeded in camouflaging his shock, Pestonji seemed to have suffered a minor convulsion. He wondered if the old man would ask Mani Shankar Varadharajan to vanish from the scene before the sun rose on the morrow.

Mark decided to play with the old man. 'I'm sorry to hear about the loss of their pilot friend. Surely you could've done them a favour by arranging a meeting with John this evening.'

'I don't think so,' said Pestonji rising from his chair. 'He doesn't like meeting his fans.'

'He could make a concession for an Air Force couple.'

Pestonji walked away without looking back.

Later that evening, Mark approached the Air Force couple as they sat in the lounge having their drinks. 'Good evening. I hope you're enjoying your stay.'

'Yes, of course,' said the lady, glowing under the amber lights of the chandelier. 'I'm sure we'll visit again.'

'That would be a pleasure. May I join you?'

'Please,' the officer said. 'May I order a drink for you?'

'I've already ordered, thanks. So how was your day?'

'Oh, we had a great time on the beach,' said the lady. 'The sea here is incredibly blue and calm.'

Mark felt anything but calm as he engaged her eyes in a manner only he could. She blushed, and held on to his gaze a trifle longer than her husband would have approved, but Mark knew what his eyes could do to a beautiful woman. Unfortunately, this was not the time to flirt, but to get rid of the couple as fast as he could.

'I'm sorry to hear about the tragic loss of your friend in the air crash.'

The soldier took a deep breath. 'That's the way it is in the Air Force. You never know when your time is up.'

The woman shuddered at the suggestion and sipped her drink.

'Part of the game,' he added.

Mark raised his eyebrows. 'What happened to him?'

He shrugged. 'No one knows for sure, but it seemed his aircraft sank into the sea.'

'Didn't he bail out or something?' Mark asked.

'He just disappeared without a trace.'

A forlorn expression crept over his wife's face. 'He was very talented. I feel so sad for Grace. God knows what happened to her.'

Hearing Grace's name sent a minor tremor in Mark's stomach. '*Grace*… ?' he asked, hoping he didn't give himself away.

'Shanks's wife—she was so vivacious! We never heard from her again.'

'*Shanks*… ?'

'That's the friend we're talking about,' said the officer. 'The only decorated pilot we had in the squadron.'

'I'm still intrigued by that painting. There's so much similarity,' Simran mused.

'Perhaps your friend was influenced by John Abraham's work,' Mark suggested.

'I wish we could meet him before we leave,' she said.

Not a bloody chance! Mark wanted the couple to disappear from the resort. A meeting with Mani, despite his beard and long hair, could spell disaster for his plans. Although he had great faith in Pestonji's ability to shield the imposter, he couldn't take any chances.

'What are your plans for tomorrow?' Mark asked.

The couple exchanged a glance. 'Well, we would just laze around at the beach and leave for Goa in the evening after an early dinner,' the officer said.

'Are you planning to leave after dark?' Mark exclaimed.

'We've ordered our taxi for 8.00 p.m.'

Mark flinched. 'And you arrived in a taxi last night?'

Her brows creased. 'Is there a problem?'

Mark raked his hair with his hand and shook his head. 'We always advise our guests not to travel in these parts after sundown.'

She looked at her husband and back again at Mark.

'Didn't you read about the rape and murder of a French lady

on this part of the road, just a fortnight ago?' Mark asked.

A growing look of horror crept over her face.

The squadron leader straightened in his chair.

'You're lucky to have arrived safely,' Mark said. 'This area is full of hostile tribes. And you can't trust the taxi drivers either, especially at night. They can be very dicey. You're taking a big risk, Squadron Leader.' Smoky Eyes chewed at her lower lip. 'We didn't know,' she managed to croak.

Mark knew he would have to drive them away first thing in the morning. 'I'm driving down to Goa tomorrow morning. You can come with me if you like…or catch that rickety bus in the afternoon, famous for breaking down in the middle of nowhere.'

'What time are you leaving?'

'Around nine.'

She didn't even wait for her husband's nod. 'We'll come with you.'

'But, sweetheart, we've hardly spent a day in this paradise,' protested the brave soldier. 'Besides, I'm carrying a gun.'

She squirmed. 'I'm not in a mood to confront some terrible hooligans with bows and arrows. Thank you very much, Mr Braganza. We're leaving with you.'

'Your husband seems to be more adventurous.'

'He can be adventurous in air,' she puttered. 'But on the ground, I make the rules.'

The squadron leader shook his head and raised his hands. 'As you wish, boss.'

The brave ones never failed to surrender their arms before their better halves.

Pestonji appeared in the lounge and greeted the couple. 'I hope I'm not intruding.'

'Not at all,' Smoky Eyes said. 'Mr Braganza has offered to drive us to Goa tomorrow morning.'

'Oh, that's good,' Pestonji said with apparent relief. 'I came to tell you that Mr Abraham will not be able to meet you as he's taken ill.'

'Never mind,' she said, 'perhaps next time.'

Mark pursed his lips. Reaching home in one piece was more important for the lady than meeting the artist. But he wanted to have some more fun.

'Taken ill? He was all right this morning.'

Pestonji scowled. 'Bad stomach.'

Mark was not one to let him off easily. 'Perhaps he chewed off more than he could digest.'

Pestonji's lips quivered a bit but he kept silent.

Smoky Eyes stood up. 'Thank you, Mr Braganza, we'll be ready at eight. Now if you'll excuse us, we must have our dinner and pack our bags.'

'I hate to disappoint a guest,' Mark said, after the couple left. 'John Abraham is no Picasso.'

Pestonji shoved his hands in his trouser pockets and slipped away.

At eight o'clock sharp the next morning, Mark whisked the couple away from harm—in the red convertible. Pestonji would never have allowed Mark to take Mani's car, but that day he stood by without complaining.

Mark sped away, raising the dust of Paradise Resort. The only trace left behind when the dust cleared was the Panama hat Mark saw in the rear view mirror.

He didn't stop, and the lady didn't seem to care.

33

With Grace's note in his pocket, Mark possessed the ultimate weapon to strike at his adversaries, but he didn't want to use it so soon after Grace's exit. He wanted public memory to fade a little before he took the next step, even if he had to wait for a couple of months. He had nothing to lose. Besides, Tanya ran the show well, leaving him free to pursue his interests: partying hard and chasing hot women.

The prospect of getting rich a third time around brought a fresh glow on Mark's face. Single and back in circulation with a vengeance, Mark enjoyed his reputation of being a potential threat to the ladies of high society—married or otherwise.

Mark had no dearth of admirers, but he had his eyes set on a raven-haired beauty of mixed parentage, whose oriental curves fit beautifully on her English chassis. She was a temptress and an angel wrapped in an intoxicating and delightfully challenging package—and Mark wanted her more than he'd wanted anyone in years.

Miss Margret, in her mid twenties, had arrived from London to spend an extended holiday with Mrs Parveen Spencer, her Indian mother. Now separated and living alone, Mrs Spencer, according to the grapevine, was looking for a prospective son-in-law to take charge of her landed property in a prime location in central Bombay. The combination was perfect and Mark wanted to quickly fill that slot before Miss Spencer considered any Tom, Dick or Harry from the British Isles.

After a couple of meetings at social dos, Mark invited Miss Spencer and her mother to a lavish party on the terrace at Paradise Resort. He also invited some of his close friends, ignoring Mani and Pestonji altogether. Single malt and champagne flowed freely. The variety of food on the table ranged from Chinese to Continental to Indian. Music and dancing went on till the early hours of the morning. By the time the party ended, Parveen Spencer seemed convinced that the suave owner of the resort was a prize catch for her daughter. For most of the evening, Miss Spencer remained glued to Mark, dancing and giggling, as though she had finally met her Prince Charming.

When Pestonji presented Mark the hefty bill for the party, Mark shrugged. 'That's part of the promotional activity. We have to entertain people to bring in business.'

'I understand, but these were your personal friends, not travel agents.'

'They're all well connected. Besides, word-of-mouth publicity is very important.'

Pestonji cringed. 'It was the word-of-mouth publicity that brought you down in the first place. Don't you think you've gone overboard with this kind of expenditure?'

Mark threw his hands in the air. 'This is quite normal.'

Pestonji threw him a steely glance before leaving Mark's office. Mark couldn't care anymore. It was time to put the bloke in his place.

A week later, Mark invited the Spencer women again, along with a dozen of his friends for an all-night party on the beach. When the staff started preparing for the event and the tempting aroma of kebabs reached Tanya, she decided enough was enough and confronted him.

'Do you mind telling us why you're having this party?' she asked.

Mark arched an eyebrow and raised his chin. 'Sales promotion.'

Tanya stared at him. 'I beg your pardon?'

'No, you don't,' he said, pointing a finger at her. 'This is the way I work, and I'm not going to change that just because some smart chick from Silvassa or wherever thinks otherwise.'

Smarting from Mark's comment, Tanya said, 'If you're so deprived of common sense, which no doubt you are, it's your problem. But we cannot tolerate such senseless extravagance.'

'I'm not about to learn how to run my business from you. And I don't need to seek your sanction for what I do.'

With an icy stillness in her voice, Tanya declared, 'Very well then, you do what you like, but it will go on your personal account.'

Mark lit a cigarette and blew smoke into her face. 'You wait and see when I finally settle accounts with you.'

Tanya pinned him with a steely glance and walked out of his office.

The party lasted until early dawn and continued for two more nights as the Spencer ladies decided to stay on as Mark's personal guests, much to the discomfiture of Pestonji and Tanya.

Before the Spencer women left the shores of Paradise Resort, Mark proposed and Margret accepted. Mrs Spencer didn't bother to seek the consent of a Mr Spencer, who was reportedly too busy with his horses and didn't care anyway.

The cordiality and camaraderie that existed between Mark and Pestonji, thin as it was, disappeared overnight. If the two got within ten feet of each other, things turned sour. Matters came to a head when Pestonji slapped Mark with the astronomical bills for the extended party that ran into a few thousand rupees.

Pestonji lay down the bills on Mark's desk. 'I'm charging this to your personal account. And from now on, your so-called sales promotion activities will require joint sanction.'

Mark placed his legs on his desk and leant back on his chair. 'I'm afraid not. This is the way I like to run the show.'

Pestonji clenched his jaws. 'I'm afraid the show has to end, because now we run it jointly and not unilaterally.'

Mark regarded Pestonji with a smirk. The old man didn't know that a much bigger show awaited them. A month had been long enough for Mark to get his mathematics right and work out his strategy. His patience had long been tried— it was time to serve notice to John Abraham and party.

Mark slowly rose from his chair and faced the old man. 'I think it's time to have a one-on-one meeting with Mr Abraham to sort out matters, once and for all.'

'I think so, too.'

'Shall we say eight o'clock this evening, at my place?'

'Sure.'

'John and I alone, if you please?'

After the sun went down into the Arabian Sea, heavy clouds veiled the sky. With the blustery winds becoming stronger by the minute, a storm seemed imminent. Mark pulled out a bottle of Smirnoff for his partner and Royal Salute whisky for himself. After all, he *was* about to give a *royal salute* to the man who had literally bought him over and caused much humiliation. The stage was set for a final showdown. He poured himself a stiff drink. The whisky tasted even better than when Grace had transferred all her money into the local branch.

He glanced at the antique grandfather clock that stood in a corner. His beloved father had inherited it from his ancestors. There were still ten minutes to go before it would strike eight gongs. By the time he was halfway through his first drink, it had started to rain. When the clock struck eight, and the tantalising aroma of mutton kebabs from the kitchen wafted in the air, he instructed Saira to put the dishes into the oven and sent her packing.

John Abraham arrived a couple of minutes later and, much to Mark's consternation, with Pestonji in tow. Mark greeted John at the door and threw an inquisitive glance at Pestonji.

Mani removed his raincoat and folded his umbrella. 'There's a storm brewing.'

Pestonji did the same and placed his protective equipment on the stand in the verandah. 'And it's very chilly too.'

'I'm sorry, Mr Pestonji, I thought this meeting was between only me and John. I'd rather talk to him privately, if you don't mind.'

Pestonji shrugged. 'I didn't come here on my own accord.'

'It's all right, Mark,' Mani said, 'I've nothing to hide from Pestonji. Besides, he's as much a part of this resort as I am.'

'I'm afraid it's far too personal to have an audience. It may be detrimental to your interests.'

'Never mind, Mr Pestonji knows more about my interests than anyone else. Please feel free to discuss anything you want, personal or otherwise.'

'As you wish,' Mark said. 'Don't say I didn't warn you. Please come in.'

'That's a cozy little bar you have in the corner.' Mani remarked as he entered the living room.

'Grace designed it. She was never short of ideas.'

Mani edged closer to the bar. 'I like the all-black granite backdrop with the subtle display of crystal.'

'Grace had expensive tastes and an eye for beauty.' Mark said, wondering what she saw in this man who wouldn't have known how to tie his pajamas back home.

A sudden gust of wind from the open window caused the

curtains to balloon. No one spoke. Mani noticed a picture of Grace on a corner table; it seemed to him that she mocked him with her eyes and the hint of a smile that played on her lips. He turned away and walked to the window at the other end of the room.

'Let me fix the drinks.' Mark moved to the bar. 'What would you like to have, gentlemen?'

'The usual for me, if you please,' said Mani.

Pestonji settled for orange juice.

Mani sat on a sofa near the window, Pestonji on a cushioned chair by his side. After passing the drinks to the visitors, Mark positioned himself at the bar.

Seconds ticked away like minutes. Mani spoke. 'I think it would be a fitting tribute to Mrs Braganza if we put up something in her memory... like a bar on the terrace as she once suggested to you.'

Mark raised his glass. 'I'd appreciate that.'

'Let's get cracking before the next season starts,' Mani said. 'Shouldn't take more than a month, I suppose.'

'Let me put on some music. Grace has left behind an impressive collection of records.' Mark put on Beethoven's Symphony No. 9, one of the composer's most haunting, to set the mood for the final act.

Mani was surprised. 'I didn't know she had an ear for such classical stuff.'

Mark looked at him sharply.

Mani recovered quickly, 'Err... I mean I only heard fast music whenever I passed by your cottage.'

The bloody man was about to hear a different kind of music. Mark excused himself and went inside the kitchen to fetch hot mutton kebabs from the oven.

Mani helped himself to the chunks of meat. 'Thank you.'

Visibly tense, Pestonji remained quiet. The old man's anxiety to finish with business was evident from his long face. But Mark believed in feeding the lamb well before taking it to the sacrificial altar. He extended the plate to him, 'Have some, Mr Pestonji.'

'No thanks.'

'So, what is it you wished to discuss?' asked Mani.

'I'm sure Mr Pestonji must have briefed you.'

'He did say something about sales promotion.'

'And the people I invite to do just that?'

Pestonji worked a muscle in his jaw.

'I do believe social networking helps a great deal in promoting goodwill. Word-of-mouth publicity goes a long way in promoting a place of leisure.'

'I see no harm in occasional social interaction,' Mani nodded, 'but we have to work as a team and respect each other's views.'

Pestonji folded his arms across his chest. 'I'm sorry, I don't agree. The kind of social networking you've been practicing has done more harm to you than good.'

'I beg to differ,' Mark snapped. 'I'm prepared to pay for the bills if it's hurting you.'

Pestonji retracted. 'I didn't mean—'

'I know precisely what you mean, Mr Pestonji. But that is not what I wanted to discuss this evening. There's something more vital that will change your attitude permanently.'

Pestonji's face turned red. He opened his mouth, but Mani waved him to stop.

'Gentlemen, let's not argue about this petty matter. You're both entitled to your opinions. But let us try to accommodate each other and function amicably in the broader interests of the resort.'

As Beethoven's symphony turned into a crescendo, the rain erupted into a hailstorm that rattled the roof tiles, making further conversation difficult. Mark raised his voice above the din to announce, 'We're not here to discuss teamwork, but something more important.'

'Like what?' asked Pestonji.

Mark lit a cigar and blew smoke in the air.

'Your roof is leaking, Mark.' Mani pointed to the corner from where water started dripping. 'We should get it fixed before it gets worse.'

Mark feared that his esteemed guest would be leaking in his pants before the evening wore out. 'Please don't bother. I won't be staying in this shack beyond a month at most.'

Pestonji narrowed his eyes. 'Where do you think you're going?'

Mark walked to the rear window with a swagger. 'Back to where I belong,' he said, gazing at his ancestral cottage on the hillock.

A bemused smile curled Mani's lips. 'Is this a joke?'

Mark knew that any smile, voluntary or otherwise, will vanish from his smug face forever. 'No, it's not,' he sneered. 'I'm dead serious.'

Pestonji couldn't desist anymore. 'Are you out of your mind?'

'I was, when I allowed you to sneak into my domain, but not anymore.'

Mentor and protégé gaped at each other.

Mark took a long drag of his cigar and raised his voice over the background music provided by the rattling roof tiles. '*Mister John Abraham,* or should I say, *Flight Lieutenant Mani Shankar Varadharajan*...your game is over.'

34

Flight Lieutenant Mani Shankar Varadharajan…your game is over…

Mark's words seemed to hit Mani like a bolt of lightning. He shrank into his sofa—more a corpse than a living being.

Pestonji wiped the sweat from his forehead.

Seconds ticked by.

'It's all over, Shanks,' Mark said menacingly.

Pestonji's face turned white. 'What are you saying?'

Mark placed his glass on the counter and pulled out the 'million dollar' note from his pocket. 'Never mind what I'm saying. Listen to what Grace has to say.'

Mark read Grace's note aloud, leaving out the portion where Grace had accused him of Irene's murder.

I do not want to live in this world anymore. Before I end my troubled life, I wish to reveal a few facts about the men who ruined my life. Mr John Abraham, who came to Paradise Resort to humiliate me, is none other than Flight Lieutenant Mani Shankar Varadharajan, my ex-husband. He deliberately ditched his aircraft in the sea near Kalaikunda air base, on 22 November 1963, and escaped to assume a new identity, with the sole objective of cashing in on his insurance money. That I deprived him of realizing his dream is a different story, but I shall rest in peace if he is made to pay for his crime.

Mani's face turned pale. His glass slipped from his hand and dropped on his lap, wetting his pants. Perhaps he did so on purpose to hide a malfunction in his water works. Mark enjoyed the hunted expression on his face—his world was about to crumble.

Mark pocketed the note and edged closer to Mani. 'And now it's payback time, Mister John Abraham.'

Eyes filled with horror, Mani sank further into his sofa.

Mark turned to Pestonji. 'I know why you visited the resort so clandestinely, with all those creepy jokers following. You came here to throw us out of our home and humiliate Grace to the point of insanity.'

Pestonji's face lost all colour. 'John never meant to cause any harm to you, Mark.'

'No harm to me?' Mark flared. 'You drove my wife to her grave, and you have the audacity to say he meant no harm? You are responsible for her death…you will bloody well pay for it through your nose.'

'He has done a lot for you.' Pestonji whimpered.

'What he did for me is inconsequential in view of what he did to Grace.'

Howling winds pounded the roof. A bolt of lightning flashed outside the window. Despite the chill, Mani broke out into a cold sweat.

Mark, the victor, ambled to the window that looked onto the wonderful cottage he was about to reclaim. Playing hide and seek, the moon winked through the gaps in the clouds rushing home.

'What do you want, Mark?' Pestonji wouldn't look at him as he spoke, his shoulders hunched and hands clasped in a tight grip.

'I want you both to pay for Grace's death,' he said in the manner of a conqueror dictating terms of surrender to the defeated. 'And return to where you came from, without any fuss.'

'We're terribly sorry for what happened to Grace.' Pestonji said, with a false tone of congeniality. 'But you shouldn't hold us responsible for what she did in her moment of distress.'

Mark pointed a finger at them. 'You two drove my wife to her grave with your wicked plans.'

Mani reached for his cigarettes and fumbled for the match box.

Mark stepped forward and offered him the light and gazed into his blood-shot eyes. 'You don't wish to rot in a prison for the rest of your life, do you?'

'Don't do this, Mark.' Pestonji pleaded. 'He doesn't deserve this.'

'Neither did Grace deserve what she got from you.' He faced Mani. 'And now, listen carefully…' Mark began to spell out his terms in the manner of a judge delivering his final verdict.

'First, I'll grant you one month to get the hell out of my paradise.'

Mani didn't lift his head.

'Second, I want ten lakhs in cash.'

Pestonji gasped. '*A hundred thousand—*'

Mark paced the floor and faced Mani. 'And third, you will leave all your paintings behind. I wouldn't like to see empty walls in the resort.'

Mani rose from his chair and staggered to the window.

Pestonji reacted like a wounded animal—his anguish seemed greater than that of his protégé. 'This is preposterous,' he spluttered, furious, but fear lurked beneath the steel in his eyes.

Mark sneered at Pestonji. 'Perhaps it is, but that's the price for keeping your master out of jail.'

'John doesn't have that kind of—'

Mark cut him short. 'Which brings me to point number four: You will sign all the necessary papers to terminate the contract, and no further claims.'

A sudden chill descended in the room. Mani, who had not spoken a word since the devastating disclosure, turned to face Mark. 'What if I don't agree to your outrageous demands?'

Mark laughed. 'Then I'll arrange a date for you with Inspector Dara.'

'Right, and what do you get out of your noble gesture?' Mani asked not looking at Mark.

Mani's words struck Mark like a boxer's punch. He knew if the stupid moron refused to pay, Mani would go to jail, and Mark Braganza would get nothing but a lot of sleepless nights. His stomach churned at the thought of police translating the damaging part of Grace's note into plain language, without employing the services of an interpreter. Although Grace had not cited any specific proof, her reference to Mark's role in Irene's disappearance could provide enough incentive to Mr Dara to re-open the long-buried case. He could never share the contents of the note with the police if he wanted to get something out of the situation—and save his own skin.

Feeling a bit jittery, Mark scowled, but then a cunning smile bloomed on his face again. 'I don't think you would want to book a presidential suite in prison for the rest of your life. You wouldn't wish to leave Tanya, practically a widow, to fend for herself, would you?'

Blood rushed to Pestonji's face, but no words came out of his mouth.

Mani tilted his head and gazed at Mark. 'Has it occurred to you that by punishing me you stand to harm yourself?'

'I've done no wrong.'

'Maybe not this time, but when the police start probing, many things would tumble out. Besides, you will stand to lose everything

I've invested in your property, and maybe more.'

Despite his wretched state, the bloody man could still hurt him. Mark definitely wanted to keep the police away. He was sure Mani would want the same.

'Mr Mani Shankar Varadharajan, let's not beat around the bush,' Mark said, with a flippant wave of his hand. 'I'm making an offer for your own good, take it or leave it.'

Mani paced the floor. 'You don't understand, Mark. Let me apprise you of what happened on that ill-fated November night. The truth is I never ditched the aircraft as you might like to believe. No pilot in the world would have the guts to abandon his aircraft unless he has a serious emergency. That is precisely what happened—a case of total control failure, one of the worst emergencies a pilot can ever experience.'

Mark gazed at him with apprehension.

'The horrific incident shook me so violently that I never wished to fly again.' Mani continued. 'True, I ejected safe and survived, but in those dreadful moments, I decided to disappear. I'm a deserter and am prepared to face the consequences.'

A tingle of suspicion raced through Mark's mind. He would bet his ass the man was telling a lie, and a good one at that, which might be difficult to prove otherwise. 'You mean to say what Grace is saying in her note is all rubbish?'

Mani narrowed his eyes. 'Even in death, Grace seemed to be settling some old scores with me. I've no other explanation.'

Pestonji leant back in his chair and pursed his lips.

Mani continued, 'So, my friend, I wouldn't mind spending a few months as state guest and pay fines, rather than giving in to your ridiculous demands.'

Mark lost a bit of colour, but he was no chicken. 'Really, and I would like to watch your face when the insurance company catches up with you and claims all the money, with interest. I'm sure it will be many times over what I'm demanding.'

'I never claimed a penny from the insurance company.'

'No, you did not,' Mark snapped, 'but there's enough proof in this note that you ditched your aircraft deliberately to gain from your insurance.'

Mani sat down in a chair. 'I'm afraid Grace's note will not stand in a court of law, since she's the one who gained from the insurance, not me.'

'Yes, and most of which went to clear your debts and finance your luxurious lifestyle.' Pestonji rebounded admirably. 'In fact, it is you who gained from the ill gotten money—not John or Grace.'

Mark swallowed hard. He realized that all the arguments presented pointed towards a compromise formula. But he was not one to give in so easily. 'Let's cut the crap, Flight Lieutenant. If you wish to dig your own grave a second time, I've no problem with that. There won't be any mourners this time, except a couple of prison guards. I've nothing to lose.'

'You're forgetting something, Mark Braganza,' Mani said. 'When the ship goes down, you go down with it.'

'Please, gentlemen, let's not get carried away,' intervened Pestonji. There's always room for compromise. I don't see why we can't find a middle path to sort things out amicably, instead of hurting each other.'

Mark conceded. 'Very well then, let's talk business.'

'You ought to be reasonable, Mark,' said Pestonji. 'John has already spent a fortune in your resort. Does it not count for anything?'

'He did it for his own nefarious designs, not for the resort.'

'Come on, Mark. Don't forget for one moment that any inquiry into this case will not be in your interest. You may harm John, but you won't escape unhurt either, I promise.'

'And how so, may I ask?'

Pestonji stared at him contemptuously. 'Why were you sitting on this note for so long in the first place? Why did you not hand over the note to the police when you discovered it? Don't you see? You'll have much more to explain to the police, my friend.'

The reply caught Mark off balance. For a moment, Mark didn't have a ready answer for that one. He never had any doubts about Pestonji's IQ, but the old man seemed to have underestimated his.

'You want to know why? Because I found the note only now, that's why.'

Pestonji mocked at him. 'Huh? You expect me to believe that? Surely the police would have found it during their search.'

'If the police were efficient, they would have solved many a crime.'

'Including that of Irene, I suppose,' Pestonji snapped. 'You wouldn't want to burn your own ass by going to the police with that note. It should make greater sense, therefore, to make a reasonable demand instead of asking for the moon.'

Mark wanted to demolish Pestonji's hard-boiled attitude by telling him to go to hell, but he knew he could trust him to bring Mani to the negotiating table. He certainly did not want to extend an invitation to the police dogs to visit his home, sniffing for meat, especially in view of what Grace had stated in the first half of her note. With his bargaining position somewhat weakening, he decided to be more practical. 'So what's your definition of "reasonable"?'

Pestonji glanced at Mani.

Mani rose from the chair. 'I think I've made myself quite clear. If you're determined to harm me, I won't stop you. But I'm not giving in to your ludicrous demands.'

Mark threw his hands in the air. 'Fair enough, let the headlines strip you of your mask and tell the whole world who you really are.'

For once, Mani shot off his mouth like a fighter pilot, a trait Mark could never have suspected. 'I could do with some publicity, even if it is of the wrong kind. I'm sure it will create a sensation that will enhance the value of my paintings. And, after I tell the whole story, there will be another headline, much bigger, to reveal what a blood sucker and murderer, you are.' He paused, raised his eyebrows and pointed his finger at Mark. 'You, Mark Braganza, will not be going without chains in your ankles... and not a penny in your pocket.'

The two locked eyes for several seconds without exchanging another word.

Pestonji interjected, 'Calm down, please. It'll hurt you both if you take such a belligerent stance.'

Mani was fuming. 'I'm not about to give in to a man who has a lot to answer for his own misdeeds?' Mani hobbled to the door and left. Once Mani was out of earshot, Mark relaxed. Although Pestonji had no financial position in the resort as such, he carried himself with a lot of authority. He had no doubt the old man would bring Mani to terms.

❧

In the den of thieves, Pestonji found himself the odd man out—mister clean who wanted to save his protégé not because he approved of what Mani had done, but for his loyalty towards the man whose talent he had admired and nurtured from day one. He could never have imagined getting entangled into this web of intrigue wherein any escape route would be painful. Besides, he thought of Tanya, and dreaded to imagine how their marriage might be harmed if the truth were ever revealed. Which is why he was more concerned with saving Mani's skin from Mark, who had the potential to ruin John's life a second time.

Pestonji and Mark negotiated the deal late into the night. An unusual calm descended on the resort after the rain stopped and the breeze became a mere whisper. After a great deal of persuasion, Mark settled for a sum of five lakhs, plus the paintings and two months for them to leave the resort.

Pestonji rose to leave and stopped at the door. 'We'll pay you the money after you hand over that note to us.'

Mark grinned. 'I'm afraid not.'

'What do you mean?'

'I would like to retain the note as a precious gift from my beloved wife.'

'Then the deal is off.'

'That piece of paper doesn't matter anymore, Mr Pestonji. Now that I know all about Flight Lieutenant Mani Shankar, a word from me to the police would be good enough to destroy him.'

'It matters to us, because we wouldn't want you to come knocking at our door again.'

Mark didn't want to part with that note for his own safety. Grace had left enough material in it for the police to reopen the case of Irene. He considered the issue and made an offer. 'All right, I'll destroy the note in your presence when you bring the money.'

'Fair enough, but not before we see the contents of it.'

Pestonji was a tough customer. He wasn't going to give up easily, and Mark wasn't willing to reveal the first part of the note.

Pestonji waited for the answer.

'I'll show you the relevant portion of the note that concerns you before destroying it.'

Pestonji shook his head. 'You must have good reason to protect your own skin, but never mind, I accept your proposal.'

A few weeks later, after he supposedly complained of breathing difficulty, Mani was advised to relocate to a drier climate, preferably a hill station, on the advice of a doctor clandestinely arranged by Pestonji. Concerned about Mani's health, Tanya didn't object. It suited both the parties perfectly, since otherwise a lot of dust would have to be raised.

A few days before their departure, Mani went to his favourite spot on the beach and sat on a rock for a long time, gazing at the ocean. Briefly, Grace's divine beauty floated in his mind. Despite the hatred he had nursed for so long, he knew her image would linger for a long time to come. Like the crashing waves on the shore, Grace would knock at his conscience again and again. He closed his eyes and raised his head towards the sky. The journey of life had taken him through incredibly strange twists and turns, culminating into something that he had never expected. And now, after paying off Mark, and deprived of his precious paintings, he had no choice but to start all over again.

As he rose to leave, he saw Pestonji standing a few paces behind him. He had no idea when he came on the scene. Neither spoke for a while.

Mani broke the silence. 'I can't live with the untruth anymore. I promise to confess everything to Tanya after we move away to the hills, maybe some place in Lonavala.'

Pestonji nodded. The sea was unusually calm, and so was Pestonji. An uneasy feeling crept into Mani's mind. He'd never found Pestonji so quiet.

After a long pause, Pestonji spoke. 'I suppose it's time to part company.'

'What do you mean?'

Pestonji picked up a stone and threw it into the sea. 'This is as far as I can go.'

Mani gazed at him. 'You don't say...?'

'I can't be with you forever, John. We have to move on with our lives.'

'You still call me John.'

'You'll always be John Abraham for me. Mani Shankar died when you first met me in Bombay.'

'You wish to ditch me like Grace did?'

Pestonji stood still.

'You want to bury John Abraham, do you?'

'No, but there might be some other John sitting on the steps of Jahangir Art Gallery, waiting for someone to show him the right path.'

'And then abandon him midway to fend for himself?'

'I don't think you'll need me anymore.'

'I thought this bond had crossed the threshold of *need* long ago and gone much beyond that. You're family, remember?'

Pestonji's eyes turned moist. 'That bond will remain intact, even if we live miles apart.'

'You're not getting any younger, Pestonji. Someone will have to take care of you when you get too old. I don't think Shehnaz or Navroz would fit into that role.'

'I don't think so either. But I'll knock on your door when such a situation arises.'

'I'm sure we'll work out something.'

Pestonji put his hand on Mani's shoulder as they walked back to the resort.

A couple of days before leaving the resort, Mani met with Mark one last time. 'May I ask you for a favour?'

'Sure.'

'Can you part with one of the paintings?'

'I suppose I can. Which one is that?'

'*Lovers' Rock.*'

Acknowledgements

I would like to thank the following for their invaluable support and help during the writing of this book:

Joyce, Carla, Charles, Jean Davis, Amelie, Faith, Katherine, Helen, Zellakate, Gail, Ciara, Sky, Mahima, Shalini, and the editorial team at Rupa Publications comprising Kausalya Saptharishi and Shyama Laxman.

www.ingramcontent.com/pod-product-compliance
Lightning Source LLC
LaVergne TN
LVHW020655110826
845149LV00012B/2004
* 9 7 8 8 1 2 9 1 2 4 7 9 1 *